MW01626299

CLEMENTE

CLEMENTE

Guggenheim MUSEUM

Published on the occasion of the exhibition
CLEMENTE
Organized by Lisa Dennison

Solomon R. Guggenheim Museum, New York
October 8, 1999–January 9, 2000

Guggenheim Museum Bilbao
February 14–June 4, 2000

ISBN 0-89207-222-9
ISBN 0-8109-6917-3

Guggenheim Museum Publications
1071 Fifth Avenue
New York, New York 10128

Hardcover edition distributed by
Harry N. Abrams
100 Fifth Avenue
New York, New York 10011

Design: Matsumoto Incorporated, New York
Editor: Edward Weisberger
Production: Elizabeth Levy, Esther Yun

Printed in Germany by Cantz

Cloth cover: Alpana Bawa and Francesco Clemente
Dust jacket and paper cover, front: Francesco Clemente, detail of *Scissors and Butterflies*, 1999 (cat. no. 148); back: Clemente, detail of *Skull*, 1999 (cat. no. 147).
Frontispiece: Robert Mapplethorpe, *Francesco Clemente*, 1982.

"The Gold Paintings" by Gregory Corso, from Francesco Clemente, Corso, and Adam Füss, *The Gold Paintings* (Zurich: Edition Bruno Bischofberger, 1990). Reprinted by permission of Gregory Corso. "Flower" and "Place" by Robert Creeley, from Francesco Clemente and Creeley, *It* (Zurich: Edition Bruno Bischofberger , 1989). Reprinted by permission of Robert Creeley. "Chain" by Robert Creeley, from *Echoes*. © 1993 Robert Creeley. Reprinted by permission of New Directions Publishing Corp. "Loop," "The Swan," and "The Skull" by Robert Creeley, from *Life and Death*. © 1998 Robert Creeley. Reprinted by permission of New Directions Publishing Corp. "Pastel Sentences" by Allen Ginsberg, selections published in Ginsberg, *Death & Fame: Poems 1993–1997* (New York: HarperFlamingo, 1999). Printed by permission of Allen Ginsberg Literary Trust.

Contents

Lenders to the Exhibition

Albright-Knox Art Gallery, Buffalo
Doris Ammann, Thomas Ammann Fine Art
Kelly-Gilles Bensimon
Bruno Bischofberger, Zurich
Galerie Bruno Bischofberger, Zurich
Stephanie Seymour Brant
The Brant Foundation, Greenwich, Connecticut
Carmignac Gestion, Paris
Francesco and Alba Clemente, New York
The Cleveland Museum of Art
Como Group
Contemporary Art Fundació "la Caixa," Barcelona
Beat Curti
Mia and Patrick Demarchelier
Anthony d'Offay Gallery, London
Stefan T. Edlis
Raymond Foye
Gagosian Gallery, New York
Walter Haas, Zurich and Puerto Vallarta, Mexico
Alex Katz
Thomas and Janine Koerfer-Weill
Robert and Mary Looker
Dr. Erich Marx, Berlin
Mugrabi Collection
Museum für Moderne Kunst, Frankfurt am Main
Tatum O'Neal
Öffentliche Kunstsammlung Basel, Kupferstichkabinett
PaineWebber Group Inc., New York
Patricia Phelps de Cisneros, Caracas
Philadelphia Museum of Art
Jean Pigozzi, Switzerland
Ron and Ann Pizzuti, Columbus, Ohio
Cynthia Hazen Polsky
Rubell Family Collections
David Salle
Sanders Collection, Amsterdam
Jacqueline Schnabel
Sezon Museum of Art, Tokyo
Joan Sonnabend
Gian Enzo Sperone, New York
Sperone Westwater, New York
Stedelijk Museum, Amsterdam
Matthew and Iris Strauss, Rancho Sante Fe, California
Virginia Museum of Fine Arts, Richmond
Angela Westwater
Anonymous lenders

The Solomon R. Guggenheim Foundation

HUGO BOSS is the sponsor of this exhibition as part of its ongoing support of the Solomon R. Guggenheim Foundation.

Additional support provided by the National Endowment for the Arts.

Sponsor Statement

The artist Francesco Clemente is a traveler between two worlds. His paintings and drawings combine a mysterious Eastern symbolism with elements of Western cultural tradition. He fashions a closely woven web of the familiar and the strange in images that ultimately defy interpretation.

At home in Madras, Rome, and New York, Clemente has explored the depths of cultural differences like no other artist. The transcultural quality of his work lies in his ability to forge a link between the rational currents of Western tradition and the intuitive tendencies of Eastern culture.

Clemente, the first comprehensive retrospective of the artist's work in all mediums, brings to light a visual poetry composed of amusing stories, symbolic eroticism, and profound self-revelation.

Cultural curiosity and tolerance are important sources of inspiration, both in art and in fashion. Our support of the Clemente exhibition is an emphatic expression of this conviction and of our long-term collaboration with the Solomon R. Guggenheim Foundation in support of contemporary art.

HUGO BOSS

1. ***My House***, 1982. Tempera on linen, 157 ½ x 118 ⅛ inches (400 x 300 cm). Private collection.

Foreword

Thomas Krens

The history of contemporary art at the Solomon R. Guggenheim Museum began in 1937, with the establishment of the Solomon R. Guggenheim Foundation, whose core mission encompassed collecting and exhibiting the art of the present. In recent decades, retrospective exhibitions devoted to contemporary artists have occupied a special place in this history, and have included artists of different generations and nationalities, from Joseph Beuys and Roy Lichtenstein to Ross Bleckner and Rebecca Horn.

With the Clemente retrospective, the Guggenheim takes on the role, as it has in the past, of interpreting the art of its time. Although Francesco Clemente has lived in the United States since 1981, no museum in this country has mounted a survey of comparable scale or range. This exhibition thus offers audiences the first opportunity to assess the artist's production from the 1970s through the present. Expanding the internal logic of Clemente's work, the show is organized around eight themes that graph the artist's labyrinthine cosmology of images and ideas.

At the Venice *Biennale* in 1980, Clemente commanded the attention of an international audience, and his rich and eclectic visual imagery was considered deeply influential in the international revival of Expressionism in the 1980s. Working simultaneously in different mediums, such as oil, watercolor, pastel, ink drawing, fresco, and sculpture, Clemente draws with great erudition and intuition from diverse cultural periods and stylistic sources to give body to the vast range of his visual and conceptual ideas. The exceptional scope and quality of his artistic production and the singular personal vision it expresses has determined the Guggenheim's decision to close the millennium with this retrospective exhibition.

Our friendship dates back to 1987, when I invited Clemente to give a lecture at the Williams College Museum of Art, where I was then Director. The artist and I have remained friends since; we share an affinity for the art and culture of India, where I worked in the early 1980s, and where the artist has traveled regularly since 1973. I began discussions with Clemente about this particular project in 1994, and since then, he has had a steady involvement in our collecting and programming activities at the museum in New York as well as at the Guggenheim Museum Bilbao.

In 1997, the museum acquired ten extraordinary works on paper by the artist, which were then included in the exhibition *From Dürer to Rauschenberg: A Quintessence of Drawing, Masterworks from the Albertina and the Guggenheim*. The artist was also commissioned to execute a site-specific cycle of paintings for the Guggenheim Museum Bilbao. Exploring such diverse subjects as the family, the Empedoclean philosophy of the four elements, and the complexity of the self, the seventeen monumental paintings that make up this installation, entitled *La Stanza della Madre*, are among the most important works the artist has accomplished to date.

With great enthusiasm, Lisa Dennison, the museum's Deputy Director and Chief Curator, assumed curatorship of the exhibition, and her expertise in contemporary painting has been invaluable in dealing with the artist and his evolving interactions with the museum. I would like to express sincere thanks to her for her expert direction of this retrospective and to the Guggenheim's staff who have been instrumental in realizing this project.

We also acknowledge with gratitude the generous support of our sponsors. Special thanks must be given to Hugo Boss, whose continuing support of the Guggenheim programs internationally is a shining example of corporate support at its finest. Hugo Boss has sponsored numerous programs at the Guggenheim Museums over the last five years and is an invaluable partner of the institution. Special thanks must go to Chairman and CEO Werner Baldessarini for his support. In addition, this long-term partnership would have been impossible without the commitment, enthusiasm, and support of Isabella Heudorf, who is responsible for arts sponsorship at Hugo Boss.

Additional thanks must be given to the National Endowment for the Arts, Isabella del Frate Rayburn Eich, and the Murray and Isabella Rayburn Foundation for their continuing support of the museum's programs.

Finally, I extend my warmest thanks to Francesco Clemente. He has been deeply involved with all aspects of this exhibition and catalogue. Without his efforts, it would not have been possible to realize this project, which explores fully the richness and complexity of his extraordinary oeuvre.

Acknowledgments

Lisa Dennison

This retrospective of work by Francesco Clemente has been realized with the generous participation of many individuals, to whom I offer my deepest thanks. Foremost, I thank the artist, who embraced every aspect of this project with remarkable thoughtfulness, focus, and attention. The time we spent together—on the ramps of the Solomon R. Guggenheim Museum in New York, at his studios, and at the Guggenheim Museum Bilbao—has been extremely rewarding, and it has been a privilege to work with him in every respect. Throughout the process of putting together this exhibition, Clemente's creation of new work was unflagging, and we are delighted that the selection of works represents the artist from the beginning of his career to the present day.

This exhibition would not have been possible without the remarkable generosity of the lenders. On behalf of the museum, I extend sincere gratitude to the institutional and private lenders whose names appear elsewhere in this book. I would like to single out in particular those individuals who have collected Clemente's work in depth, lent most generously to the show, and shared their advice, including Doris Ammann; Bruno Bischofberger; Peter and Stephanie Seymour Brant; Anthony d'Offay; and Dieter Koepplin, Head of the Department for Prints and Drawings, Kunstmuseum Basel. My appreciation also goes to Francesco's principal dealers, including Bischofberger, d'Offay, and Larry Gagosian, for their commitment to the artist and their support of our project. Angela Westwater and Gian Enzo Sperone were also instrumental in helping us locate important works. Thanks are due as well to gallery staff members, specifically Tobias Müller and Frédérique Hutter of Galerie Bruno Bischofberger, Zurich; Christophe Van de Weghe, Jessie Washburne-Harris, Stephania Bortolami, and Robert McKeever of Gagosian Gallery, New York; Lorcan O'Neill and Joanna Thornberry of Anthony d'Offay Gallery, London; Karen Polack and Sophie Prieto of Sperone Westwater, New York; and Maria Brassel of Thomas Ammann Fine Art, Zurich. We also benefited from the able assistance of Jean Bickley of the Brant Foundation, Greenwich, Connecticut; Peter Fischer of Alesco AG, Switzerland; and Rupert Burgess and Tina Sotel on behalf of a private collector.

A special acknowledgment is due to Bill Katz, who acted as exhibition designer and was in every way an essential collaborator on the project. His knowledge of Clemente's work is profound, due in part to his close friendship with the artist over the years, and his unique perspective on the artist's work is reflected in the exhibition's elegant design. Tal Varech, who works with Katz, was also helpful in realizing the design.

I am truly indebted to Takaaki Matsumoto for his superb design of this catalogue. He has captured the essence of the artist's sensibility in this monograph, which is the largest and most comprehensive publication of Clemente's work to date. I also thank Matsumoto's staff designer, Kathryn Hammill, for her valuable input. I am deeply grateful to Anthony Calnek, Director of Publications, Elizabeth Levy, Managing Editor, Esther Yun, Assistant Production Manager, Edward Weisberger, Editor, Meghan Dailey, Assistant Editor, and Jennifer Knox-White, freelance editor, for their skillful handling of all aspects of the realization of this book. My appreciation also goes to Alpana Bawa for realizing the cloth production and embroidery for the hardcover editions. She was ably assisted in this endeavor by Chandana Bawa.

In addition, the catalogue has benefited greatly from the knowledgeable and illuminating texts written by Robert Creeley, Raymond Foye, the late Allen Ginsberg, Jyotindra Jain, Gita Mehta, Francesco Pellizzi, Rene Ricard, Ettore Sottsass, and Gus Van Sant. All distinguished cultural figures in their own right, they are quite familiar with the artist and deeply engaged in his work, which is reflected in their insightful contributions. In addition, the catalogue has benefited from the inclusion of previously published poems by Creeley, Gregory Corso, and John Wieners, who have directly collaborated with the artist on specific projects and/or written verse in response to individual works by the artists.

During the planning of this exhibition, individuals who have followed Clemente's work have given advice and support, among them Michael Auping, Rafael Jablonka, Ann Percy, Diego Cortez, Peter Blum, Jerome de Noirmont, C. T. Nachiappan, and Prema Srinivasan. Others were not available to offer input but have nonetheless been inspirational to us, such as the late Stella Kramrisch and Henry Geldzahler.

Clemente's wife, Alba, and his family have been most gracious in dealing with the museum, and I hope they have enjoyed this experience as much as I have. The artist's assistants have also been a pleasure to work with during the planning of the project. I thank Simeral Achenbach and Kara Vander Weg, without whose collaboration this exhibition would not have been possible. Barry Frier, Clemente's framer, also provided essential information.

The staff of the Guggenheim Museum has been supportive and meticulous in all aspects of planning this project, and to everyone involved, I extend my sincere gratitude. Above all, I am enormously grateful to Craig Houser, Curatorial Assistant, who has overseen all aspects of the project with extreme diligence and intelligence. Melanie Mariño, Curatorial Assistant, has also played a critical role in the organization of this project, and her extensive research on the artist has been indispensable for the exhibition catalogue. I would like to thank Michael Govan, Director, Dia Center for the Arts, and Nancy Spector, Curator of Contemporary Art, for reading the texts of the catalogue. J. Fiona Ragheb, Associate Curator, provided useful input during the early stages of the project, and Anna Vallye, Curatorial Administrative Assistant, helped me throughout the process of planning the exhibition. Additional assistance has been provided by interns Jennifer Hochhauser, Jennifer Kingsley, Anna Andrea Lehmann, Lee Ann Pomplas-Bruening, Günther Salzmann, Julia Katharina Schawe, Claire Schneider, and Lisa Zeitz. The exhibition team including Sean Mooney, Exhibition Design Manager, Marylouise Napier, Project Registrar, Carol Stringari, Senior Conservator, and Joe Adams, Assistant Manager of Art Services and Preparation, was a pleasure to work with in coordinating this retrospective. Thanks are also due to Melanie Forman, Director of Development, Ben Hartley, Director of Corporate Communication and Sponsorship, and Kendall Hubert, Manager of Corporate Sponsorship; Karen Meyerhoff, Director of Exhibition and Collection Management and Design, Marion Kahan, Exhibition Program Manager, and Jocelyn Groom, former Exhibition Design Coordinator; Marilyn JS Goodman, Director of Education, Pablo Helguera, Education Program Manager, Rebecca Shulman Herz, Education Program Manager, and Amy Whitaker, former Education Program Coordinator; Scott Wixon, Manager of Art Services and Preparations, Richard Gombar, Construction Manager, Jocelyn Brayshaw, Chief Preparator, Barry Hylton, Senior Exhibition Technician, and James Cullinane, former Senior Exhibition Technician; Peter Read, Jr., Manager of Exhibition Fabrication and Design; Meryl Cohen, Head Registrar; Paul M. Schwartzbaum, Chief Conservator, and Gillian McMillan, Senior Conservator; Alison M. Gingeras, Curatorial Assistant, and Janice Yang, Curatorial Assistant; and David Heald, Director of Photographic Services and Chief Photographer, and Ellen Labenski, Assistant Photographer. I would also like to recognize the efforts of many individuals in the museum's departments of Budgeting and Planning, Finance, Marketing, Membership, Public Affairs, and Special Events. And finally, I express my sincere gratitude to Thomas Krens, Director, for his continuous support of this project.

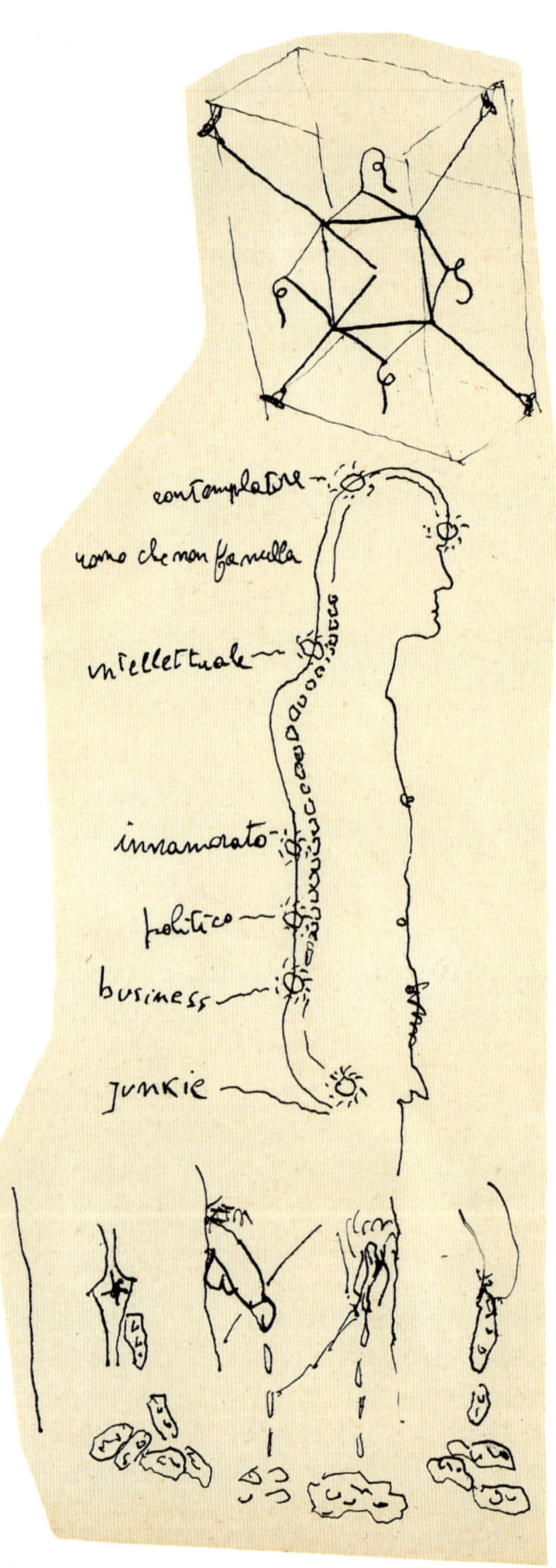

2. *Uomo che non fa nulla*, from ***Il viaggiatore napoletano***, Rome, 1971. Ink on paper, 9 ⅝ x 3 $^{11}/_{16}$ inches (24.5 x 9.3 cm).
Öffentliche Kunstsammlung Basel, Kupferstichkabinett, 1984.12.

Francesco Clemente: Once You Begin the Journey You Never Return

Lisa Dennison

The Guggenheim Museum's last exhibition of the twentieth century, *Clemente* charts over twenty-five years of the artist's career, including works in all the mediums that make up his prodigious oeuvre. In comparison, the institutional exhibitions that have previously marked the career of Francesco Clemente have been limited in scope. *Francesco Clemente: The Fourteen Stations* at the Whitechapel Art Gallery, London, in 1983 and *Funerary Paintings* at the Dia Art Foundation, New York, in 1988–89, for example, unveiled single bodies of work soon after they were created. Clemente's first retrospective, at the John and Mable Ringling Museum of Art, Sarasota, in 1985 was billed as an "introduction" to barely a decade of work. Otherwise, the retrospective format has been generally confined to specific mediums: pastel at the Nationalgalerie, Berlin, in 1984; fresco at the Fundación Caja de Pensiones, Madrid, in 1987; drawing and watercolor at the Museum für Gegenwartskunst, Basel, in 1987; and works on paper at the Philadelphia Museum of Art in 1990. Entitled *Francesco Clemente: Three Worlds*, the Philadelphia exhibition took as its point of departure Clemente's migratory existence, with residences in Italy, India, and the United States, and proceeded from the premise that his subjects, materials, and working methods were inextricably bound to locale.[1]

A museum retrospective is always a glance backward. It begins with a selection process—a period of intense scrutiny and reflection on a particular artist's career—in order to arrive at specific choices of those works that best illuminate that artist's contribution to the history of art. The objects in the exhibition space are arranged to provide a compelling visual impact and a coherent narrative. The customary organizing principle is that of chronology, for the curator's objective is to demonstrate the artist's development through an evolutionary course that extends from early work to maturity.

While the Guggenheim's retrospective and the accompanying publication include the defining works of Clemente's career, their arrangement runs counter to tradition. Remaining true to the artist's vision, the works are ordered not by chronology but rather through the various systems of metaphysics, numerology, mythology, and astrology that form the basis of his singular artistic language. The exhibition is shaped more as a journey than a career overview. As Clemente says:

> Certain constellations of work[s] are formed even at a distance of years; the same format, the same technique, the same subject, the same images that the technique evokes. . . . If you were to show my work chronologically, you would have a discontinuous representation since the same formats disappear for years and then return, then disappear and then return again.[2]

In general, the majestic Frank Lloyd Wright spiral of the Guggenheim building lends itself especially well to the chronological unfolding of an artist's career. The individual bays frame groupings of similar works, and the vistas across the ramps grant a sweeping panorama of a span of time. It is significant to note that Clemente's engagement with Wright began as early as 1970, when he was an architectural student in Rome, and it continues to be evident today in the artist's New York studio, which is sparsely furnished with Wright chairs. The installation of *Clemente* takes advantage of the architect's conception of space as a "continuous becoming," which has been translated by Clemente as a process of constant metamorphosis and transmutation, rather than as linear development.

For this exhibition, as the spiral folds in on itself, theme and chronology are juxtaposed and overlapped. Starting at the bottom, the visitor travels through the museum's space and at each turn of the ramp is guided by a poetic title that suggests the theme for that particular group of works. In the course of ascension, the viewer is diverted to the flat, tower galleries adjacent to the spiral, encountering rooms devoted to "Books, Palimpsests, Collaborations"; *The Fourteen Stations* painting cycle of 1981–82 (cat. nos. 154–65); frescoes; and *The Indigo Room* of 1983–84 (cat. no. 167), an environment of four wall hangings made of indigo-dyed paper and fabric. The final ramp brings the visitor to the summit: the domed skylight that opens onto the heavens—a metaphor for the cosmos and an emblem of Wright's utopian ideas.

Clemente himself provided the narrative trajectory that informs the exhibition's organization:

> "I" is the ground of the show. First you establish the Self. Then you give up the Self with "Unborn." Next, you cross a field of transformation ["Bestiary"]. Then you are reconciled with your powers ["Conversion to Her"]. At that point, you can collect your weaponry ["Amulets and Prayers"]. And then everything dissipates into nothing, "Sky." Once you begin the journey you never return.[3]

Of course, this is only one possible narrative for the retrospective, but it is also a possible narrative for the artist's entire body of work, quite aside from this particular presentation. At the core of his thought is the notion that there is no single truth but many truths, so that, at any other moment in time, the story might be formulated differently. Each element of Clemente's experience, and each object of his artistic production, is a fragment:

> I have always thought of each one of my works as if they were the only work I would ever do: a total constellation of objects that had to suggest the idea that they came from another place; as if they had been dug up from under the earth, from a forgotten place. This is the way I feel, that I approach my work. It is very difficult for me to think only of a single object. An object is a fragment of a more complicated discourse. There are other fragments and one story or another can be images from these fragments, but basically it is not important which one it is.[4]

3. *Untitled*, from ***Il viaggiatore napoletano***, Rome, 1971. Ink on paper, 8 11/16 x 11 15/16 inches (22 x 30.3 cm). Öffentliche Kunstsammlung Basel, Kupferstichkabinett, 1984.20.

4. ***Tutto***, from ***Il viaggiatore napoletano***, Rome, 1971. Ink on paper, 4 7/8 x 6 15/16 inches (12.4 x 17.6 cm). Öffentliche Kunstsammlung Basel, Kupferstichkabinett, 1984.22.

Although this publication mirrors the intentions of the exhibition, it cannot totally simulate the ascent from "I" to "Sky" up the spiral of the Wright building with side trips to "Rooms" and "Books, Palimpsests, Collaborations" in the tower galleries. By its nature, as a book, it has an entirely linear arrangement in which "Rooms" and "Collaborations" appear after "Sky," the section that is otherwise the terminus of the journey that begins with "I."

The authors, who call upon prophets and gods as well as mystical and sacred texts as reference points for the artist, explicate Clemente's themes from the vantage point of their own respective disciplines. They work on the cutting edge of contemporary culture and share an affinity of sensibilities. Like Clemente, they blend their own genres or disciplines with those of others. They have figured so prominently in the artist's personal pantheon as friends and colleagues that it would be truthful to classify them as being among the eclectic muses of civilization from whom he has drawn inspiration.

Gita Mehta, author, documentary filmmaker, and resident of New York, London, and Delhi, is an integral part of New York's literary-publishing world. Her first book, *Karma Cola: Marketing the Mystic East* (1979), is the ultimate satire on the pilgrimages of 1960s hippies to India in search of spiritual unity and harmony. Mehta's texts for "Unborn" allude to the fluidity of Clemente's imagery and draw on Indian philosophical concepts of form and formlessness to explore how his art moves between East and West, matter and spirit, unconsciousness and consciousness. Also in the "Unborn" section is Gregory Corso's evocative poem "The Gold Paintings," which was originally published as part of a collaboration with Clemente and Adam Füss. Corso is one of a number of Beat writers whose work the artist admires.

Ettore Sottsass, a radical driving force in contemporary design and a central figure in avant-garde culture, has been active in the realms of anthropology, psychology, poetry, literature, and art. In 1967, he founded a magazine, *Pianeta Fresco*, with Fernanda Pivano and Allen Ginsberg, bringing together an American and European artistic and literary avant-garde. He is renowned in international circles for infusing new life into the prevailing rationalist aesthetic in architecture and design. Through his work with the Memphis Design Group, which he founded in 1981, he has introduced a figurative language to the iconography of objects and the environment. Sottsass's essay for "Bestiary" illuminates a theme inspired by twelfth- and thirteenth century books that are devoted to the theological explication of beasts. His personal ruminations, in a stream-of-consciousness style, evoke the trope of travel that is shared by medieval allegories and Clemente's paintings. The "Bestiary" section is also graced by the first complete publication of Ginsberg's "Pastel Sentences," which the poet wrote in response to specific works by Clemente. The artist had read Ginsberg's works when he lived in Rome, through translations by Pivano, who was married to Sottsass at the time. After Clemente and Ginsberg met in 1983, they immediately began a collaborative relationship that they sustained until the poet's death in 1997. The synergy that Clemente felt with Ginsberg extended to the poet's contemporaries, but Ginsberg holds a place of honor in Clemente's pantheon.[5]

Robert Creeley, poet, essayist, novelist, short story writer, taught at Black Mountain College in the 1950s at the invitation of Charles Olson. Through his own critical writings, he helped to shape and define an emerging countertradition to the literary establishment. This countertradition began with the poetry of Ezra Pound and William Carlos Williams and extended through the works of Ginsberg, Olson, and others. Creeley has also written about many of the Abstract Expressionist artists. He has, on several occasions, composed poems for Clemente's work, and the artist credits him with giving voice to his art. For "Conversion to Her," Creeley wrote a poem-introduction that addresses the allusions to polymorphous sexuality in Clemente's images and a cycle of poems that reflect on individual artworks.

Jyotindra Jain, Senior Director of the National Handicrafts & Handlooms Museum (also known as the Crafts Museum) in New Delhi, is recognized as one of the most eminent historians of Indian tribal and folk arts. He has conducted extensive ethnographic field research in a number of states in India, focusing on the folk and tribal religions of the western part of the country. In "Amulets and Prayers," Jain examines the elements, senses, and symbols that proliferate throughout Clemente's work. Weaving together resonant details drawn from Indian folk history and mythology, Jain brings into relief the magical and spiritual aspects of Clemente's esoteric systems.

Gus Van Sant is a filmmaker well known for directing such independent classics as *Drugstore Cowboy* (1989) and *My Own Private Idaho* (1991); as well as *To Die For* (1995) and *Good Will Hunting* (1997), in which Clemente played a cameo role as a hypnotist; and the remake of Alfred Hitchcock's *Psycho* in 1998. Clemente characterizes Van Sant as a director "who likes to put a pill of poison under a coat of sugar."[6] Van Sant attended the Rhode Island School of Design and is himself a painter. He is also involved in photography, music, fashion, design, and fiction; his novel, *Pink* (1997), is about the power of the image in contemporary society. In "Sky," the filmmaker constructs a wry, scenographic narrative of a visit to the artist's studio. Through his excentric approach to Clemente's work, he captures how the complex structures and processes of the artist's unique pictorial universe function analogically in relation to one another.

Francesco Pellizzi is the editor of *Res*, a journal of aesthetics and anthropology, and a collector of primitive and contemporary art. Pellizzi was one of the earliest collectors to recognize Clemente's talents and began acquiring his work in 1980. Pellizzi's thinking, like Jain's and Clemente's, extends beyond the boundaries of pure art to social and cultural history in general. His commentaries for "Rooms" address the individual spaces that connote refuge, rest, an invitation to contemplation, a space for the soul. He approaches the technique and iconography of frescoes in terms of Clemente's passage through painting and through his native Italy; provides penetrating interpretations of *The Fourteen Stations* based on ancient alchemical texts that reflect on notions of time and metamorphosis; and describes his experience of *The Indigo Room* in terms of "hiding and revealing," movements intrinsic to both sexuality and visuality.

Raymond Foye, editor and book publisher, has had a long engagement with the literary and art worlds and has bridged the two through collaborative projects initiated by him, many of them involving Clemente. Foye was introduced to Clemente by Henry Geldzahler in 1983 and in turn introduced the artist to many Beat writers, including Corso, Creeley, and Ginsberg. Together Foye and Clemente founded Hanuman Books in 1986, adopting the small format of Hindu prayer books for publications of artist's writings, Lower East Side poets, overlooked Sanskrit scholars, and rock musicians, among others. Foye himself has written extensively and authoritatively on Clemente's work. In "Books, Palimpsests, Collaborations," he focuses on Clemente's early notational drawings; collaborative projects with poets in the United States and with artisans in India; and watercolor portraits of contemporaries.

The various strands of Clemente's biography are brought together for the first time in Rene Ricard's chronology. Ricard is a poet, critic, Warhol "superstar" (he appeared in the underground film classic *The Chelsea Girls* in 1966), and wit. According to Foye, the poet and the artist met during Clemente's first visit to New York, when Ricard was at "the height of his reign of terror over high society and the New York art world."[7] Ricard's text is as much a narrative biography as a chronology. It highlights not only the major cultural influences and life experiences of the artist but also the more intangible elements that have been the ingredients of Clemente's creative process.

Ezra Pound, whose poems are quoted throughout Pellizzi's texts, played with the ideogrammatic notion of poetic image, and he has been particularly important to the artist, who found in Pound's writings, as well as those of James Joyce, a structure that mirrors his own approach to image-making. Clemente says:

> It is in the literary tradition, in literary invention, that one most often finds this situation, in which seemingly meaningless imagistic elements rub against one another to

> spark a flame of indeterminate meaning. What these writers do that interests me very much is to use a collection of arbitrary choices to create a field of meaning. In their writing, the distinctions between private and public, important and unimportant, trivial and overwhelming, the big scheme and the little detail all fall away. They create a secular world of meaning, a constellation of familiar qualities that have an unfamiliar meaning, which makes us happy, and which is the task of art to do.[8]

Indeed, Clemente's absorption of American culture occurred in part through the literature and music of the Beat generation, especially such dominant figures as William Burroughs, Ginsberg, and Jack Kerouac. His empathy for the Beats was grounded in their embrace of Eastern thought and mysticism, their irreverence for authority, their relentless mobility, and their celebration of everyday life and the commonplace. The Beats brought art out of the institutions and into the streets. The 1950s and 1960s, characterized by the fluid commingling of the worlds of avant-garde dance and theater, independent film, Abstract Expressionism, Fluxus, and Happenings, set the tone for the atmosphere of crossover and collaboration between the arts that Clemente found so invigorating when he first moved to New York in the 1980s.

Clemente cultivates the randomness of the world. As Edit deAk so eloquently states, "He is footloose in time, culture, and metaphor."[9] The geographies of the different places he knows—as well as the people, history, culture, and religions that define each locale—accumulate in the artist's memory and emerge as imagery after being filtered through his unique persona. To this, Clemente adds his exceptional craftsmanship, demonstrating proficiency in many mediums: from "drawing" (whether using pen and ink, charcoal, watercolor, gouache, pastel, or pencil) to fresco, oil painting, sculpture, and handmade artist's books. He maintains an indifference toward subject and materials that frees him to move randomly through them:

> My overall strategy or view as an artist is to accept fragmentation, and to see what comes of it—if anything. . . . Technically, this means I do not arrange the mediums and images I work with in any hierarchy of value. One is as good as another for me. All the images have the same expressive weight, and I have no preferred medium.[10]

The internal model of fragmentation that characterizes Clemente's oeuvre did not emerge by chance. It is inextricably linked to his biography. The artist was born in Naples, a city that began as an ancient Greek settlement and since the collapse of the Roman empire has been governed by a succession of foreign rulers, from Byzantine to Spanish. The historically diverse layers of culture in Naples, Clemente's extensive travels throughout Europe in his youth, and his early schooling in Latin and Greek profoundly affected his artistic and intellectual sensibility:

> I read *The Golden Ass* by Apuleius and *Satyricon* by Petronius. This was one of the periods when there was a kind of world culture. The world was at the same time one and totally split in a thousand different possibilities. You could find Egyptian people painting Greek pictures, Greeks singing Latin songs, and Latins praying to Eastern gods.[11]

In 1970, Clemente moved to Rome to study architecture. The fractured political, social, and cultural landscape of post-1968 Italy—its ideological rigidity on the one hand, and its dissolution of national and regional character on the other—incited the artist's need to configure a different understanding of the world. But it was the trips he made to India between 1973 and 1978 that had the strongest and most transforming influence on his world view. In India, his romantic notions about travel and the exoticism of the East were quickly supplanted by a sense of disorientation and by the discontinuity of social experience he felt.

5. *Untitled*, from ***Il viaggiatore napoletano*,** Rome, 1971. Ink on paper, 8 3/8 x 5 7/8 inches (21.3 x 14.9 cm). Öffentliche Kunstsammlung Basel, Kupferstichkabinett, 1984.25.

As Foye writes:

> The cultural multiformity of India led Clemente to accept fragmentation and stylistic diversity in art, in contradistinction to the prevailing cultural hegemony of the West. By abandoning the traditional hierarchical ordering of experience, Clemente was seeking a more open form that was able to accommodate the influx of new factors brought to the fore in India: eros, the psychic imagination, the mutability of meaning.[12]

During an extended stay in India in 1977, Clemente's home was the Theosophical Society in Madras. The time he spent in the society's compound overlooking the Bay of Bengal, its garden harboring the oldest and largest banyan tree in India and its vast library filled with esoteric and occult literature, had a formative influence on the artist. Clemente's synthesizing impulse in the face of the awesome diversity of experiences and cultures is close to the spirit of Theosophy, a theological and philosophical movement that blends the teachings of the world's religions into a common spiritual narrative. The teachings and writings of Theosophy, espoused by Helena P. Blavatsky, the movement's founder in 1875, have been a persistent influence in twentieth-century art. Among the most prominent of those who have professed their interest in the tenets of the Theosophists were the artists Vasily Kandinsky, Piet Mondrian, and Joseph Beuys. Clemente's attraction to India extended beyond its mystical heritage to the contemporary arts of Madras and Bombay, including the cheap and gaudy products that advertise its popular culture to the masses: movie billboards, statuary and relics, souvenir books sold at temples and shrines, and Hindu comic books.[13] Over time, he found great stimulation in collaborating with local artisans and craftspeople on the making of his art.

Clemente returned briefly to Italy in 1980. At that time, he and such Italian figurative painters of his generation as Sandro Chia, Enzo Cucchi, Nicola de Maria, and Mimmo Paladino were grouped by the art critic Achille Bonito Oliva under the banner of Transavanguardia. Of all these painters, Clemente perhaps best exemplified, stylistically and in his nomadic lifestyle, the transcultural art described by Bonito Oliva:

> Every work becomes a vicissitude carrying and returning to the place of work, crossing multiple fields of reference, using every utensil . . . allowing the work's fragments to maintain a mobile relationship which is never bolted and never seeks shelter in the idea of unity. . . . Today, making art means having everything on the table in a revolving and synchronous simultaneity which succeeds in blending inside the crucible of the work both private and mythic images, personal signs tied to the individual's story and public signs tied to culture and art history.[14]

In 1981, drawn to the plurality of nationalities and cultures that populated New York, Clemente moved permanently to the United States with his family. New York was a fertile breeding ground for culture, high and low, and within the city there was a strong esprit de corps between the worlds of art, poetry, avant-garde theater and film, fashion, and popular music. It was a period that recalled the energy and creativity of the 1960s. Clemente found a congruence of interests within a community of painters, graffiti artists, composers, musicians, poets, and critics. He quickly integrated into this milieu, painting portraits of his new friends, illustrating a poetry collection for Ginsberg (the first of their many projects together), and collaborating on a group of works with Jean-Michel Basquiat and Andy Warhol.

Clemente returned to India and Italy regularly. An inveterate traveler, he continued to wander the globe—Europe, the Caribbean, Egypt, Japan—synthesizing his experiences into always new painterly narratives. His visits to the American Southwest had a particularly strong impact:

> I went to New Mexico and walked around in the desert and saw this very slight makeup the American Indians had left on the desert, just this thin layer of graffiti and broken pots. Where a village had been you see a slight curve. . . . Wherever else you go, in India

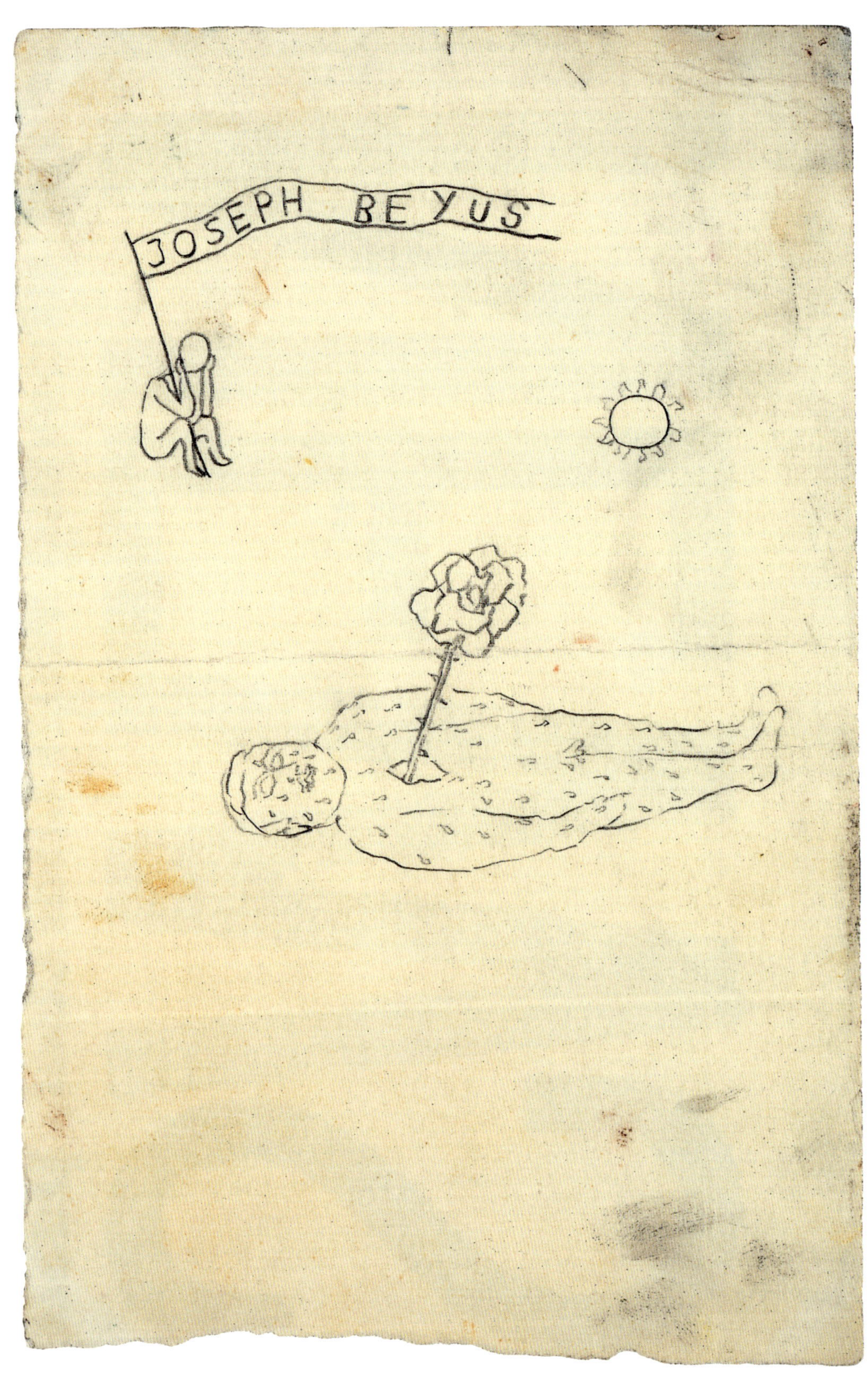

6. *Untitled* (JOSEPH BEYUS), 1974. Pencil on paper, 8 3/4 x 5 13/16 inches (22.3 x 14.7 cm). Öffentliche Kunstsammlung Basel, Kupferstichkabinett, 1987.262.

> or in Europe you have foundations that go miles down into the earth. But here it seems that civilization has always, for thousands and thousands of years, been a matter of a very light film.[15]

Drawn to the vastness of the landscape, visibly marked by these traces of earlier civilizations, Clemente established a home and studio in the desert of New Mexico, adding yet another layer to the web of experience that defines his personal cosmology.

A combination of Indian mystic and Beat poet, Clemente is a wanderer who cultivates friendships with fellow artists, poets, and seers in the course of his journeys. He fashions himself as a cult figure, not unlike those artists who served as mentors and inspirations to him, four of the most legendary figures of Italian, German, and American postwar art: Alighiero Boetti, Beuys, Warhol, and Cy Twombly.

Clemente met Boetti in 1972 in Rome, and the two developed an immediate spiritual kinship, stemming in large part from their interest in the East. In 1973, Clemente made his first trip to India. In 1974, he traveled with Boetti to Afghanistan, staying initially in Kabul, where Boetti ran a hostel and café, and eventually traveling further afield. For both artists, their voluntary exiles to other cultures were formative influences on their lives and work. Boetti was a nexus of personal and professional relationships, of artists and friends, around which Clemente shaped some of his own interactions.

Boetti had been a major figure in Arte Povera, the dominant movement in Italian art in the late 1960s and early 1970s. Through an engagement with "poor," or humble, materials, either organic or industrial, the sculpture, installations, and performances created by the artists of this movement investigated the relationships between art and life, as well as art's relationship to institutions and the marketplace. Clemente saw that Boetti's field of ideas was much bigger than his roots in Arte Povera suggested. Already a postmodernist of sorts, Boetti had opened the door to a wider world through his art. He was interested in languages and systems of classification, in things that have prescribed orders, such as maps, numbers, and alphabets. He then set out to undermine and disorder these very systems through an intuitive, almost metaphysical, approach to them.

Some of Boetti's most important works were collaborations. In Afghanistan, he engaged local artisans, weavers, embroiderers, mosaicists, poets, and philosophers—amateurs and professionals alike—to realize his work. Often, he hired these collaborators through an intermediary, so that they were unknown to him in person. In this way, he opened his art to the randomness and unpredictability of unmediated experience. Boetti gave Clemente the sense that if the hand of the artist is removed from the procedures of making art, far from reducing creativity, another mystery enters into the equation. The ego of the artist is not projected whole through the work but is tempered through an engagement with the "other." Clemente would adopt this spirit of collaboration in his work with the miniature painters of Jaipur and Orissa, papermakers of Pondicherry, and sign painters of Tamil, allowing his creativity to flow through others, merging his own world view with that of another.

Beuys served as Clemente's inspiration for the medium of drawing. Beuys used drawings as a personal codex, a way of thinking, and an intrinsic element within his working process. In the 1950s, Beuys created thousands of drawings, working in series, or what he called "blocks," with themes ranging from alchemy to religion, folklore, science, and mathematics. His pictorial language initially centered on female figures and animals, all possessed with extraordinary powers. The swan, for example, a personal totem of sorts for Beuys, suggests the unification of male and female in a single being, its feminine aspects connected to a phallic neck.

Clemente also uses the swan as subject or as attribute in his work, drawing upon its symbolic function in history and myth. During the 1970s, he drew incessantly—in his studios and while traveling—producing hundreds of small drawings, executed in ink or pastel on irregular sheets of paper, which were sometimes ideogrammatic in nature, sometimes hieroglyphic, and sometimes combined figure and text. Clemente pays homage to Beuys in *Untitled* (JOSEPH BEYUS), a pencil drawing from 1974 (cat. no. 6), in which a large male nude sprouts a flower, and a smaller seated figure holds a banner etched with the misspelled name "Beyus." Like Beuys, he explores the medium of drawing as a generative process, yielding a vocabulary of visual sources from which to draw again and again. In this particular image, the spontaneous growth of the flower also points to the function of drawing in the two artists' oeuvres as a metaphor for human creativity or thought.

Beuys's earliest drawings were imbued with a sense of ritual and myth, both historical and personal. Clemente shared Beuys's belief in the transformative power of art through ritual. In the 1960s, Beuys used draftsmanship, much like sculpture and performance, as a vehicle for social change, to further his greater aspiration for the unification of divided aspects of the universe, as well as the healing of a divided Germany. Clemente's art, however, does not culminate in activism. His objective is not the reconciliation of opposites but rather a fracturing of experience.

The reigning deity of the New York art world in the 1960s, Warhol remained an inescapable and ubiquitous presence, and he and Clemente became friends soon after the younger artist arrived in New York. Warhol's public persona was as much an artistic creation as his paintings. Clemente was drawn not only to that persona but also to Warhol's unique blending of art and life, to his willingness at any moment to mix high and low culture, and to his ability to recognize the equal importance of art history, media, fashion, and social gatherings. As Clemente has said, "Andy Warhol found his subject matter in common places and asked the questions that everybody was too intelligent to ask. He was the exemplary mediator between the meaningful, the meaningless, and what is simply vague."[16]

Warhol's engagement with society—from movie idols and celebrities to the contemporary art world—was demonstrated most convincingly in his portraits. Portraiture has been a similarly important vehicle for Clemente, although he eschewed Warhol's society portraits in favor of commemorations of his friends and acquaintances, muses and patron saints. In 1983, Warhol painted a portrait of Clemente, and in that same year Clemente began a collaboration with Warhol and Basquiat on a group of paintings and drawings that were passed from studio to studio in a contemporary variant of Surrealism's exquisite corpse.

Another figure of tremendous importance to Clemente was Twombly. Unlike Boetti, Beuys, and Warhol, who stood as dominant figures in their respective cultures, Twombly was a reclusive artist, caught between cultures: Italy and the United States, ancient and modern. At first associated with Abstract Expressionism, Twombly moved to Rome in 1957 and made use of Italy's classical heritage, especially mythology, to form his personal painting style, which is characterized by an elegant and fluid draftsmanship and graffiti-like scribblings replete with sexual or erotic overtones.

Clemente first saw Twombly's work in Rome in 1968, at Galleria La Tartaruga, and was attracted to the artist's penchant for classical civilization, engagement with past and present, and sensibility driven by a linear impulse. Clemente, who understood distance and dislocation as crucial to cultural perspective, first as a pilgrim to India, then as an Italian expatriate in New York, found a kindred spirit in his inverse—Twombly—an American expatriate living in Rome.

7. *Symbolon*, Venice, 1977. Ink on paper, 6 x 8 3/16 inches (15.3 x 20.8 cm). Öffentliche Kunstsammlung Basel, Kupferstichkabinett, 1984.60.

8. *Io*, 1978. Watercolor on paper, 12 3/16 x 8 1/2 inches (30.9 x 21.6 cm). Öffentliche Kunstsammlung Basel, Kupferstichkabinett, 1987.265.

In the years following Bonito Oliva's call for artists to take a "nomadic position" in order to roam freely through all the realms of art and art history, such landmark exhibitions as *Westkunst* in Cologne in 1981, *A New Spirit in Painting* in London in 1981, and *Zeitgeist* in Berlin in 1982–83 heralded the arrival of a return to figuration in painting. Clemente's work was integrated into the framework of this international phenomenon, which was labeled Neo-Expressionism. His utilization of traditional mediums, the cultural diversity of his sources, his natural inclination to fragmentation, and his openness to contingency reflected the larger critical and theoretical concerns of the movement.

Looking back, however, it is clear that Clemente was never bound by the rhetoric of Neo-Expressionism. He set his work apart in ways that can perhaps only be evaluated today, now that the clamor for figurative painting has subsided. The complexity, subtlety, and breadth of his project was from its inception more profound than the collage of transcultural and transhistorical notions of Bonito Oliva's Transavanguardia. While many of his fellow Italian painters remained deeply rooted in the past, interweaving a national-historical consciousness with private myth, Clemente immersed himself in more than one culture simultaneously and took on more than one history at a time, releasing himself from any specific style or convention of making art. And it was precisely in this collision of diverse geographies, cultures, and histories that he found his voice.

What sets Clemente even further apart from his contemporaries, in the United States as well as Europe, is his eschewal of juxtaposing different styles and images, and other strategies of appropriation, in favor of a method of synthesizing images into an extremely personal mythology. Drawing directly on literary as well as visual sources, Clemente has taken the risk of creating his own images. References in his work function as the echoes, the scents, the ghosts of his experiences, of other cultures, of the "other."

Clemente has understood that what we call "art" is an extremely arbitrary distinction within a larger field of visual culture, and he has confronted the ambiguity of this situation through collaboration, whether making use of high or low culture. Rather than simply appropriating kitsch and craft, he chances an actual engagement with them, assimilating them totally into his process, especially through the collaborations with artisans in India. And the involvement of the craftsperson actually lends an additional layer of authenticity to the work, rather than taking it into an ironic mode. Clemente's engagement with the literary community is also an important component of his art, and his close relationships with poets have borne particular fruition through the numerous collaborative book projects he has realized. Here, the ego of the artist is not subverted, but rather drawn into a symbiosis where, at its most successful moments, "the painter's line and the poet's line are one and the same."[17]

Viewed through the lens of 1990s art, Clemente's work is prescient in its obsession with the human body. He has explored the body as a permeable membrane for absorbing and releasing experiences, both sensual and intellectual, in other words, as an organism through which a visualization of the world is possible. Ultimately, the substance and nature of the body is the theme that unifies the artist's oeuvre.

In the 1980s, the reemergence of figurative painting coincided with a new interest in the body's representation as a site of larger issues. A focus on the AIDS crisis, on issues of gender and race, and on representation in media and advertising, located the body as a site of contest and debate, as a locus of critical and political discourse tinged with the tragedy of disease. Representational painting was sometimes seen as inadequate to communicate the implications of these weighty topics of loss and identity. Instead, in nonfigurative painting, sculpture, and photography, the body was abstracted and described through its absence or by association. The direct, erotic, dimension of Clemente's work, in which sexual taboos are prevalent and sexual orientation is confounded—where birth, coitus, and excretion are often one and the same, and where the body is viscerally and vociferously present—runs counter to most of the appropriated or abstracted figurative art of the 1980s. Clemente's insistence on the body as a provocative libidinal space has made an impression on a younger generation of artists willing to allow the body an unmediated presence.

Clemente has made a new and unique contribution to the art and culture of his times. His method is contemplative, meditative, and indulgent. He maintains a fantastical, exotic vision, even when dealing with the commonplace. The paradoxes in his work—the blurring of boundaries between interior and exterior, between self and others, between the physical and psychical—are what sustain its interest for us most deeply, and what continually open up its possibilities for the future.

1. Raymond Foye, "Locale," in Ann Percy and Foye, *Francesco Clemente: Three Worlds*, exh. cat. (Philadelphia: Philadelphia Museum of Art, 1990), p. 15.
2. Francesco Clemente, quoted in "Conversation with Francesco Clemente, Danilo Eccher and Francesco Pellizzi," in Danilo Eccher, *Francesco Clemente: Opere su carta*, exh. cat. (Turin: Umberto Allemandi & C., 1999), p. 165.
3. Clemente, conversation with the author, June 18, 1999.
4. Clemente, quoted in "Conversation with Francesco Clemente, Danilo Eccher and Francesco Pellizzi," p. 165.
5. For an excellent in-depth discussion of Clemente's collaborations with Gregory Corso, Robert Creeley, Allen Ginsberg, Rene Ricard, and John Wieners, see Foye, "New York," in Percy and Foye, *Francesco Clemente: Three Worlds*, pp. 118–24.
6. Clemente, conversation with the author, June 18, 1999.
7. Foye, "New York," p. 122.
8. Clemente, quoted in Donald Kuspit, "Clemente Explores Clemente," in *Contemporanea* (New York) 2, no. 7 (Oct. 1989), p. 40.
9. Edit deAk, "A Chameleon in a State of Grace," *Artforum* (New York) 19, no. 6 (Feb. 1981), p. 40.
10. Clemente, quoted in Kuspit, "Clemente Explores Clemente," p. 40.
11. Clemente, interview with Robin White, *View* (Oakland) 3, no. 6 (Nov. 1981), p. 2; this issue is devoted entirely to the interview.
12. Clemente, quoted in Foye, "Madras," in Percy and Foye, *Francesco Clemente: Three Worlds*, p. 51.
13. Ibid., p. 58.
14. Achille Bonito Oliva, "The Italian Trans-Avantgarde," *Flash Art*, nos. 92–93 (Nov. 1979), p. 18.
15. Rainer Crone and Georgia Marsh, *Clemente: An Interview with Francesco Clemente* (New York: Vintage Books, 1987), p. 39.
16. Clemente, quoted in "A Collective Portrait of Andy Warhol," in Kynaston McShine, ed., *Andy Warhol: A Retrospective* (New York: Museum of Modern Art, 1989), p. 447. Quotation revised by Clemente.
17. Foye, "New York," p. 121.

I

The journey began with "I" and "eye." "I" is the self-portrait Francesco Clemente returns to again and again. "Eye," the instrument of the artist's vision, is one of the body's holes that separate inside from outside and through which the self becomes porous to the world.

The journey began in 1978 when a simple drawing entitled *Io* (cat. no. 8) became an ideogram of the self. Simultaneously language and image, the letters "i" and "o" (spelling *io*, the Italian word for "I") are body and head, male and female, an I and an eye. That same year, informed by four extended trips to India, Clemente broke with his Conceptual style and turned toward predominantly figural expression, starting with a self-portrait.

The extensive series of self-portraits and portraits that have emerged throughout the artist's career are keys to understanding the nature of his vision. The enlarged, exaggerated eyes of many of his faces and figures suggest that the ocular openings allow access to the body (but not the soul, in the artist's secular iconography) and form a reciprocal boundary between body/artist and the world. In Clemente's work, the orifices of the flesh are both sensory and sexual, allowing for ingestion and excretion; in Edit de Ak's words, they are "receptors through which the world is channeled into personalized existence, points of high tension where interaction with the world takes place, and they are the domain of direct negotiation."[1]

Clemente says, "All my early works revolve around the image of holes in the body. There are nine, there are ten, there are five million pores; the interior, the perception of that which is inner becomes just as important as the perception of what is outer. They are like two oceans which are separated by nothing. By what? By these millions of empty holes."[2]

In a series of dislocated situations or places, the artist depicted himself nude or clothed; truncated, decapitated, or otherwise deformed; transmuting between human and animal or between male and female. Images are coupled, doubled, or split in two. Ruptures, and sometimes bullet holes, add yet more apertures. The bodily cavities are themselves filled with smaller heads, creating an infinity of reflection.

The self-portraits, in their endless variety, suggest that not only may one subject have many forms but also that the artist reflects his own unique state of consciousness: "The self-portrait for me is justified . . . by the idea that the ego re-emerges, continually new. . . . The idea of the self-portrait is tied to the repetition of the ego and the rebirth of the ego. It is the contrary of the mirror."[3] The same self, always new, Clemente's ego itself is permeable and indefinite. Absorbing, synthesizing, and releasing the substance of sensual and cultural experience, the artist remakes the ego in each encounter with an *other*, whether the other is something in the world, is another, or is the self in reflection.

In Romantic philosophy, the I, or ego, projects, or expresses, itself as an other among others, placing the self in relationship to that which is outside the self. Conversely, in Clemente's formulation, the representation of the ego is porous enough for the other to pass through it. As a permeable membrane of orifices and pores, the skin allows for an osmosis between external and internal, and provides for the relationship to the other of the world.

The metaphor of the sensual bodily encounter extends to Clemente's immersion in other cultures. His engagements with Italy, India, and America take on sexual and sensual dimensions, as does the meeting and blending of cultures and cultural narratives in his work. Indeed, isn't culture a body with borders like skin?

The artist's choice of subjects in his portraits is meaningful in itself. His sitters represent a community of kindred spirits: "I started with painters, continued with poets, ended with women."[4] The watercolor portraits of the 1980s are marked by the freshness and translucency of their medium. In his renderings of friends and collaborators—Jean-Michel Basquiat, William Burroughs, Morton Feldman, Allen Ginsberg, etc.—the borders of his own body are expanded through its association with other human sensibilities and through shared experience. Collectively, these images are a kind of self-portrait.

The blur of identity between Clemente and his subjects is perhaps nowhere more evident than in the 1982 watercolor *Alba & Francesco* (cat. no. 26), in which husband and wife, male and female, dissolve into one superimposed image. Here, "I" and "other" are overlapped as seamlessly as his eyes and those of his other. Clemente's portraits of women, a preoccupation of the 1990s, include a series of larger-than-life pastels of female heads and paintings of recumbent women. The artist blends the living subject with art-historical artifice, drawing upon the stylistic conventions of Parmigianino's mannered, long-necked madonnas and Ingres's idealized and exoticized odalisques. Clemente's contemporary odalisques include artists and writers, all close friends, but the heart of the group is again the person closest to him: Alba.

Clemente's universe is more diverse than the monolithic and positivist goals of Western culture. His artist-self, neither genius nor prophet, is a body through which relations are established between things, between cultures, between people and thoughts.

Lisa Dennison

1. Edit de Ak, "A Chameleon in a State of Grace," *Artforum* (New York) 19, no. 6 (Feb. 1981), p. 38.
2. Francesco Clemente, quoted in "Conversation with Francesco Clemente, Danilo Eccher and Francesco Pellizzi," in Danilo Eccher, *Francesco Clemente: Opere su carta*, exh. cat. (Turin: Umberto Allemandi & C., 1999), pp. 129–30.
3. Ibid., p. 127.
4. Clemente, quoted in Ingrid Sischy, "Francesco Clemente," *Interview* (New York) 27, no. 7 (July 1997), p. 79.

Self-Portrait, The First (1979, cat. no. 9) marks the beginning of Francesco Clemente's focus on depicting his own form. Executed without the aid of a mirror, this self-portrait and others that have followed are less like straightforward, mimetic self-portraits and more like explorations of the artist's psychic imagination. Clemente's body serves as a vehicle for realizing ambiguous and provocative visions, each of which brings together an amalgam of motifs.

In this work, Clemente used Chinese ink to render himself in a linear manner across a neutral gouache background. Placing himself in the position of an artist's nude model, he becomes both the subject and the object. He has bared his body, showing his willingness to be vulnerable, yet his figure confronts us directly, and his eyes penetrate.

The birds converging on Clemente's shoulders add to the ambiguity of the image. The inclusion of these feathered creatures is possibly a reference to Alberto Savinio. Part of the Italian Metaphysical School, Savinio sometimes painted historical figures with heads of fowl, giving hybridized forms nightmarish overtones. By comparison, Clemente's birds are more abstracted, reading as flattened, less threatening forms; upside down and right side up, they fit together like pieces of a puzzle. Mimicking the posture of a bird, the artist leans forward, his head jutting out. As a result, viewers may feel as if they are looking down upon the artist from a bird's-eye perspective. *Self-Portrait, The First* equates human and animal—an idea Clemente would continue to explore in his oeuvre—and its peculiar juxtapositions create a psychologically charged scene.

Craig Houser

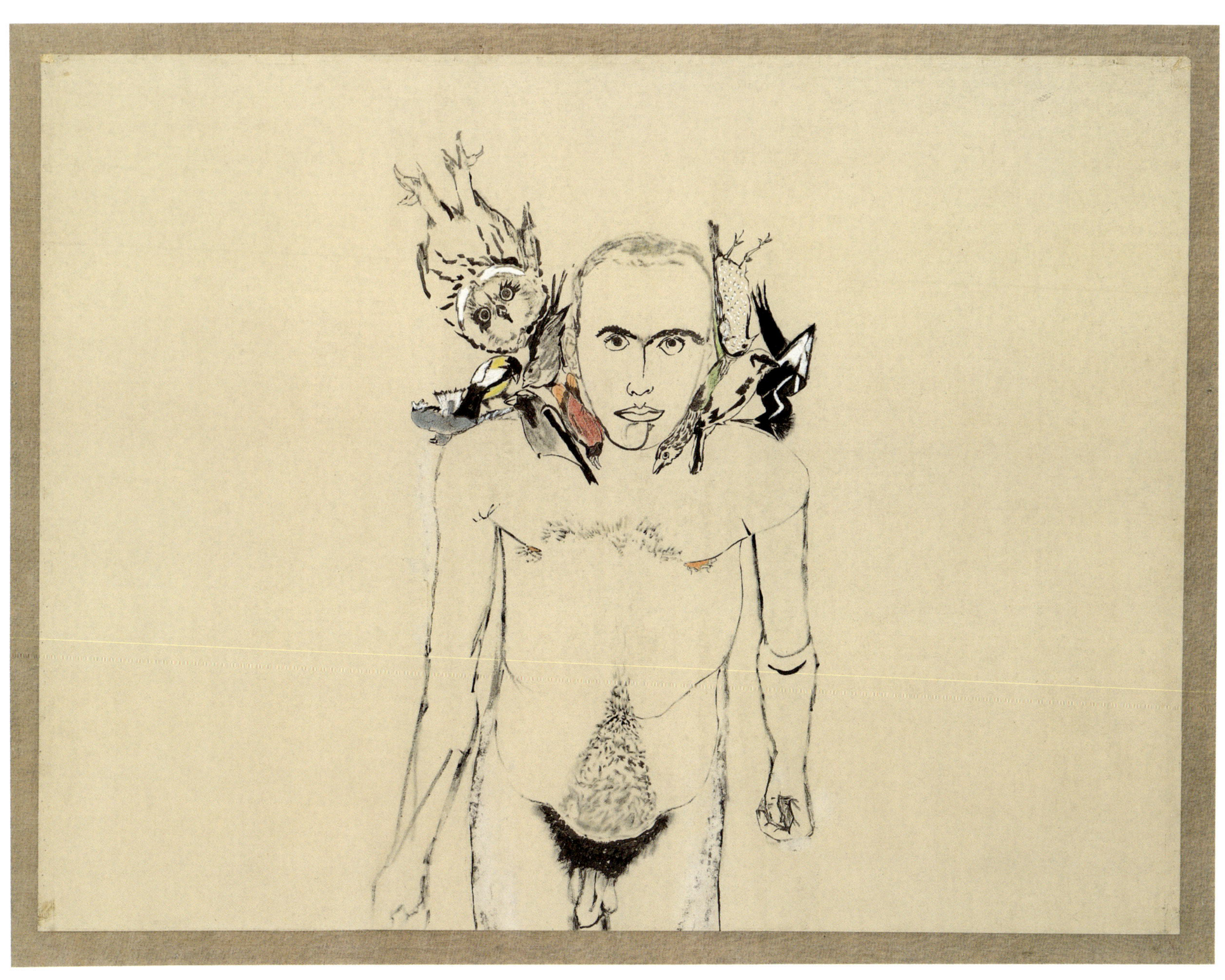

9. *Self-Portrait, The First*, 1979. Chinese ink, pastel, and gouache on paper, mounted on linen, 44 x 58 inches (111.8 x 147.3 cm). Collection of Bruno Bischofberger, Zurich.

10. ***Self-Portrait without a Broom***, 1979.
Chinese ink and gouache on paper, mounted on linen,
83 7/16 x 127 15/16 inches (212 x 325 cm). Private collection,
courtesy Galerie Bruno Bischofberger, Zurich.

In 1980, Francesco Clemente painted a series of small self-portraits, rendering himself in unusual situations. Although his work focuses on the human body, he does not think of himself as a figurative painter per se; for example, many of the 1980 self-portraits conflate corporeal representation with elements of abstraction. In *Self-Portrait* (cat. no. 11), a depiction of a diseased body is combined with imagery related to formal, abstract aspects of painting. Clemente portrayed himself with red markings that look like acne or inflammations resulting from an infection. These marks, however, are not clearly ingrained within the skin but almost float above it, creating a decorative pattern on the canvas. In a reverse effect, the surrounding field of blue in the background and shirt is treated like a skin itself; random stipple marks puncture the otherwise smooth surface of the paint, revealing what look to be imbedded, open, fleshy sores. In this work, Clemente bridged the gap between the figurative and the abstract, an assumed dichotomy that has so often dominated twentieth-century art practice and theory.

C. H.

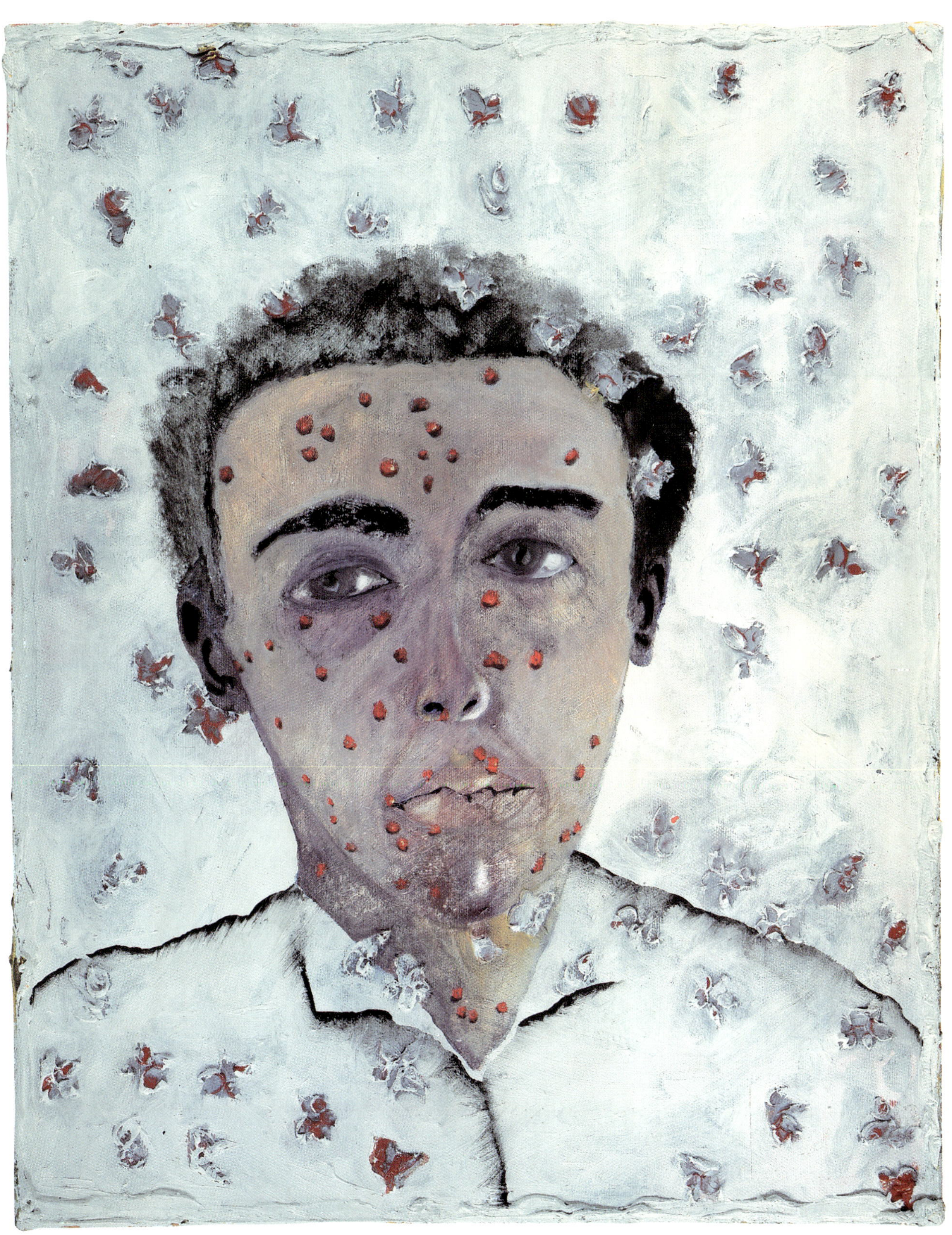

11. ***Self-Portrait***, 1980. Oil on linen, 19 11/16 x 15 3/4 inches (50 x 40 cm). Private collection.

12. *Self-Portrait*, 1980. Oil on linen, 17 $^{11}/_{16}$ x 13 $^{5}/_{8}$ inches (44.9 x 34.6 cm).
Collection of Gian Enzo Sperone, New York, courtesy Sperone Westwater, New York.

13. *Self-Portrait*, 1980. Oil on linen, 17 5/8 x 13 11/16 inches (44.8 x 34.8 cm).

Collection of Gian Enzo Sperone, New York, courtesy Sperone Westwater, New York.

14. *Self-Portrait,* 1980. Oil on linen, 15 3/4 x 23 7/16 inches (40 x 59.5 cm). Private collection.

Throughout the history of portraiture, the face, or the head, has been privileged over the rest of the body in artists' attempts to record a "true" sense of the self, as it represents the psyche, the intellect, or one's personality. In *Self-Portrait* (cat. no. 15), perhaps his most bizarre self-portrait from 1980, Francesco Clemente played with this tradition. Although the head is placed in the center of the canvas, it is completely severed from the body, so that the two forms meet frontally tête-à-tête. In a savage gesture of domination, the hand grips the cropped hair of the head. Positioned to service the body sexually, the head appears to fellate the artist's erect penis. In this fantasy of self-gratification, Clemente problematized the familiar concept of Cartesian mind-body dualism. In addition, he inverted his color scheme, using hatch marks and patches of red on a dark background; the resulting image looks like an inked printer's block or, put more abstractly, the negative of a positive image. Employing strategies of fragmentation and inversion in this self-portrait, Clemente revealed that to render a so-called true representation of the self is indeed an elusive task—whether privileging the mind, the body, or a confrontation between the two.

C. H.

15. *Self-Portrait*, 1980. Oil on linen, 16 x 17 ¾ inches (40.6 x 45 cm). Courtesy The Brant Foundation, Greenwich, Connecticut.

16. *Self-Portrait with Bird*, 1980. Oil on linen, 15 ¾ x 11 ¾ inches (40 x 29.8 cm).

Collection of Ron and Ann Pizzuti, Columbus, Ohio.

17. *Pagan Self-Portrait*, 1980. Oil on linen, 20 $^{1}/_{16}$ x 16 inches (51 x 40.6 cm). Private collection.

18. *Self-Portrait with a Hole in the Head,* 1981. Oil and wax on linen, 20 1/16 x 29 15/16 inches (51 x 76 cm). Stedelijk Museum, Amsterdam.

19. *Fortune and Virtue*, 1980. Oil, pencil, and pastel on paper, mounted on linen, 59 1/16 x 108 1/4 inches (150 x 275 cm).

Private collection, Switzerland.

OTA DELLA FORTUNA

During his continuous travels to and from Italy, the United States, India, and elsewhere, Francesco Clemente has absorbed the diverse references of each culture. In this spirit, *Perseverance* (1982, cat. no. 20) contains imagery of ancient Rome and markings that relate to twentieth-century American painting, particularly Abstract Expressionism. The rigidity of classicism, which emphasizes balance and order, is juxtaposed with the looseness of gestural abstraction. Standing amid a stormy abstract composition, Clemente's figure of himself appears strong and virile, with the hulking legs of a gladiator. At the time he painted this image, which came to him in a dream, he had recently moved from Rome to New York. His dream and the resulting painting may be perceived as his working through a radical period of transition, and the tender protectiveness with which he clutches a miniature Pantheon close to his face may be read as an expression of nostalgia for his homeland.

Perseverance recalls the paintings of Cy Twombly, whose unique style grew directly out of Abstract Expressionism and often references classical mythology. In addition, both artists have alluded to the body and its emissions in their work. In *Perseverance*, the brown oblong shapes hailing across the white background suggest the scatological. The contrast reads as peculiar: a symbol of high classicism—an "ideal" of humankind—is juxtaposed with the most abject material in any culture.

C. H.

20. ***Perseverance,*** 1982. Oil on linen, 78 x 93 inches (198.1 x 236.2 cm). PaineWebber Group Inc., New York.

21. ***Self-Portrait with Tears***, 1983. Oil and wax on linen, 40 1/8 x 34 1/8 inches (101.9 x 86.7 cm). Collection of Alex Katz.

22. ***Self-Portrait***, 1983. Oil and wax on linen, 66 x 42 ½ inches (167.6 x 108 cm). Collection of Jacqueline Schnabel.

In 1982, Francesco Clemente painted a series of watercolors, largely self-portraits and portraits of the friends, family, and colleagues who populated his universe and helped shape his sense of self. He took full advantage of the aqueous medium, which allowed forms in his imagery to easily flow together. In *I* (cat. no. 23), he depicted himself without glamour, distorting the features of his face by using patches of red and green. His head held high, he appears aloof, yet tears fill his eyes in sadness. These two different states of mind are merged into one expression. In *Alba & Francesco* (cat. no. 26), the artist extrapolated on this idea of consolidation, superimposing his wife's face with his own, so that distinctions between the two are purposely obfuscated. The new, combined head, a visual realization of their bond together in matrimony, displays two sets of eyes and two mouths. Questioning the concept of individuation, the image takes inspiration from Arthur Rimbaud's remark, "I is an Other."[1]

C. H.

1. Arthur Rimbaud to George Izambard, May 13, 1871, in Rimbaud, *Oeuvres completes* (Paris, 1972), p. 249.

23. ***I***, 1982. Watercolor on paper, 14 ¼ x 20 inches (36.2 x 50.8 cm). Private collection.

24. *Morning*, 1982. Watercolor on paper, 14 3/16 x 20 1/16 inches (36 x 51 cm). Courtesy Galerie Bruno Bischofberger, Zurich.

25. *Laugh*, 1982. Watercolor on paper, 14 3/16 x 20 1/16 inches (36 x 51 cm). Private collection.

26. *Alba & Francesco*, 1982. Watercolor on paper, 14 1/4 x 20 inches (36.2 x 50.8 cm). Private collection.

27. *Distance*, 1982. Watercolor on paper, 14 3/16 x 20 1/16 inches (36 x 51 cm). Courtesy Galerie Bruno Bischofberger, Zurich.

28. *Rama*, 1982. Watercolor on paper, 14 ¼ x 20 inches (36.2 x 50.8 cm). Private collection.

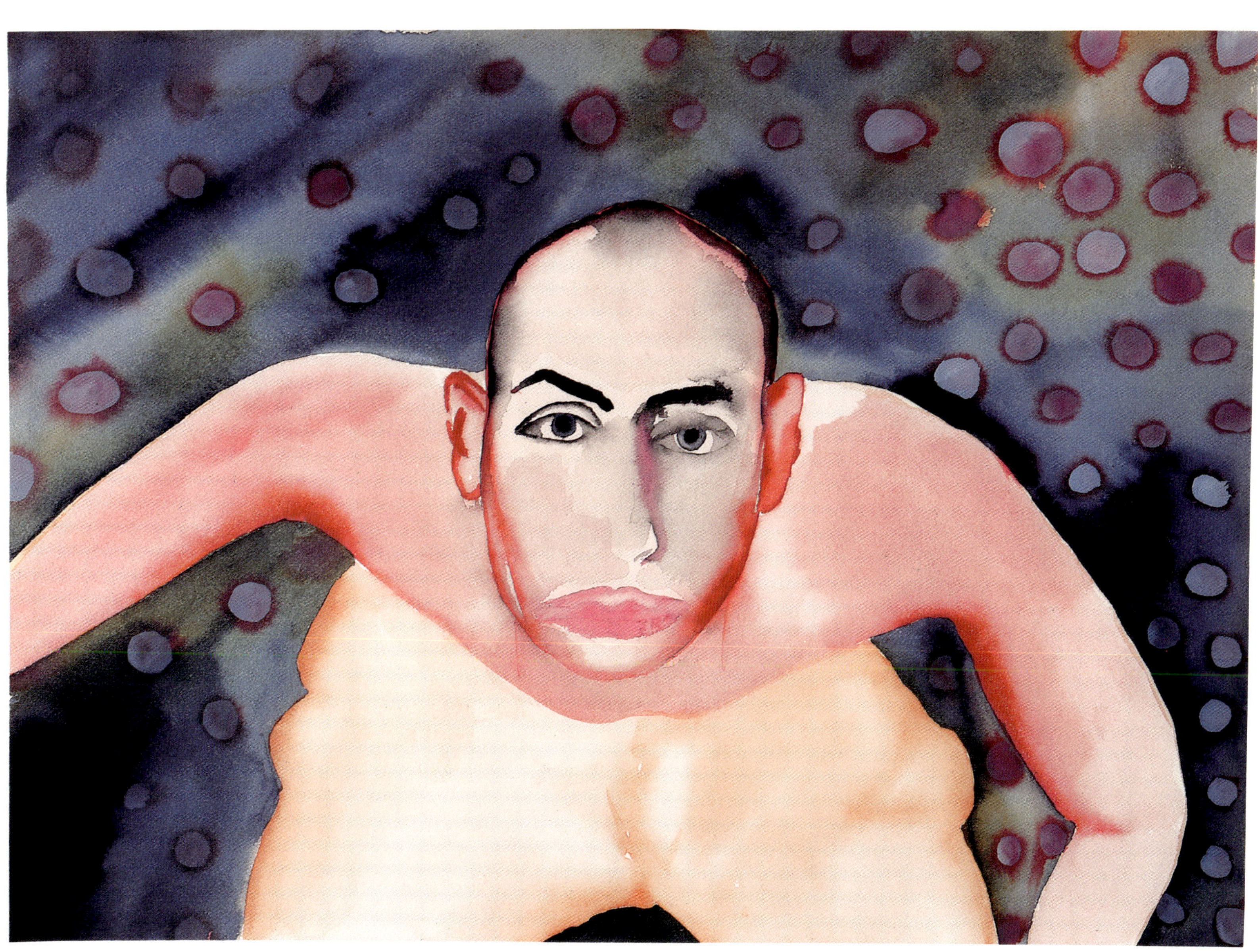

29. *Waiting*, 1982. Watercolor on paper, 14 1/4 x 20 inches (36.2 x 50.8 cm). Collection of Stephanie Seymour Brant, courtesy The Brant Foundation, Greenwich, Connecticut.

Francesco Clemente's *New York Muses* series (1993, cat. nos. 30–32) recalls Zeus and Mnemosyne's nine daughters, the goddesses who presided over the arts and sciences. During the Greek and Roman empires, the Muses were thought to be the source of inspiration for creative endeavors. According to Plato, poets were possessed by the Muses and thus touched by divine madness. Similarly, the women depicted in Clemente's *Muses*, with their enormous, close-cropped faces, possess their onlookers. They wear stoic expressions, and their large eyes penetrate—as if hypnotizing or casting spells—looking at, through, and beyond the viewer.

In his revival of classical ideas, Clemente recast them in a contemporary context. Describing his *New York Muses* from a broader, cultural perspective, the artist said, "There is a very unique, martial, New York woman, a kind of Amazon, who walks the street without looking left or right. She is strong enough to attract your attention, to not participate in 'the game.' To me that carries a sense of poetry. I draw these women larger than life. And though you feel very close to them when you are looking at them, the picture keeps a part of them private, because their bodies are left out."[1]

C. H.

1. Francesco Clemente, quoted in Ingrid Sischy, "Francesco Clemente," *Interview* (New York) 27, no. 7 (July 1997), p. 79.

30. ***Fabiola***, from ***New York Muses***, 1993. Pastel on paper, 40 x 28 inches (101.6 x 71.1 cm). Collection of Francesco and Alba Clemente, New York.

31. ***Akure***, from ***New York Muses***, 1993. Pastel on paper, 40 x 28 inches (101.6 x 71.1 cm). Collection of Francesco and Alba Clemente, New York.

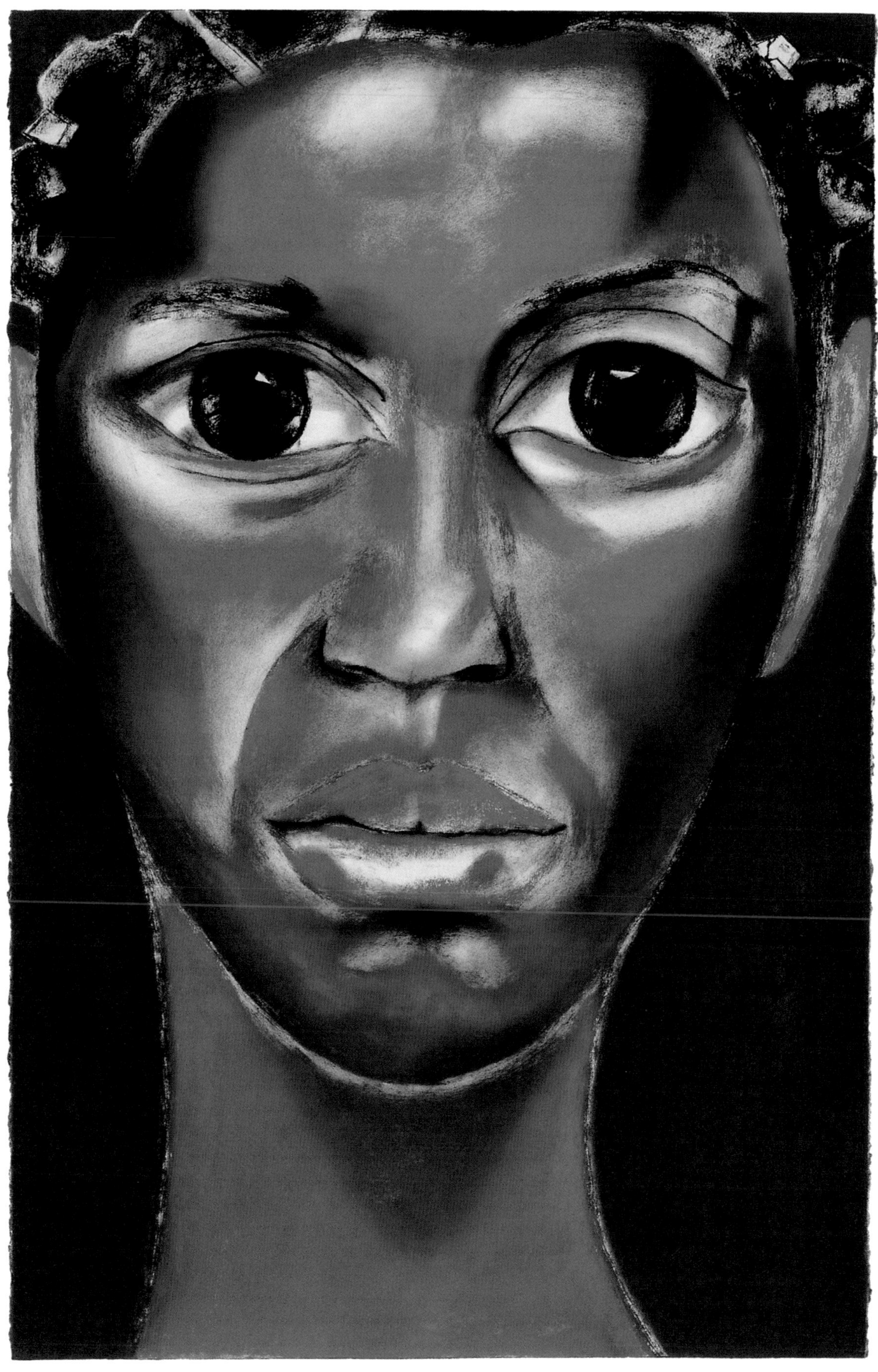

32. ***Lysa***, from ***New York Muses***, 1993. Pastel on paper, 40 x 28 inches (101.6 x 71.1 cm). Collection of Francesco and Alba Clemente, New York.

The subject of the self-portrait remains a constant in Francesco Clemente's oeuvre, yet his recent work differs from his earlier self-portraits, in which he depicted himself with a decapitated head or multiple breasts or juxtaposed himself with animals, flora and fauna, or inanimate objects. The *Grisaille Self-Portraits* of 1997–98 (cat. nos. 33–35) are reduced to a basic palette, a simple black background, and concentrate on just the artist's visage. He looks directly at the viewer and also inward at himself, revealing sadness and even a sense of shyness. As this series progressed, the brushstrokes became looser, and the eyes became more abstract, eventually bulging out of their sockets, larger than life. An inner psychological state took over. It is as if Clemente internalized the peculiarities of his earlier work and ended up communicating them, with unusual intensity and focus, through the eyes.

C. H.

33. ***Grisaille Self-Portrait,*** 1997. Oil on linen, 24 x 20 inches (61 x 50.8 cm). Private collection, Milan.

34. *Grisaille Self-Portrait*, 1998. Oil on linen, 17 x 15 inches (43.2 x 38.1 cm). Courtesy Anthony d'Offay Gallery, London.

35. ***Grisaille Self-Portrait***, 1998. Oil on linen, 16 x 15 inches (40.6 x 38.1 cm). Courtesy Anthony d'Offay Gallery, London.

36. ***Self-Portrait with Black Gloves***, 1996. Pastel on paper, 42 x 59 inches (106.7 x 149.9 cm). Collection of Kelly-Gilles Bensimon.

37. *Alba*, 1997. Oil on linen, 46 ³⁄₈ x 92 inches (117.8 x 233.7 cm). Collection of Francesco and Alba Clemente, New York.

Unborn

"I don't believe in a single truth, but in many truths," Francesco Clemente has stated, and he nailed his colors to the mast in the 1981 painting *Arme Clemente* (cat. no. 38). The heraldic images of his art are there: The death's head contemplated both in the art of Christianity and the meditations of the god Shiva's ascetic followers. The dark flowing background as an amniotic fluid in which the artist struggles to be reborn and, equally, as the swirling energy in which the universe struggles to be reborn while the god Vishnu slumbers. Between the skull's teeth—the pearl of the drowned Western sailor or the mythic egg of India?

"Painting is one of the few things left in the Western world which is close to the oral tradition of the East. You need to be an initiate," says the artist, describing the credo that gives him the flexibility to draw on contradictory worlds.[1] It is a view that allows him to move between West and East, exchanging forms, colors, backgrounds, and materials without self-consciousness. "Craft is the enemy of the artist. For a century there has been no such thing as a given craft in Western art—a breakdown reflecting the general breakdown. Art is now such a fragile thing, reinventing itself in starts and jumps."

For Clemente, one of India's attractions lies in her rejection of knowledge as an objective entity. "I have always been very diffident about the suggestion that knowledge can be seen as objective, that art is something objective that can be taught. I still believe any artist has to break away from his tribe. Tribes are based on confirming each other's idea of knowledge. But what is vital about knowledge cannot be confirmed. It has to be discovered fresh every time."

Equally important to Clemente is India's long and profound meditation on issues central to the artist—form and formlessness, the manifest and the unmanifest, *arupa* and *rupa*. It is a preoccupation Clemente finds restful. "Formlessness is made approachable in India. Death is made approachable. Color is always in motion, something you can't experience anywhere else."

In *Unborn* (1983, cat. no. 40), a crouching tiger is seen through iron bars, expectant, its ears forward, while a man slumbers within the tiger. The tension between the wakeful tiger and the unconscious man reinforces the Indian philosophical concept that to be unborn is to be in a state of blind unconsciousness, while to be born is to be conscious, to see. Eyes are a recurrent theme in Indian iconography; single figures created from composite images are a recurrent obsession with connections. Clemente acknowledges the inspiration but notes, "I never really quote in my work. It is more like a ritual, like trying to renew the memory of an experience. All rituals have an inventor. In my head I try to mimic that first experience—the origin of the ritual."

Nonetheless, India's fascination with synthesis seeps through his art. "All my work—if it is an image, a form—is always a reconciliation. Otherwise it could not come together in completion as a form."

Reconciliation—or put another way, rejection of tribal certainties—is shown in the vitality of Clemente's flower pictures. The image of a Western rose contained in the domesticity of a Western vase, symbolizing the Rosicrucian view of beauty and pain in the petal and the thorn, is sundered when the vase is replaced by the torso of a woman, with parted thighs revealing an open vulva, in the classic pose of Indian and African fertility goddesses. The rose remains, but now it has gained the Tantric symbology of Kundalini energy.

"I have a notion in my head that there are commonplace notions which are a mystery. Which is why you can work with them. Everyone thinks they understand them. But no one really does."

And what is more commonplace than a rose or a vulva? But while the first is a common theme in Western art, the second has been eliminated. A Western lineage of the phallic image exists. Images of fertility and female sexuality were displaced by those of virginity so long ago; little remains, except in the threat of witchcraft. Maybe it is no coincidence that Clemente can observe, "My work was first shown in Amsterdam, Cologne, Basel—a funny map of the most liberal European cities. Three cities in which they never burned a witch."

Such mysteries of the commonplace no less than the movement between worlds and traditions allow Clemente to return again and again to rest inside the tiger of consciousness. Suspended in the state of the unborn, the artist attends the next awakening, the next discovery to be shared in his next work. As he says, "I have always felt art implied a relationship, an emotional deal between people. The first thing you have to do is imagine an audience for your picture. Then you have to imagine the place where this work comes from. Then there is the audience that is actually there. Without patronage an artist can't exist. After all, painting is a communal activity."

Gita Mehta

1. This and all subsequent quotations are from the author's conversations with the artist in January 1999.

38. *Arme Clemente*, 1981. Enamel on linen, 16 15/16 x 21 11/16 inches (43 x 55 cm). Private collection.

39. ***Purgatory***, 1983. Oil on linen, 94 7/8 x 101 $^{15}/_{16}$ inches (241 x 259 cm). Private collection.

40. *Unborn,* 1983. Oil on linen, 77 $^{15}/_{16}$ x 83 $^{7}/_{8}$ inches (198 x 213 cm). Private collection.

In Francesco Clemente's work, the artist's unconscious seems to lie just below the surface of his conscious images, and in *Multitude* (1983, cat. no. 41) these twin states are so close it is as if both are seen through refraction. Indeed, the swirling color suggests water or amniotic fluid, while the vivid red evokes the Eastern or Buddhist palette used in mandalic art to explore states of awareness. Even the title, *Multitude*, reinforces the enigmatic quality of this painting. Is the floating figure asleep or dreaming? Is an appetite for the sensual world suggested by the full lips, the open nostrils, the glass, the eyelid closed perhaps in pleasure or in saturation? At the same time, the other eye is submerged, lost in inner contemplation. This is a portrait not just of the artist's external features but also of his interior state, reinforced by the use of white around the visible face, as if indicating a force field of stimulation from the external world. Within the overpowering red, the white suggests an innocence that rejects moral judgment, implying that withdrawal from the multitude is essential to creation but acknowledging that the world of the senses is serious fun.

G. M.

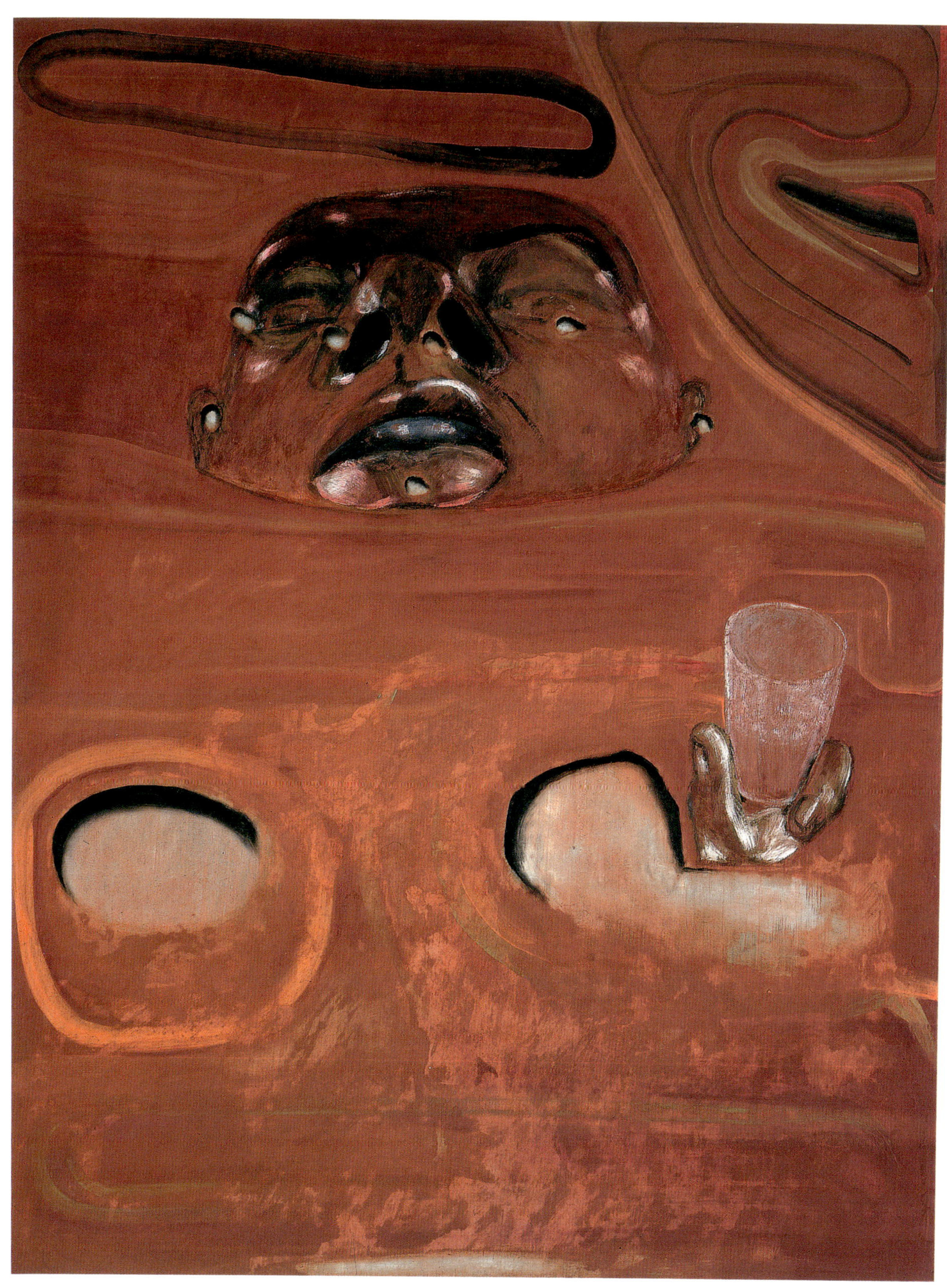

41. *Multitude*, 1983. Oil on wood, mounted on aluminum, 42 x 32 1/16 inches (106.7 x 81.5 cm). Private collection, Switzerland.

In 1983, Francesco Clemente was teaching at Skowhegan School of Painting and Sculpture in Maine when he painted *Multitude* and *Son* (cat. nos. 41, 42). If the reds of *Multitude* evoke the sensuality of his native Naples and his long sojourn in India, *Son* evokes bleak Northern winters. Yellow globes hang like ornaments from a tree, but the foreground is dominated by a gray-black trunk that rises from a mysterious undergrowth, its menacing presence dispelling any notion that this is a cozy Christmas tree. The shades of gray that culminate in the brooding darkness of the trunk also seep through the glass globes, suggesting the dread of uninhabited forests, and the bright yellow of the balls, with their artisan handles, evokes the very human need for light, warmth, association. This juxtaposition of menace and gaiety is a frequent motif in Clemente's work. So too is a dominant image—like the tree—rising from a mysterious, even primal, source, as if the artist is always struggling to free himself from the very subconscious that inspires his creative impulse.

G. M.

42. *Son*, 1983. Oil on linen, 112 1/8 x 91 1/8 inches (284.8 x 231.5 cm). Albright-Knox Art Gallery, Buffalo, George B. and Jenny R. Mathews Fund, 1985.

43. ***Usary of Love***, 1986. Oil and gold leaf on linen, two panels, 78 3/4 x 173 1/4 inches (200 x 440 cm) overall. Private collection.

Flower

All my peculiar sense
of life I've wanted to
tear out of the bounds
of it be less or more
than meat and feel the
edges less bloody now I
circle am conscious now
the exact pieces of oblong
world make a leaden place-
ment I watch the colors follow
the articulate limits measure
the black flower of weights.

Robert Creeley

44. *Flower*, 1988. Pastel on paper, 26 3/16 x 19 inches (66.5 x 48.3 cm). Private collection, courtesy Galerie Bruno Bischofberger, Zurich.

45. *Clouds*, 1988. Pastel on paper, 26 3/16 x 19 inches (66.5 x 48.3 cm). Collection of David Salle.

46. ***I Hear,*** 1988. Pastel on paper, 26 3/16 x 19 inches (66.5 x 48.3 cm). Private collection.

Chain

Had they told you, you
were "four or more cells
joined end to end," the Latin,
catena, "a chain," the loop,
the running leap to actual
heaven spills at my stunned
feet, pours out the imprison-
ing threads of genesis,
oh light beaded necklace,
chain around my neck, my
inexorably bound birth, the sweet
closed curve of fading life?

Robert Creeley

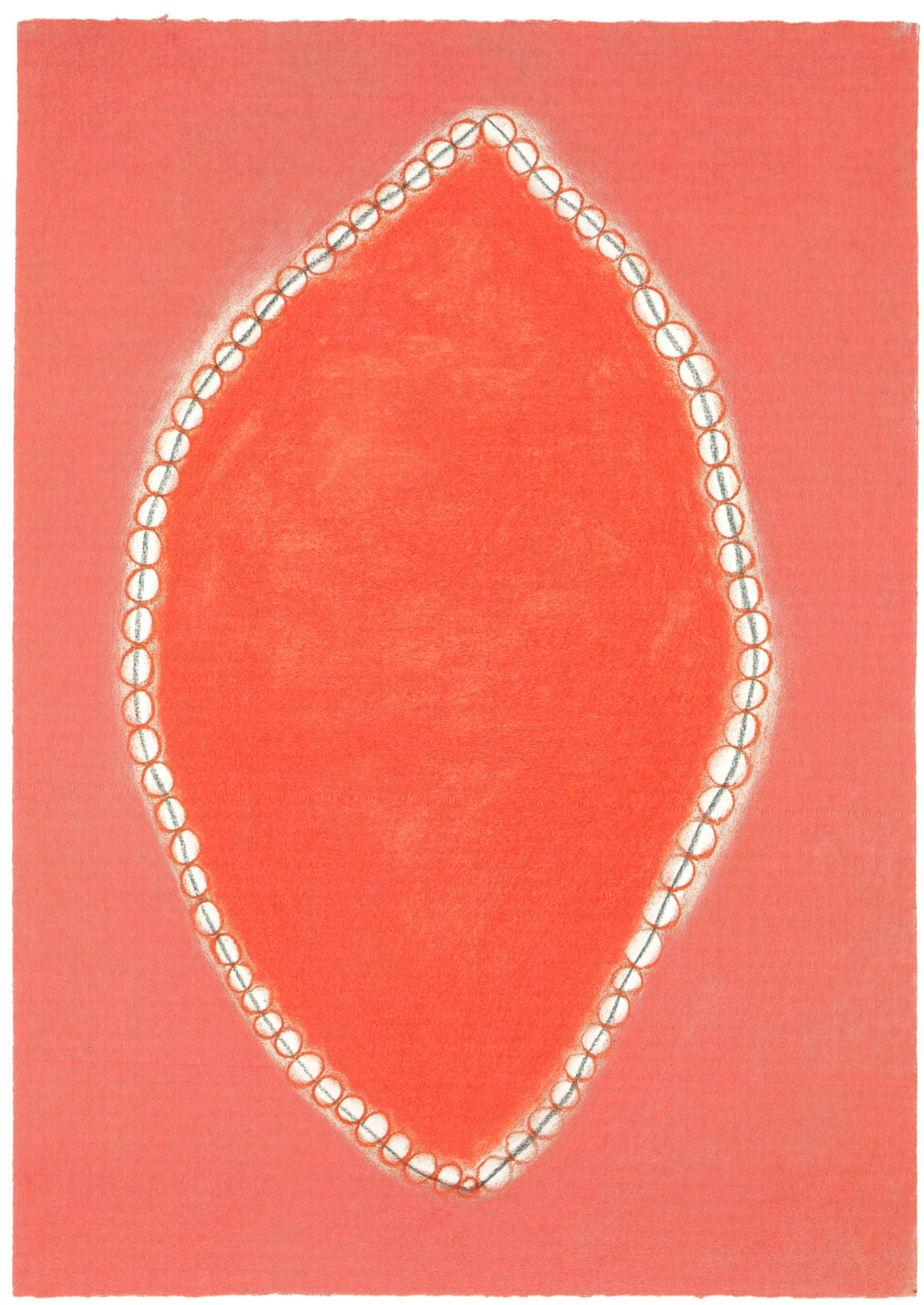

47. ***Unus omnes***, 1988. Pastel on paper, 26 $^{3}/_{16}$ x 19 inches (66.5 x 48.3 cm). Private collection, courtesy Galerie Bruno Bischofberger, Zurich.

Place

That amoebic threadlike place
it finds itself to be grayish
waiting this presence you have
anticipated the deep tinged
space of darkness all for you
it hovers the dots of intense
gleaming light poised through
it and back of it an invitation
to the other world the bargain of
simple existence all your words
so label there and out there waiting quietly it keeps waiting.

Robert Creeley

48. *Silence*, 1988. Pastel on paper, 26 3/16 x 19 inches (66.5 x 48.3 cm). Private collection, courtesy Galerie Bruno Bischofberger, Zurich.

The Gold Paintings

I come for the pies

Carpets covered with leather'd-silver
shoes, sandals, gloves, gold-woven purses
and garish trinklets
ah, Etruria, speak not of Byzantium

Thanks to the dark in me
I can be seen

O domes, arches, fiery galleries!

Stockings, garters, ribbons, feathers, and soft silk
Coats, capotes, and cloaks
long and short
furs of different hues
and wide-brimmed hats

These eyes glint like a skinless sun
in the Februarian sky

Gold unlike fire doesn't go out

49. *The Dark in Me*, 1988. Oil, pigment, and gold leaf on linen, 94 1/2 x 78 3/4 inches (240 x 200 cm). Mugrabi Collection.

Terra cotta
        was angry
"You get me pine trees
and a side saddle
        and mind yr
                own business"
                     she screamed
Gold went after the
        horses
"We'll go up to Italy
get the pines and cypresses to boot—
I'm hungry for fingers, wrists, necks"
Gold took terra cotta to Umbria
"This is on me," he said
"and so is Tuscany."
"Good," she said
Gold statues look at terra cotta figurines
slyly—O—they always start to say something
then they change their minds.

Any place is a good place
to make love
when one is not burdened with property
The roof leaked in a hundred places
and dinner was a long time coming

I'd love to shove a rose up your heart

If one must do wrong things
one must always try
to do them
in the right way

                      The trouble was
                      I was too real
                      And death wasn't

Why can't I
walk away from me
a good knowing man
and take my place
no more hereafter?

The magic fink
        he may dress in pink
And the fat lady
she may wipe
        the nude Norseman
But the weather that's known
in New Jersey
is also known in New York
with no cost to Penn. or Conn.

Here be the terra cotta
anus of a
gold aphid

The whites of her Fra Angelican blue eyes
glistened like eyes under a March sun

You'll be followed
home if you
display wealth
O Etruria!
Ah, Roma!

Dogs, young or old
yellow or black
are the bane
of the burglar's life—
gold inside a house
where people are sleeping
invites burglary
and the dog
it prohibits

Two men prowling about in the house
in the dark are apt to get confused
if anyone wakes up, they can
shoot each other
it has happened.
To the thief, the moon is a stool pigeon—

Ever see moonlight
alight a wedding ring?

Where there's gold
There has to be a code of ethics
In a wild shoot-out

Besides the nuts and bolts
a small fry
runs counter to himself

There never was any question about it
until everybody
started answering it

Life
We often think how difficult it must be
Until a Greek comes along wearing shorts—

Why do they do that?
Why do they do anything?

I'm the only guy
who knows the gold dealers
by their first name.

Are you looking for Gold?
No, I'm asking for it.

Take an Etruscan
        subway ride
in a terra cotta car
let the newly buried
        gold
                slide
in a grandma
        mason jar

50. ***Speak Not of Byzantium***, 1988. Oil, pigment, and gold leaf on linen, 94 11/16 x 78 15/16 inches (240.5 x 200.5 cm). Private collection, Switzerland.

The gold 6's
are horned 9's
—the oval dab
be a scarab
And the hole of it
a pile of tit

Ah—and now the
neo-Etruscan
buys a house
in Etruria
and what happens?
Guys come up from
Rome
with geiger counters
looking for buried gold
He complains.

When in Etruria, do as the Romans do.

What's the oldest goldest?

November 19–25, 1988, New York City

Gregory Corso

51. ***Februarian Sky***, 1988. Oil, pigment, and gold leaf on linen, 94 1/8 x 77 15/16 inches (239 x 198 cm). Private collection, courtesy Galerie Bruno Bischofberger, Zurich.

52. *Funerary Painting*, 1987. Tempera on linen, 73 1/4 x 183 inches (187.3 x 464.8 cm). Private collection.

Bestiary

People—those people who starting from a special monkey very slowly became Homo sapiens and then, so they say, Homo sapiens sapiens (i.e., those pacing up and down streets and sidewalks clutching mobile phones and knowing almost everything)—have always been in hot pursuit of the idea that somewhere, hidden in the sky or in the sea or in the forests or underground or at worst above ground, there must be someone all good and wise, some light, some sun, some mighty presence armed with thunder and lightning or a being armed with a sword, who could keep everything in order or at least know what order should be like and know where order, which is destiny, might be concealed on this miserable, muddled planet; there must be someone who could unveil the answer to every question persecuting us about the "thing" in general. In fact, there always happens to be a dire need for wisdom and knowledge, forecasts, programs, and destinies—given the daily stress of having to cope with the opposite, the daily trouble of looking into the face of the truth, the only truth we've got, that we are living and in the meantime also dying.

Even the brilliant scientist Stephen Hawking is looking for an ultimate bliss; he says that if he finds the one total formula for the universe, he will know what God thinks. Finally, everybody would like to know what God thinks or at least what the high and mighty—the ones evidently protected or enlightened by some god—think.

Precisely because of these uncertainties and this obscurity we're wrapped up in, many people have always attempted to outline, draw, paint, carve, and describe in order to get on friendly terms with some invisible being, so that his or her presence might be imagined and worshiped as the one in charge of order, of truth, indeed, of everything, of the entire "thing." Francesco Clemente is someone who doesn't try to draw the "thing"; he doesn't draw global answers. He knows too well that the answer to the question has no shape or figure or even speech. He doesn't get worked up, doesn't gasp or shout or destroy, doesn't send messages. Francesco doesn't draw figures of those truths that some believe are right or of the truths that some believe are wrong. Vast numbers of such truths exist; they are virtual truths, provisional, uncertain, fragile, blurred conventions.

Francesco stays absolutely calm. He just keeps on drawing the ambiguity of what's going on around him. Rather than what's actually happening around him, he draws the non-truth of everything that's happening, the non-dependence on a possible visible truth or an invisible truth, the non-dependence of the human comedy or drama on a set script. He draws the non-dependence on that truth set by the mere fact that the comedy takes place at all. Whenever something happens, at that same moment it has already happened. It only remains for us to reinvent it. And then in any case what happened, if by chance it began between the legs, also happened in the middle of the forehead, in the middle of the heart, in breathing, in the distance, in betrayal, in nostalgia, in fear, in joy, in dying. What has happened and happens always, happens inside an unstoppable kaleidoscope of combinations, variants, vicissitudes, wonders and horrors, gains and losses, continuities and interruptions, beginnings and farewells.

Francesco invited me to write about the group of works that he calls his *Bestiary*. I was very pleased and got out the encyclopedia to look up "bestiary." The encyclopedia says that in the Middle Ages there was a book in which real or imaginary beasts were described by telling fantastic allegories of true or imaginary cases in life. The allegories travel through landscapes over or above (or maybe below) the ups and downs of life, travel into supermarvelous or superterrifying landscapes—spaces and places that smell more of dragons than of minestrone and are closer to spectacular apparitions than to afternoon sermons. These are the landscapes through which the innocents imagine they journey to feel their hearts beating, to be able to laugh or to be scared out of their wits, to keep their eyes wide open and glued on life. These are the landscapes where wise men and women float over the ground, making no noise, almost no noise.

I don't know if Francesco is innocent or wise. The innocent usually can't help being wise, and the wise can't help being innocent. Maybe it is Francesco's destiny to journey through life with his feet off the ground, making no noise, looking here and there, as if going through an infinite amusement park of stories—happy, unhappy, heroic, wretched, shining, shadowy stories—his heart thumping, his eyes peeled to make sure he misses nothing and sees absolutely everything that can be seen and everything that cannot be seen or even known. The "cannot be seen" and the "cannot be known" are irremediably attached to what can be seen, as moving clouds are attached to the blue visible sky, as the distant noise of a river (which can't be seen) is attached to a mountain. Is it so?

When one is in a boat, one is also in the sea. One swims in the boat and sails on the sea. When one grows old, one gets sadly into the yellow boat of the beyond, no need to row anymore. The big eye of darkness is expecting us. When you kiss your beloved in the dark, don't you sink into a gigantic mysterious ball of light? Is it so?

The amusement park of stories never ends. One story is that of "painting," an ancient way of representing other stories, known and unknown, by using ocher, fingers, brushes, colors, pencils, pastels, all the means once used but hardly used anymore. (Nowadays, people prefer to represent ideas, not stories that happen, and there are movie and video cameras and all those other technologies.) In his journey through the amusement park, Francesco has bumped, as an innocent, into the story of painting, into the mysteries of painting. It is as if he were crossing a wide river of purifying, special water, of special, hidden, dangerous waves and currents, leading far into a deep orgasm, into a total physical ecstasy. The ecstasy ends in a fantastic exhaustion. It always happens after a deep, very deep, orgasm.

Painting is ultimately a challenge, an aggressive existential hope, a total self-abandonment of body, veins, blood, and breath in the arms of life, a deep erotic self-representation, with many complicated pleasures along the way, nothing else but pleasures. Francesco never gives up what some call "the sin of the flesh," which is noble painting. He never gives up the pleasure, the abandonment, the tenderness, the only distraction left: the erotic background of existence. He cannot deny himself the subtle pleasures of painting. As a Mediterranean man, a man of the South, he knows too many perfumes, too many tastes and colors, too many lights and skies, and too much melancholy, as well as too much empty space and solitude, poverty and prisons—hence, cleverness and cunning, long songs and exhausting dances, Dionysian escapes. All this, it seems to me, is what Francesco gives us as he travels, his feet off the ground, making no noise, almost no noise. He is a bit like that Sadhu, with eyes looking far into the distance, who held out his hands to offer us leaves of fresh mint and lumps of sugar.

Dear Francesco, now I apologize. Maybe I have used too many words, and we know that words never get to the point. Words slide all over the place. This time, it went like this. Next time, though, I hope we'll be playing cards by the seaside with our beloved ladies. Will it be so?

Ettore Sottsass

Translated, from the Italian, by Rodney Stringer.

53. *Circuito*, 1980. Pastel on paper, 24 x 18 1/16 inches (61 x 45.8 cm). Private collection, East Sussex.

54. *Everything I Know*, 1983. Pastel on paper, 26 x 18 $^{7}/_{8}$ inches (66 x 48 cm). Private collection, courtesy Galerie Bruno Bischofberger, Zurich.

55. *She and She*, 1982. Pastel on paper, 24 x 18 inches (61 x 45.7 cm). Private collection.

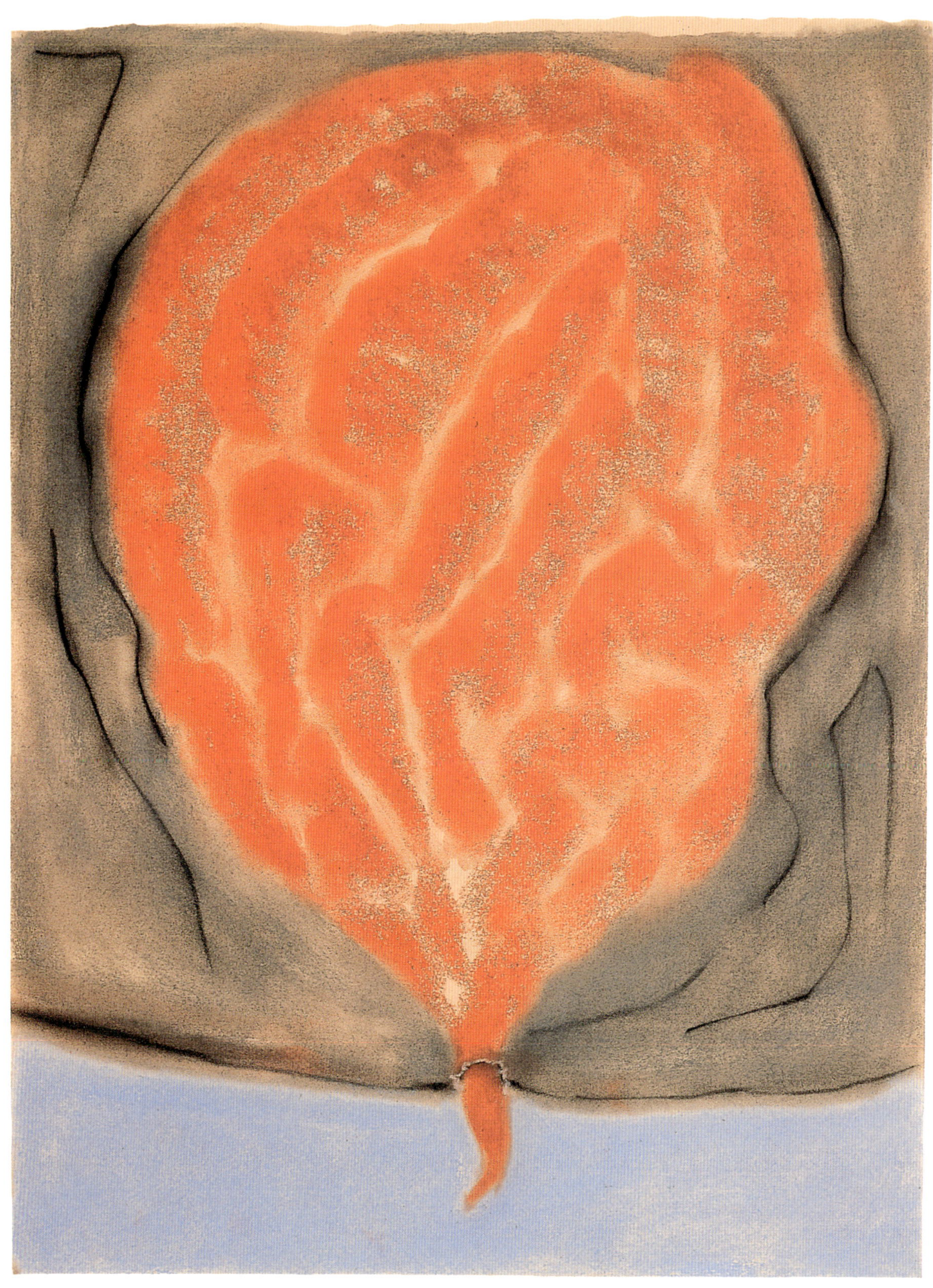

56. *Interior Landscape*, 1980. Pastel on paper, 24 x 18 inches (61 x 45.7 cm). Private collection.

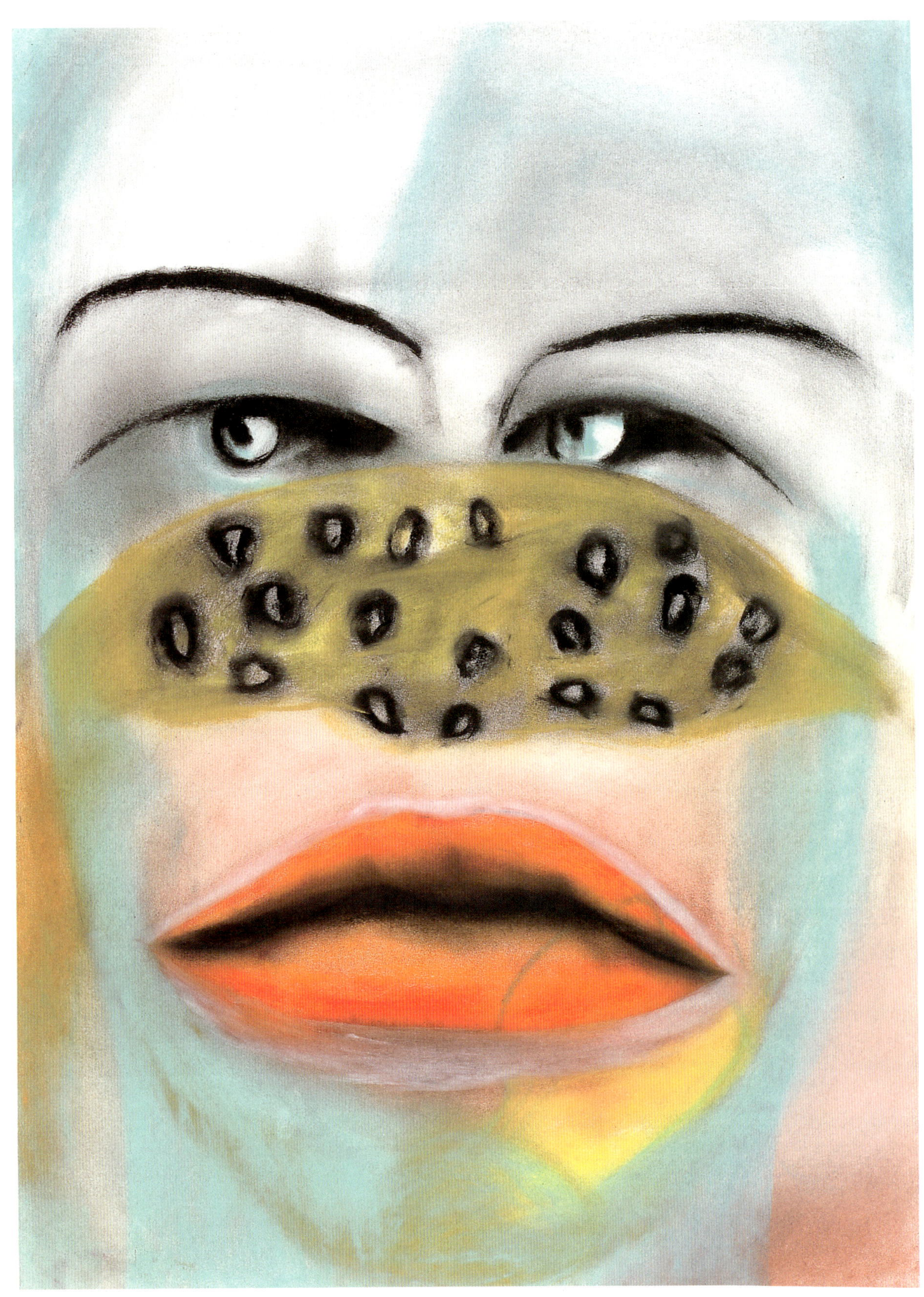

57. *Naso*, 1983. Pastel on paper, 26 x 19 inches (66 x 48.3 cm). Collection of Francesco and Alba Clemente, New York.

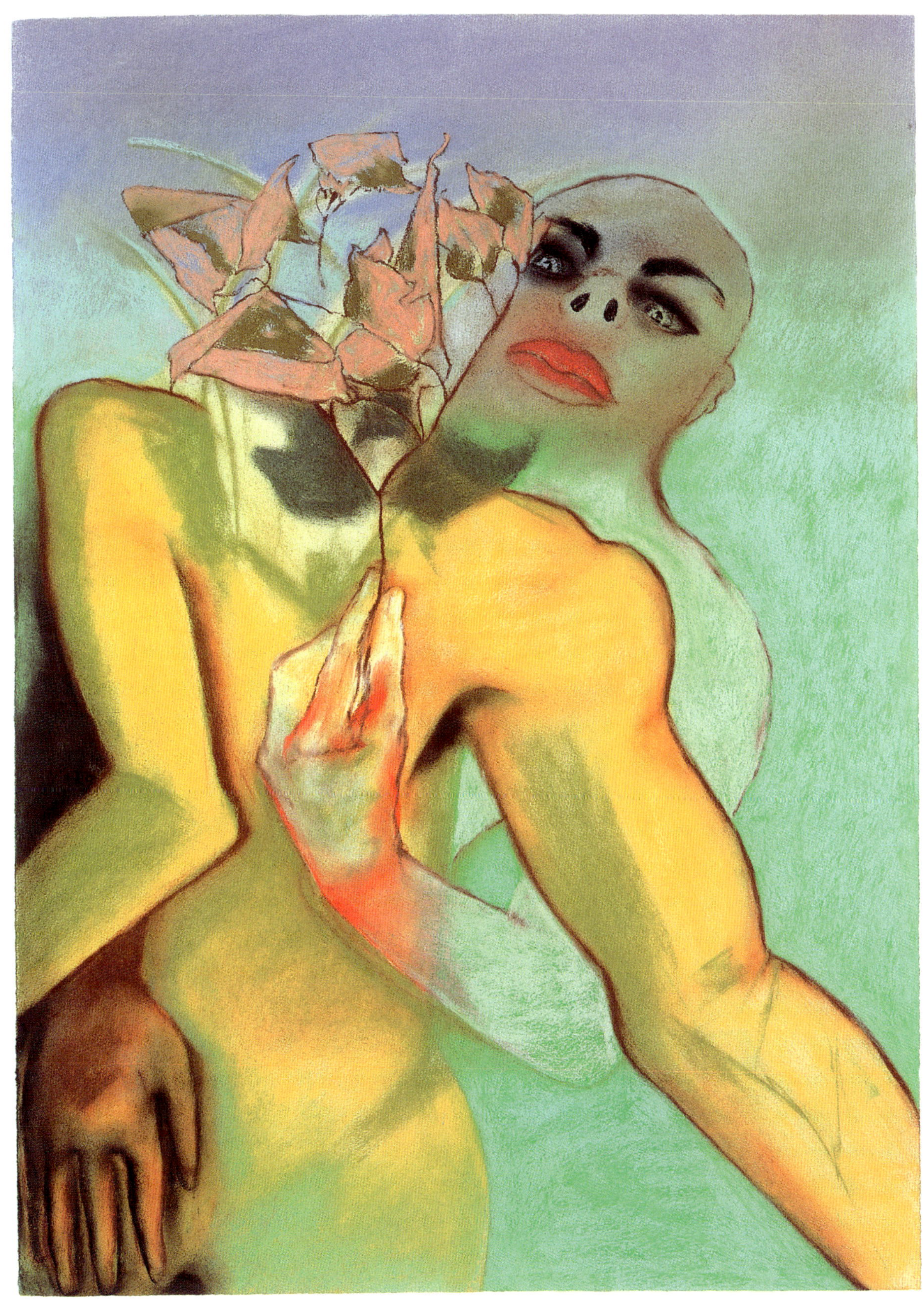

58. ***Abbraccio*****,** 1983. Pastel on paper, 26 x 18 7/8 inches (66 x 48 cm). Private collection, courtesy Galerie Bruno Bischofberger, Zurich.

59. *Non ti ricordi*, 1982. Pastel on paper, 24 x 18 1/16 inches (61 x 45.8 cm). Collection of Bruno Bischofberger, Zurich.

60. ***Kiss***, 1983. Pastel on paper, 26 x 19 inches (66 x 48.3 cm). Collection of Francesco and Alba Clemente, New York.

61. ***Secret***, 1983. Oil on linen, 78 x 93 inches (198.1 x 236.2 cm). Collection of Mia and Patrick Demarchelier.

62. *Name*, 1983. Oil on linen, 77 15/16 x 92 15/16 inches (198 x 236 cm). Private collection.

63. ***Untitled***, 1983. Oil and wax on linen, 82 x 28 1/2 in (208.3 x 72.4 cm). Private collection.

64. *General Animal*, 1984. Oil on wood, mounted on aluminum, 39 x 68 7/8 inches (99 x 174.9 cm). Private collection, Switzerland.

65. ***Suitcase***, 1984–85. Oil on wood, mounted on aluminum, 41 3/4 x 67 11/16 inches (106 x 172 cm). Private collection.

66. *Breathing*, 1984. Oil on wood, mounted on aluminum, 72 1/16 x 42 15/16 inches (183 x 109 cm). Private collection, Switzerland.

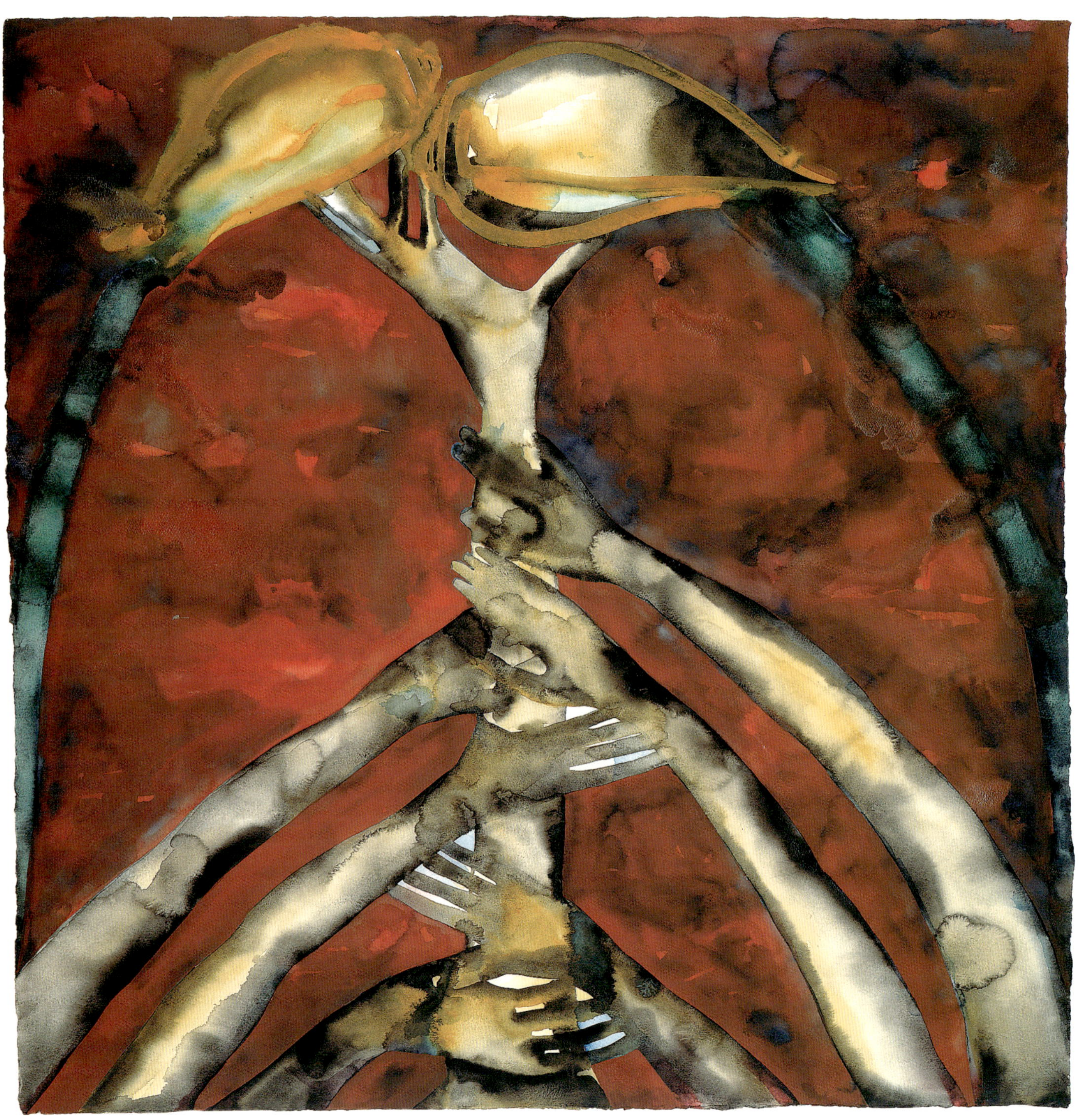

67. *Fountain*, from ***The Book of the Sea***, 1993. Watercolor on paper, 44 1/4 x 45 1/8 inches (112.4 x 114.6 cm). Collection of Francesco and Alba Clemente, New York.

68. ***Symmetry***, from ***The Book of the Sea***, 1991. Watercolor on paper, 46 1/2 x 44 1/2 inches (118.1 x 113 cm). Collection of Francesco and Alba Clemente, New York.

69. *Tree*, from ***The Book of the Sea***, 1993. Watercolor on paper, 44 1/4 x 46 inches (112.4 x 116.8 cm). Private collection.

70. ***The King and the Corpse***, from ***The Book of the Sea***, 1992. Watercolor on paper, 44 1/4 x 46 inches (112.4 x 116.8 cm). Collection of Tatum O'Neal.

Loop

I left it behind
Only me
in the dark
like they say

for others to find
no one more
as they came in
than another

two and two
if there
the doubles of desire
it's enough

their bodies' architecture
inside flesh
myself still inside
I could be

singing small gray bird
more than reflection
caught by design
fixed as an echo

upright cock breast
be myself more
hips the rope's loop.
like passage like door.

Robert Creeley

71. ***Loop***, 1993. Tempera on linen, 76 x 72 inches (193 x 182.9 cm). Collection of Matthew and Iris Strauss, Rancho Santa Fe, California.

Pastel Sentences

Perfume bottle between thighs, she appreciates blue human odor.

Soles & palms stare out wide-eyed under World War I's low monoplane skies.

Snail brows, chakra eyes, iron nose, portico mouth, oak beard, ears hear the sea.

Mice ate at the big red heart in her breast, she was distracted in love.

Peek through the keyhole big blue sky, man & woman support empty space.

He kneels & slurps orange lips between spread knees that lift up blind joy birds.

Big Mother bent on knees head down hands on ass still can come by herself.

Bowed down by the weight of nebulae he crouches underneath the hill.

A bat that's bigger than your ear watches you sleep while you dream him there.

Protect your black electric octopus plexus with red parasol.

Protect your low dark secret eye-crotch with long pink fingers intertwined.

Earth birdhead prow, Dead Man cargo; Earth manhead prow, passenger Big Bird.

One brown bird impassive eyes her crotch, two black birds backs turned watch what's up.

A round blue eye work red lipped 'neath this century's gigantic lightbulb.

One points ahead from moon-whale's jaws; one's caught his moon-whale, looks up surprised.

He kneels on all fours red hot, she sits Lotus & mouths the blue apple.

Lantern-jawed Bismarck dreams a rich red rose blossoms thorn-stemmed through his skull.

In an oval blue womb a full-grown girl curled up eyes closed dreams her birth.

Big little people do yab yum in their ten petal'd yellow daisy.

Long hand over left eye Mother Sudan sees big bellied kids' thin ribs.

In midst of coition a blood-red worm spurts out his heaving rib-cage.

Death sweats blood in Earth's black womb, yearning as clouds wing 'round blue horizons.

The one eyed moon-whale watches you weep, drifting pale seas in a pale boat.

Climb Snowtooth Mountain, put your staff in the moon's beak, fall down from the sky.

Thirty Kingdoms' keys chainmailed down his chest, the Pope dreams he's St. Peter.

Perfume bottle 'twixt his asscheeks, they smile to inhale human odor.

The black hermaphrodite squats on black spheres upholding square black slave-blocks.

He lies back eyes half shut stupefied by Sun that hovers far too low.

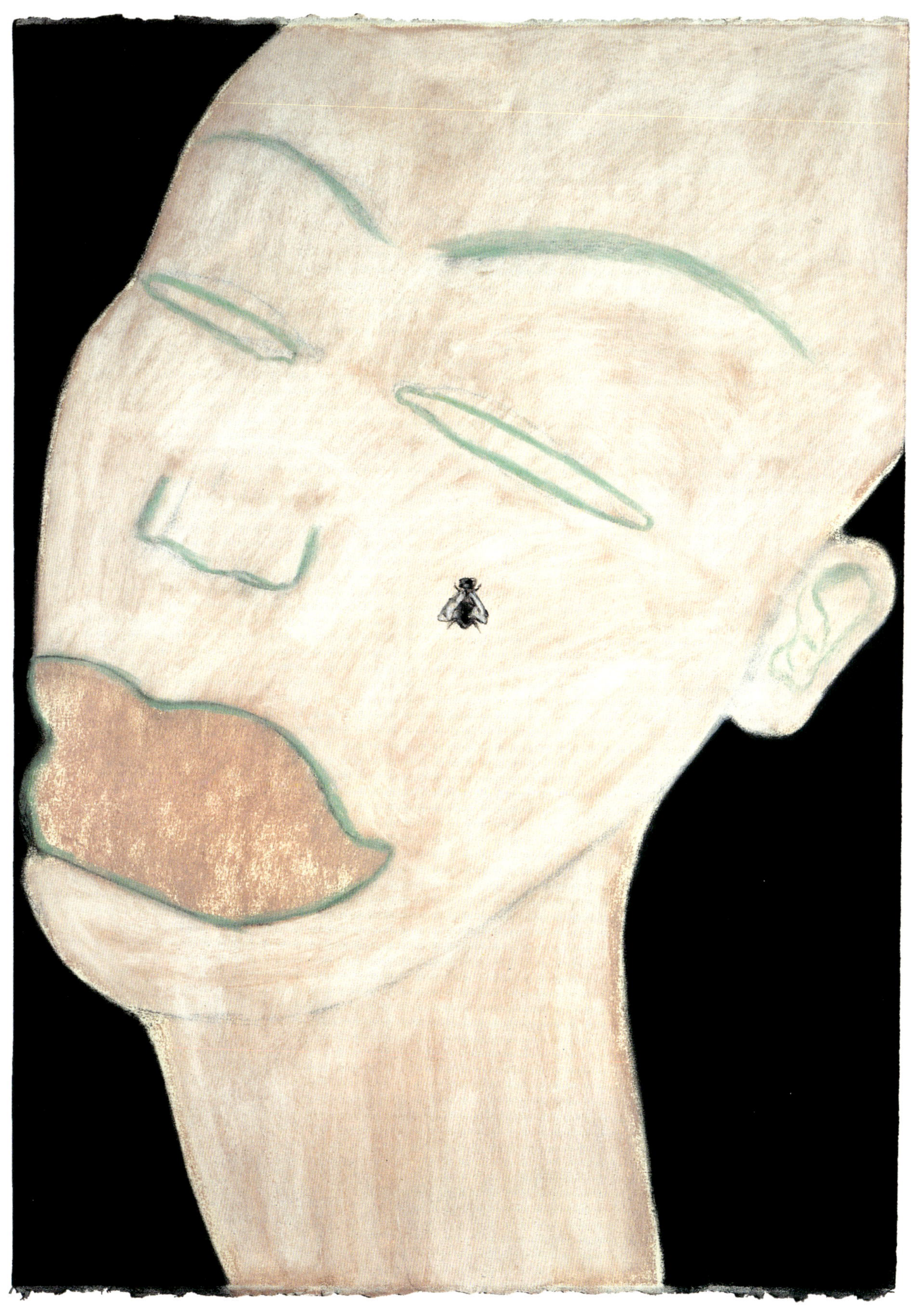

72. *She*, from ***Ex Libris Chenonceau***, 1994–95. Pastel on paper, 26 x 19 inches (66 x 48.3 cm). Private collection, courtesy Galerie Bruno Bischofberger, Zurich.

Jeannie Duval's cheek tickled by a Paris fly, 1852.

Angels pour amphorae of black water on her rainbow parasol.

Octopus sun cracks red legs above th' umbrella'd dreamer's rain rock stream.

The Czar's green felt greatcoat hangs in Hermitage's Hall of Mirrors now.

Sun manhead prow, passenger Big Bird; Sun birdhead prow, passenger Dead Man.

Red sun on yellow seas, pale boats float a bird's and dead man's heads, necks cut.

Spiraled above ghost earth Christ faints in blue sky floating black lightning clouds.

She watches three black birds question us at th'entrance to her green spread thighs.

Meteors flash down, skulls wait under earth, one green leaf breaks through black soil.

Standing between black door keys in Afric graveyards she births a white ghost.

Puff a cigarette between skullfleshed lips, smoke gets in your empty eyes.

A funnel, a knife, & eight-legged Ant stand upside down the night's black floor.

What bluefaced sin! he holds a white-hot candle between her sunny thighs.

Jonah gives his high sign to a man who cuddles the whale at his breast.

Sphincter-wound in his chest, he kneels and lifts both hands in surprise to pray.

All mixed up breasts feet genitals nipples & hand, both fall into sleep.

Adam contemplates his navel covered with a bush of jealous hearts

Body spread open, black legs held down, she eats his ice cream-white sex-tongue.

On grey moon crescent, green thumb-pinkies raise a brown champaigne shoe-last.

The black serpent vortex rises round-eyed, fist & black heart arrow-pierced.

One centaur palm raised thru earth-crust lifts a red live dog barking at stars.

Her dog licks the live red heart of th' African lady curled up in bed.

The green tree dreams a pink sun, the root-buried head dreams an egg-brown globe.

Naked in solitary prison cell he looks down at a hard-on.

Hands hold her ass tight with joy to lick and eat the blue star 'twixt her thighs.

Small pink-winged Lady-Heart hovers, rose-cunt legs spread nigh his stiff black dick.

The one-eyed twat squats on his head, scissors at masked Pinocchio's nose.

Willendorf Venus stands on Mars' shoulders, arms stretched up hold sky's blue bowl.

Her Shield: third eye, armpits, eye boobs, navel, pussy ass split on star-field.

Grave ghosts guard the chthonic cellar door steps out to cypress, sky & clouds.

Chic shoes rest in a black rose vortex of sociable fashion money.

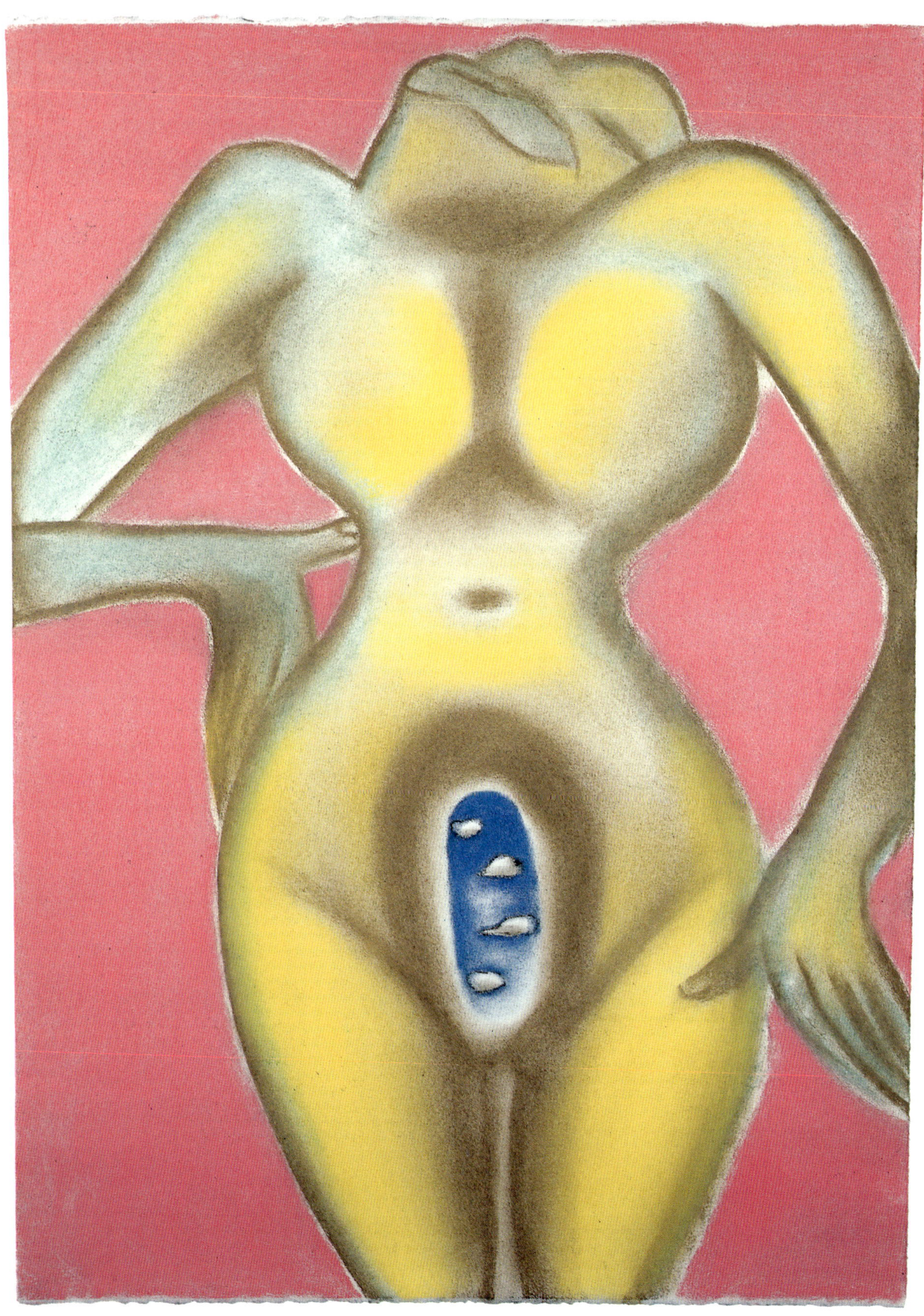

73. *Sky*, from ***Ex Libris Chenonceau*,** 1994–95. Pastel on paper, 26 x 19 inches (66 x 48.3 cm). Collection of Francesco and Alba Clemente, New York.

She poses self-confident, blue sky & clouds borne in her oval womb.
White clit, brown nipples, rose smile, legs up, dark eyes stare through her cross-hand mask.
Lady Buddha sleeps on blue air in a green leaf, knees raised spread naked.
Repose open-eyed on starry blue pillows under a star-roofed sky.
Two girls show big dildos—or is one a boy with his dick in the air?
The black guy steps in the shade, glancing back at the sunlit boy he screwed.
Hard-on stuck thru beachtowel folds, hands telescope an unashamed eye.
Legs behind neck, arms hung down, Yogi's solar anal navel burns red.
Blowing bubbles in blue sky he squats on his own blue bubble planet.
Star, bird, cane & big thigh bones, the ghost baby dreams life beyond the womb.
Regarding their long thick tails, blue demons wrestle with golden scissors.
One dances in red fire, one leaps in blue sea, no one burnt or drowned yet.
He steps on his own breast lying in bed with red half hard-on.
He kneels with big dong toenails to marvel the radiant snake in his breast.
Tongue hung out, he hangs near his orange bicycle exhausted to death.
Kneeling nude he upholds a big newt on each palm, doesn't know why yet.
Lady snails delicately climb naked thighs to stir his genitals.
A human white leopard kneels hard on top the pink zebra on all fours.
Left forefinger probed into his own left hand proves a Doubting Thomas.
Half-man Half-woman share their head, a fish gasping one big sad blue eye.
Smiling eye, hand cupped to her ear, a huge red egg prophesies twin boys.
They exchange glances, a bee shadows her tail, a rose grows on his hip.
William Burroughs' skeleton twists a towel, he's got the bloody rag on.
The rose-girl kneels weighed down, iron tanks on shoulder, coccyx, calves & footsoles.
Horse stands on horse upon horse, lie back on top & take your forty winks.
He dives from naked sky past the sun's nimbus into space-blue ocean.
Curtains part on a nail and its shadow, Samsara's drama Act I.
The red lip'd fat billionaire appeals you try out his wee twat or dick.
Arms to neck, his tit, her belly, prong-twat, the President and his wife.
Pale green headless phantoms upside down dipsy-doodle with thin hard-ons.

74. *Story*, from ***Ex Libris Chenonceau***, 1994–95. Pastel on paper, 26 x 19 inches (66 x 48.3 cm). Collection of Francesco and Alba Clemente, New York.

Eyes' nose mouth's secret place's white tusks wound importunate magicians.

Lady Day bows her neck under a pyramid of oily black rocks.

Cloud-shoulders balloon a pale headless dame above his brooding chalk face.

Beneath breast-eyed wasp-beaks the pink rose opens, better get in there quick!

Insider her red womb the hermaphrodite fetus closes a third eye.

Wiping blood-black tears from hard labor, try holding up your big sad head.

Jealousy! Jealousy! Chin in hand he ponders the Unfaithful Muse.

Young Don Juan bravely displays his girlish red-sexed lips and eyeshadow.

Caught in the burning house of my brown body I fainted openeyed.

Black legs spread wide, arm 'neath neck relaxed, a hand shakes gold leaves down her crotch.

A golden lady's pink lips and fingers soothe her lover prone in sleep.

Comets fly, sperm shoots forth, man kneels erect, woman climbs him glancing back.

Blue Adam kneels on blue clay earth, Eve dances his neck in gold-washed sky.

Big phallus, black womb lined with reddish flesh, look at the monkey we birthed.

One bird pecks her double's breast on a ghost-white lingam's unblinking head.

The thin brown man studies his stuck-up prong, a tall pink conchshell shrinks back.

The red-lipped ladyman's head rests eyes calm on bright mineral pillows.

Cut by the green knife neck to crotch, he grins in pain, blue guts rolling out.

Bird beaks poke in his eyeball skull and heart's eye while his red thing spurts seed.

She flies down thousands of stone steps for years, aged climbs them all back up.

for Francesco Clemente
Château Chenonceau, June 24, 1995
Naropa Institute, July 5, 1995
Lawrence, Kansas, July 22, 1995

Allen Ginsberg

75. *Nose*, from ***Ex Libris Chenonceau*,** 1994–95. Pastel on paper, 26 x 19 inches (66 x 48.3 cm). Collection of Francesco and Alba Clemente, New York.

76. *Seal*, from ***Fifty-one Days on Mount Abu***, 1995. Watercolor on handmade paper, 21 $^{1}/_{8}$ x 27 $^{7}/_{8}$ inches (53.7 x 70.8 cm). Private collection.

77. *Food*, from ***Fifty-one Days on Mount Abu***, 1995. Watercolor on handmade paper, 21 1/8 x 27 7/8 inches (53.7 x 70.8 cm).
Courtesy Anthony d'Offay Gallery, London.

78. *Anima*, from ***Fifty-one Days on Mount Abu*,** 1995. Watercolor on handmade paper, 21 1/8 x 27 7/8 inches (53.7 x 70.8 cm).
Collection of Francesco and Alba Clemente, New York.

79. *Muse*, from ***Fifty-one Days on Mount Abu***, 1995. Watercolor on handmade paper, 21 1/8 x 27 7/8 inches (53.7 x 70.8 cm).

Collection of Francesco and Alba Clemente, New York.

80. ***Tree***, from ***Fifty-one Days on Mount Abu***, 1995. Watercolor on handmade paper, 21 1/8 x 27 7/8 inches (53.7 x 70.8 cm). Private collection.

81. ***Silence***, from ***Fifty-one Days on Mount Abu***, 1995. Watercolor on handmade paper, 21 1/8 x 27 7/8 inches (53.7 x 70.8 cm). Carmignac Gestion, Paris.

82. ***Skin***, 1996. Oil on linen, 48 x 60 inches (121.9 x 152.4 cm). Private collection.

83. ***Heart***, 1996. Oil on linen, 48 x 60 inches (121.9 x 152.4 cm). Courtesy The Brant Foundation, Greenwich, Connecticut.

84. *Memory*, 1996. Oil on linen, 48 x 60 inches (121.9 x 152.4 cm). Private collection.

Conversion to Her

Parts of each person,
Lumber of bodies,
Heads and legs
Inside the echoes—

I got here slowly
Coming out of my mother,
Herself in passage
Still wet with echoes—

Little things surrounding,
Little feet, little eyes,
Black particulars,
White disparities—

Who was I then?
What man had entered?
Was my own person
Passing pleasure?

My body shrank,
Breath was constricted,
Head confounded,
Tongue muted.

I wouldn't know you,
Self in old mirror.
I won't please you
Crossing over.

Knife cuts through.
Things stick in holes.
Spit covers body.
Head's left hanging.

The hole is in the middle.
Little boy wants one.
Help him sing here
Helpless and wanting.

•

My odor?
My name?
My flesh?
My shame?

My other
than you are,
my way out—
My door shut—

In silence this
happens, in pain.

•

Outside is empty.

Inside is a house
of various size.

Covered with skin
one lives within.

Women are told
to let world unfold.

Men, to take it,
make or break it.

All's true
except for you.

•

Being human, one wonders at the others,
men with their beards and anger,

women with their friends and pleasure—
and the children they engender together—

until the sky goes suddenly black and a monstrous thing
comes from nowhere upon them

in their secure slumbers, in their righteous undertakings,
shattering thought.

One cannot say, *Be as women,*
be peaceful, then. The hole from which we came

isn't metaphysical.
The one to which we go is real.

Surrounding a vast space
seems boundless appetite

in which a man still lives
till he become a woman.

Robert Creeley

85. *Bestiarium*, 1989. Pastel on paper, 30 x 26 5/16 inches (76.2 x 66.9 cm). Museum für Moderne Kunst, Frankfurt am Main.

Sleeping birds, lead me,
soft birds, be me

inside this black room,
back of the white moon.

In the dark night
sight frightens me.

86. ***Bestiarium***, 1989. Pastel on paper, 30 x 26 5/16 inches (76.2 x 66.9 cm). Museum für Moderne Kunst, Frankfurt am Main.

Who is it nuzzles there
with furred, round headed stare?

Who, perched on the skin,
body's float, is holding on?

What other one stares still,
plays still, on and on?

87. *Bestiarium*, 1989. Pastel on paper, 30 x 26 5/16 inches (76.2 x 66.9 cm). Museum für Moderne Kunst, Frankfurt am Main.

Stand upright, prehensile,
squat, determined,

small guardians of the painful
outside coming in—

in stuck-in vials with needles,
bleeding life in, particular, heedless.

88. *Bestiarium*, 1989. Pastel on paper, 30 x 26 5/16 inches (76.2 x 66.9 cm). Museum für Moderne Kunst, Frankfurt am Main.

Matrix of world
upon a turtle's broad back,

carried on like that,
eggs as pearls,

flesh and blood and bone
all borne along.

89. *Bestiarium*, 1989. Pastel on paper, 30 x 26 5/16 inches (76.2 x 66.9 cm). Museum für Moderne Kunst, Frankfurt am Main.

I'll tell you what you want,
to say a word,

to know the letters in yourself,
a skin falls off,

a big eared head appears,
an eye and mouth.

90. *Bestiarium*, 1989. Pastel on paper, 30 x 26 5/16 inches (76.2 x 66.9 cm). Museum für Moderne Kunst, Frankfurt am Main.

Under watery here,
under breath, under duress,

understand a pain
has threaded a needle with a little man—

gone fishing.
And fish appear.

91. ***Bestiarium***, 1989. Pastel on paper, 30 x 26 5/16 inches (76.2 x 66.9 cm). Museum für Moderne Kunst, Frankfurt am Main.

If small were big,
if then were now,

if here were there,
if find were found,

if mind were all there was,
would the animals still save us?

92. *Bestiarium*, 1989. Pastel on paper, 30 x 26 5/16 inches (76.2 x 66.9 cm). Museum für Moderne Kunst, Frankfurt am Main.

A head was put
upon the shelf got took

by animal's hand and stuck
upon a vacant corpse

who, blurred, could nonetheless
not ever be the quietly standing bird it watched.

Not lost,
not better or worse,

much must of necessity depend on resources,
the pipes and bags brought with us

inside, all the sacks
and how and to what they are or were attached.

93. *Earth*, 1988. Tempera on linen, 84 x 135 inches (213.4 x 342.9 cm). Private collection.

Everybody's child
walks the same winding road,

laughs and cries, dies.
That's "everybody's child,"

the one who's in between
the others who have come and gone.

Turn as one will, the sky will always be
far up above the place he thinks to dream as earth.

There float the heavenly
archaic persons of primordial birth,

held in the scan of ancient serpent's tooth,
locked in the mind as when it first began.

94. ***Everybody's Child***, 1990. Tempera on linen, 79 1/8 x 108 1/4 inches (201 x 275 cm).
Private collection.

95. ***Constellation***, 1990. Tempera on linen, four panels, 47 5/8 x 220 1/16 inches (121 x 559 cm) overall. Private collection, courtesy Galerie Bruno Bischofberger, Zurich.

Inside I am the other of a self,
who feels a presence always close at hand,

one side or the other, knows another one
unlocks the door and quickly enters in.

Either as or, we live a common person.
Two is still one. It cannot live apart.

Oh, weep for me—
all from whom life has stolen

hopes of a happiness stored
in gold's ubiquitous pattern,

in tinkle of commodious, enduring money,
else the bee's industry in hives of golden honey.

96. *Paradigm*, 1988. Tempera on linen, 82 x 56 inches (208.3 x 142.2 cm). Collection of Angela Westwater, New York, courtesy Sperone Westwater, New York.

97. ***Honey and Gold***, 1988. Tempera on linen, 81 7/8 x 55 7/8 inches (208 x 142 cm). Private collection.

98. ***Signature***, 1988. Tempera on linen, 82 x 56 inches (208.3 x 142.2 cm). Collection of Thomas and Janine Koerfer-Weill.

He is safely put
in a container, head to foot,

and there, on his upper part, wears still
remnants of a life he lived at will—

but, lower down, he probes at that doubled sack
holds all his random virtues in a mindless fact.

The forms wait, swan,
elephant, crab, rabbit, horse, monkey, cow,

squirrel and crocodile. From the one
sits in empty consciousness, all seemingly has come

and now it goes, to regather,
to tell another story to its patient mother.

99. *Oblation*, 1990. Tempera on linen, 79 1/16 x 108 1/16 inches (200.8 x 274.5 cm).
The Cleveland Museum of Art, Dorothea Wright Hamilton Fund 1993.164.

Reflection reforms, each man's a life,
makes its stumbling way from mother to wife—

cast as a gesture from ignorant flesh,
here writes in fumbling words to touch,

say, *how can I be,*
when she is all that was ever me?

100. ***Contemplation***, 1991. Tempera on linen, 44 x 64 $^{1}/_{4}$ inches (111.8 x 163.2 cm). Collection of Gian Enzo Sperone, New York, courtesy Sperone Westwater, New York.

101. ***Oblation***, 1990–91. Tempera on linen, 44 x 44 inches (111.8 x 111.8 cm). Collection of Robert and Mary Looker.

Around and in—
And up and down again,

and far and near—
and here and there,

in the middle is
a great round nothingness.

102. *Seed*, 1991. Tempera on linen, 24 x 24 inches (61 x 61 cm). Collection of Francesco and Alba Clemente, New York.

Not metaphoric,
flesh is literal earth.

turns to dust
as all the body must,

becomes the ground
wherein the seed's passed on.

103. ***Foot***, 1990. Tempera on linen, 23 x 25 inches (58.4 x 63.5 cm). Collection of Raymond Foye.

Entries, each foot feels its own way,
echoes passage in persons,

holds the body upright,
the secret of thresholds, lintels,

opening body above it,
looks up, looks down, moves forward.

104. ***Necessity***, 1991. Tempera on linen, 40 3/16 x 40 3/16 inches (102 x 102 cm). Private collection, courtesy Galerie Bruno Bischofberger, Zurich.

Necessity, the mother of invention,
father of intention,

sister to brother to sister, to innumerable others,
all one as the time comes,

death's appointment,
in the echoing head, in the breaking heart.

105. ***Friendship***, 1991. Tempera on linen, 30 x 24 inches (76.2 x 61 cm). Private collection.

In self one's place defined,
in heart the other find.

In mind discover *I*,
in body find the sky.

Sleep in the dream as one,
wake to the others there found.

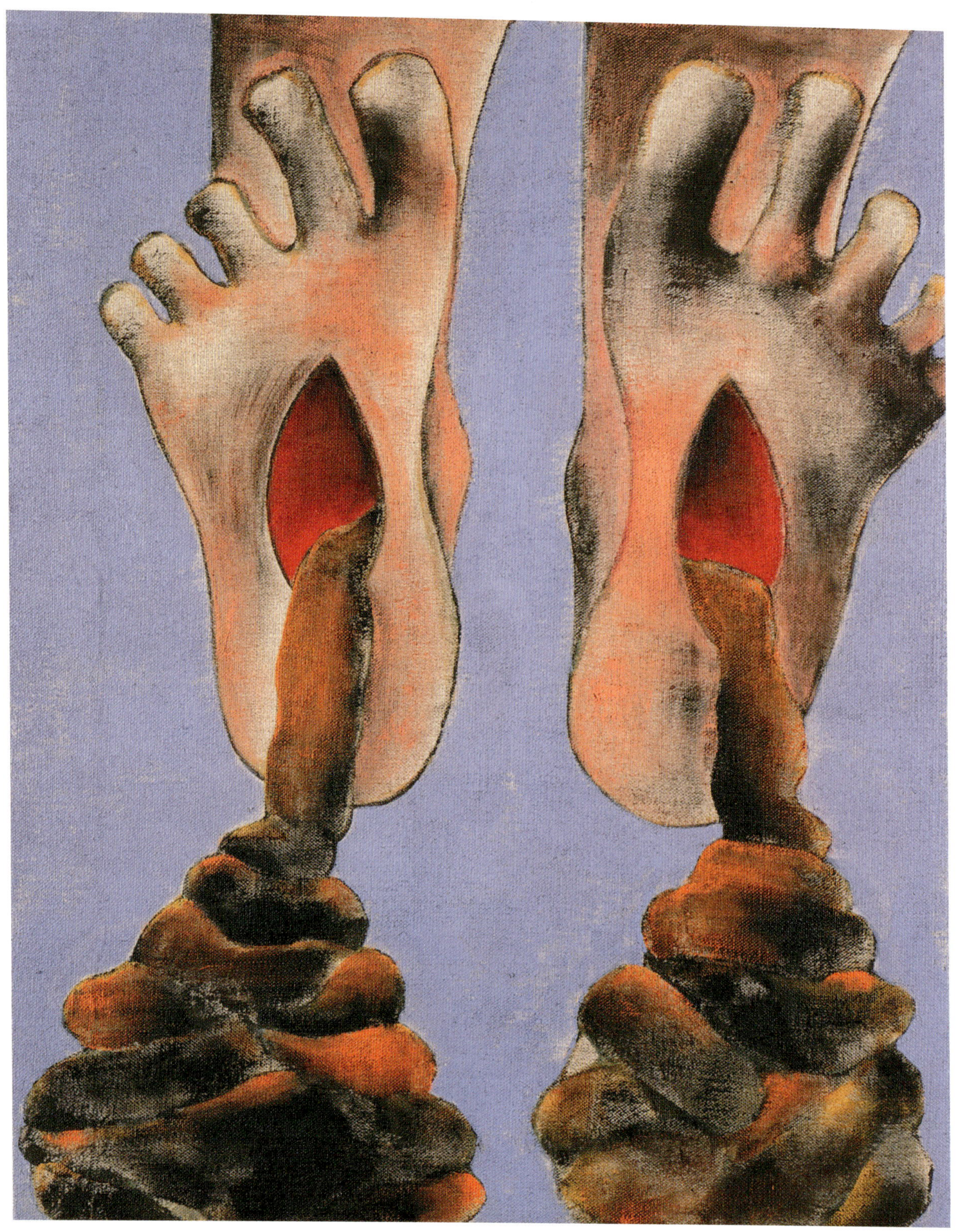

106. ***Foot,*** 1990. Tempera on linen, 26 x 21 inches (66 x 53.3 cm). Private collection, courtesy Annika Barbarigos Fine Art.

Emptying out
each complicating part,

each little twist of mind inside,
each clenched fist,

each locked, particularizing thought,
forgotten, emptying out.

107. *Meditation*, 1991. Tempera on linen, 29 15/16 x 24 inches (76 x 61 cm). Collection of Bruno Bischofberger, Zurich.

What did it feel like
to be one at a time—

to be caught in a mind
in the body you'd found

in yourself alone—
in each other one?

108. ***Broken Hearts***, 1990. Tempera on linen, 52 x 42 inches (132 x 106.7 cm). Courtesy Sperone Westwater, New York.

Broken hearts, a curious round of echoes—
and there behind them the old garden

with its faded, familiar flowers,
where all was seemingly laced together—

a trueness of true,
a blueness of blue.

The truth is in a container
of no size or situation.

It has nothing
inside.

Worship—
Warship. Sail away.

Robert Creeley

109. ***Black Muse Twice***, 1990. Tempera on linen, 87 1/2 x 106 3/4 inches (222.3 x 271.1 cm). Collection of Jean Pigozzi, Switzerland.

Amulets and Prayers

Francesco Clemente does not perceive any inherent incongruity in his concurrent explorations of images from his own "dominant" culture and from India's "alternative" one. He probes the classical Upanishadic ideas of the elements and the five senses, as well as the flood of contemporary popular imagery in Madras, such as cinema billboards and campaign posters. The artist says, "The gods who left us thousands of years ago in Naples are still in India,"[1] and "in Indian diversity there is still the memory of very refined expressions, which we have lost."[2] The Indian concept of *parampara* (one permeating the other), a sort of simultaneous and polymorphous transmigration of images, each rooted in its essence but equal in relation to the other, appeals immensely to Clemente, for whom one image is as good as another, each having the same expressive power.

Fragmented, decontextualized, self-contained images, imbued with their own radiance, were reconfigured as Clemente's *The Pondicherry Pastels* (1979–80, cat. no. 111) without a hierarchical order. Full of transcultural quotes, not vying for a known referential context, they dwell in an ambivalent space and speak in what the Tantrics would call "twilight language." Ruptured hierarchies are replaced by a fantasizing and reschematizing personal order, searching for new possibilities of representation. Clemente's transient, symbolic images adopt forms concrete enough to evoke definite history and illusive enough to elicit mythology.

For Clemente, fascinated by variations on a theme, the Indian literary form of *kathachakra* (cycle of stories), as employed in the revolving narrative of *The King and the Corpse* (1994, cat. no. 120), had to be alluring. Each time the king pursues the corpse to bring it under his control, he has to carry it on his shoulders from one magical place to another. As he does so, he has to solve riddles posed by the corpse. The idea of riddle—what is real and what is deceptive, what is manifest and what is concealed—appeals to Clemente's highly articulated sense of fantasy. Once the riddle is solved, the story ends. Decoding an image would be tantamount to emptying it of its spell, its power. It would then no longer remain an amulet. In *The King and the Corpse* sculptures, Clemente brings into play a transmuting permeation between the corporeal and the imaginary, often marked by a metamorphosis of genders. King and corpse are entangled like a riddle; the answer is encapsulated in bodies of copper, tin, bronze, brass, and lead.

The alchemical powers of metals pervade the elements of the cosmic order. The formula for fashioning Hindu divine images entails the use of five metals, which are also the essence of the five elements and the five senses. Clemente's planets *Mercury* and *Saturn* (1992, cat. nos. 117, 118) emanate as anthropomorphs of tin and lead. Each is in the image of the other, shooting off a burst of light through a pair of open palms, forming a radiant halo, echoing the Brhadaranyaka Upanishad: "His voice enters into the fire, his breath into the wind, his thought into the moon, his hearing into the four directions."

Clemente's intellect may have been charged by the classical Indian tradition, but his painter's eye was drawn to the bright and florid imagery proliferating in the bazaars of Madras. He saw the continuity and fragmentation of Indian tradition in the gigantic cinema billboards, staring fixedly at the onlooker from all directions, with their simplified, almost emblematic, renderings of eyes, ears, noses, and lips, imagery that virtually underlines the notion of senses. In all this, however, what interested Clemente most was the possibility of having his work attain an immense artistic transformation of history, imagery, meaning, symbolism, and, above all, the scale of the picture plane. He employed the services of the bazaar painters of cinema billboards and created the *Five Senses* series (1990, cat. nos. 121–23), as well as *Sun* (1980, cat. no. 113), *Moon* (1980, cat. no. 114), *Contemplation* (1990, cat. no. 124), *Birth* (1990, cat. no. 126), etc., on vast surfaces composed by joining sheets of handmade Pondicherry paper. Wide areas of flat gaudy colors, vestigial shadings, sharp outlines, and grids of horizontal and vertical lines of joinery, in combination with quotes from the "three worlds" that he effortlessly maps, turn his images into haunting new icons.

The same magical transformation marks Clemente's erotic imagery. In *The Black Book* (1989, cat. no. 131), orgiastic coital diagrams, reminiscent of the Kamasutra and Khajuraho, bathe in a distant twilight atmosphere of brilliance and celebration. While the doe-eyed women of *The White Book* (1989, cat. no. 130)—their faces in profile, their yonis worn like emblems—wander in another resplendent space of liberation, their counterparts in *The Red Book* (1989, cat. no. 129) appear to have been synopsized from a performative context.

Clemente sees himself rooted in the highly eclectic environment of the Roman Empire of the third century, when Egyptians painted Greek themes, Greeks sang Latin songs, and Latin Romans worshiped the gods from the East.[3] *Story of My Country I* (1990, cat. no. 127) is an intertwined narrative of two raconteurs: Clemente and the Other. As he painted this work, in layered improvisations, he forged time into the vast spaces of many mythologies, histories, and ideas, looking through the consciousness of the Other, letting the Other think through his consciousness; the I is always the Other.[4] Clemente constructed the story through sketches in which he has a distant Orissan painter build up the fictive narrative. The story—from Clemente's own imagination—of violence, intrigue, fragmentation, love, separation, jealousy, and rape is told through another's language, images, and symbols. In the process, an unanticipated world of surprise and wonder is brought into being. Clemente seeks to find himself through these surprises, these elements of the unknown.

Jyotindra Jain

1. Francesco Clemente, quoted in Raymond Foye, "Madras," in Ann Percy and Foye, *Francesco Clemente: Three Worlds*, exh. cat. (Philadelphia: Philadelphia Museum of Art, 1990), p. 50.
2. Clemente, quoted in Donald Kuspit, "Clemente Explores Clemente," in *Contemporanea* (New York) 2, no. 7 (Oct. 1989), p. 40.
3. See Clemente, interview with Robin White, in *View* (Oakland) 3, no. 6 (Nov. 1981); this issue is devoted entirely to the interview.
4. See Dieter Koepplin, "Offener Zyklus," introduction to *Francesco Clemente CVIII*, exh. cat. (Zurich: VerlagsHausZürich; and Basel: Museum für Gegenwartskunst, 1987), p. 9.

110. ***Map of What Is Effortless***, 1978. Gouache on paper, 60 x 57 inches (152.4 x 144.8 cm). Courtesy Anthony d'Offay Gallery, London.

Pondicherry, the former French colonial city near Madras, was where Francesco Clemente obtained the unevenly grained handmade paper he used for *The Pondicherry Pastels* (1979–80, cat. no. 111). Imbued with a certain sense of lightness, joy, freshness, immediacy, and a percipient distancing from "meaning," the images exalt the commonplace: a ceiling fan, a bucket, a plate, a tumbler doll, a carrot or a banana, a palm tree or a rose, a pair of scissors or a rosary. These are iconized in a liminal space between their momentary and eternal existences. At times, they are amulets infused with magical powers; at times, they are merely deconsecrated charms waiting to be immersed in the river of transmigration, to be born again in other forms, other contexts.

Conscious of the futility of finding meaning in hierarchical ordering, Clemente configured his swiftly recorded "notes," "quotes," and "raw material" into a series redolent with his personal associations, leaving open to his viewers the possibility of an alternative configuration.

For Clemente, "Pastels reveal the primeval qualities of colour. Pastels are colours just born. In India . . . in the evening all colours are born and they are pastels."[1]

J. J.

1. Francesco Clemente, statement in *Francesco Clemente: Two Horizons*, exh. cat. (Tokyo: Sezon Museum of Art, 1994), p. 23.

following nine pages:

111. Thirty-one drawings from ***The Pondicherry Pastels***, 1979–80. Ink, pastel, charcoal, gouache, paint, and pencil on paper, smallest: 6 3/8 x 3 1/2 inches (16.2 x 8.9 cm); largest: 13 x 13 3/4 inches (33 x 34.9 cm). Courtesy The Brant Foundation, Greenwich, Connecticut.

Please note that drawings shown as full-page reproductions are also shown as part of groupings.

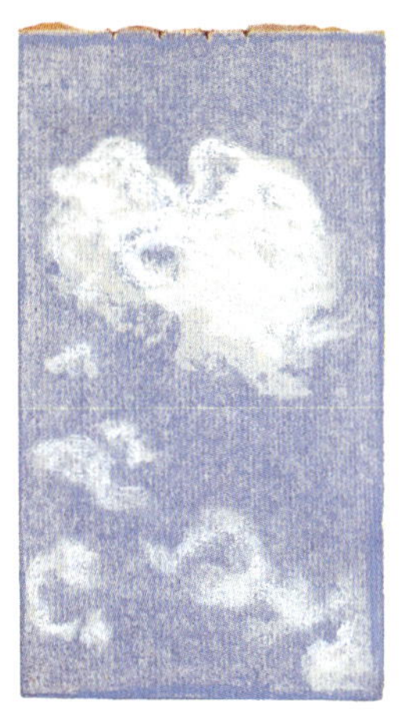

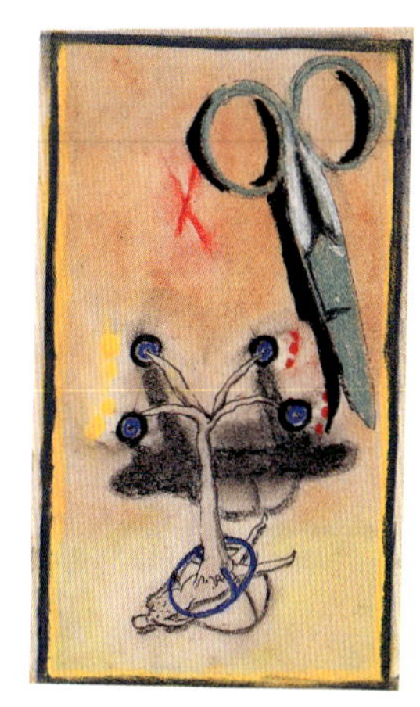

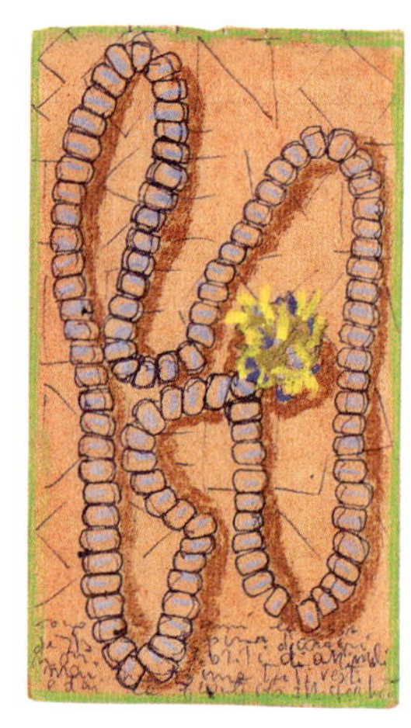

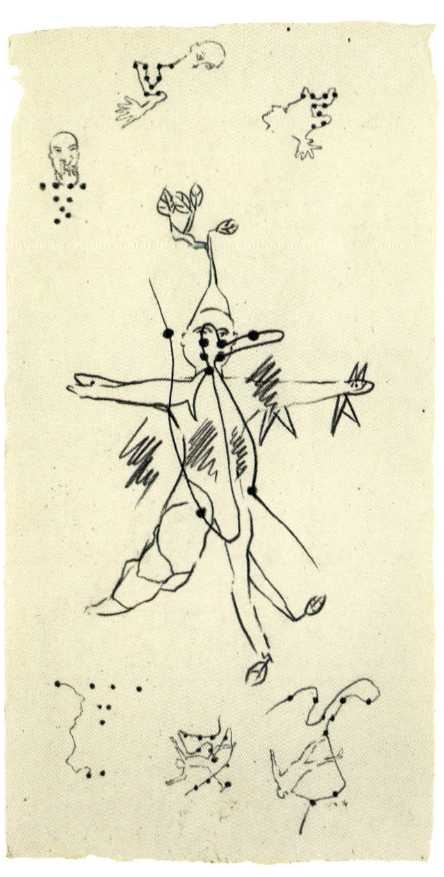

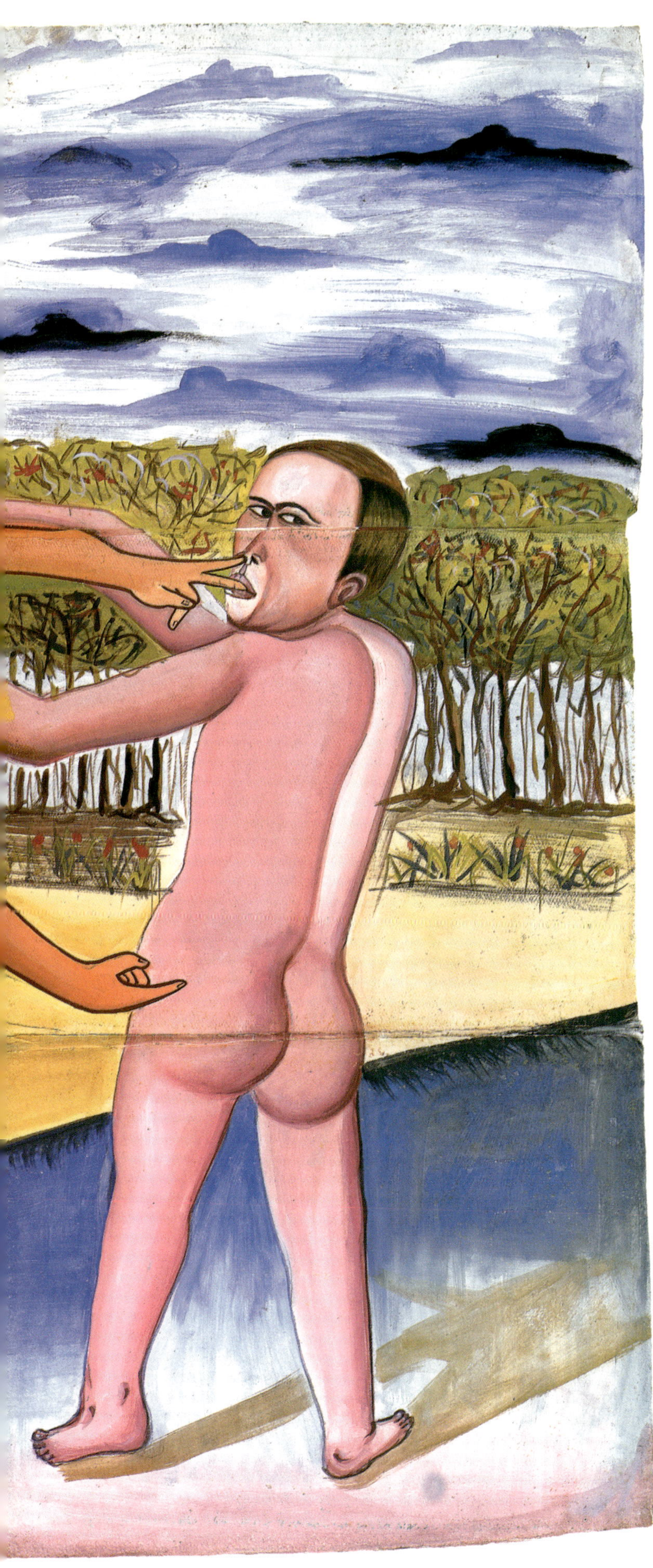

112. *Two Painters*, 1980. Gouache on nine sheets of handmade Pondicherry paper, joined with handwoven cotton strips, 68 x 94 1/8 inches (172.7 x 239 cm). Private collection.

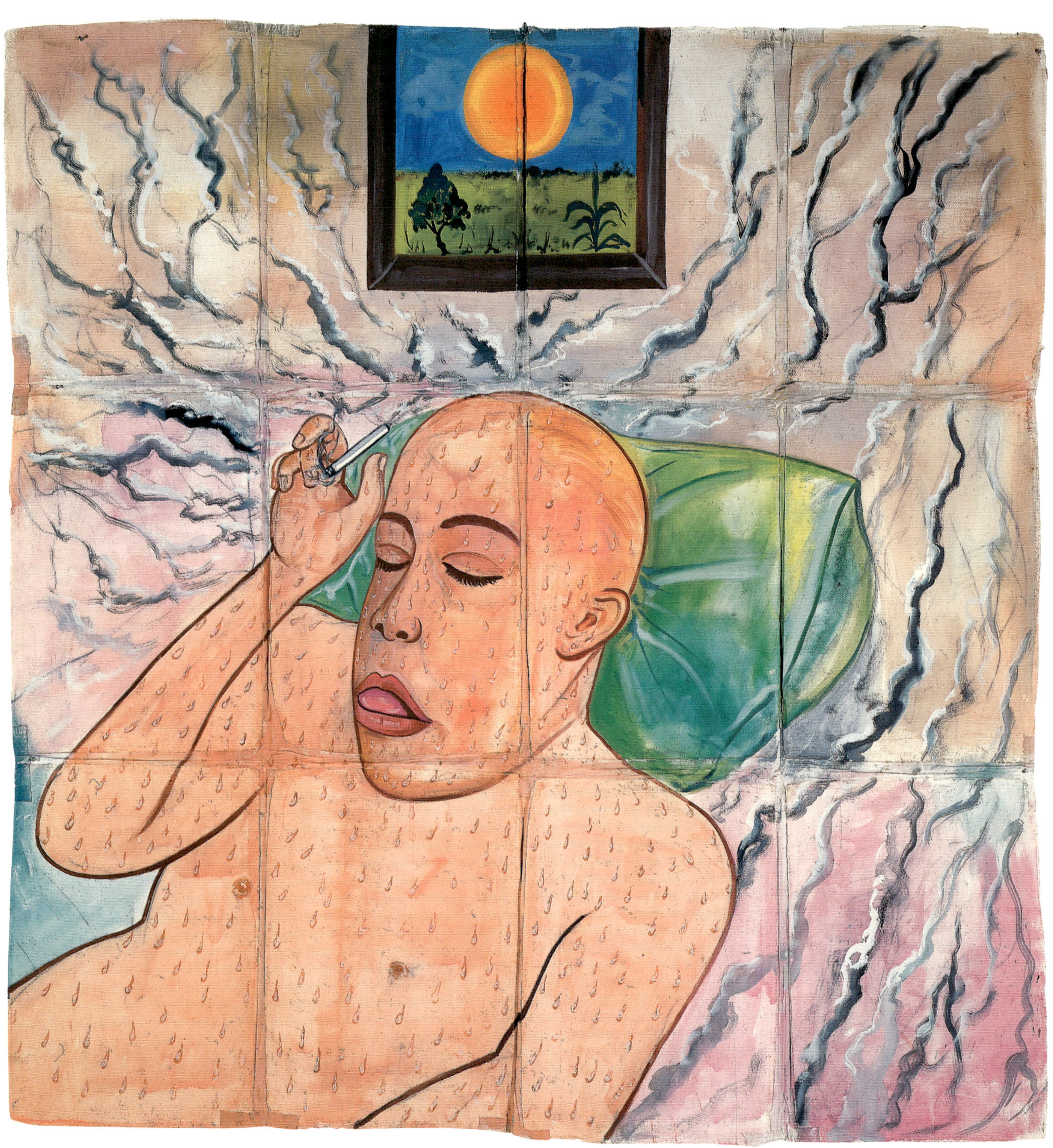

113. *Sun*, 1980. Gouache on twelve sheets of handmade Pondicherry paper, joined with handwoven cotton strips, 91 x 95 inches (231.1 x 241.3 cm). Philadelphia Museum of Art, Edward and Althea Budd Fund, Katharine Levin Farrell Fund, and funds contributed by Mrs. H. Gates Lloyd.

114. *Moon*, 1980. Gouache on twelve sheets of handmade Pondicherry paper, joined with handwoven cotton strips, 96 3/4 x 91 inches (245.7 x 231.1 cm).
Private collection, courtesy Sperone Westwater, New York.

115. ***Inside/Outside***, 1980. Watercolor, pastel, and pencil on fourteen sheets of handmade Pondicherry paper, joined with handwoven cotton strips, 63 x 164 inches (160 x 416.6 cm). Rubell Family Collections.

116. ***The Four Corners***, 1985. Gouache on twelve sheets of handmade Pondicherry paper, joined with handwoven cotton strips, 96 $^{1}/_{16}$ x 94 $^{1}/_{2}$ inches (244 x 240 cm). Private collection.

Cast from the same mold, born from the same womb, Francesco Clemente's *Mercury* and *Saturn* (1992, cat. nos. 117, 118) adopt different mediums—tin and lead—evoking the eternal powers of *dhatu*, the essential substances of the matter that pervade all the senses.

The serially multiplying image, while projecting a sense of drama and mystery, amplifies and reinvents the idea and also has reverberations from the Upanishad: "I am One who becomes Many." The fingers of two open palms, forming a dazzling nimbus behind the heavenly bodies, reiterate the artist's obsession with the number five.

J. J.

117. ***Mercury***, 1992. Tin, 16 3/4 x 18 1/2 x 14 9/16 inches (42.5 x 47 x 37 cm). Private collection.

118. ***Saturn***, 1992. Lead, 16 3/4 x 18 1/2 x 14 9/16 inches (42.5 x 47 x 37 cm). Private collection.

following ten pages:

119. Thirty watercolors from ***CVIII***, 1985. Watercolor on paper, smallest: 4 7/8 x 7 1/2 inches (12.3 x 19.1 cm); largest: 10 1/16 x 10 3/16 inches (25.6 x 25.9 cm). Öffentliche Kunstsammlung Basel, Kupferstichkabinett, Gift of CIVA-GEIGY, AG, Basel.

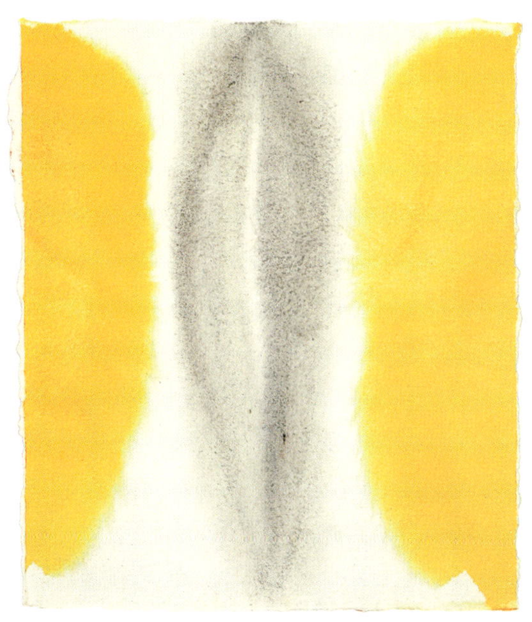

In 1992, with the creation of a series of analogous figures of planets, one mirroring the other—*Moon, Sun, Mercury* (cat. no. 117), and *Saturn,* (cat. no. 118) cast in copper, brass, tin, and lead—Francesco Clemente discovered the spirit of the elemental powers of the metals that pervade the heavenly bodies.

In 1994, Clemente further enunciated this idea in *The King and the Corpse* (cat. no. 120), a series of metal sculptures. Here the entangled bodies of king and corpse, also cast in different metals, appear to be organically growing from and into each other. Surging, bending, enveloping, and convoluting, the bodies at times change their gender, like Roman Polanski's vampires.

The King and the Corpse series was inspired by the medieval Indian fable that revolves around the valiant King Vikrama in his efforts to bring Vetala, a ghost residing in a corpse, under his control. He carries the corpse from one place to the other "bound to his body like a beggar's wallet." On his way, the king listens to a cycle of interconnected stories, each in the form of a riddle.

Clemente apparently begins where the fable ends; the metamorphosed bodies of king and corpse have become iconized images.

J. J.

120. ***The King and the Corpse***, 1994. Copper, tin, bronze, brass, and lead, respectively, five pieces, smallest: 8 x 6 1/4 x 2 inches (20.3 x 15.9 x 5.1 cm); largest: 9 x 7 3/4 x 1 1/4 inches (22.9 x 19.7 x 3.2 cm). Unnumbered edition of 10. Private collection.

The words "sense," "sensorial," and "sensual" are interrelated. The senses transmit the external world to human beings through sense organs. Francesco Clemente imagines "the body to be a line. The boundary between inner and outer worlds. . . . Outer worlds leak inside, inner worlds pour out."[1] The senses are the medium through which the two worlds meet. The body is perceived to be a negative space within the outer world, and the outer world is construed as a negative space around the body.

In *Five Senses* (1990, cat. nos. 121–23), Clemente turned senses into vast anthropomorphic icons, each personified as a separate entity or an element. He amplified a sense symmetrically within the checkered grid of the picture plane, which was created by joining together several rectangular sheets of handmade paper in the same way in which the bazaar painters of Madras enlarge, square by square, a sketch or photograph into a cinema billboard of giant proportions.

J. J.

1. Francesco Clemente, statement in *Francesco Clemente: Two Horizons*, exh. cat. (Tokyo: Sezon Museum of Art, 1994), p. 23.

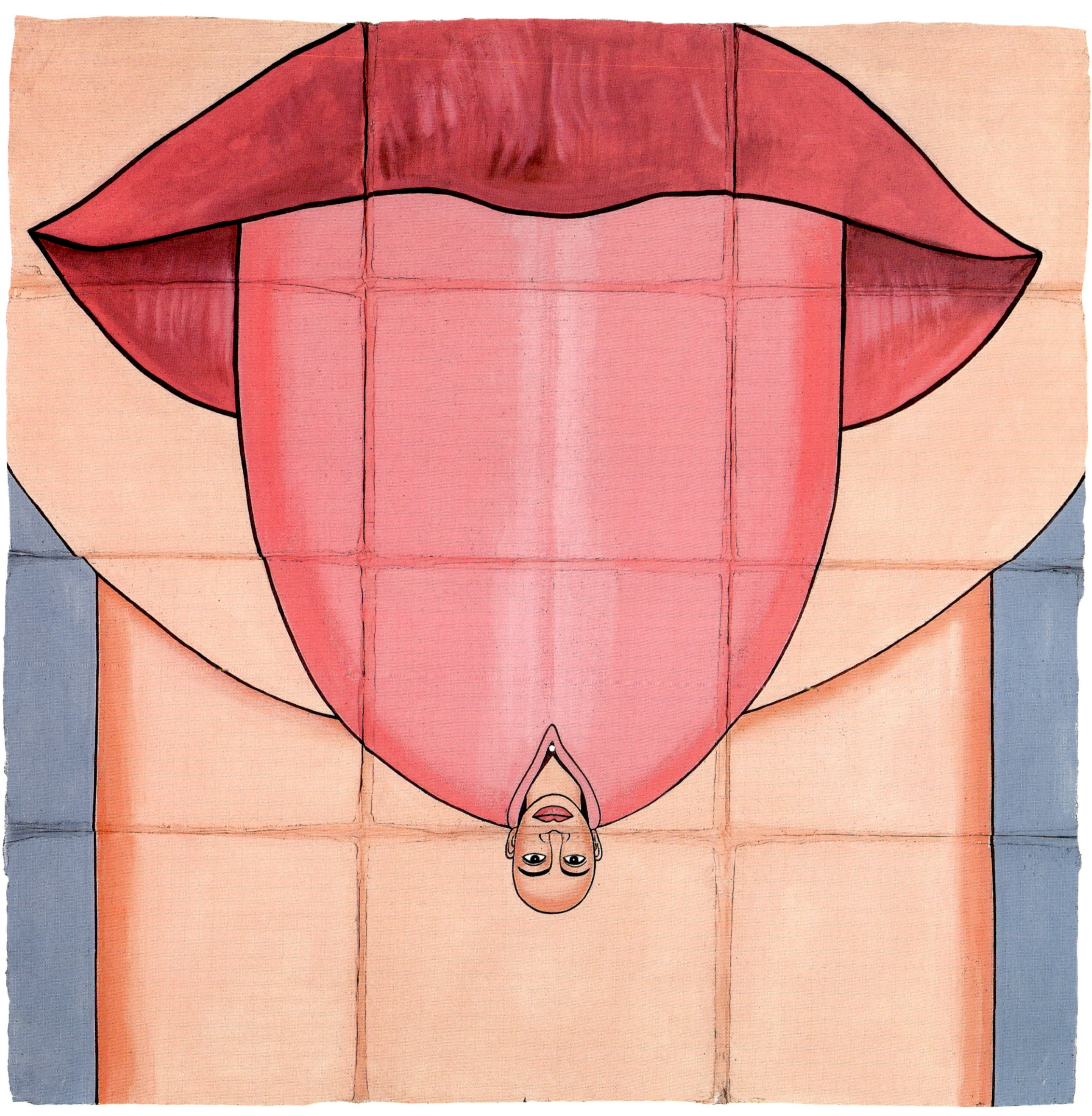

121. ***Five Senses***, 1990. Gouache on twelve sheets of handmade Pondicherry paper, joined with handwoven cotton strips, 94 $^{1}/_{8}$ x 96 $^{1}/_{16}$ inches (239 x 244 cm). Stedelijk Museum, Amsterdam.

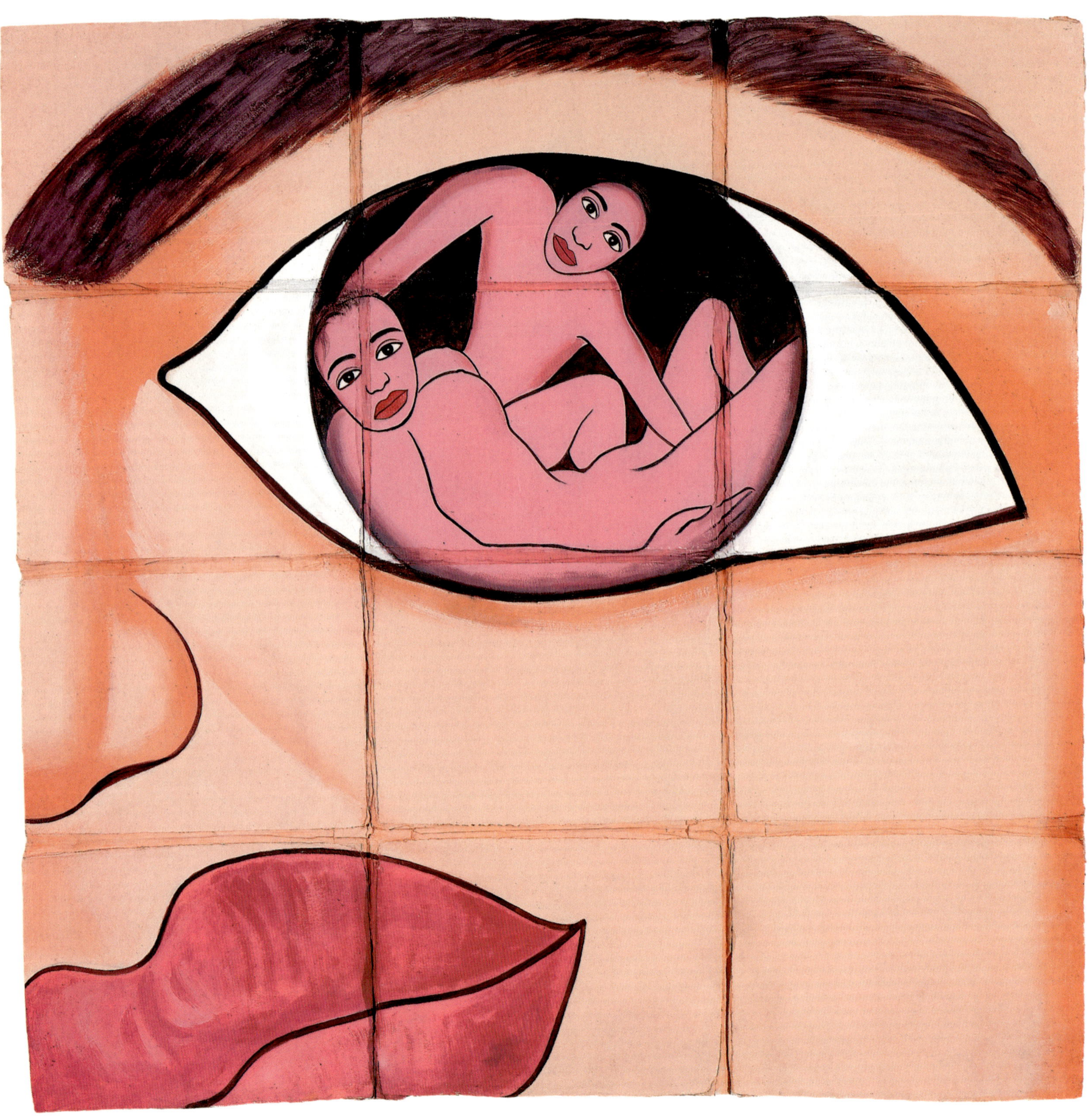

122. *Five Senses*, 1990. Gouache on twelve sheets of handmade Pondicherry paper, joined with handwoven cotton strips, 94 1/8 x 96 1/16 inches (239 x 244 cm). Stedelijk Museum, Amsterdam.

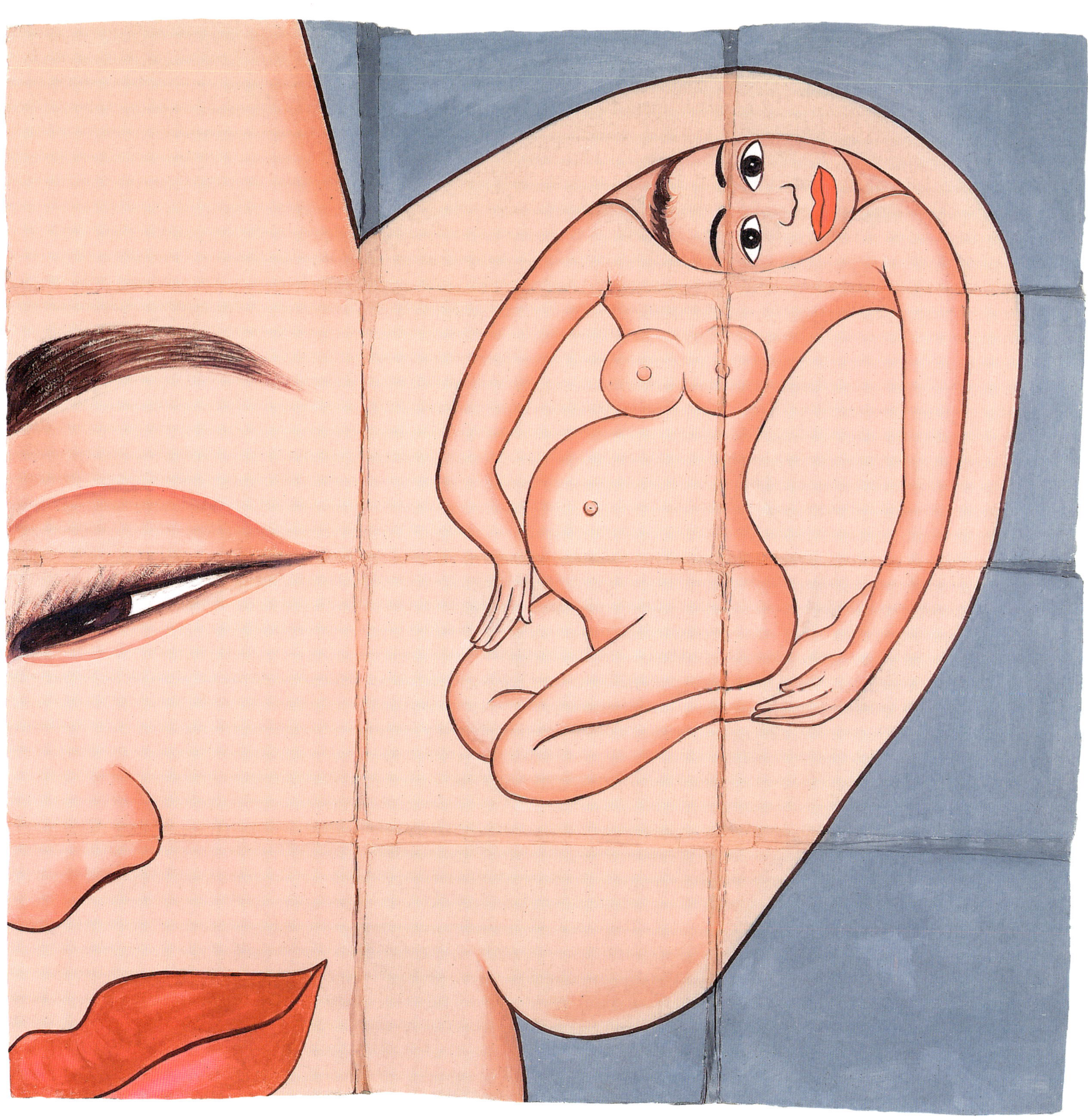

123. ***Five Senses***, 1990. Gouache on twelve sheets of handmade Pondicherry paper, joined with handwoven cotton strips, 93 $^{1}/_{2}$ x 95 $^{1}/_{2}$ inches (237.5 x 242.6 cm). Stedelijk Museum, Amsterdam.

The images of *Story of My Country I* (1990, cat. no. 127) are those of stories from many countries, histories, times, and mythologies. These are the perpetual images of fragmentation, separation, duality, isolation, and boundaries, represented by water and earth, ocean and sky, man and woman, woman and woman, torso and legs, lotus and sword, circle and square, object and reflection.

As Clemente sought to speak through the voice of an Orissan painter, he let the men, women, trees, birds, animals, oceans, mountains, rain, and even the picture frames of medieval Orissan painting enact the ancient Mediterranean stories that surfaced from his own "memory." The transient and otherworldly space emanates from the disparate visions of two artists, alien to each other for that very reason.

By changing the setting and speaking through another's language of pictorial narration, Clemente transformed the same people, the same geography, and the same flora and fauna of *patachitra* (the conventional ragboard painting of Orissa) into omnipresent symbols and metaphors. *Story of My Country I* invites repeat visits and offers surprises in return.

J. J.

following four pages:

127. ***Story of My Country I***, 1990. India ink and gouache on Tamarind vellum, eighteen sheets, approximately 9 x 18 inches (22.9 x 45.7 cm) each. Courtesy Anthony d'Offay Gallery, London.

125. *Sound, Point*, 1990. Gouache on twelve sheets of handmade Pondicherry paper, joined with handwoven cotton strips, 95 11/16 x 97 5/8 inches (243 x 248 cm). Courtesy Anthony d'Offay Gallery, London.

126. *Birth*, 1990. Gouache on twelve sheets of handmade Pondicherry paper, joined with handwoven cotton strips, 95 11/16 x 97 5/8 inches (243 x 248 cm). Courtesy Anthony d'Offay Gallery, London.

124. *Contemplation*, 1990. Gouache on twelve sheets of handmade Pondicherry paper, joined with handwoven cotton strips, 95 11/16 x 97 5/8 inches (243 x 248 cm). Sezon Museum of Art, Tokyo.

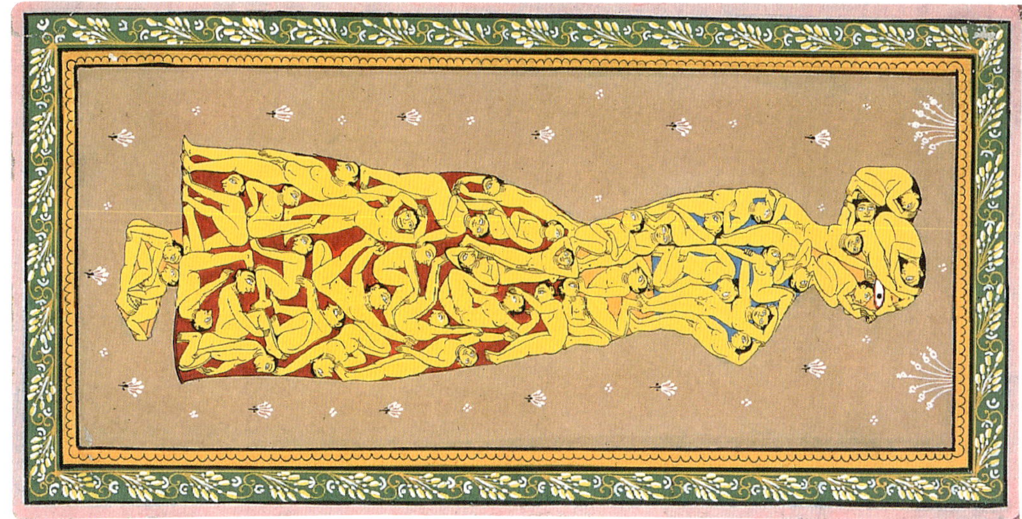

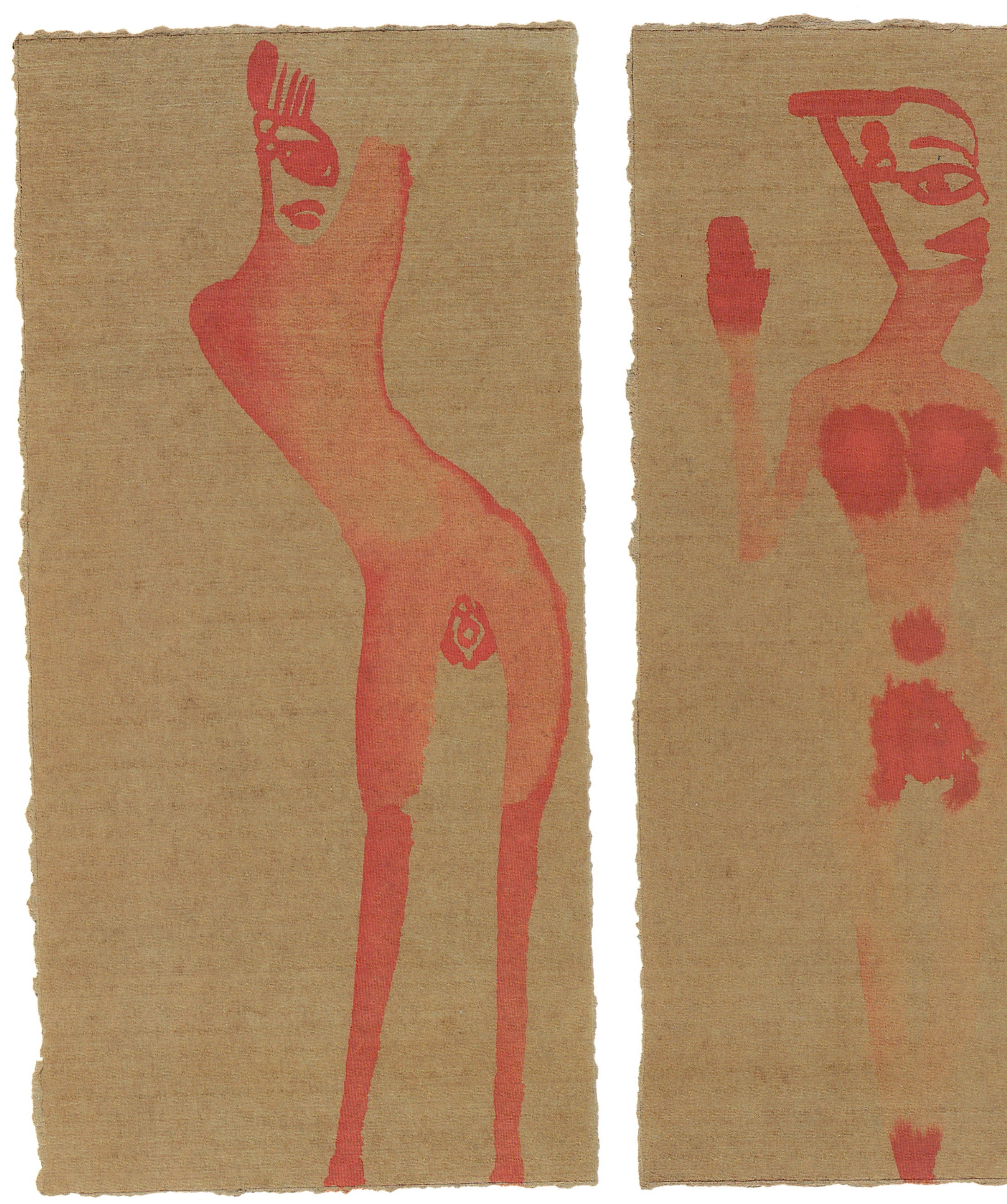

129. Four pages from ***The Red Book***, 1989. Watercolor on handmade paper, 11 1/2 x 5 1/2 inches (29.2 x 14 cm) each. Collection of Francesco and Alba Clemente, New York.

128. ***Mothers of Letters***, 1992. Iron, twenty-one pieces, 22 1/16 x 19 1/8 x 1 inches (56 x 48.6 x 2.5 cm) each.
Collection of Francesco and Alba Clemente, New York.

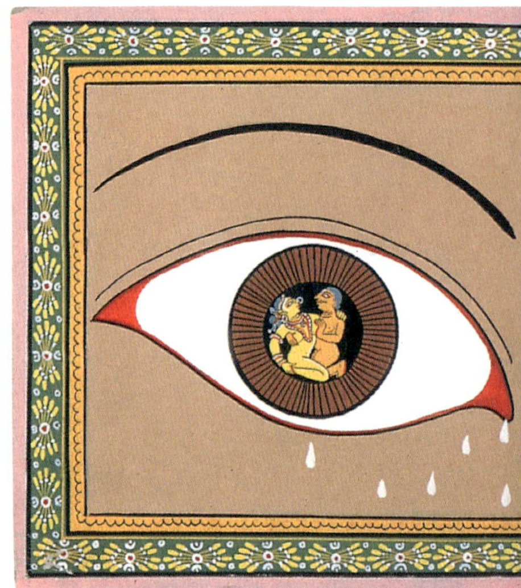

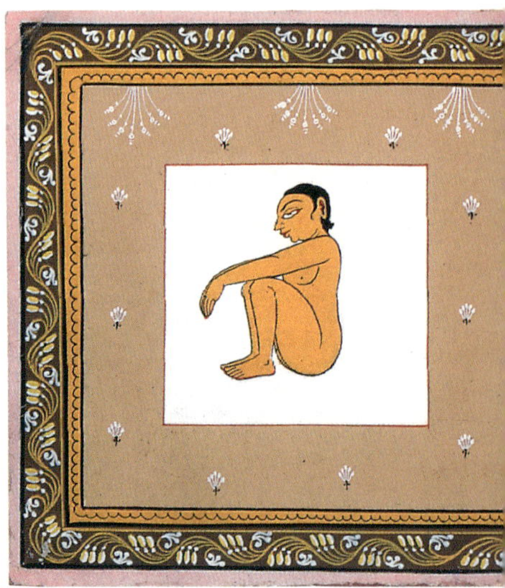

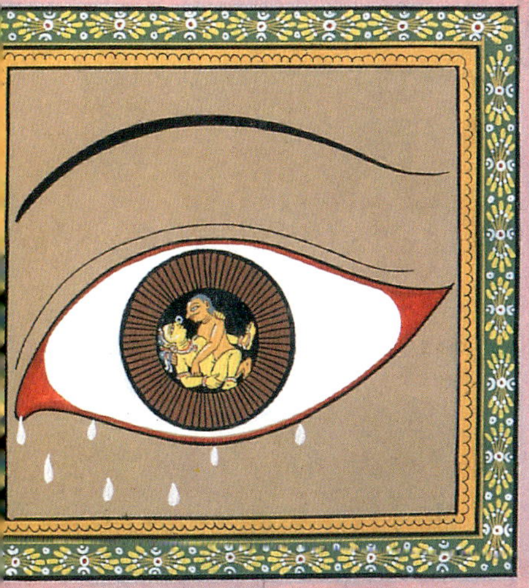

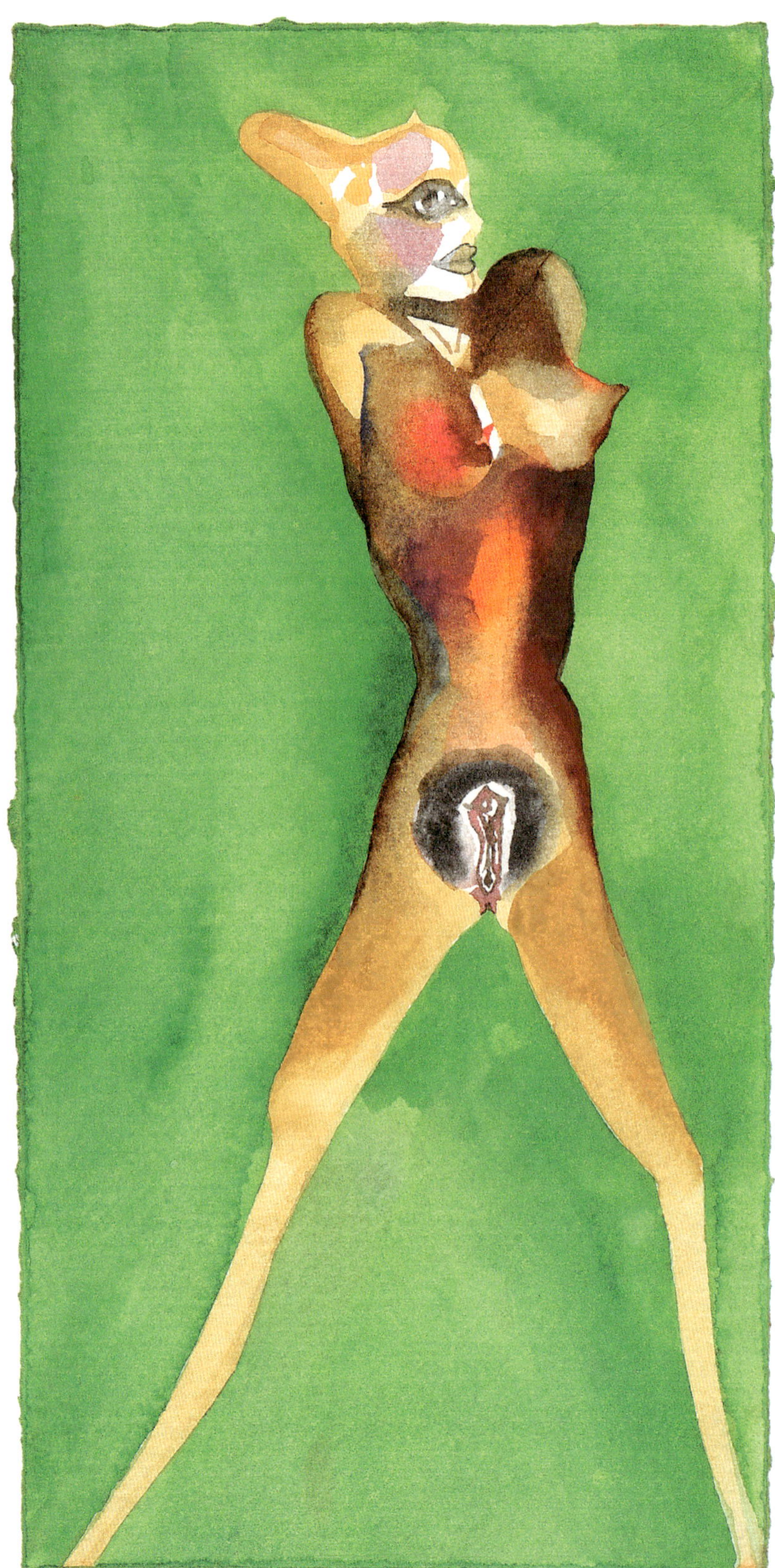

130. Four pages from ***The White Book***, 1989. Watercolor on handmade paper, 11 1/2 x 5 1/2 inches (29.2 x 14 cm) each. Collection of Francesco and Alba Clemente, New York.

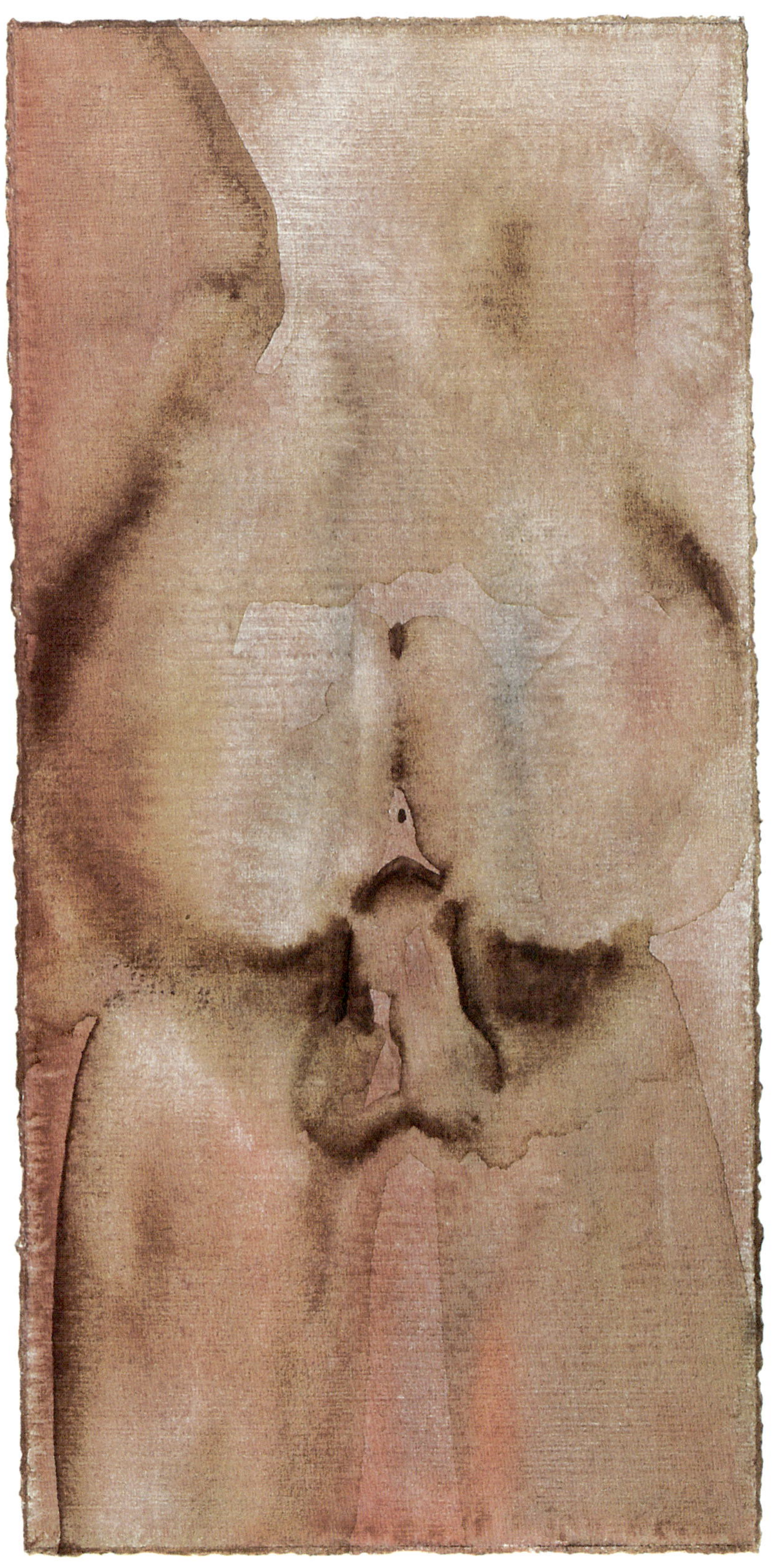

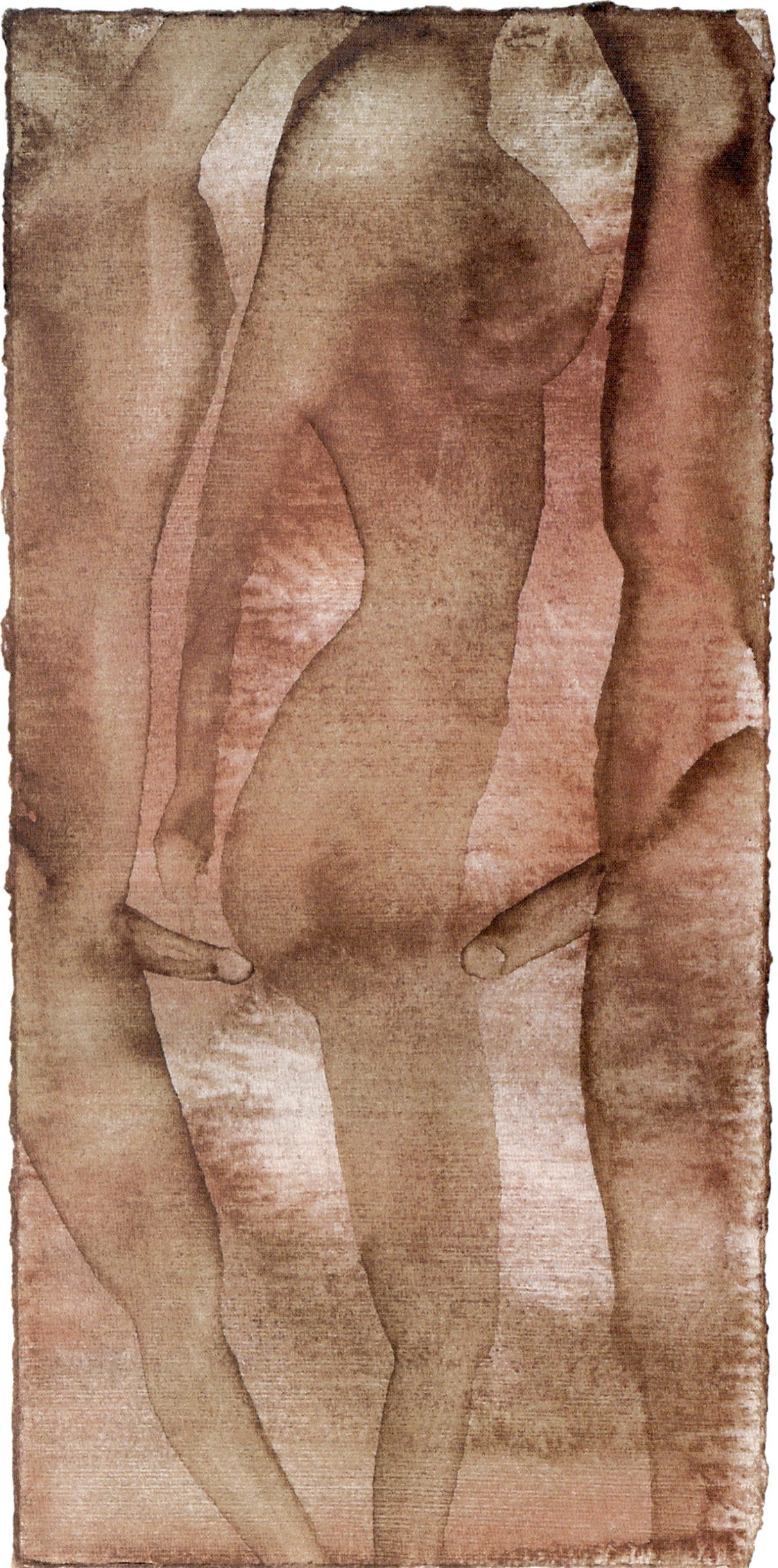

131. Four pages from ***The Black Book***, 1989. Watercolor on handmade paper, 11 ½ x 5 ½ inches (29.2 x 14 cm) each. Collection of Francesco and Alba Clemente, New York.

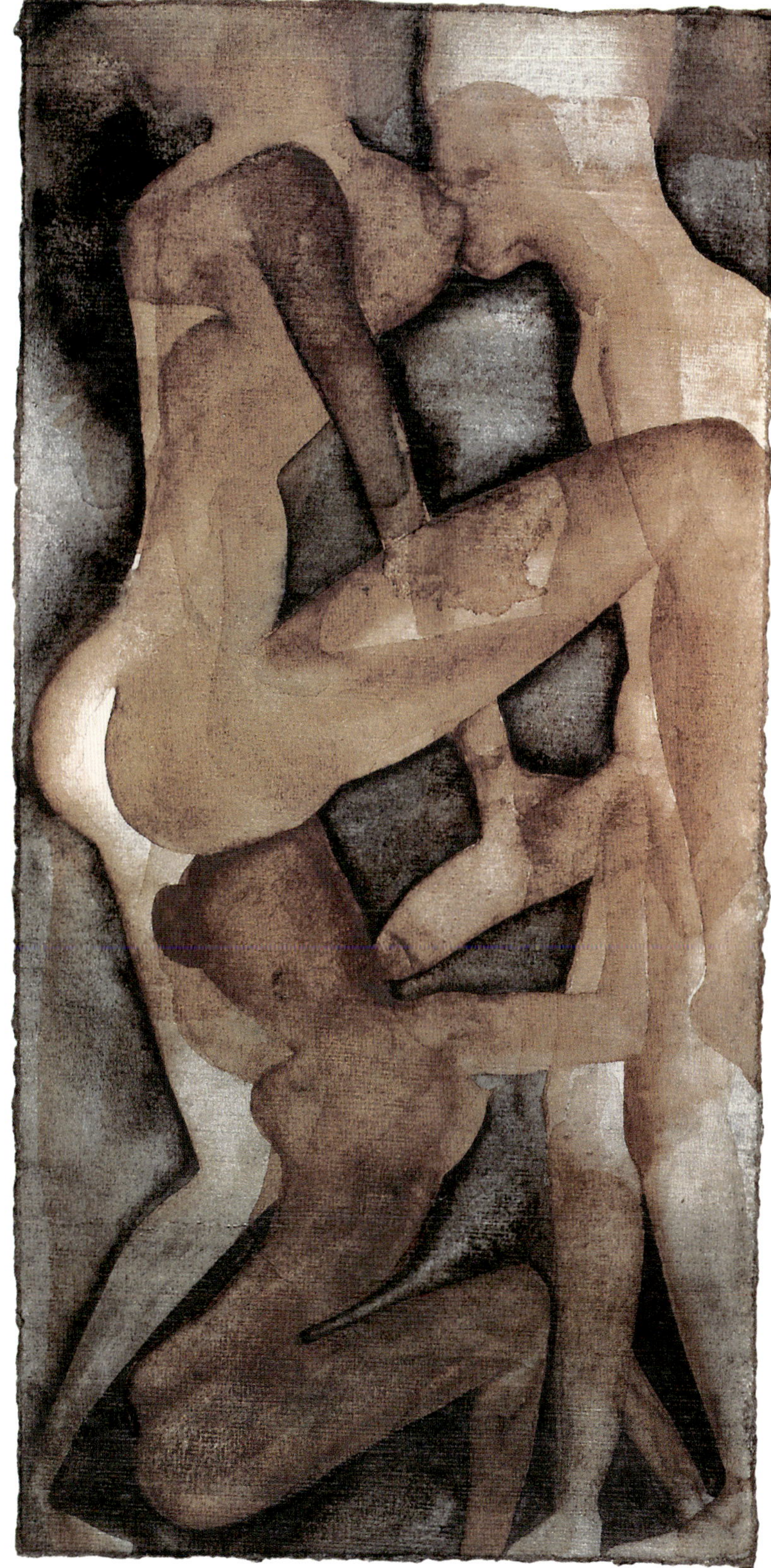

Sky

The daylight from Francesco Clemente's studio window is muted; because of the filter of fine New York bus and truck filth, it is refracted on its way to a floor of rough wood streaked with paint. It brightens up this large room, which feels like India but is New York. Open books and items lie on a table in the center of the space, and Francesco's larger paintings are against a far wall. They are whopping in person. People in the neighboring building watch Francesco paint in front of the smeary windows. On the table, I see tiny drawings and scribbles. Some are on napkins he has worked on in restaurants and have religious, metaphysical, or allegorical themes. He tells me the history of some of the scribbles, how one is from a Buddhist text and how another, of a worm becoming a man, was inspired by a scientific finding that the people in a small village were telling him about when he last traveled to India. His focus is intense, and his eyes are azure crystals when he is explaining the drawings to me.

I ask about the many jars of mixed paint lined up together on the floor. "I mix all the colors," he says, "before I start on a painting. This might take a little time before I start something. I mix even more paint when I think that there will be more than one painting." I ask him, "Then you know what colors you are going to use before you start to paint?" He lifts his shoulders and holds his palms up in a shrug. I notice he is wearing a very nice wool suit. "Something like that. I think of the colors that I am going to use, and I get into that in the beginning. It is part of the painting ritual. It is not an exact science," he laughs. "If there are any other colors I've forgotten, I can mix them later, but that usually doesn't happen because by then I will have convinced myself that these colors are the only ones that I need." Francesco points to paintings as we walk around his space. "You need a lot of paint when the painting is ten feet tall, which is really why all the paint is mixed first." A few dented dishpan lights on the floor here and there light up the paintings that are standing farther from the window. He likes to have guests and asks for a cigarette from another visitor, saying he doesn't want to smoke, but. . . . He lights the cigarette that he doesn't want to be smoking and says to his friend that we have addictive personalities, that we are not necessarily in control of our impulses; he charmingly pulls us all into his small excuse. The phone rings, but Francesco doesn't want to pick it up. It has been distracting him, and I wonder if we are a distraction as well.

We examine one of the *Meditation* paintings, *Helvétius and Tracy* (1993, cat. no. 138). Hmm. I wonder what to say about it, but I feel comfortable that a response isn't expected or particularly needed. I point to the little bird in *Helvetius and Tracy*. "I like that," I say. Francesco pauses before he offers, "Yes, I think I do too. It's growing on me." After a few more moments, he says, "You can tell me when you are finished looking at this one." I help Francesco move the paintings from behind one another, which is somewhat difficult because they are so big. Two other *Meditation* paintings are before us, *Trigonometrie* and *Fioriture* (1993, cat. nos. 136, 137). While we prop them up and look them over, I think of the Indian celebrations at Chidambaram, where Francesco has traveled, able to pose as an Indian and walk in and witness the ceremonial dances of Siva. I think of vaudeville, Berlin in the 1920s. I think of a psychological mindscape and of a movie theater showing curiously symbolic or psychosexual or ceremonial movies; I don't know.

He is consumed by sex. Sexuality. Which is beauty. He wants to paint sexuality and does. He wants to paint literal intellectual and metaphysical and psychological and scientific and religious origins. Which often leads to sex. Which I understand through some of his paintings.

Gus Van Sant

132. ***Trophy***, 1990. Pastel on paper, 26 1/4 x 40 1/4 inches (66.7 x 102.2 cm). Courtesy Anthony d'Offay Gallery, London.

133. ***Porta Coeli***, 1983. Tempera on linen, 103 x 93 inches (261.6 x 236.2 cm). Collection of Stefan T. Edlis.

134. ***Semen***, 1983–84. Tempera on linen, 93 x 106 inches (236.2 x 269.2 cm). Collection of Patricia Phelps de Cisneros, Caracas.

135. ***Sky***, 1984. Oil and shale on linen, 107 7/8 x 187 13/16 inches (274 x 477 cm). Private collection.

136. ***Meditation: Trigonometrie***, 1993. Enamel and silkscreen on linen, 73 ¼ x 77 ¼ inches (186.1 x 196.2 cm).
Private collection, Switzerland, courtesy Galerie Bruno Bischofberger, Zurich.

137. ***Meditation: Fioriture***, 1993. Enamel and silkscreen on linen, 73 1/4 x 77 1/4 inches (186.1 x 196.2 cm).
Private collection, Switzerland, courtesy Galerie Bruno Bischofberger, Zurich.

138. *Meditation: Helvétius and Tracy*, 1993. Enamel and silkscreen on linen, 73 1/4 x 77 1/4 inches (186.1 x 196.2 cm).
Private collection, Switzerland, courtesy Galerie Bruno Bischofberger, Zurich.

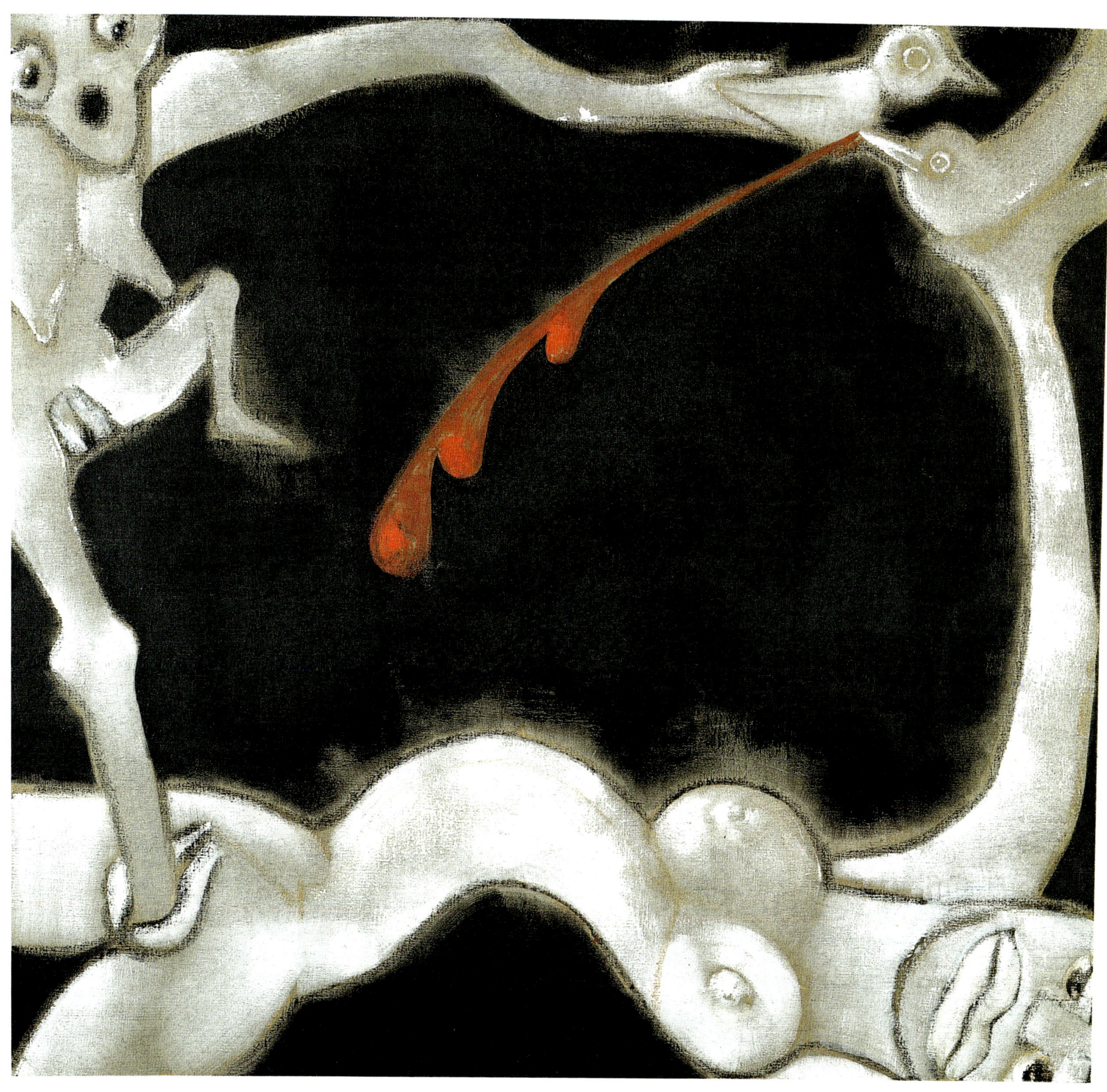

139. ***In Silence***, 1993. Tempera on linen, 49 $^{3}/_{16}$ x 52 $^{3}/_{8}$ inches (125 x 133 cm). Private collection.

140. ***Mandala***, 1993. Tempera on linen, 44 1/8 x 44 1/8 inches (112 x 112 cm). Collection of Bruno Bischofberger, Zurich.

141. ***Mother of Hope***, 1993. Tempera on linen, 49 7/16 x 52 inches (125.5 x 132.1 cm). Collection of Francesco and Alba Clemente, New York.

142. ***Mother of Paintings***, 1995. Tempera and oil on linen, 84 1/4 x 302 inches (214 x 767.1 cm). Courtesy The Brant Foundation, Greenwich, Connecticut.

The Swan

Peculiar that *swan* should mean *a sound?*
I'd thought of gods and power, and wounds.
But here in the curious quiet this one has settled down.

All day the barking dogs were kept at bay.
Better than dogs, a single swan, they say,
will keep all such malignant force away

and so preserve a calm, make pond a swelling lake—
sound through the silent grove a shattering spate
of resonances, jarring the mind awake.

The Skull

"Come closer. Now there is nothing left
either inside or out to gainsay death,"
the skull that keeps its secrets saith.

The ways one went, the forms that were
empty as wind and yet they stirred
the heart to its passion, all is passed over.

Lighten the load. Close the eyes.
let the mind loosen, the body die,
the bird fly off to the opening sky.

Robert Creeley

143. *The Swan*, 1997. Oil on linen, 46 x 92 inches (116.8 x 233.7 cm). Private collection, Switzerland.

144. ***The Skull***, 1997. Oil on linen, 46 x 92 inches (116.8 x 233.7 cm). Courtesy Gagosian Gallery, New York.

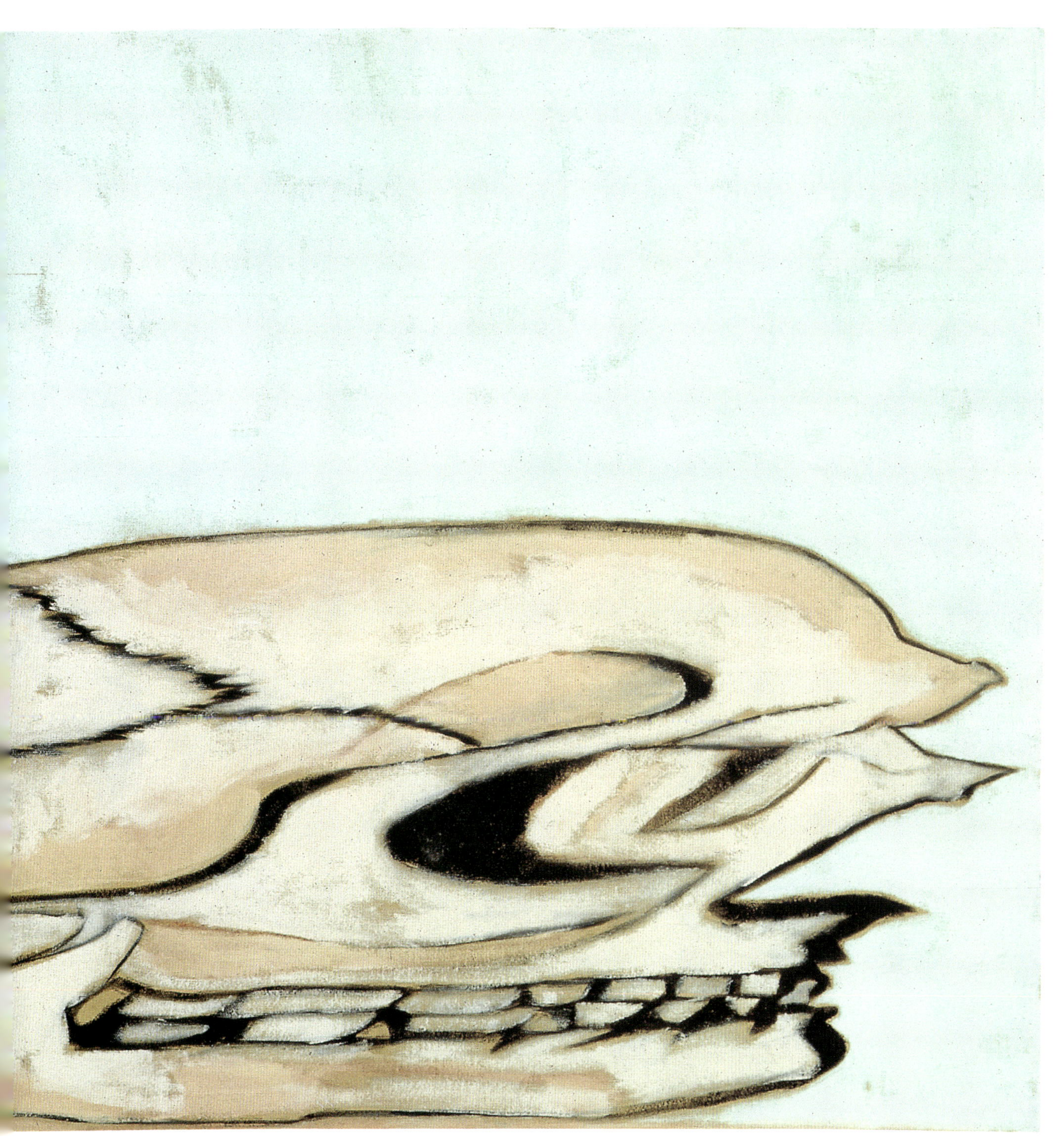

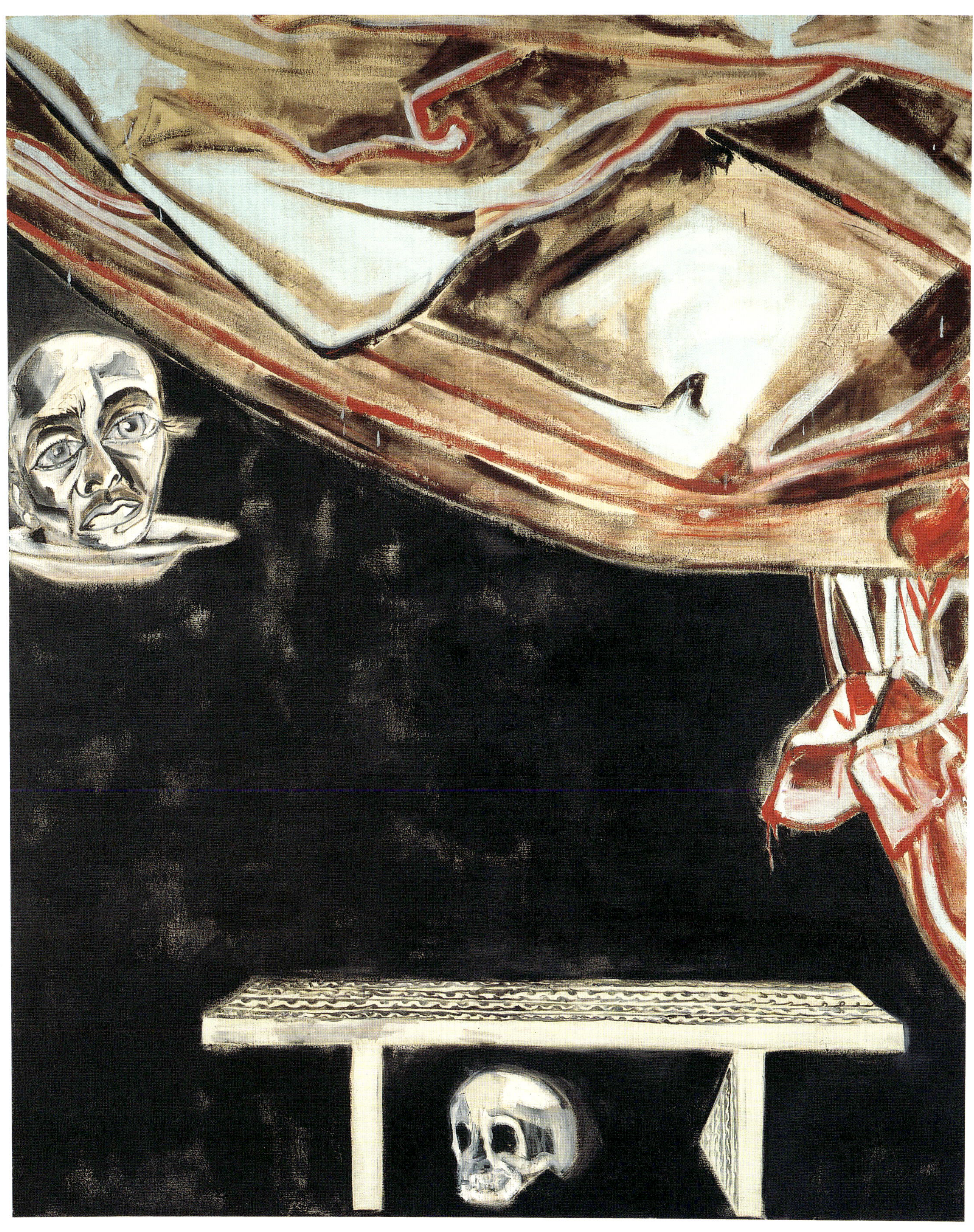

145. ***Black, White, and Red,*** 1998. Oil on linen, 112 x 92 inches (284.5 x 233.7 cm). Courtesy Gagosian Gallery, New York.

146. ***Circle***, 1998. Oil on linen, 46 x 92 inches (116.8 x 233.7 cm). Courtesy Anthony d'Offay Gallery, London.

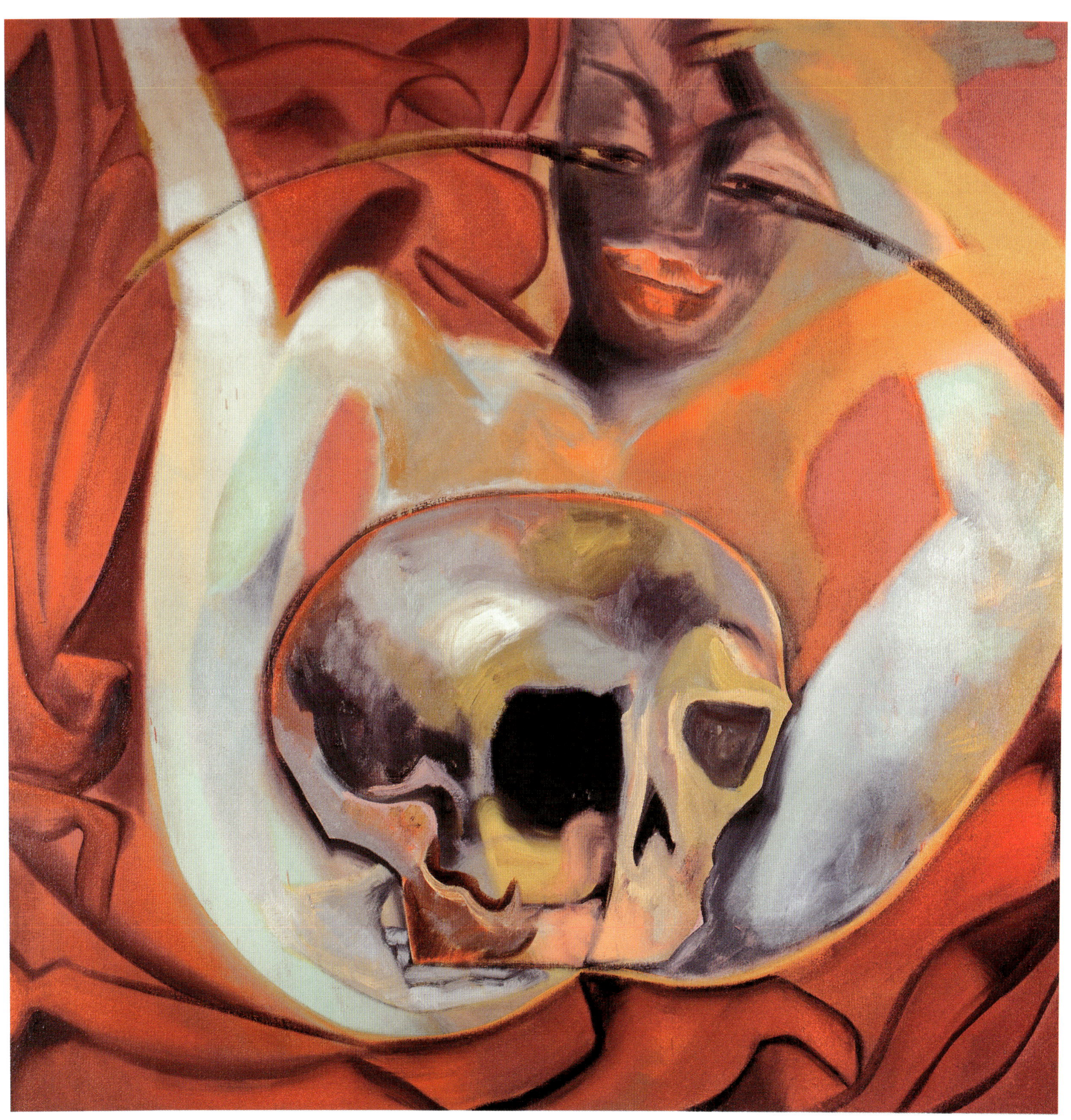

147. ***Skull***, 1999. Oil on linen, 48 x 48 inches (121.9 x 121.9 cm). Collection of Francesco and Alba Clemente, New York.

148. *Scissors and Butterflies*, 1999. Oil on linen, 91 x 92 inches (231.1 x 233.7 cm). Collection of Francesco and Alba Clemente, New York.

Rooms

When you open windows and doors for a room it is where there is nothing that they are useful to the room. Therefore being is for benefit, nonbeing is for usefulness.

—*Tao Te Ching*, XI (trans. T. Cleary)

There is something dizzying and profound, as though we are on the edge of an abyss, in the first known decorated "rooms," those dark caves reached by narrow, oppressive shafts, carved by water into malleable and living rock. Sixteen thousand years ago, the barely visible images danced like ghostly presences on the irregular walls as long as a flame flickered in the subterranean breezes, then were swallowed up once more by the geological night.

In the heart of Mexico's Mazatec Mountains, a wooden, windowless hut was lined with sheets of newsprint. In the candlelight, amid clouds of incense smoke and under the influence of the psilocybin mushroom, the swirl of images and words was no less exquisite than the most palatial rococo interior. As in a Paleolithic cavern, the chanting and dancing seer, gathering time and space into his state of trance, fought the night with light, and the day with darkness.

That the shaman's disposition may forever be lost to modern man is a given that no contemporary experience can alter, for the artist or anyone else. But echoes of classical spaces—such as the mantic ones still resonating from the sibyl's cave in Neapolitan Cumae—offer, to any who can feel it, a sort of intermediate space, poised between passion and reason. For Francesco Clemente, passion is an antinomic category, and it is rooted in his receptive nature. This is a "Mediterranean" disposition whose power still emanates from Demeter, the Great Mother. In our age, it must take new forms since we are living in Kali-Yuga, a time of apocalyptic reabsorption into the room of Nothingness, silvery moon and indigo night.

Meister Eckhart said in a sermon, "that which must be received must be received into something" ("On Detachment"); the soul is also a room. Yet the idea of room-as-container may be too limited; *who*, as Ramana Maharishi would say, or *what* is to be contained? Making the room a site uncovers its muted wall: a discovery, the invention of Inside and Outside, as the mountain sides open up (as they did for the prehistoric painter), and we are there within the secret (*secretum*). One does not need to suffer from claustrophobia to dread the grip of enclosures or from agoraphobia to imagine the panic associated with amorphous places in the shadowless hours of midday or a moonless night. If the usefulness of the primitive shelter derived from its hidden access, the modern room favors an easy entrance and open views that ideally expand its *roominess* to the infinite. Even television, the ubiquitous "tube," is both an opening to the world, a channel, and a contraption that boxes it in, and the image it relays is seen as through a window, as if we were looking in. Clemente's "rooms" have paintings in the place of windows, and we see into them, not through them; in relation to their first habitation—in the studio—they appear to function more as mirrors than as openings, reflecting particular states-of-being of that original setting. Thus, the walls of these rooms expand the enclosure indefinitely, while also holding it in *place*. Clemente has spoken of the false perspectives on the wall decorations of Rome's Palazzo Spada, of the impression they made on him early on, but the inwardness of his own walls is radically nonillusionistic, the opposite of *faux-semblants*, as if we were made to intrude on a most private realm. Yet, one finds his walls the expression of a relation being negotiated, rather perilously, between inner and outer realms, between the room itself and "the world."

Clemente's rooms also suggest the experience of the simultaneous. They are time-traveling capsules of sorts and also out of time, representing not so much a moment as a suspension. He has actually stated how, as a painter, he is "naturally" inclined to be more interested in "space" than in "time." A room is a place in which to stay, in which to sit or lie down. Since antiquity, and notably since the Renaissance (from the *stanze*, the rooms, of Poliziano and Lorenzo to those of Raffaello), the room has implied an invitation to rest, to linger. Between rest and movement, the room embodies a discontinuity different from the stop-and-go flow of the gallery, the serpent, spotted with images, that coils and uncoils up and down the ramps of Frank Lloyd Wright's Guggenheim Museum. *Stanze* are not galleries; they are like refuges from life's unstoppable flow. And if death is the ultimate *resting place*, it is appropriate that, after *The Fourteen Stations* (1981–82, cat. nos. 154–165), Clemente's most coherent group of works should have been his *Funerary Paintings* (1987, see cat. no. 44), even though human figures were absent from them.

In the Piramus and Thisbe play-within-the-play of *A Midsummer Night's Dream*, the wall, a barrier separating one reality from another, an obstacle to love and desire, also carves out a fatal landscape of inwardness; it is a symbol of the Limit (of desire), hence of Death, death encountered but also perhaps, through that transformative encounter, conquered. Clemente's rooms also lie within the walls of life and death, guarding intimations of eternity. He has said that everything began with a vivid vision of his own death, and it is in *The Fourteen Stations* more than anywhere else in his oeuvre that one finds the alchemical precipitation of that singular and defining experience; it permeates every surface, every image, and almost every brushstroke. The implication, as in a traditional initiation, is that the possibility of resurrection is also encoded within these and his other rooms. Beyond the practice of painting as a therapeutic act, these paintings were conceived as if around the memory of a perilous journey to and from "the undiscovered country." In almost pragmatic terms, resurrection, for Clemente—the survivor who has lived and painted his way through Naples, Rome, many parts of India, New York, and beyond—stands for a daily reincarnation, for an almost miraculous series of epiphanic life-acts: "The point is that we do reincarnate in our daily life—I am only providing a record of this process of being."

If all expression is in some way autobiographical, Clemente's—far beyond the surface of his self-referential imagery—is certainly so. Biography, true experience and the experience of truth, with its mixture of recollection, appropriation, risk, and abandonment, is embedded in the work itself (opus, Vedic *apah*:

"religious action, sacrifice"). It could be that between the Beginning and the End, somewhere between Lascaux and Mark Rothko's chapel in Houston, the image-in-the-room, the secreted image, became the counterpart, and the trace, of sacrifice, and sacrificial substitution constituted the price of consciousness. It is as if in some fundamental way self-awareness implied an objectification of the space occupied by one's spirit, and inner space has been visualized and transmuted into an artificial environment. Certain Eastern forms of this reification intersect with Western ones in the way they come to express, through imagery, the longing for a dissolution of the Subject. But this spiritual goal is pursued though an extreme heightening of self-awareness, which in turn can be seen as the ultimate sublimation of sacrifice itself and also of any idea of "relic." Thus, the modern painted room became a transsacrificial abode in which the relevance of the Vedic conception that "Man is sacrifice," "Sacrifice is Man," faded away, like the polyvalent erotic imagery in *The Indigo Room* (1983–84, cat. no. 167). Yet, what would human life be if it were truly free of sacrifice?

From the distended surfaces of Clemente's frescoes to the concretions of *The Fourteen Stations*—which have something of the imaginary vividness of waking dreams—to the absorption of *The Indigo Room*, it is as if we are made newly aware of the connection between the outer surface of our skin and the inner one of our world, the world as our enveloping cave or womb. Then comes the question: what can we make of this relation? In the translation of motives and affections, through line—which, according to the painter, "is a continuation of the surface that separates the inner room of the body from the outer one"—and pigment, the hell of the world, or the world as hell, is transmuted into a half-hidden paradise (*bienestar oculto*), or the world as bliss. That both worlds should be simultaneously present and visible is the allegorical magic, and the secret, performed by Clemente's environments; it is one aspect of the meeting of opposites, or mystical wedding (*mysterium coniunctionis*), which they evoke with engulfing effect. And it is as if the very walls of his rooms are not still but approach and recede, leading us into a perceptual and conceptual dance. They are plastic rooms in more than one sense, forming a cosmology in which single-focus perspective is undetermined. They are centerless circles of being and nonbeing, which certain alchemists called "the Round" (*il Rotondo*) and which Clemente may be inviting us to contemplate as mirrors of our own and his own displacement (*dépaysement*).

"I wish I could change sex as I change shirts," André Breton proclaimed. Disarticulated desire, floating on and off Clemente's surfaces, permeates the images' many "openings," which are analogous to the body's and the person's own porosity. There is, first of all, the painter-magician conjuring up the illusions of permanence and impermanence. What is built up, on the wall, rather than the appearance of an Ego "always under construction," in C. G. Jung's expression, is a cumulative Ego subtraction. Something transpires that is at once most intimate, even secret, and yet out there for all to see: perhaps the ultimate, unmasking mask that the painter had seized from within his own heart. So, the room, this familiar refuge, also becomes terra incognita, a wilderness of adventures and encounters in the painter's studio. One has the impression of embarking on a journey through the debris of interiority. Perhaps we have come full circle from the ancient subterranean painter—the masked shaman dancing in the cave at Les Trois Frères who may have translated the power of direct perception (experience), and perhaps dreaming, by projecting the moving images captured within his heart—the Greeks' *thumos*—in glorious parades of vivid forms (a Paleolithic cinematography).

Clemente, a modern explorer of deep recesses and *monts analogues* gives life to images that are liminal. One cannot situate them out there, among the wild creatures of an unpeaceful kingdom, nor in the soul, which Jung called the "rubble of destruction." It is as if they belong in the passages between those two realms and that this accounts for their frequent depiction of bodily orifices. Their orality may also stand for an understated metaphysical hunger. If they radiate that "tension towards that which is primary," which Jung saw as the mark of true art, it stems from the painter's rigor in simultaneously keeping himself present and forgetting what he has been doing. The forms, even his manner, are familiar, yet it is as though he rediscovered them every time, even within different parts of a single work. "Always remember what you are doing and abandon it," the painter has said, and this is true of his earlier work as much as of the rest of his oeuvre, with its transformations of leitmotifs through different mediums. It is a peculiar contest (*tenzone*), this striving for a certain passivity, in which the elusive evidence of the immediate is sought, each moment, through painting as a meditative act. Particularly in Clemente's rooms, all thoughts are accepted at face value, neither countered nor suppressed, as transient mind-states unworthy of attachment. The by-product is as much a record of occurrence as of passing into nothingness. "Have no discrimination, behave unconcernedly with all things, resembling an idiot" is one of the Bodhidharma's sayings that were discovered at Tun-Huang.

In the framework of the present volume, one can isolate three early phases of Clemente's journey to the center—three phases of his rooms: frescoes, *The Indigo Room*, and *The Fourteen Stations*. As with other groups of works, these should be seen not in sequence but as recurring existential and aesthetic patterns that represent three basic exchanges between the traveling room of the spirit and its worldly and otherworldly conditions. The walls of *The Indigo Room*—soaked in the color of the heavenly depths, the purity of night interspersed with silvery moon rays, like Paul Klee's *Nacht der Liebe* (1937)—are an immersion into a paradise remembered, a product of travel to the East and a sense of participation in the great chain of being (Dante's "*Amor che muove il sole e l'altre stelle*"). In the painter's own words, he discovered the "huge inner space" of India, a space wherein, as Stella Kramrisch said of Clemente's images, "forms unite." And *Indigo* is also, in some way, a music room, where, if one listens intently, one hears not just echoes of the tamboura's drone, "the sound of the universe," or the Kirana-style spiritual virtuosity of a Pandit Pran Nath, but that of modern sound too, such as Morton Feldman's eddying journeys through minimal variations and repetitions, in his long, late compositions—a music more of space than of time.

The oil paintings of *The Fourteen Stations*, at the opposite end of the painter's broad register of states of being, transfigure the here and now, the hellish and exhilarating confrontation with modern life ("I am a modern painter")—within the "huge outer space, soulful and full of hope" of America. Thus the *Stations* provide an inventory of wordly lures, with all their frightful excesses (a sort of "panic" eros), but also, in my view, an intimation of possible escape, as through transformative action of, and on, spiritualized matter—matter invested with transmuting desire. This may have been a prevalently "Oriental" approach, originally, but also one that had Western hermetic counterparts—witness Paracelsus, Kepler, and even Newton—at the very beginning of our scientific revolution. Between these two approaches—which are also mediums (indigo dye, silver, and charcoal on paper and cloth, on the one hand, and oil and wax on linen on the other)—but in another sense at the root of all forms—the frescoes may be seen as standing for the "purgatorial" moment (this is, despite all, *art catholica*, i.e., *universalis*). They function as both a filter of pristine immediacy and a reservoir of archetypal elements that makes all other expressive experience possible, through classical memory—Pompeii, but also Villa Adriana; Rome as "door to the Orient"—and through the irrepressible reflections of Italian light.

Between India's distensions of the spiritual body (which are just as contemporary as we are, the painter reminds us) and America's pragmatic tightening of the physical one, Italy functions as the eye of the hourglass, filtering one into the other. Two spaces and two time-frames stand side by side in *The Indigo Room* and *The Fourteen Stations*, perfectly self-contained, yet pressing at the boundaries to meet. The connection—osmotically, organically, almost bodily—is provided by the epidermal quality of the frescoes. Italian space-time shares traits with both the Indian and the American and here transmutes, through the immediacy of the medium, the inexhaustible inwardness of India into America's vast outwardness and freshness of gaze. Nothing is ever lost in such translations, but in each instance, the specific and intrinsic nature of the body's experience of different environments is quite evident in the temperature—and temper—of each of the rooms. If any medium can be said to be closest to Clemente's true nature (together with pastels and watercolors) it is certainly fresco: all the expressive strains of his work seem to come together in the simplest, most subtle way. In fact, each fresco in this exhibition could be said to make up a room by itself: the frescoes are about origins.

A leitmotif of Hindu mythology that is startling in the face of our tragic, Greco-Semitic penchant for rebelling against the dictates of fate is the deities' own full and lighthearted acceptance of the consequences of spells, sometimes spanning entire eons: no hell is forever ("Hari, the Blessed Lord, sportive and gracious, accepted her curse"—Tulasidasa, *Shriramacharitamanasa*). Since blame is inevitably attached to all action—even ritual action (especially sacrifice)—destiny, even that of supernatural beings, is necessarily shaped by the consequences of those actions, and the sooner this *karman* is spent —as inevitably it must be—the better. Far from being a dark persecution, guilt is what makes it possible to take on the curse of living with joyous intent: "'No one is wise or foolish,' said the great Lord Siva with a smile" (ibid.). The descent of gods and heroes into hellish realms is not just an instance of paradise lost, nor a capricious or willful intrusion of the numinous irrational in human affairs, but constitutes a sacrificial act (*karman*), a human incarnation: "men who have committed crimes and have been punished by the sovereign go to heaven" (*Manu Smrti*, VIII, 318).

Sacrifice implies subtraction, an act of diminishing—an important metaphor in Clemente's aesthetic strategy. But there should be no confusion: Arte Povera is one thing; this art of impoverishment is quite another. It is not abstraction, but, rather, a game of subtraction, of adding by taking away. The way of the cross leads to a shedding and purification through suffering (*dolore*, an Italian word, whose resonances, Clemente has noted, are richer than those of any of its English equivalents). For a Westerner, this attenuation can only come of reason stripped bare—as in Marcel Duchamp's *The Bride Stripped Bare by Her Bachelors, Even* (1915–23), and perhaps anticipated in Titian's late painting *The Flaying of Marsyas* (1575–76). It is so that painting asserts its diminished presence in the itinerary of the *Stations*. Unmoving movement is convulsive stillness, seeking somehow to reverse the order of desire, possibly toward a "Love that moves the sun and other stars," which concludes the *Divine Comedy* and shapes our consciousness. What the painter might seek, and what the viewer should find, is not a sense (*aisthesis*) of liberation, but the transmodern sense of a shifting place of origin; every step, every station, is the first and last in this vortex, a maelstrom animated by an eros that is enveloping and inevitable but also, in the end, joyous, soft, and welcoming. The deconstruction is within painting, but the painter is saved.

An entire artistic generation has come and gone between the sensuous reductionism of Barnett Newman's *Stations of the Cross* (1958–66)—or the nihilism of Rothko's chapel—and Clemente's rooms. The difference is not one of abstraction versus representation, for a circularity of movement and stillness is apparent throughout. It is a question of metaphysical versus nonmetaphysical painting, or of a modern reinterpretation of the mythological. More accurately, one might see in the two forms distantly related manifestations of a common, post-metaphysical, search for "suchness." Whatever their immediate source, whether Italian, Indian, or American, Clemente's images often appear as forms-before-form in their willful roughness and immediacy. In Indian terms, they might be defined as *kalpa* representations, personal glimpses of finite yet infinitely recurring eons. In Italian terms, they digest and dissolve the classical. In the American perspective of a world empire (and an empire state) they reflect a new uncloseted expression of the daily encounters with the immediate perils and exhilaration of present life.

Francesco Pellizzi

I especially thank Gini Alhadeff for her invaluable help with my texts.

A fresco is done swiftly, before its supporting surface has a chance to dry (the opposite of oil paint, which needs a dry ground to take hold). That accounts for its air of freshness and transparency of touch, from ancient Roman walls to the Cappella Paolina. The nerve-racking process that makes the swiftness of execution possible goes unrecorded—very much as in the case of a great jazz virtuoso or an Indian traditional singer of ragas. The tension between the immediacy of improvisation and the groundedness of the wall gives frescoes their special character. In Francesco Clemente's case, of course, thanks to a technique developed for him by an ingenious Roman restorer, frescoes do travel, and his hybrids of water, light, soil, and air can transcend the site and float between continents. The chance effect that the painter cultivates in making his watercolors (the uneven spreading of diluted hues and their varying absorption into the paper's fiber) is reduced here to a spontaneous, yet always definitive gesture. No pentimento is possible, but the constriction is voluntary; the word fresco should not be confused with *al fresco*, which in Italian means "imprisoned." Self-imposed "limitations"—technical, formal, of color, perceptual strategy, even of manner—define the work of the painter. So do ropes, laces, enclosures, scissors, etc., as well as groups of beings linked by ties of desire and by ritualized (hence, theatrical) forms of pain and pleasure. A limitation and definition of color schemes and registers is also possible with fresco as well as other mediums (recently in oils) to free the hand, so to speak, and permit a great fluidity of form. That all refuge is a prison, yet that we cannot help seeking it, is a constant in the climate of Clemente's journey through painting.

The discipline of technique is a mask that the painter impersonates, in each instance, imagining and interpreting the medium as a filter, what he has called a "distancing of the hand." His original use of the photograph, in the 1970s, which was connected to the approach to factura of his fellow-travelers Alighiero Boetti, who worked with traditional craftsmen, and Luigi Ontani, who disguised himself and "performed" stereotypical impersonations. In employing such a specific technique, the painter fully adopts it as a "mediation"—which also happens to be the basic attitude that links Modernism to the traditional crafts, and makes any true Modernist, including Clemente, a "primitivist." In a recent oil, *Untitled* (1998), the painter himself is shown holding his palette and pointing to a female model whose face is covered by a red mask.

The precise planning that goes into preparing for the fresco demands perhaps a more rigorous clarity about specific aesthetic and representational aims than for any other medium. The group of frescoes presented here (which do not truly constitute a room, since they were painted at different times and in different places), from *Priapea* (1980, cat. no. 149) to those that were in Clemente's fresco exhibition at Madrid's Fundación Caja de Pensiones in 1987 (see cat. nos. 149–52), echo the playful daring of murals in Pompeian brothels as much as the formal sophistication of those gracing the walls of Augustan palaces.

F. P.

149. ***Priapea***, 1980. Fresco, 78 3/4 x 125 13/16 inches (200 x 319.5 cm). Collection of Dr. Erich Marx, Berlin.

150. ***Coi sentimenti insegna alle emozioni***, 1980. Fresco, three panels, 118 ⅛ x 236 ¼ inches (300 x 600 cm) overall.
Private collection, courtesy Galerie Bruno Bischofberger, Zurich.

Bodily changes follow directly the perception of the exciting fact, and . . . our feeling of the same changes as they occur is the emotion.
—William James

In *Coi sentimenti insegena alle emozioni* (1980, cat no. 150), at the top of the left panel, are *la civetta e il coniglio*, the owl and the rabbit: one who sees in the dark, one who acts in fear. These are symbols, and, as such, contradictory: the owl is blinded by the sun and attacked by inoffensive, vocal larks; the lecherous and prolific rabbit lives in fear of its own vitality. What is the rabbit's wisdom, what is the sensuousness of the owl? Are the zig-zags behind the owl flashes of lightning (insight), and the crosses behind the rabbit a reference to keeping some kind of score? That might relate to the bright yellow field beneath, in which the subject is immersed; does it hint at their common source of jealousy and curiosity? It is as if Francesco Clemente's identity could only be established when his hands are tied and every opening of his body is being touched (obstructed?). But Who is he? There is also a gentleness to the erotic theme here as elsewhere. As the painter said, "I am as interested in small wounds as I am in big wounds. It relates to the idea of fragments, emotional fragments, fragments of time, fragility, softness."

Between the "physis" of feeling and emotional "metaphysis"—a remembered sensation—lies the image of the body-as-presence. Tactility is the preeminent "feeling." Sensation-as-feeling becomes the substance of emotion—not as depicted, though, but through a sort of tactful evocation: a painting about touch as much as one to be touched by—and painting, particularly fresco, is eminently a form of touching, *prière de toucher*.

F. P.

The enigma of beginnings, of nascent form, lies buried deep in the sea. The sign, the gesture of the hand, is like a calligraphic evocation of being and non-being, of forgotten and unforgotten origins. The horizon, symbol of our final room, terra incognita, unites and separates all shapes and colors. Eros reverts to an airy, watery ground, basic and nurturing.

In Francesco Clemente's *Maternal* (1986, cat. no. 151), there seems to be a clockwise progression from the flower—a generative form in nature—to pure shapes. (Or is it due to the eye's habits? It is hard to forget Piet Mondrian's "vanishing" tree.) These shapes retain a sensuousness—a sort of hollow concreteness—that is almost Chinese: "Form comes to life before ideas," Stella Kramrisch told the painter. There may be an affinity, here, with the use of certain found materials, surfaces, and shapes by Brice Marden (and the influence may work both ways).

The meditative atmosphere of *Maternal* is split between the yantralike geometries below and the dreamlike visions above. In the faint landscape of body parts floating above, the surface of the painting seems pierced from the back (a distancing device that may also remind us of Keith Haring's work), as if to point to a physical connection between painting and space-time before, and after, painting. Or perhaps, in another sense, this points to painting and life as one, at least in the realm that many traditional cultures refer to as dreams or the "soul world," which is that of a parallel awareness having little to do with ordinary dreams.

F. P.

151. ***Maternal***, 1986. Fresco, three panels, 118 ½ x 236 ¼ inches (301 x 600.1 cm) overall.
Stephanie Seymour Brant, courtesy The Brant Foundation, Greenwich, Connecticut.

152. ***Honey, Silver, Blood***, 1986. Fresco, three panels, 78 ¾ x 236 ¼ inches (200 x 600 cm) overall. Contemporary Art Fundació "la Caixa," Barcelona.

Honey, silver, blood—nourishment, speed, libation. Quicksilver as *clair de lune*. Purgatory and yoga, a realm between the honey-gold of eternity and immortality (sweet transmutation), and the regenerative infernal powers (sacrificial reincarnations). But the horsefly stings the heavens while the breasts, mouth (*oscula*), and tongue (*non dixit*) may magically take us there: "*e risalimmo a veder le stelle.*" The only way out, symbolically, is to follow the spiral movement suggested by this uplifting well.

Classical memories, such as those of monochrome stucco panels of Roman villas, are transformed in Francesco Clemente's *Honey, Silver, Blood* (1986, cat no. 152) by an expansive modulation of Indian hues. Here, color, in all its luscious understatement, represents the quintessence of the wall. This wall "moves" (and is movable) like a screen: *paravento*, in Italian, a barrier to drafts in a room. Vertical streaks and "hinges" articulate the panels in a deceptively simple hanging of color curtains. One might recall the floating decorations on the tents of Central Asia, but here the abstraction is both countered and enhanced by a heraldry of female body parts, like banners of a depersonalized eros (a post-Surrealist reinterpretation of Indian yantras). Yet space is also enclosed. How is one to enter such a place, to inhabit such a room? The only doors are emblems of soma: the body of desire subsumed into archetypal fields, and into impersonal moments.

F. P.

Francesco Clemente's *Meaning of Sacrifice* (1989, cat. no. 153) is closely related to *Honey, Silver, Blood* (1986, cat no. 152) but also, despite great differences in color register and imagery, to the earlier *Coi sentimenti insegna alle emozioni* (1980, cat no. 150). It could be subtitled "repetition as contrition," because of the prominence of the sacrificial-erotic theme. Excess may be hinted at (there are, after all, less human figures than there are duck bodies and heads!), and so too its Augustinian counterpart, penitence, another form of sacrifice (note that the male organs are cut off by the painting's edge).

Though the connection between the altered spiritual states of Western (and Eastern) ascetic practices and the experience of rechanneling and sublimating sexual energies—more developed in the Indo-Tibetan tradition—is obviously familiar to the painter, one should not interpret the content of any of his paintings as religious. What appears particularly relevant here is that, as in most religions, pleasure is an issue.

F. P.

153. ***Meaning of Sacrifice***, 1989. Fresco, three panels, 118 1/2 x 238 inches (301 x 604.5 cm) overall. Collection of Francesco and Alba Clemente, New York.

The Fourteen Stations

> Our oneiric being is one. It continues in the light of day
> the experience of the night.
> —Gaston Bachelard, *The Air and the Dreams*

On the title-page of the original catalogue for *The Fourteen Stations* (Whitechapel Art Gallery, London, 1983), Francesco Clemente drew the black-and-white image of a clock surmounted by two Janus-head donkey profiles, one with eyes shut, the other with eyes open. The hands of the clock are represented by what looks like a male sexual organ; here is movement, desire, looking forward and backward, sensing, through memory, recurrent deaths and rebirths. The cycle announces itself at first as dumb time plodding along through stations—sites at which action, and time itself, have stopped, transfixed in the stillness of the room.

The ancient voyage *ad infera* entailed a confrontation with shadowlike creatures—diaphanous emanations of departed bodies forever reenacting the entrapments of their existence; the shadow images of modern souls, as in Gogol, are but numbers locked in vacuous, formless permutations. This room is a place in which such spirit concretions—after appearing and vanishing in the studio—are reevoked. Disposition (Aristotle's *Diathesis*) is a condition of emotional receptivity, corresponding to a specific situation, in which physical states are evaluated in relation to higher intellectual functions. In this room, the disposition is like that of someone awakening from a dream (perhaps not always a pleasant one)—or of returning from a trancelike state. It is the *stanza* as "space of the soul," in which time is both the memory and site of the everlasting present, as in Martin Heidegger's version of Saint Augustine: "In you, my soul, I measure time . . . I measure the feeling-of-myself in present existence" (*The Concept of Time*).

The harsh impact of progress through *The Fourteen Stations*, the way the images always seem to break the very aesthetic habits into which they have lured us, is achieved by cultivating imperfections. These demand our attention, so that, as in Sukracharya's precept, their "defects" may "constantly be destroyed by the power of the virtue of the worshiper." At one time, love and faith signified a surrender to ultimate Imperfection, the *via dolorosa* of resurrection. Today, an orphic voyage, and a pilgrim's progress, might be no more than a "voyage to the end of night," although it could be—as Fernando Pessoa, wearer of many masks, once wrote—that "this Night is light" (*Fiat Lux*). Certainly, in these paintings, the analogical play between the forms of the world (matter, reality) and those of emotion (spirit, soul) still points to the workings of true experience, to an *initiation*. In the words of one of Clemente's favorite poets:

> Being no longer human, why should I
> Pretend humanity or don the frail attire?
> Men have I known and men, but never one
> Was grown so free an essence, or become
> So simply element as what I am.
> The mist goes from the mirror and I see.
> Behold! the world of form is swept beneath—
> Turmoil grown visible beneath our peace,
> And we are that are grown formless, rise above—
> Fluids intangible that have been men,
> We seem as statues round whose high-risen base
> Some overflowing river is run mad,
> In us alone the element of calm.
> —Ezra Pound, "Paracelsus in Excelsis," *Personae*

F. P.

Unattributed quotations in the following entries are statements by Francesco Clemente. Many of the alchemical references may be found in Lyndy Abraham, *A Dictionary of Alchemical Imagery* (Cambridge: Cambridge University Press, 1998) and the alchemical studies of C. G. Jung; all of these writings are well known to Clemente.

154. *The Fourteen Stations I*, 1981–82. Oil and wax on linen, 77 15/16 x 88 inches (198 x 223.5 cm). Private collection, loan to the exhibition in memory of Thomas Ammann.

Quaterna. "Others act as if the world were a 'paradise' of which they must reveal the hidden horrors, I see it more as a hell, of which I must uncover the blessings." Beginning and end, and the end within the beginning. Volcanic *prima materia* embracing *nigredo*, and incandescence holding the gaping treasure of *albificatio*: the great, moonlike whitening effected by mercurial waters and by fire. Like an alembic, the exotic world holds the "water of life" that "whitens the body" and purifies it (Artephius). But sulphur (i.e., the devil and fire) is a fundamental aspect of *prima materia*, its male principle in our Western alchemical tradition (*opus alchemicum*) and, fundamentally, its form, and that tension between form and formlessness (again, mercury) is ominously depicted here.

In *The Fourteen Stations I* (1981–82, cat. no. 154), the *selva oscura*—an almost Gauguin-like setting in which Francesco Clemente himself has become the primitive—forms a devilish cave for the containment of light, in which the four elements (air, fire, earth, water) are conjoined around the "white foliated earth" (Michael Maier, *Atalanta Fugiens*). Yet, if the transmuting forces are awakened, we are still within the furnace.

> I join these works for four people,
> Others may overhear them,
> O world, I am sorry for you,
> That you do not know those four
> —Ezra Pound, "Causa," *Personae*

F. P.

Uroboros. And then there were three. If we proceed with an alchemical reading, after the four figures of *The Fourteen Stations I* (1981–82, cat. no. 154), the three women in Francesco Clemente's *The Fourteen Stations II* (1981–82, cat. no. 155) may be seen as standing for the three primary principles (*tria prima*) of Paracelsus—salt (the body), sulphur (the soul), and mercury (the spirit)—linked into what the great alchemist-scientist called circular work (*opus ciculatorium*): through the cycle of "melting and coagulating" (*solve et coagula*), of separation and union, endlessly reiterated, a unification of qualities is brought about. This "philosophical wheel," also a wheel of fortune, is inscribed within the rectangular painting as a sort of "squaring of the circle," and its aim, through a "shifting of the elements" (George Ripley), would be the attainment of ultimate harmony, or, more precisely, peace—as in John Donne's description of "elements and passions living at peace." Peace is the joining of opposing principles that results from this opus, a resurfacing of the ancient archetype of the cosmic serpent biting its own tail (*Uroboros*).

Unlike the uniform whiteness of two figures in *The Fourteen Stations I*, permutation is reflected in the changing colors of the three women in *The Fourteen Stations II*, with a rainbowlike effect; in alchemical terms, this would be a movement toward the perfect whiteness of the albedo, perhaps descending from the painting's upper right-hand corner. There are, of course, many other possible readings of the three women, whirling against a stormy sky; formally they look somewhat like those Tiepolesque apparitions that grace so many of the ceilings and cupolas in Venetian villas. Their realism, even garishness, is a perfect disguise for their archetypal trinitarian resonance. Multicolored desire above and below; look up!

F. P.

155. *The Fourteen Stations II*, 1981–82. Oil and wax on linen, 77 15/16 x 88 inches (198 x 223.5 cm). Private collection, loan to the exhibition in memory of Thomas Ammann.

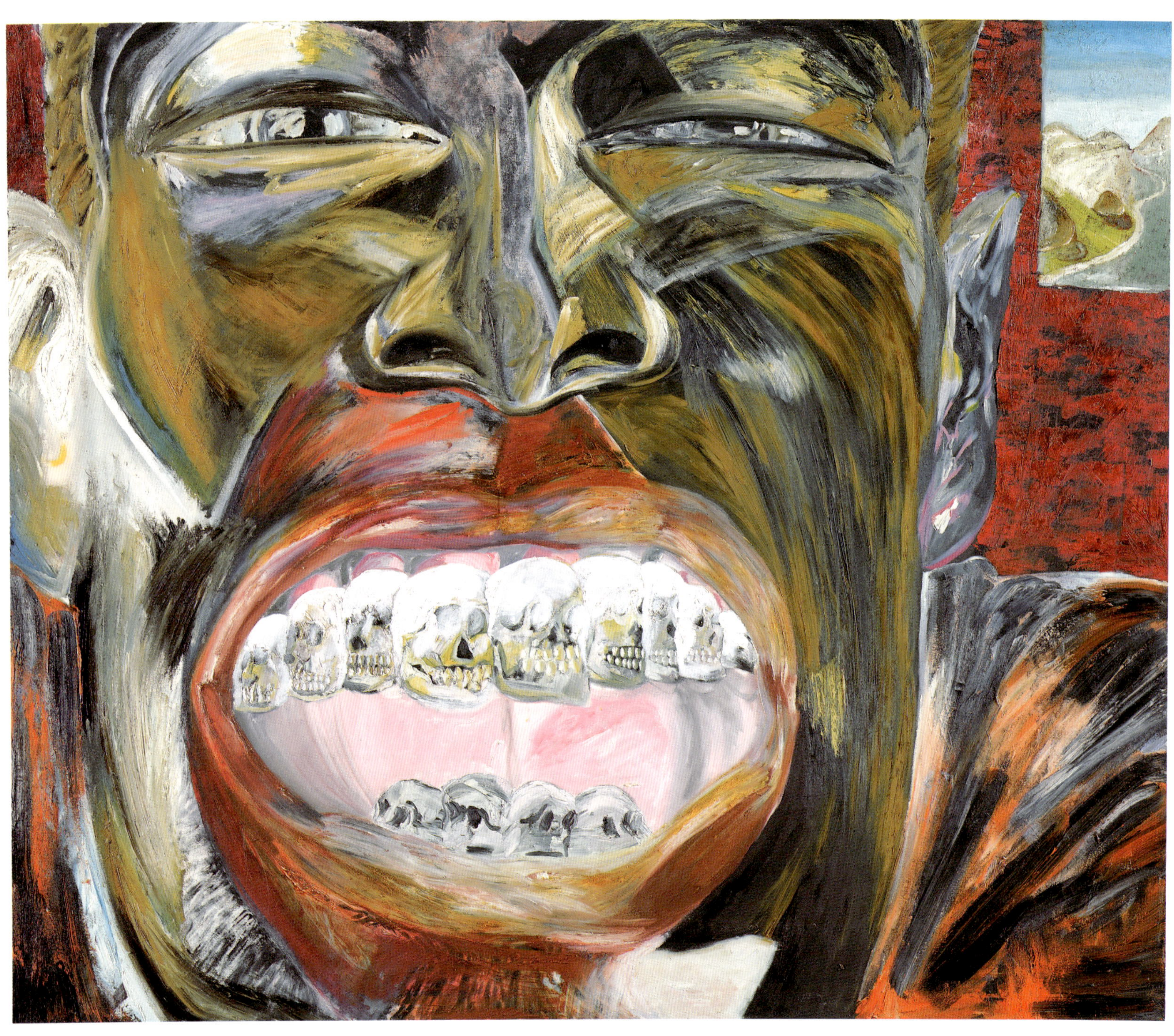

156. ***The Fourteen Stations III***, 1981–82. Oil and wax on linen, 77 15/16 x 92 15/16 inches (198 x 236 cm). Private collection, loan to the exhibition in memory of Thomas Ammann.

Mona Lisa. At least since the fabled journey of Gilgamesh to the Western land of death, entering the ancestors' time and space has marked the initiation into higher existence. A landscape with a winding mountain path, framed by a Renaissance-like window in the background, as in Francesco Clemente's *The Fourteen Stations III* (1981–82, cat. no. 156), may remind us of our search for, and encounter with, shadows. In many traditional cultures, funerary remains were literally consumed, then carefully polished (only theatrically so in our Baroque ossuaries); here, skulls are almost devoured, becoming ornaments of the mouth in the form of golden, intarsioed teeth. (There are thirteen skulls, as many as there are levels in the Mayan dream world, but this may just be coincidental.) The self-portrait close-up, though suffused with a symbolist aura, clashes with the impersonality of the skulls. Yet, they seem almost alive—in the color reflections around their teeth, for instance—while the subject is half lost in a hypnotic state, like a python digesting. Where, in all this, is the Ego in its transformative journey? And where are we and where is Clemente—within the limits of his body, or outside of them? Are we, and he, to (re)enter their precincts?

To see close up can be chaotic (as Hugo von Hofmannsthal's character, Lord Chandos, condemned to see microscopically, frighteningly attests), and chaos is associated with the dark beginnings of any *opus alchymicum*. In alchemy, the dead head (*caput mortuum*) is both the "residue" and the "symbol of the initial stage of the opus, the black *nigredo*, during which process the old form . . . is 'killed,' dissolved into the *prima materia* or original stuff of creation" (Lyndy Abraham). But here a certain redness of the subject and its surroundings would seem to indicate that there is life and regeneration in this encounter with death, as in the alchemist's journey where *rubedo* indicates the final stage of transformation: "sublimation . . . calcination [the skulls], rubification" (John Lily, *Gallathea*). The operation stood for the resurrection of the body into immortality, but also for being bloodied; the life of the white soul, vivified by its conjunction with the spirit, is in its inner redness.

F. P.

Spoils. The ever-increasing concentration on an image of the self can be seen, historically, as the expression of art's progressive journey inward. It is also, in another sense, a feminization of representation, as the old fighter and hunter turns in on himself, examining his own existential condition. (But are we really sure that those reclusive geniuses who painted our Paleolithic caves were not women? How better to while away the hours waiting for a bison *entrecôte* or a leg of gazelle?) Self-mutilation—in fact, castration—was the supreme ecstatic gesture for devotees of certain Great Mother cults of antiquity, which may also have included sacred whores—and their lineage also connects to that of extreme ascetic practices of the desert outcasts of early Christianity.

The animal of the hunter was sacrificed in effigy, deep in mountain recesses, as though the prey should not see what was done to its image, and to its soul, forever transformed into a vividly fleeting shadow. The shedding of mortal spoils in life is one of the themes of Francesco Clemente's *The Fourteen Stations*. In particular, it is the image in *The Fourteen Stations IV* (1981–82, cat. no. 157)—the shadow skin, the clothing, or the mask—that is sacrificed, while Nandi, Siva's bull, prances across a stormy end-of-the-world landscape. One may be reminded of Michelangelo's quasi-anamorphic semblance as disembodied, or flayed, skin, held up by Saint Bartholomew in *The Last Judgment* (1534–41), and perhaps echoed by Titian's *The Flaying of Marsyas* (1575–76), in which the grieving Midas represents the painter himself: self-portrait as a painful distancing from the worldly self.

F. P.

157. ***The Fourteen Stations IV***, 1981–82. Oil and wax on linen, 77 15/16 x 88 9/16 inches (198 x 225 cm). Private collection, loan to the exhibition in memory of Thomas Ammann.

158. ***The Fourteen Stations V***, 1981–82. Oil and wax on linen, 77 15/16 x 92 1/8 inches (198 x 234 cm). Private collection, loan to the exhibition in memory of Thomas Ammann.

Ockham. The cat has nine lives—many too are those of desire. Light and darkness, water and air, duality and self-sufficiency. Sanskrit logicians are masters at splitting hairs into infinitesimal threads; if you do it long and rigorously enough, all distinctions are ultimately effaced. The cat has a long tail. (Is it also a sad one, like that of the mouse in Alice's wonderland? *Animal post coitum triste*, said the philosopher.) But in Francesco Clemente's *The Fourteen Stations V* (1981–82, cat. no. 158), the cat is cut in half, and all redness is flowing out of it. Ockham's razor calls for simplicity—"*entia non sunt multiplicanda praeter necessitatem*" (plurality should not be posited unnecessarily)—and images are multiplications of reality of sorts; two half-cats are less, not more, than one whole cat.

The top of the painting cuts off the subject's head, yet playfulness will not make one lose one's head; as Rumi sang, "ask the severed head the secrets of the heart" (*Diwan Shans-i Tâbrizi*). The alchemist Van Melmont reportedly did it by experimenting with certain witches' herbs. For Stéphane Mallarmé, the experience is referred back to John the Baptist (significantly, an androgyne in Leonardo da Vinci's famous depiction), whose overflowing and boiling blood, the origin of all desire, like that from the head of Raktabija, held up by Kali as she couples with Siva, signifies the rising sun of "clarity, intensity, and peace."

F. P.

Creche. The reclining tree, here, is not quite an *arbor inversa*, as in the alchemical figure signifying nourishment from above, or from a bottle of virgin's milk, like the one kept by Athanasius Kircher in his personal museum—another of alchemy's innumerable images of mercurial water. With its look of a discarded Christmas tree in a heap of snow, it evokes the truncated tree, symbol, once more, of the dark labor of *nigredo*, in which the worker confronts death, his own and that of the Object of his work, as the *prima materia* is buried and becomes subject to "putrefaction" (Lyndy Abraham).

The bright red balls in Francesco Clemente's *The Fourteen Stations VI* (1981–82, cat. no. 159) are there as a sign of hope, without which there is no surviving the *noche oscura*, and the flood of whiteness engulfs the spotted hide of an enticing and fearsome leopardess. This painting, which reminds us of Dante's own symbol of lechery—"*e non mi si partia dinanzi al volto*" (she would not pull back from before my face)—reappears in later works by Clemente. In this midwinter night's dream, though, the whitening light at the center, as in many of *The Fourteen Stations*, supplies raw energy to the whole sacred representation, and this is an indication, in my view, that it is not a Manichaean struggle that is being depicted. Is that the painter's own face, barely visible within the vulva-shaped opening at the center?

The tree has entered my hands,
The sap has ascended my arms,
The tree has grown in my breast—
Downward
The branches grow out of me, like arms.

Tree you are,
Mob you are,
You are violets with wind above them.
A child—so high—you are,
And all this is folly to the world.
—Ezra Pound, "A Girl," *Ripostes*

F. P.

159. ***The Fourteen Stations VI***, 1981–82. Oil and wax on linen, 77 15/16 x 88 inches (198 x 223.5 cm). Private collection, loan to the exhibition in memory of Thomas Ammann.

160. ***The Fourteen Stations VII***, 1981–82. Oil and wax on linen, 77 15/16 x 89 15/16 inches (198 x 228.5 cm).

Private collection, loan to the exhibition in memory of Thomas Ammann.

Breathing. In or out? Big fish and small fish always find each other. The spot of whiteness makes it all rather distant, and yet so present; the goal is not forgotten. Three nipples around water flowing from the lips—or is it being sucked back through them? Inhale and exhale. And so we reach the stage of ablution, also called mundification, which might be seen as the breathing in and out of all the water of the seas—as in the Chinese tale of the little fisherman. Water into air, soul into spirit, receptivity into meditation; the thought of awakening is entertained.

"Some alchemists say that, during or after washing or whitening the blackened earth or body of the stone at the ablution, there appear pearls or fishes' eyes in the vessel. It is the appearance in the dark solution of the spark or light of pure consciousness. . . . Then the work is complete in the first part" (Benjamin Lock, "His Picklock to Ripply His Castle").

The white splash in Francesco Clemente's *The Fourteen Stations VII* (1981–82, cat. no. 160) is like a bright sun opposite the barely visible blue crescent moon, but it is also a distancing device in relation to both the iconographical content of the painting and the picture plane, providing a counterpoint to the wide, somewhat vacuous pool of the subject's eyes. Despite their realism, the eyes are asymmetrical, looking in different directions and with different expressions. Yet we have come a long way from the piercing blindness of the subject's eyes in *The Fourteen Stations III* (1981–82, cat. no. 156). Meister Eckhardt comes to mind: "When detachment reaches its zenith, by knowledge it is made unknowing, by love, not-loving" (*On Detachment*). Or Ezra Pound, not long before his death:

> But to live as flowers reflected,
> as moonlight,
> free from all possessiveness in affections
> but, as Chu says, egoistical.
> —Pound, "Canto 99," *Thrones*

F. P.

Suspension. Lazarus *redivivus.* Excrement, crumpled sheets, and vermin. Painting is not resurrection, but description cannot kill the painting either. Equivalence between curiosity and *voluptas;* pleasure is the force that opens the doors of the body, does it also cause the transfusion of soul and spirit that points to a transcendence of the body? The deceptions of pleasure, transformed into bittersweet memories, may lead to higher understanding. In our inverted materialistic world, the sweet carnal fruit has fulfilled the deceitful promise of Eve's apple, though perhaps the gift of knowledge has been lost.

Levitation in a white and black field. Lightness above, darkness below; what goes up, must come down; humility in detachment. In Francesco Clemente's *The Fourteen Stations VIII* (1981–82, cat. no. 161), it is as if the male, the spirit (C. G. Jung's "animus"), the androgynous child, rises up despite being trampled by the leftover marks of the soul's uncontrolled affections. But *anima* also activates the energy centers of being, suggested by the woman's shoes distributed over the body, placed roughly at Hindu *chakra* sites.

Distillation and sublimation are equivalent in alchemy, and spiritual sublimation, according to all traditions, is a journey that must be rooted in filth and darkness. This is the alchemist's *putrefactio,* which also appears, to dramatic effect, in the Baroque sermons of John Donne. Rabelais, on the other hand, gives a hilarious description of an alchemical "kingdom of the quintessence": "I saw one calcinator artificially extracting farts from a dead donkey. . . . Another was putrefying . . . abstractions" (*Pantagruel,* 651). In *The Fourteen Stations VIII,* we can once more find *nigredo* below—the nocturnal mice and excrement: "The faeces . . . are the dross and *terra dannata*" (Artephius)—but also the material of the alchemist's *pharmaka,* potions for worldly aims. In the same vein, the blood-stained, crumpled sheets may stand for both the yet unclean matter of the (philosophical) stone, which must be washed and dried at the ablution (see *The Fourteen Stations VII,* 1981–82, cat. no. 160) to attain the pure white matter of the albedo (i.e., the "body" of the stone; note the whiteness of the levitating body) now ready to receive the imprint of form (the spirit of the stone), and "the staining of the white sheets with the red blood of the precious red elixir or tincture" (Lyndy Abraham).

F. P.

161. ***The Fourteen Stations VIII***, 1981–82. Oil and wax on linen, 77 15/16 x 92 15/16 inches (198 x 236 cm).

Private collection, loan to the exhibition in memory of Thomas Ammann.

162. ***The Fourteen Stations IX***, 1981. Oil and wax on linen, 77 15/16 x 92 15/16 inches (198 x 236 cm). Private collection, loan to the exhibition in memory of Thomas Ammann.

Beginnings. Closeness can come in many ways, as between the evanescences of odor (never twice) and the rigidity of shadow (never again). What is the magic of the moment? Aura and persona, soul and mask; yet something is fishy here! Early hunters may have started washing so as to better sneak up on their prey. In "high" civilizations, the extreme, dandyesque disregard for bodily-care of the sannyasin/world-renouncers—our saintly *odore di santità*—fits well with a tripartition of being: the solar body (object of desire); the shadow (the soul and language); and in between the two, perhaps as an evocation of the marriage of sun and moon, of male and female, the "*tingeing arcanum*" that "has the power to bring wisdom to the heart of man," the volatile, mercurial substance of spirit, "whose rejoining with the purified body of the Stone constitutes the culminations of the opus" (Lyndy Abraham).

In Francesco Clemente's *The Fourteen Stations IX* (1981–82, cat. no. 162), there is, once again, black, white, and red, mediated by gold, but still separate, with the evocation of the alchemist's *stinking gumme*, proceeding from the unclean body in the first distillation. The whole play of body-soul-spirit is immersed in a green-gold field that may evoke a germinating and transformative condition which, like the alchemical "green lyon," is "multiplicable, spermatick, and not yet perfected by nature" (St. Dusten).

F. P.

Jonah. I see Francesco Clemente's *The Fourteen Stations X* (1981–82, cat. no. 163), this complex and central painting, as providing a sort of cosmology of transition: the Great Goddess—a Western Kali—the subject subsumed (but not subjugated) within her, with flaming hair (Pentecost), the compass held out in the egg-shaped, distant azure (for Paracelsus, the "arcane substance"; for Thomas Vaughan, the "body of heaven"), the vessels on the left, navigating dark waters, and a whaler on the right, with its open womb, ready to receive Jonah, the twice-born traveler. It all amounts to an unsettled and unsettling stream of worldly and other-worldly emblems that are not easy to navigate; "child's play" (*ludus puerorum*), or "woman's work" (*ars nostra est ludus puerorum cum labor mulierum*), turns "undermost that which before was uppermost," the hard (body) into soft (spirit), while the soft spirit, in turn, is "congealed into form" (Lyndy Abraham).

The Fourteen Stations X depicts within its strong horizontal/vertical four-part divisions, a harmony in disorder that comes together in spite of itself (*contro voglia*). It does so through an obstinate, obsessive pursuit of imbalance, which might also be traced to alchemical imagery—notably, in the progression from the "white king" to the "ruby king" ("a little island in the middle of a feminine ocean"; "what is feminine includes what is masculine"), or in the "incest" between the red man and the white woman, which is one metaphor for the chemical wedding that must produce the all-transforming stone of wisdom. But it is the gesture itself, both as depicted and in depiction, that manages to juggle everything in a vertiginous swirl and yet also convey an uncannily serene vision.

F. P.

163. ***The Fourteen Stations X***, 1981–82. Oil and wax on linen, 77 15/16 x 92 15/16 inches (198 x 236 cm). Private collection, loan to the exhibition in memory of Thomas Ammann.

164. ***The Fourteen Stations XI***, 1981–82. Oil and wax on linen, 77 15/16 x 92 15/16 inches (198 x 236 cm). Private collection, loan to the exhibition in memory of Thomas Ammann.

See no evil. And then there were five. Eye that sees and eye that is seen; piercing eye and eye transfixed. Witchcraft and fame, and foresight (as in the all-embracing gaze of the shaman). The shadow is the body—a nocturnal constellation of innumerable eyes. Night prevails in *The Fourteen Stations,* as it did in the life of Francesco Clemente at the time that he painted them. The alchemist's work is also mostly nocturnal, and the soul-spirit conjunction of the opus may be seen to spring from Clemente's analogous experience in the form of a handheld lotus flower. The left hand may indicate the *via oscura,* the tantric way of Hindo-Tibetan traditions.

There are five bodies in *The Fourteen Stations XI* (1981–82, cat. no. 164), and it is tempting to think of the Grand Oeuvre: "Gerhard Dorn stated that the quintessence was needed for the purification and preparation of the body. The purified body or *caelum* became *the corpus glorificatum,* a substance capable of being united with the already united soul and spirit, in the final *coniunctio* or chemical wedding of the opus, [and one must combine] the four contrary elements into an integrated, harmonious whole," an effect of the *opus circolatorium,* a circular movement that is evident in this painting. Lyndy Abraham also evokes Isaac Newton's statement that "quintessence is a thing that is spiritual, penetrating, tinging, and incorruptible, which emerges anew from the four elements when they are bound to each other."

The classical positioning of the main figure (reminiscent of a Bernini river god on a Roman fountain), the central cluster of intertwined bodies, and the *agro romano* pine trees in the distance convey the feeling that the modern alchemist/painter is somehow being supervised in his work and is not quite free to act alone.

F. P.

Deposition. It is mysterious, and momentous, how duality reemerges from the expression of quintessence—the end is also the beginning. Now the spiritual body is worn, so to speak, outwardly, looking somewhat like a fallen idol from Easter Island, while the heart rests tranquil in its duplicity whose symmetry is never absolute, or the eternal generative cycle would be stilled. "Between *Winterreise* and Nativity," says Lyndy Abraham's *Clangor Buccinae*, "the sublime Body [of the Stone] . . . [will] ascend most purely, like Snow, which is our pure Quintessence." The ultimate albedo, which the alchemists represented as a "landscape . . . cold, white, still and silver under the illumination of the moon," may have been reached. It is in such a landscape that the twin brothers, the *adelphoi*, "burn" as "Asiatic male twins," their union forming "one perfect whole" (Abraham).

In Francesco Clemente's *The Fourteen Stations XII* (1981–82, cat. no. 165), as in *The Fourteen Stations I* (1981–82, cat. no. 154), a foursome, but here their arrangement is as different as their transformed nature. The soulful, white female head rests on the knees of a dark male while the devils have become the twins within; in Paracelsus's words, "'Tis dissolved by itself, coupled by itself, and conceives by itself" (Aurora). Incest is traditionally represented as that of mother and son, which may be sublimated, in *The Fourteen Stations XII*, as a reversal of the Deposition. A Western, hyperborean Parvati rests her head on the knees of a melancholic, brooding Siva. The natural, spiritual order is reversed—albedo below, *nigredo* above—but hope swirls through the darkness in luminously white snowflakes, and the reversal may also be an invitation to move around the room—perhaps in the opposite direction?—one more time: "*d'opra non star, se di fe' non se' sciolto*" (Cino to Dante).

F. P.

165. ***The Fourteen Stations XII***, 1981–82. Oil and wax on linen, 77 $^{15}/_{16}$ x 92 $^{15}/_{16}$ inches (198 x 236 cm). Private collection, loan to the exhibition in memory of Thomas Ammann.

Self-Portrait

Each consciousness must emigrate
And lose its neighbour once.
—Emily Dickinson

Rembrandt may have invented the self-portrait as disguise: exteriorization through fancy dress. Francesco Clemente brings a new use to portraiture; through his innumerable self-portraits, it becomes clear that he may have intended from the start to dissolve his own image, both his presence as person (persona: mask) and as artifact. Repetition is not meant to affirm but to weaken any illusion of continuity: "For I do not exist: there exist but the thousand mirrors that reflect me. With every acquaintance I make, the population of phantoms resembling me increases. Somewhere they live, somewhere they multiply. I alone do not exist. . . . A fetus in reverse, my image, too, will dwindle and die within that last witness of the crime I committed by the mere fact of living" (Vladimir Nabokov, *The Eye*). In the Christian reading of *Self-Portrait* (1982, cat. no. 166), personal existence is not a crime to be expiated in a binary relation to the transcendent, but a moment in the circular movement of an epiphanic and healing Trinity. Self-sacrifice is only one of the transmuting vehicles, and compassion starts at home.

As we look further, there is something disquieting about the iconography of the image. Is the shape of the crucified animal that of a frog? Or, perhaps the memory of a woman's body, or (not mutually exclusive) of an alter ego? Certainly, the factura of this portrait-mask accentuates a sense of extraneousness: the odd, asymmetrical nostrils, the bright, parrotlike shadow beneath the left eye, the quadripartition of the face (close-up as microcosm), the whites of the eyes overflowing their confines (a Matissean device). The subject hovers between the figures of cross and amphibian, mediators from opposite worlds: "Perhaps he will think with a bit of melancholy that Greek mythology does not know the word 'resurrection'" (Zbigniew Herbert, "Antaeus"). It all makes one wonder whether the experience of the Crucifixion, in a Blakeian echo, has touched something as deep and phylogenetically remote as the murderous neural strains that humans share with serpents. "Yes, he thought, between grief and nothing, I will take grief" (William Faulkner, *The Wild Palms*).

O strange face there in the glass!
O ribald company, O saintly host,
O sorrow-swept my fool,
What answer? O ye myriad
That strive and play and pass,
Jest, challenge, counterlie!
I? I? I?
  And ye?
—Ezra Pound, "On his own face in a glass," *Personae*

F. P.

166. ***Self-Portrait***, 1982. Oil on linen, 40 x 34 inches (101.6 x 86.4 cm). Private collection, Basel.

The Indigo Room

> Night now! Tell me, tell me, tell me, elm! Night Night! Tell me tale of stem or stone.
> Beside the rivering waters, hither and thithering waters of. Night!
> —James Joyce, *Finnegan's Wake*

Many years ago, in a Madras garden, I saw thick, immaculate sheets of porous, handmade Pondicherry paper being dipped again and again into basins filled with indigo ink. Gigantic overhanging trees shaded the operation in dappled green. As the blue deepened, sapphire drips speckled Francesco Clemente's dhoti and body. I didn't know then what would become of these color saturations, which drew their feel and technique from traditional handcrafted cloth dyeing, until years later, in Philadelphia, when I saw *The Indigo Room* (1983–84, cat. no. 167).

Materials cohere in this room, where paper has the consistency of papier-mâché and cloth the gauzelike delicacy of weavings produced by Gandhi cooperatives. The whole space is like an enveloping sari, and its modulated dominant hue reminds me of the old indigo cloaks of Dogon men in Mali and wraparound skirts of Mayan women in Mexico. Here, there is hiding and revealing, with elegance as the overriding theme. This is the realm of *rasa*, where the test, and taste, of seeing is believing. There is much sensuousness on these walls; in traditional Indian aesthetic theory, *rasakule*—literally, "filled with rasa"—refers to the emotion of being "overcome with sexual passion" (J. Moussaieff Masson).

And this is also a tantric room, in which one is caught in a net of illusions yet also enticed to slip beyond appearances into the world of the unseen: "The wall of Maya, the wall of illusion, is not a wall but a net. And what is a net? Your eye focuses on the threads that block your vision, but if you were to change focus, you would see the holes, the void." Through this "net," one perceives barely visible chains of sexually interlocked figures, faintly reminiscent of the reliefs of Konarak in Orissa.

In this softly resonating space, I am reminded of the poetically obsessive atmosphere in Satyajit Ray's *The Music Room* (1958), where, in the end, music becomes a silent presence, associated with the sea.

F. P.

left and following six pages:

167. ***The Indigo Room***, 1983–84. Indigo dye, charcoal, and silver pieces on 123 sheets of handmade Pondicherry paper, joined with handwoven cotton strips, four parts, 148 13/16 x 164 3/16 inches (378 x 417 cm); 123 1/4 x 235 1/16 inches (313 x 597 cm); 97 5/8 x 235 1/16 inches (248 x 597 cm); 147 1/4 x 163 3/4 inches (374 x 416 cm). Como Group, courtesy Diego Cortez Arte, Ltd., New York.

Books, Palimpsests, Collaborations

The idea of collaboration in art is often viewed with mistrust by critics and audiences; it frustrates the impulse to identify and label, as well as the desire to elevate individual authorship. This prejudice overlooks thousands of years of actual practice by artists, from the times of ancient Greece and Rome to the Renaissance and after. In regard to production and the specialized division of labor, an artist's studio has as often resembled a small film set or a couturier's workshop as it has the solitary atelier of lore. In tune with the spirit of the past, Francesco Clemente has stated:

> I enjoy being part of a standard—that's exactly what I'm missing as a painter in the twentieth century. Everybody always says to me, "Do whatever you want to do." That's a terrible situation to be in. So it was a great relief and joy to hear someone in a Jaipur workshop say, "No, it must be this color." . . . The image is totally mine, but the craft I'm relating to is the craft that is used in the decoration of temples or for movie posters or souvenirs for the tourist trade. In India I never go to the museums, I go to the streets and look at all the things I like. The most beautiful things you see in India are the ones that only last for a day. I hate the whole authorship frenzy we have in the West. I don't believe in it, I don't care about it—how everything has to be known down to the last brushstroke. If you look at Mantegna, you know this man had some fourteen-year-old boy helping him, and they were modestly doing the best they could. And now Mantegna is up there with the immortals. But the reason why he's up there is because the work was done without flaw, modestly, to the craft.[1]

Throughout his career, Clemente has consistently worked against the notions of fixed identity that are denoted by a "signature" style. Diversity in mediums and execution is characteristic of his work. By using another person's sensibility as a tool—the way one might use a pencil or brush—Clemente at times exchanges his own view for that of another, in the process expanding his own thought. Wallace Stevens once asked, "What are the motives for metaphor?" Clemente's self-imposed task as an artist has been to seek out the needs and desires that give rise to metaphor, as well as to invite situations from which new motives might arise. In filtering his decision-making process through that of another, and in following pathways he would not have traveled otherwise, collaboration has been essential for him.

Clemente's reticence to discuss the particulars of his collaborative efforts has less to do with any covertness of fabrication and more to do with a deep ambivalence toward dissecting the creative process: "I think painting is still about enjoyment and the more you know about it the less you enjoy."[2] To replace appreciation with analysis is something of a modern malady in art. Clemente belongs to the breed of artists who seek to guard mysteries and not unravel them.

The germ of Clemente's penchant for collaboration can be traced to the work of Alighiero Boetti:

> A great inspiration for me was certainly Boetti's work. Boetti was an extremely original, unique mind whose approach to the making of images was almost like a composer. He would orchestrate a certain process but he would not execute the work himself. He would find ways to have the work executed by other people in an anonymous way. He was traveling to the Orient, and I was traveling with him, and he was making works which were embroidered in Afghanistan. . . . That was a great inspiration to me, the wider feeling that this activity doesn't stop with you but rather extends away from you, away from your control and taste and sense of self.[3]

Another early mentor was Luigi Ontani, whose wry and operatic imagination manifested itself in a number of collaborations with artisans in India. By the end of 1977, Clemente himself had completed a series of collaborative works in India, employing local craftspeople, including tinsmiths, clay and papier-mâché model makers, billboard sign painters from the vast Indian film industry, and painters of miniatures. In the best of these works, one cannot tell where one hand leaves off and another begins. As Clemente noted of the Tamil sign painters, "I was copying them and they were copying me."[4] It was also in 1977 that he began collaborating with C. T. Nachiappan of Kalakshetra Publications in Madras, and this has been perhaps the most fruitful and personally rewarding of all his collaborative relationships. Alike in temperament, both men tend to be taciturn, cryptic in their intentions, and somewhat fatalistic in their general outlook, although not without humor. The books produced by Nachiappan contributed to the early renown of Clemente's work. Long before I'd met the artist or seen his work in the flesh, I was acquainted with these publications and was struck by their otherworldly look, like fabulous travelogues from another time and place.

In Italy, Clemente has enjoyed a long friendship with Claudio di Giambattista, a skilled restorer of Renaissance paintings, whose expertise has aided the artist not only in the execution of a great number of frescoes but also in various centuries-old recipes for mediums, grounds, and pigments. But collaboration remains a fine line, and the results must ring true to the artist's sensibility. For over a dozen years, I have seen Clemente design and commission various work in Indian embroidery and fabrics, only to abandon the work midway or dispose of the results shortly after completion. At other times, he is motivated by a sense of preservation of craft, employing artisans, mostly in India, when the fashion or demand for their work nears extinction.

When Clemente moved to America, his lifelong love of the writers of the Beat generation was suddenly actualized, and poems became a new type of canvas. Ovid's phrase "*ut pictura poesis*" (as poetry, so painting) may serve as a motto for Clemente's New York years. Almost daily contact with William Burroughs, Gregory Corso, Robert Creeley, Allen Ginsberg, Rene Ricard, and John Wieners made for a world as romantic and picaresque as anything out of John Aubrey's *Brief Lives*. In 1986, in New York, the painter and I cofounded Hanuman Books, a small press that has to date published fifty chapbooks, including all the above authors, as well as Cookie Mueller, Eileen Myles, Patti Smith, and others. Printed in Madras by Nachiappan, the project brought together the discrete worlds of Clemente's inspiration. In delving into the common roots of painting and poetry, Clemente has created a parable of connectedness for our divided age, one that may serve as an ethic and standard, as well as an aesthetic.

Raymond Foye

1. Francesco Clemente, conversation with Vishakha N. Desai, Asia Society Galleries, New York, May 27, 1993.
2. Ibid.
3. Clemente, conversation with Robert Storr, 92nd Street Y, New York, May 4, 1995.
4. Clemente, interview with the author, August 7, 1997.

If there is a single key to Francesco Clemente's art, it is drawing. It underlies both his painting and thought. Line is where his sensibility exists in its purest form: tenuous, agile, penetrating. Possessing a potent, latent elegance, Clemente's early drawings are akin to writing in their epigrammatical approach (see cat. nos. 2, 4, 5, 7, 8, 168). Rarely exhibited at the time they were made, they were presented unframed, often laid in piles on the gallery floor. Like seeds, each drawing contained a germ of thought that ultimately and voluptuously flowered into paintings, pastels, gouaches, and watercolors. These early notational studies are the aesthetic DNA, so to speak, of Clemente's later work. "Rome is the city of emblems, of grotesques and seals,"[1] the artist has noted, and there is an archaic quality to these images, like ancient graffiti or an incised glyph on a seal or tomb.

As with most of his colleagues, Clemente's artmaking activites in Rome in the 1970s took place along the lines of philosophical investigation: "The artists I knew didn't even keep studios in those days—it was such a metaphysical activity to be an artist."[2] Given that nearly all of his preceding works were photo-based conceptual installations, the early drawings represent a resolute reconciliation with the hand. In his reintroduction of traditional materials, Clemente was determined to establish a territory of his own in relation to his contemporaries, but the visual thinking behind these works was very much a continuation of that "metaphysical activity."

R. F.

1. Francesco Clemente, quoted in "Conversation with Francesco Clemente, Danilo Eccher and Francesco Pellizzi," in Danilo Eccher, *Francesco Clemente: Opere su carta*, exh. cat. (Turin: Umberto Allemandi & C., 1999), p. 114.
2. Clemente, conversation with Robert Storr, 92nd Street Y, New York, May 4, 1995.

168. *Whether the Holes in the Body Are Nine or Ten*, 1977. India ink on paper, 5 5/8 x 6 9/16 inches (14.3 x 16.7 cm).

Öffentliche Kunstsammlung Basel, Kupferstichkabinett, 1984.59.

In *The Bestiary of Christ* (1943)—an exhaustive and near-hallucinatory work by the medievalist Louis Charbonneau-Lassay—nearly twenty pages are devoted to the many attributes of the swan, "noble bird par excellence." The fabled "swan song" sprang from the belief that this animal, solar charioteer of Greek, Norse, and Hindu myth, sang a melody of unspeakable beauty at the moment of its death. As with many symbols, double meanings proliferate, from Zeus's ravishment of Leda to the steadfast symbol of purity and courage in medieval heraldry. In our age, endangered species and their natural habitats are used by advertisers to sell everything from computers to gas-guzzling vehicles.

Animals abound in Francesco Clemente's work. The fact that he is one of the few contemporary artists of note for whom animals have been an enduring subject is an example of how distanced art has become from traditional sources. From Pliny the Elder to medieval bestiaries to Matisse and Picasso, animals have been a ceaseless source of wonder for artists, a kind of ultimate metaphor for the sheer imaginativeness and improbability of God's creation. Certainly this awe is not lost on children, and in searching for subject matter Clemente had only to look around the studio to find his own children's toys scattered about. In *Untitled* (1974, cat. no. 170), the swan's image of fierce beauty retains its distance from the flotilla of bathtub toys that wallpaper the background.

Simplicity of presentation is part of the charm of *Untitled*. In forms both noble and whimsical, it is a meditation on the persistence of natural beauty, which retains its grace in pure and debased forms. It is also a visual homily to the Buddhist adage that "things are symbols of themselves." And it is very much in keeping with Clemente's project in the 1970s of constructing an iconology of everyday life—to freeze musing thoughts or daydreams into images of permanence.

R. F.

169. ***Harlequin Close Up***, 1978. Ink and colored pencil on nine sheets of paper, mounted on linen, 39 1/4 x 25 3/4 inches (99.7 x 65.4 cm). Sanders Collection, Amsterdam.

170. ***Untitled***, 1974. Gouache, ink, and pencil on paper, mounted on linen, 65 ⅜ x 74 7/16 inches (166 x 189 cm). Collection of Beat Curti.

Twins are a recurring motif in Francesco Clemente's work, as they are throughout mythology and history. Like all inhabitants of Rome, the artist lived under the city's titular gods, the twin brothers Romulus and Remus, whose balance, subsumed by rivalry, ended in destruction. As forms of natural replication, twins have always been intriguing to the traditional artist, whose very job description is to create a "double" of the original. Twins exist in all aspects of nature, and the presence of similar yet distinct entities heightens the mystery of creation, while at the same time introducing the disconcerting notion of nature as a masquerade. In the mineral world, twinned crystals form in identical, reversed position in relation to each other. The phenomenon of twin stars exists in cosmology, while in astrology the twins of Gemini are a potent symbol of duality. Polarity is another variation of equivalence, whereby invisible attraction is dependent not on resemblance but opposition.

Twins (1978, cat. no. 171) is an example of the emblematic power of Clemente's early drawings carried to a further stage of development. In a strange hieroglyph of orphic enchantment, a human hand forms the strings of the lyre shared by the paired figures. Roman signet rings—devices for affixing symbols of ownership in wax or clay—pattern the background. Enshrouding and revealing, it is an image that conjures the paradox embodied in the concept of twinning, which in Clemente's aesthetic is a metaphor for the condition of fragmentation and the yearning for unity.

R. F.

171. *Twins*, 1978. Gouache, ink, and colored pencil on four sheets of paper, mounted on linen, 93 x 59 inches (236.2 x 149.9 cm). Sanders Collection, Amsterdam.

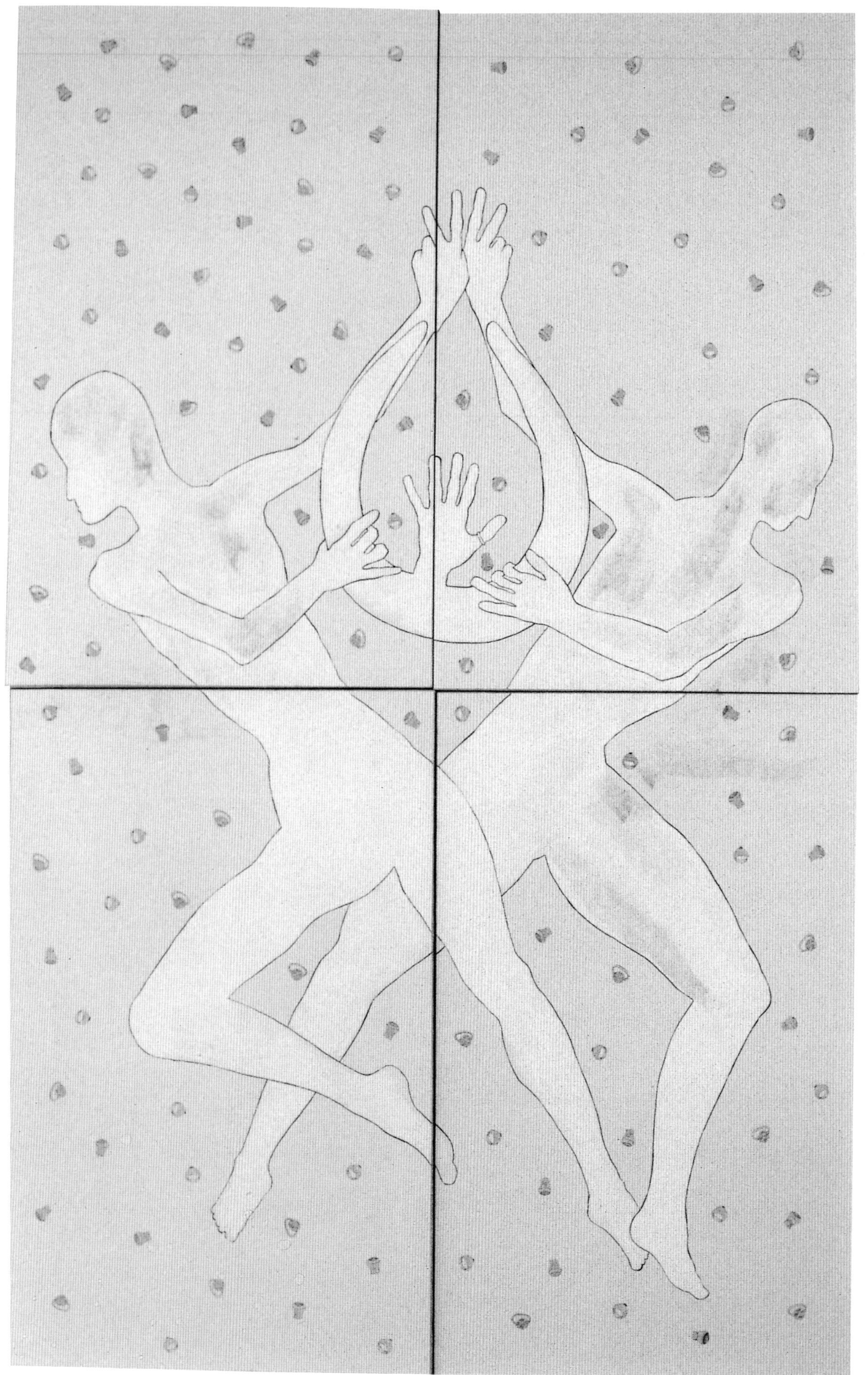

Among the more memorable works Francesco Clemente has made in India are those from the miniature-painting workshops of Jaipur and Orissa. In *Francesco Clemente Pinxit* (1980–81, cat. no. 172), the artist took on a vast and ancient tradition with a lightness of touch and whimsical detachment. In a contemporary way, Clemente availed himself of this tradition and adapted the pictorial aspects most integral to it: the architectonic division of the picture plane, a multifarious iconography that can be "read" as well as viewed, and a rhythmic grammar of ornament, employed at times with austerity and at times with a flourish.

The gouaches that make up *Francesco Clemente Pinxit* depict a world in which all things in creation are animated, enmeshed in a web of private metaphors. Some are fablelike, involving animals, while others depict Bosch-like enterprises from a garden of bizarre delights. Obscure narratives and odd minutiae abound. In their finely focused detail, these vertically arranged landscapes might almost be Sienese of the fourteenth century were it not for the Mughal settings, which are occasionally intruded upon by contemporary artifacts: a kite, a telephone, a soccer field. Transformation is the overarching activity, with one form exchanging itself for another. As Herman Hesse once observed, "India doesn't interpret symbols, it lives them."[1]

As a Neapolitan, Clemente's love of the extravagant and fanciful comes as second nature. Paradoxically this side of his imagination was only fully awakened during his early life in India, where reality everywhere took on the semblance of a folktale as told by Italo Calvino. As folktales are largely about destiny, traveling from one's home in youth to be tested by the vicissitudes of strange fate was in part Clemente's own story when these works were made. The oral tradition of the folktale satisfied his mistrust for what is written down (i.e., fixed) and therefore betrayed. Often when making these images, Clemente would not draw but rather verbally describe the image to the artisans in the workshop. The sixteenth-century Vastusutra Upanishad, possibly the earliest treatise on Hindu painting, informs us that images of Divinity were originally revealed to the sages (*rishis*) in their most subtle aspect: the mantra. In other words, the image derives from sound. The aural dimension of knowledge and experience is one that connects in Clemente's mind to painting itself: "To paint, to make images in general, is for me a form of listening. I am a believer in the voice of each level, the voice of the place in the self. This voice comes before poetry, painting, music."[2]

R. F.

1. Herman Hesse, quoted in Miguel Serrano, *C. G. Jung and Herman Hesse: A Record of Two Friendships* (New York: Schocken Books, 1968), p. 14.

2. Francesco Clemente, quoted in Donald Kuspit, "Clemente Explores Clemente," *Contemporanea* (New York) 2, no. 7 (Oct. 1989), p. 41.

above and following five pages:

172. Twelve gouaches from ***Francesco Clemente Pinxit***, 1980–81. Gouache on antique paper, 8 3/4 x 6 inches (22.2 x 15.2 cm) each.

Virginia Museum of Fine Arts, Richmond, gift of Sydney and Frances Lewis.

In Rome throughout the 1960s and 1970s, Francesco Clemente avidly read Allen Ginsberg's poetry in excellent translations by Fernanda Pivano. In New York City in 1983, he and his wife, Alba, first met the poet at a dinner with Henry Geldzahler. The following day, Ginsberg called on the artist at his loft, and within the hour the two began their first collaboration, *White Shroud* (cat. no. 173). Until the poet's death fifteen years later, Ginsberg regularly sat for portraits by Clemente, and they collaborated on dozens of watercolors, catalogues, sketchbooks, and *livres d'artiste*, most of which have never been published or exhibited.

Aside from their personal rapport, which was immediate, Clemente and Ginsberg shared a wealth of common ground, including affinities for Ezra Pound, India, and William Blake. Pound was a model for imagistic clarity, and for recasting the classical past in contemporary terms, with ancient gods and myths seen not as historical artifacts but as intimations of psychic states that are universal and timeless. In India, both Clemente and Ginsberg found dwelling places where those psychic states were viewed as sources of enlightenment and not of conflict or illegitimacy. The illuminated manuscripts of Blake embodied this visionary experience, in which the common impulse of poet and painter was ideally wedded on a single page to celebrate the glory of the imagination. Indeed, it is the long shadow of Blake that falls across all the Clemente and Ginsberg collaborations.

The relationship of image to text in Clemente's collaborations is parallel rather than derivative. The question the artist has been faced with is how to depict (or amplify) the mental space of the poem in a way that allows the image to remain true to its psychic ground, which for *White Shroud* and *Black Shroud* (1984–85, cat. no. 174) is a landscape of dream and death. Death occupies a place in Clemente's work not dissimilar to that of a drone instrument in Indian music; it supplies a background tone, which one need not focus on but which is always there. "I am under the impression that every painter or poet who has found his voice has very much based his finding on a vivid experience of imagining death," Clemente has said. "I think death is part of a great truth that I feel compelled as an artist to paint."[1]

Ginsberg's "White Shroud" recounts a dream wherein the poet discovers that his mother did not die in a mental hospital in 1957 but has been living destitute on the streets of the Bronx. The poem offers a joyful opportunity for reunion and amends, feelings that linger after awakening. True to the dream state, Clemente's illustrations depict a fluid underworld of forms—abstracted, biomorphic, and corporeal—in various stages of commingling and dissolution. Pages alternate between dynamism and repose. The changing forms of dream and afterlife are presented, as they are in Ginsberg's poem, as a world of hungry ghosts, to be dispelled only through an awareness of their unreality.

R. F.

1. Francesco Clemente, interview by Denise Darricklaw, *The Observer Magazine* (London) (Feb. 1993).

173. Double-page spread from ***White Shroud***, with handwritten text by Allen Ginsberg and illustrations by Francesco Clemente, 1983. Ink, pencil, and watercolor on paper, 17 1/2 x 26 3/4 inches (44.5 x 67.9 cm). Collection of Jean Pigozzi, Switzerland.

Where was I living? I'd remembered looking for a house
& eating in apartment kitchens, bookshelf decades ago,
Aunt's tragedies, an appendix operation, teeth braces,
one afternoon fitting eyeglasses first time, Combing wet hair
back on my skull, young awkward looking in the highschool mirror
photograph. It was like the dead looking for a home,
but here I was still alive.
I walked past a niche between buildings
with tin Canopy shelter from Cold rain - warmed by hot exhaust
from subway gratings, beneath which engines throbbed with pleasant quiet drone.
A Shopping-bag lady lived in the side alley on a mattress,
her wooden bed above the pavement, many blankets + Sheets,
Pots, pans and plates beside her, fan, electric stove by the wall.
She looked desolate white-haired, but strong enough
[to survive.
Passersby ignored her buildingside hovel many years,
a few businessmen stopped to speak or give her bread or yogurt.
Sometimes she disappeared into State Hospital back wards,
but now 'd returned back in her homely alleyway, sharpeyed,
Old Cranky hair, half paralysed, Complaining angry as I passed.
I was horrified a little, who'd take care of such a woman,

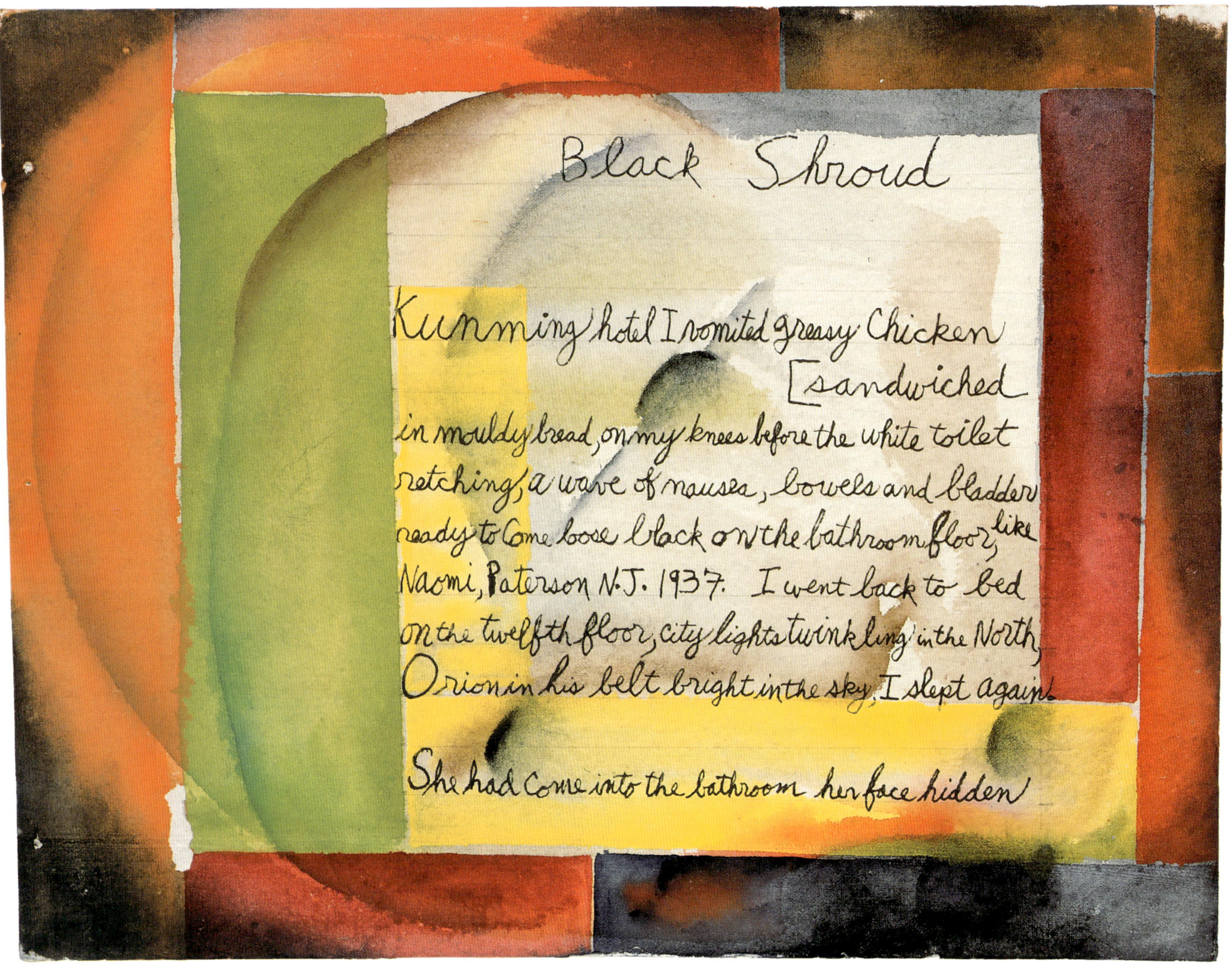

174. Page from ***Black Shroud***, with handwritten text by Allen Ginsberg, 1984, and illustrations by Francesco Clemente, 1985. Ink, pencil, and watercolor on paper, 10 1/2 x 13 3/4 inches (26.7 x 34.9 cm). Collection of Francesco and Alba Clemente, New York.

In his collaborations with Allen Ginsberg, Francesco Clemente employed a method visually congruent with the poet's own sense of open form, an organic structure able to accommodate the contours of the poet's mind: his imaginings, sexual daydreams, and visionary impulses. Treating the page as a graph of the moving mind was for Ginsberg a realization that came about in part through meditation practice. Later, a more physical realization of poetic form occurred through chant, which Ginsberg viewed as an elaboration on the strophic measure based upon breath. Clemente independently arrived at many of these same realizations in his own work, and largely though the same means.

When Ginsberg met Ezra Pound in Venice in 1967, the younger poet praised Pound's *Cantos* for their "working model of the mind" and for their "condensed perception [of] concrete image."[1] This is essentially Ginsberg's method in *Images from Mind and Space* (1983, cat. no. 175), a notebook of American haikus, most of them spontaneous, compiled late one afternoon at Clemente's studio. The haiku form involves vivid perceptions concisely deployed, what is known in Buddhism as ordinary mind. In this notebook, Ginsberg, like Clemente, was working with a brush, and did so quite adeptly, lending the pages a Zen-like aspect of empty space, much in keeping with the immediacy of both poems and images. Collaboration between poet and painter was not unlike that of two musicians who bring an entire lifetime of practice to bear on a performance that, for all its preparation, depends entirely upon the communicating spirit of the moment. Largely devoid of imagery, *Black Shroud* (1984–85, cat. no. 174) might be considered a tone poem of sorts in which vocal utterance is translated chromatically rather than imagistically.

Clemente's chosen medium for the collaborations with Ginsberg was most often watercolor, thus allowing the poet's calligraphy to emerge through the translucency of the pigment. This effect is partly the subject of these works, in the same way that transparency is one subject of Pound's last *Cantos*: the crystal metaphor for the mind, the whisper of the wind as an answer to useless speech, or pure light as the image of deity (*lux einem*, the light itself). Images are presented with such realization that one literally sees through them. Part of the special bond between poet and painter was a shared sense of the nature of the image, based on a nonhierarchical acceptance of mental pictures as they arise in the mind, and the physical dimension of thought forms as rooted in the body and its functions. The ease and naturalness of these collaborations derived from Ginsberg and Clemente's shared sense of experience (more accurately, *feeling*), which is the emotional field out of which the images emerge.

R. F.

1. Allen Ginsberg, quoted in Donald Allen, ed., *Allen Ginsberg: Composed on the Tongue* (Bolinas: Grey Fox Press, 1980), pp. 8, 13.

175. Double-page spread from ***Images from Mind and Space***, with handwritten text by Allen Ginsberg and illustrations by Francesco Clemente, 1983. Watercolor on paper, 5 ⅝ x 15 ⅝ inches (14.3 x 39.7 cm). Collection of Francesco and Alba Clemente, New York.

the whitehaired photographer fixes his image.
my mother came here in 1905.
window as cars pass up First Avenue.

Early Morning Exercises (1984, cat. no. 176) began as a handwritten folio by John Wieners. While in Boston editing his collected poems, I asked the poet to write out a selection of his verse with the idea of presenting the manuscripts to Francesco Clemente for illustration. I had serious doubts whether Wieners would comply: he kept no copies of his own books, he regularly cleaned house by discarding manuscripts, and only a few days previous had referred to his early work as "old faces I don't care to see again." But, at seven o'clock the next morning, the poet was seated at a small table in his Beacon Hill apartment assiduously copying out the poems in his usual tidy hand, only occasionally succumbing to the impulse to rewrite. The title page, of his own devising, described the yoga-like task: "Early Morning Exercises."

The poet's dedication to his book *Ace of Pentacles* (1964) reads, "For the Voices." Indeed, the plethora of voices contained in his work speaks to the mediumistic origins of his poetry. His life has been that of the classic *poète maudit*, and the subjects of his poems read like a résumé of latter-day Romanticism: urban despair, poverty, asylums, homosexual love, narcotics and drug addiction, the fraternity of thieves and loveless transients. Wieners is also the epitome of wit in poetry. The reader follows the poet's mind from one unexpected line to the next, along a knife edge of nostalgia and sentiment, august declamation, dire humor, and stunning beauty. His poems presage a great many of Clemente's motifs, most uncannily a persistent return to his own image as a metaphor for identity, a fixed point of continuity in the diversity of experience. In *Early Morning Exercises*, three of the nine poems are about looking at his face in the mirror. Displaced gender and a love of transvestism often find him writing poems in the guise of the opposite sex.

For *Early Morning Exercises*, Clemente tore apart one of his first Indian sketchbooks, from 1976, and freely collaged images and texts onto color reproductions from a facsimile edition of Indian miniatures he had purchased in Madras. He then reworked and unified the collages with watercolor and gouache. I recall being slightly shocked at the cavalier way the artist treated this sketchbook, although it was a gesture not out of keeping with the nonchalant attitude Wieners shows toward his own work. In essence, what Clemente was depicting was a state of mind, and that particular sketchbook came closest to the strange delicacy that is this poet's territory. The way text and image abut and overlap in *Early Morning Exercises* is similar to the technique of the poet's later writings and to his penchant for recreating his work at public readings through a spontaneous interweaving of poems, imagined voices, tourist brochures, advertising copy, pulp novels, and whatever else may be at hand.

R. F.

176. Page from ***Early Morning Exercises***, with handwritten text by John Wieners and illustrations by Francesco Clemente, 1984. Ink, pencil, watercolor, colored pencil, and metallic paint on paper and printed paper, 17 x 13 inches (43.2 x 33 cm). Collection of Francesco and Alba Clemente, New York.

Francesco Clemente's watercolor portraits, which he began in 1982, were a project the artist conceived when he first moved to New York. He pursued the series in earnest until the end of the decade. His intent was to chronicle the society he and his wife suddenly found themselves inhabiting. A cross section of the New York/New Wave milieu, it was a world made up of artists, writers, poets, composers, musicians, graffiti artists, rappers, deejays, rock stars, club kids, curators, art dealers, models, etc. They were the aristocracy, and he their court painter. During a two-hour sitting, Clemente would lean over a small table within a foot or two of the subject's face, utterly remote and absorbed in his work. Portraits are a unique challenge, as the illusion of a life must be conveyed, and we may each rightly consider ourselves to be an expert judge of a work since we all spend our lives looking at and reading faces. In his notebooks, Leonardo observed that a portrait must be two things: an image of man, and of his mind. Through pose, attitude, and gesture, Clemente portrayed his sitters, as well as their self-image.

With the enjoyment of a mystery novel, Clemente read John Ashbery's long poem "Self-Portrait in a Convex Mirror" (1975), combining as it does the painter's dual obsessions with anamorphosis and self-portraiture. Ashbery's portrait (cat. no. 182) is an homage to that experience. The penetration and fixity of Robert Mapplethorpe's gaze is captured, as is his humanity, in what is a study of purity in both perception and rendering (cat. no. 180). Clemente's portrait of Jean-Michel Basquiat (cat. no. 179) is a shockingly beautiful image of the intelligence and sensitivity of this painter in his youth. The portrait of Keith Haring (cat. no. 183) is an image of profound sadness, painted when Haring was already ill. (It is ironic that the two youngest artists of this generation, Basquiat and Haring, should have been its first famous casualties.) Rammellzee (see cat. no. 177) is an overlooked painter who emerged from graffiti writing but was by no means limited to it; much admired by Clemente, he evolved his own hybrid of music, art, and language. The portrait of Gita Mehta (cat. no. 184) is one of several the artist has done of an author whose wry and perspicacious love of India rivals his own.

The watercolor portraits are a series suffused with the realization that here was a special time and place, with a unique cast of characters in fragile association. As the specter of AIDS and early death encroached upon this society, the melancholy that characterizes Clemente's portraits proved an ominous presentiment. Only a dozen years later, it is largely a lost world.

R. F.

177. *Rammellzee*, ca. 1982–87. Watercolor on paper, 14 1/4 x 20 inches (36.2 x 50.8 cm). Collection of Francesco and Alba Clemente, New York.

After several decades of exile, during which he produced the multivolumed epic that chronicled the narco-empire of our times, William Burroughs returned to America in 1974, warily but gradually accepting the public acclaim that his writing brought him. Once resettled in New York, the writer's proximity to painters resulted in an important source for companionship and encouraged his own visual inclinations, which had always been at the core of his aesthetic. Burroughs liked to quote Brion Gysin: "Writing is fifty years behind painting." By adapting collage technique to the written word, Burroughs used the cutup as a key to deciphering "the word virus," as he called the habit of naming, which he believed interferes with direct observation. His most comprehensive statement on art, "The Creative Observer," originated in a series of conversations conducted with Clemente at the time the portrait shown here (cat. no. 178) was made. He told the painter, "You make something exist by seeing it. Nothing exists until it is observed. I call it 'creative observation.'"[1]

The ideas of Burroughs and Clemente have much in common: a fascination with pictographs (in the writer's case, Mayan); an acceptance of randomness, especially where technique is concerned; a recognition of the visual impact of multiple and shifting frames of time and space; an openness to synchronicity as opposed to cause and effect; the active and creative role played by the viewer in completing the work of art; and, perhaps most importantly, constructing a channel between dream and reality. In response to a question by Clemente, Burroughs replied, "What do artists do? We dream for other people. We dream for other people who have no dreams of their own to keep them alive."[2]

R. F.

1. William Burroughs, "The Creative Observer," in *Painting & Guns* (Madras and New York: Hanuman Books, 1994), p. 39.

2. Ibid., p. 46.

178. *William Burroughs*, ca. 1982–87. Watercolor on paper, 14 ¼ x 20 inches (36.2 x 50.8 cm). Collection of Francesco and Alba Clemente, New York.

179. ***Jean-Michel Basquiat***, ca. 1982–87. Watercolor on paper, 14 1/4 x 20 inches (36.2 x 50.8 cm). Collection of Francesco and Alba Clemente, New York.

180. ***Robert Mapplethorpe***, ca. 1982–87. Watercolor on paper, 14 ¼ x 20 inches (36.2 x 50.8 cm). Collection of Walter Haas, Zurich and Puerto Vallarta, Mexico.

Morton Feldman was a composer of exquisitely nuanced aural landscapes, often extending for several hours. In the mid-1980s, he was a regular visitor to Francesco Clemente's atelier, where performances of his music were presented on numerous occasions. Portrayed here with thick black hair and his characteristic hulking pose (cat. no. 181), Feldman loved to spend hours in the artist's studio, soaking up the atmosphere, conversing, and occasionally composing. Like Clemente, Feldman was an avant-gardist who used traditional materials. He favored acoustic instruments (piano, viola, French horn, flute), employing them as tenuous extensions of touch and breath. He spoke of his music as a search for structure; out of this search, his subjects emerged. Through his friendships with Philip Guston and Mark Rothko, Feldman came to conceive of his music increasingly in terms of painting, presenting each note as if a distinct and shimmering brushstroke in a soft, chromatic field. Conversely, his influence on Clemente emerged in an increased tendency to view painting in musical terms of tonality and interval, as in the *Funerary Paintings* (1987), in which vastness of space is marked by percussive incident.

Feldman revealed the contours of a new space, congruent with the painter's own instincts, as Clemente has noted: "Western music is measured and relates more to architecture than painting. Eastern music is about coincidence between two channels, let's say of rhythm and melody—they go two different ways, then they meet somewhere in a beautiful way, an unexpected, happy way. In that sense, yes, some of my work relates to this idea of happy coincidence. Morton Feldman's music is interesting in the sense of creating 'place'—a new home or locus—a place which has a spirit. It has a legitimacy but without being authoritarian."[1]

R. F.

1. Francesco Clemente, interview with Lisa Phillips, March 27, 1989.

181. ***Morton Feldman***, ca. 1982–87. Watercolor on paper, 14 1/4 x 20 inches (36.2 x 50.8 cm). Collection of Francesco and Alba Clemente, New York.

182. ***John Ashbery***, ca. 1982–87. Watercolor on paper, 14 ¼ x 20 inches (36.2 x 50.8 cm). Collection of Francesco and Alba Clemente, New York.

183. ***Keith Haring***, ca. 1982–87. Watercolor on paper, 14 ¼ x 20 inches (36.2 x 50.8 cm). Collection of Francesco and Alba Clemente, New York.

184. ***Gita Mehta***, 1998. Watercolor on paper, 14 $^{1}/_{4}$ x 20 inches (36.2 x 50.8 cm). Private collection.

Seldom are the purely plastic qualities of Francesco Clemente's painting as wonderfully concentrated as in the series of portraits in oil on wood painted in 1985 (cat. nos. 185–87). A fascination with the quasi-religious death cults of late antiquity informs these modern-day Fayum portraits, which blend styles of Naturalism and the Icon. Clemente's love of the reductivist and melancholy portraits of Francisco de Zurbarán is likewise echoed in these frontal depictions where the sitter is placed tightly and squarely within shallow planar space; one may also read the influence of the master of *tenebroso* painting, José de Ribera (like Clemente's ancestors, a Spaniard transplanted in Naples). The portraits were painted *à la prima*, in one go, on a prepared ground of variously colored oil paint; the use of wood panel instead of canvas lessened resistance to the brush and lended fluidity to the execution. During this period, it was Clemente's preference to capture a likeness on first meeting, before vision was dulled by familiarity. The oil panels fix this unrepeatable moment with the heightened immediacy of a *portrait parlant*, a speaking likeness.

R. F.

185. *Portrait of Luigi Ontani*, 1985. Oil on wood, 11 13/16 x 10 inches (30 x 25.5 cm). Private collection.

186. ***Portrait of Fab Five Freddie (Fred Brathwaite)***, 1985. Oil on wood, 14 15/16 x 11 13/16 inches (38 x 30 cm). Private collection.

187. *Portrait of Allen Ginsberg*, 1985. Oil on wood, 14 15/16 x 11 13/16 inches (38 x 30 cm). Private collection.

In the early 1980s, the rehabilitation of Andy Warhol's reputation as a painter was due in part to the esteem paid him by a new generation of European artists. By 1985, the recognition of his eminence by younger painters in New York was nearly total. Much to his credit, Warhol used this position to regenerate his own inspiration. Contact with Jean-Michel Basquiat, Francesco Clemente, and Keith Haring reawakened his engagement with popular imagery and drawing. To young painters, Warhol's example in turn offered a model that reconciled the conflicting roles of public persona and private activity. For Clemente, Warhol's irony was the antidote to the dilemma—which so plagued the Abstract Expressionist generation—of society's co-opting of private rebellion, the process through which today's drama of the soul becomes tomorrow's lyrical wallpaper. As Clemente noted, "The Abstract Expressionists went through the whole paradigm of turning your back to social conformity then going through the whole cycle and finding yourself back where you started. They implicated Warhol's nonchalance. They tragically lived what Warhol learned to live comically."[1]

In 1983, Bruno Bischofberger organized a series of collaborations between Basquiat, Clemente, and Warhol. Each artist began three canvases and one drawing, which in turn—in a variation on the Surrealists' exquisite corpse—were sent to the next artist's studio for successive stages of completion (see *Alba's Breakfast*, 1984, cat. no. 188). Although all three artists shared an affinity for images rooted in popular culture, each approached the commonplace from a different direction. (Clemente's engagement with popular imagery often goes unrecognized, in part because many of his sources are appropriated from Indian culture.) Warhol proved to be the aesthetic mediator in the group, noting in his diaries that Basquiat and Clemente "paint each other out."[2] The real success of these collaborations may have been latent: following this experience, Warhol returned to the painted image for the first time in twenty years, and Basquiat and Clemente began using silkscreens in their canvases.

R. F.

1. Francesco Clemente, interview with Lisa Phillips, March 27, 1989.

2. Andy Warhol, *The Andy Warhol Diaries*, ed. Pat Hackett (New York: Warner Books, 1989), p. 545.

ALBA
"ALBA"©
TOAST EGGS+
"LET ME GO
ECIAL"

188. Andy Warhol, Jean-Michel Basquiat, and Francesco Clemente, ***Alba's Breakfast***, 1984. Gouache on paper, 46 7/16 x 59 13/16 inches (118 x 152 cm). Collection of Bruno Bischofberger, Zurich.

Chronology
Selected Exhibition History
Selected Bibliography

Chronology

Rene Ricard

1952
On March 23, Francesco Clemente is born in Naples. His mother, Bianca Quarto, is a painter and his father, Lorenzo, a judge. He is an only child.

The Clemente di San Luca family arrived from Spain to Calabria in the fourteenth century with the Aragon, the first Spanish rulers of the Kingdom of the Two Sicilies. Like the majority of the ancient aristocracy, by the middle of the nineteenth century, the family had lost its lands and embraced professional life.

Grows up in an apartment in a seventeenth-century building in the Chiaia section of Naples. There are some good paintings on the walls by seventeenth-century Neapolitan painters, including Luca Giordano, Francesco Solimena, and Andrea Vaccaro.

1954–1960
Travels through Europe each summer with his parents—every museum, every palace and church. In Spain, they visit the Prado. Velázquez, of course, makes a great impression on the eight-year-old boy.

1962
Extensive childhood readings include Emilio Salgari, then popular for tales of adventure set in the jungles of Hindustan.

1964
Has been improvising poems throughout his boyhood and reciting them to his mother. She publishes a collection of them, *Castelli di Sabbia*, against the twelve-year-old's wishes.

1974: Francesco Clemente (left) with Alighiero Boetti in Kabul on the final day of their travels through Afghanistan. Photo by a street photographer.

1975: Alba Primiceri, performing on stage at Galleria L'Attico, Rome, in opening scene of Raymond Roussel's *Locus Solus* directed by Meme Perlini. Illuminated by single candle and splashing water from metal plate, she maintains this uncomfortable position for "so long." Photo by Antonio Sferlazzo.

1967

Continuing public school education, enters high school (Liceo Classico Umberto). The courses include ancient Greek, Latin, philosophy, and ancient history. Meets an upperclassman, Cesare Colletta, who introduces him to the writings of Jacques Lacan and the music of Bob Dylan.

1968

In tune with the rest of the world, the students of Naples riot. They occupy the Liceo Classico Umberto. One classmate leaves to become a guerrilla in Colombia, another becomes a sadhu, an itinerant beggar, in India. Clemente is reading Allen Ginsberg in Fernanda Pivano's translation and listening to Jimi Hendrix.

Meets Lucio Amelio at his gallery in Naples. They do not get along. Here, Clemente sees works by Cy Twombly. This is a revelation. Sees Arte Povera and Michelangelo Pistoletto. A film at this time, *SKMP2*, by the Roman artists Jannis Kounellis, Eliseo Mattiacci, Pino Pascali and Luca Patella, produced by Fabio Sargentini, brings home to him that painters, artists, really exist as people and not as something too distant. He has been painting throughout high school, but the film opens up the real possibility of life as an artist.

1970

Graduates high school second in class.

Moves to Rome. An older friend, an architecture student named Folco Grimaldi, has an apartment on via dei Cappellari, in the heart of criminal Rome. Clemente stays a short while. Then lives with various other friends for the next two years.

Enrolls in architecture school at the University of Rome, the national center of student unrest. Over three years, completes all the course work, losing interest before the final examination, and does not receive a diploma. Takes a special interest in the architecture of Frank Lloyd Wright.

1971

Rome at this time is cosmopolitan. Cinecittà is in full swing. There is Tina Aumont, a young beautiful actress, the daughter of Maria Montez and Jean-Pierre Aumont, and the charismatic French actor Pierre Clementi. Glauber Rocha, a Brazilian filmmaker, is part of an important South American colony. The time is political and glamorous.

During the summer, Clemente leaves Rome with Milagros Maldonado and goes to Caracas. With Benedetta Piccolomini, takes a bus from Caracas to Bolivia, then, by bus again, returns to Caracas. Flies back to Rome.

On November 13, Joseph Beuys shows his work in Naples. The invitation is a postcard of Sils Maria in the Engadine, where Nietszche worked. Written across it, *"la rivoluzione siamo noi"* (the revolution is us).

First solo exhibition: collages at Galleria Valle Giulia, Rome.

1972

A crucial encounter with Alighiero Boetti. Clemente says this takes him "from zero to a hundred." Boetti, although already established with Arte Povera in Turin, has just moved to Rome with his wife, Anne Marie, who introduces Clemente to the radical critiques of Gilles Deleuze, Michel Foucault, and Félix Guattari. He will eventually refer to Boetti as a "tragic hero." "Boetti thinks through images, but hates their materiality. Loves to teach, but his knowledge is too arcane to be taught. Recognizes the poetry of craftsmanship, but refuses to draw. Has faith in the power of asceticism, but embraces addiction."[1]

Sees *Tarzan*, a performance by Luigi Ontani in the underground parking lot at Villa Borghese: "Ontani's work in performance and photographs anticipates his generation by a decade." Ontani has just arrived in Rome from Bologna. They become friends.

Ontani introduces him to Joan Jonas. With Ontani, Clemente will follow the works of visiting American performers: Philip Glass, Simone Forti, Steve Paxton, Terry Riley, and La Monte Young. They also see the Dagar Brothers, the great Pakistani singers, and dancers from South India.

1973

The ink drawings first produced under the influence of psilocybin in the Venezuelan forest now begin to proliferate on small pieces of paper that cover the floor, two inches deep, of Clemente's via Manara studio in Trastevere in Rome (see cat. nos. 2–8, 168).

Jack Smith, the American filmmaker and avatar of performance art, is in Rome. Clemente is taken up in his entourage. This will be an education in temperament.

On a monthly or a triweekly basis, visits Milan, where he connects with Gio Ponti's daughter, Lisa, whose home is an important meeting place for the older avant-garde: Mario and Marisa Merz and Vincenzo Agnetti, a conceptual artist and contributor to *Azimuth*, Piero Manzoni's theoretical magazine.

Also in Milan, at Franco Toselli's, sees the work of tough American artists: Robert Barry, Robert Mangold, Agnes Martin, Lawrence Weiner, etc. Clemente will attend openings and then spend the night on Toselli's couch.

Back in Rome, Giordano Falzoni, Surrealist painter, Theosophist, and part-time CIA agent, trusts Clemente with his just-finished translation into Italian of the teachings of R. P. Kaushik, an Indian guru.

There is an age-old tradition in India allowing anyone to encounter a transformative experience that delivers them from the mundane. Those who have these experiences will be sought as removers of ignorance. J. Krishnamurti, Kaushik, Nasargadatta, and Ramana Maharishi have rephrased this experience into the urban language of our time.

Clemente is to carry Falzoni's translation to Delhi and present it personally to Kaushik.

Stays in India three months, first at the Hotel Crown in Chandi Chowk in Old Delhi, the infamous hippie station. Then, moves into Kaushik's ashram in the slums of Old Delhi, into a six-by-eight foot room, where he stays two months. Here, Clemente learns to speak English, absorbing the teachings from Kaushik, who speaks with the constant stream of seekers who come for his advice. He keeps a small notebook of ink drawings.

1974

In April, meets Alba Primiceri, an actress in the burgeoning Italian theater scene, in Rome. She is famous. She performs nude. Her head is shaved. She has appeared in almost every theater in Italy. Clemente introduces himself.

1976: Alba and Francesco Clemente on the Ghats of the Ganges in Benares.

Her hair is growing in, and his has just been cut. For the moment, they are the same length. Photo by a street photographer.

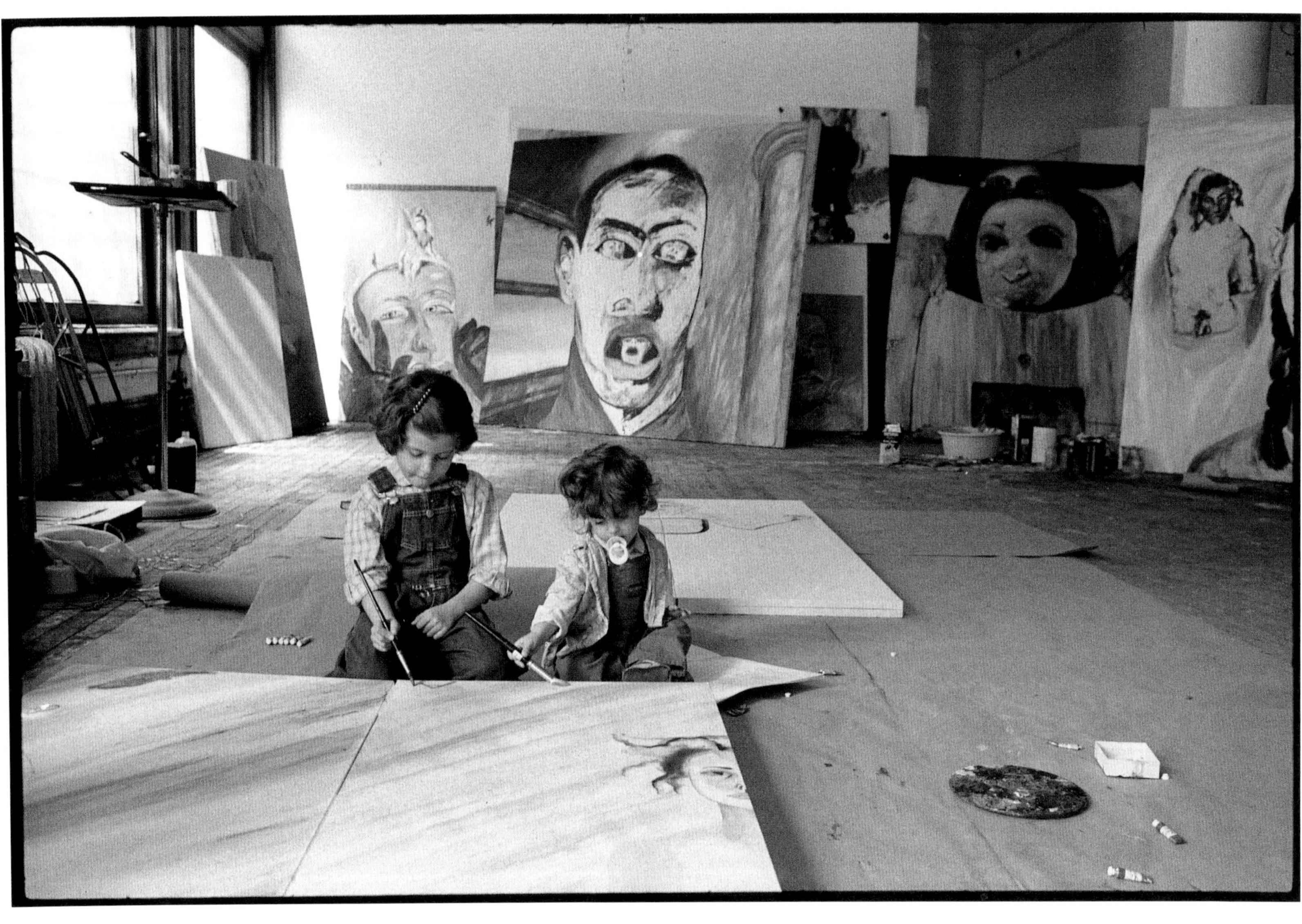

1983: Chiara (left) and Nina Clemente assisting Francesco Clemente, their father, in the studio.
The piece they are painting is one of several screens the artist was working on at the time. Photo by Gian Franco Gorgoni.

The following day, leaves for Afghanistan with Boetti. There, they travel by truck on the old silk road up to Pamir and the Hindu Kush on the Chinese border. They reach Feizabad, the meeting point of all the nomadic tribes. Today, it no longer exists. In Kabul, they stay in the hostel that Boetti purchased in the 1960s. Boetti has begun to collaborate with local craftswomen to produce his embroidered maps. Clemente does not draw in Afghanistan.

During the autumn, his hair long, curly, and blond, he runs into Alba in Rome. They do not separate again.

1975

In January, he and Alba move to a slightly larger and quieter studio on via dei Riari. This is a simple and clean space with literally no furniture. They sleep on the floor. Although he has been drawing almost without interruption for three years, to the young artist the drawings do not seem impressive enough to compete with the serious art from America and the grave weight of Beuys.

Becomes concerned with format. Distances himself by photographing an eclectic range of obscure objects: small details of dress prints and little piles of tea scattered on the floor. These photos are framed and arranged in various patterns—cruciforms or parallel strips. This is an important step: a group of works. They are enigmatic and demand or beg attention.

During the spring, in response to the new pieces, Boetti brings to Clemente's studio the art dealer Gian Enzo Sperone. In his early twenties, Sperone introduced Pop art to Italy and Arte Povera to the rest of the world.

Agrees to a summer show at Sperone's gallery in the Palazzo del Drago, Rome.

Boetti also brings Corrado Levi, the distinguished connoisseur and artist.

On June 26, opening day, the exhibition at Sperone is deserted, except for Leo Castelli, Sarah Charlesworth, Joseph Kosuth, and Roy Lichtenstein, who were traveling through Rome at the time.

By the end of the year, he will have exhibited solo in Brescia, Milan, and Turin, and in a group show in Rome.

1976

With the thousand dollars Clemente earns, takes Alba to India. She is pregnant.

On arrival in India, the couple stay on the banks of the Yamuna in a Tibetan refugee camp. They sleep in the temple with the monks. These accomodations are free.

They move to the Ghats of the Ganges in Benares.

Later, they arrive at the lovely estate of the Theosophical Society on the Adayar River in Madras.

Rendezvous with Ontani, Falzoni, and Sargentini in Madras. Sargentini proposes an exhibition of the four.

Madras, like any Indian city, is papered with spectacular hand-painted movie billboards. Having learned the Boetti lesson of local collaboration, Clemente is inspired to work with the Madras sign painters. Produces three breakthrough works and shows them in a cheap lodging behind Mylapore Temple. The day of the opening, Alba becomes seriously ill and is hospitalized for two weeks.

1977

In April, returns to Rome.

In June, while visiting the Venice *Biennale* (where he is not showing), sells a work to Paul Maenz. Due to a miscalculation in the exchange rate, Maenz makes the check out for three thousand dollars, twice the actual price.

On August 12, Chiara Clemente is born in Piacenza.

With the three thousand dollars from Maenz, the Clementes are able to spend a year in Kashmir and Madras.

It is a good time to leave Italy. The generation gap of the 1960s is still in force with the Italian police. An entire generation is made guilty for the behavior of the few. It is unsafe to dress a certain way. To Clemente and Alba, with a new baby, India looks good.

In October, the family is at the Theosophical Society's compound in Madras for an extended stay. The physical location, on a beach in the Bay of Bengal, is seductive, and the oldest and largest banyan tree in India (already described as a prodigy in the fifteenth century by the Chinese traveler Han Hsi) is sheltered by the gardens. Still in residence at the society is the man who had taken J. Krishnamurti to England in the 1920s.

The society's library has one of the great occult collections. It becomes a focus for Clemente, who immerses himself in reading everything from Vedic literature and the Tao to Saint John of the Cross and *The Cloud of Unknowing*. Also reads Gregory Bateson's *Towards an Ecology of the Mind*.

Older and younger seekers are meeting at a café run by an Australian sadhu.

Clemente is drawing (see cat. no. 7). His English is improving.

During Christmas week, attends daily lectures by J. Krishnamurti.

"By 1977, I realized that no matter how much I had tried to fit in, I had to give it up and be on my own. In 1977, the degree of fragmentation and bankruptcy of all the ideas and all the people I knew was so high, so tragic for me that I didn't really feel bound to anything anymore."[2]

Italy is far away.

1978

The monsoon is three months late. All wells in Madras become polluted, and the entire family contracts hepatitis. Clemente loses half his weight. Alba and Chiara are only mildly affected. Ill, he is working, assembling a group of pieces for an exhibition at Adrian van Ravenstein's gallery Art & Project in Amsterdam in July.

Temples sell postcard books that are still made in a very old-fashioned style. Using these idiosyncratic publications as a

1985: C. T. Nachiappan, Chiara Clemente, and Francesco Clemente at the Chidambaram Temple in Tamil Nadu.
Here, an enormous ruby in the natural shape of the deity Nataraja is bathed twenty-four hours a day.
Notice Chiara's bangles; she is totally acclimated to India. Her first words were in Tamil. Photo by Alba Clemente.

1985: Photographed by Robert Mapplethorpe, here is the fashionable, iconic Francesco Clemente. If he looks awkward, he is. He is balancing on the top of a ladder.

prototype, he determines to make a book of the Amsterdam show. The works reproduced are in a variety of styles, the most characteristic is still in sign-painting technique. In search of a printer for this volume, meets C. T. Nachiappan who is astonished that anyone would want to do something so tacky. They will produce many books together over the years.

1979

Early in the year, recovering from illness, Clemente is preparing his second exhibition for Art & Project, to open in May. This will contain *Harlequin Close Up* (cat. no. 169), *Twins* (cat. no. 171), and three other related works. In *Harlequin Close Up*, lets loose with virtuoso drawing for the first time. Has now made work that resembles no one else's, and ever more looks like Clemente. There are important formal things happening here, things that will become relevant to other artists in a few years—the overlaying of the harlequin, for instance—but that is in the future. This is new now. All those little drawings done over the years are not so little any more. They are a body of work.

David Salle sees the Art & Project show. He is one of the first New York artists to see this new work.

In April, shows an artist's book at Emilio Mazzoli's gallery in Modena. Mazzoli has recently presented Sandro Chia and Enzo Cucchi in a two-man exhibition. The next show will be Mimmo Paladino.

During June–July, Clemente, Chia, Cucchi, and Paladino are shown together at Paul Maenz's gallery in Cologne, in an exhibition called *Arte Cifra*.

Clemente, Chia, Cucchi, Nicola de Maria, and Paladino will be packaged by Achille Bonito Oliva as the Transavanguardia in the October issue of *Flash Art*.

During the summer, in Rome, purchases a roll of photographer's seamless paper, the type used for backgrounds. Using Chinese ink, ground on a stone with water, produces about eighteen very large self-portraits (see cat. nos. 9, 10).

In November, Clemente, Chia, Cucchi, de Maria, and Paladino are shown together at the Palazzo di Città, Acireale, in Sicily, in an exhibition organized by Bonito Oliva.

In December, Sperone shows the large self-portraits in his gallery in Turin. These include *I*, *Non Scopa*, and *With Gold*. *With Gold* will be the first Clemente seen in New York, in a group exhibition at Annina Nosei's gallery in 1980.

In December, the family returns to India.

Aurobindo Ashram is located in Pondicherry. This ashram, the largest in India, is also one of the great papermaking centers in the world. Using paper from the ashram, makes his first pastels, *The Pondicherry Pastels* (1979–80, cat. no. 111).

1980

In January, working again with local sign painters in Madras, makes large billboard-style gouaches, including *Two Painters*, *Sun*, and *Moon* (cat. nos. 112–14). Each consists of large sheets of paper joined with handwoven cotton strips, a format that permits him to work on a large scale without the physical inhibitions of stretched canvas. They are also conveniently foldable and can be easily placed in a small cotton bag. He will carry them to Kamakura, Oakland, and to his first New York exhibition at Sperone Westwater Fischer in April.

In February, spends three weeks at a small seventeenth-century Buddhist temple in Kamakura. Reads Oswald Spengler's *Decline of the West.*

In March, works on about twenty plates in etching and drypoint at Crown Point Press in Oakland. This important artists' print shop is owned by Kathan Brown, who is Tom Marioni's companion. The plates are published in small editions.

In April, stays with Alba and Chiara in a small apartment attached to Sperone Westwater Fischer on Greene Street. At the opening of his solo exhibition, meets Donald Baechler, Edit deAk, Eric Fischl, David Salle, and Julian Schnabel.

Francesco Pellizzi, editor of the journal *Res*, buys *Two Painters.* He and Clemente become lifelong friends.

Anthony d'Offay buys *The Pondicherry Pastels.* A London dealer in early avant-garde art, he asks Clemente to show with him. Don and Mira Rubell buy *Inside/Outside* (1980, cat. no. 115).

During May–June, participates in a group show with other Italians at the Kunsthalle Basel, curated by Jean-Christophe Ammann. Meets Bruno Bischofberger, who buys *Self-Portrait as a Garden.* A dealer of Jean Tinguely and Andy Warhol, Bischofberger asks to represent Clemente's work.

During May, in Rome, prepares for his first Venice *Biennale.* Having decided to paint a large fresco, seeks out someone to assist him and meets Claudio di Giambattista, a young and skilled conservator. They devise a light, portable fiberglass support for frescoes. *Coi sentimenti insegna alle emozioni* (cat. no. 150) is in three panels.

In June, the *Biennale* is a revelation to Clemente. An international generation of painters is brought together: the Americans Salle and Schnabel, the Germans Anselm Kiefer and Georg Baselitz (both of whose work he sees here for the first time), and a veritable manifesto of artists from Italy. He realizes that he now has accomplices.

At the tiny Camuffo gallery in Venice, simultaneous with the *Biennale*, Clemente, Chia, and Cucchi have a show entitled *I tre C (The Three C's).*

During the summer, at the via dei Riari studio, paints a dozen small self-portraits from reflections in a seven-metal Tibetan ritual mirror. These are his first oil paintings (see cat. nos. 11–16).

Later in the summer, in di Giambattista's garden in Rome's Pasoliniesque suburb of Mandrione, paints three large frescoes, including *Priapea* (cat. no. 149), a self-portrait in a necktie surrounded by putti derived from Raphael and Bronzino.

In September, participates in an exhibition with Chia and Cucchi, at Sperone Westwater Fischer in New York. It includes the three frescoes, which display a far-flung range of visual sources and will go far in determining how Clemente's work will be perceived. A feature article by Kay Larson in the *Village Voice* is entitled "Bad Boys at Large: Three C's take on New York."

1981

In January, stays in Jaipur. Alba is pregnant. At the dilapidated Jaipur Museum, had become fascinated by the technique of Mughal miniatures. Had located a small atelier of miniature painters on the top floor of a cavernous six-story

1984: Clockwise from top left: the legs of Francesco Clemente, Andy Warhol, and Jean-Michel Basquiat. This photograph was taken while the three artists were collaborating. They are at Francesco Pellizzi's house, and it appears as if they are standing on a Carl Andre. Clemente wore this kind of Chinese slipper for years. Photo by Pellizzi.

John Giorno, Henry Geldzahler, Allen Ginsberg, Francesco Clemente, William Burroughs
(behind him Jim Grauerholz & Ira Silverberg) with Alan Ansen, visiting from Athens,
the afternoon of Francesco Clemente's giant vernissage in Soho Galleries, March 30, 1985
– gathered in H. G.'s back garden 33 West 9th Street, N.Y.C. Allen Ginsberg
[photo snapped by Raymond Foye.]

building. Working from his drawings—with each of fifteen boys, aged eight to twelve, specializing in a different pattern—he completes a suite of twenty-four miniatures, *Francesco Clemente Pinxit* (1980–81, cat. no. 172).

In February, *Artforum* publishes "Chameleon in a State of Grace," an essay on Clemente by deAk. Publisher of the avant-garde journal *Art-Rite*, deAk is one of the most brilliant intellects in New York. She explores the cultural waywardness of Clemente and his work. At this time, *Artforum*, under Ingrid Sischy, its editor-in-chief, is at the height of its prestige, and the article places Clemente at the forefront of the young Italians.

Steve Maas, owner of the Mudd Club, gives Keith Haring the club's fourth floor to use as an ad hoc art gallery. Haring invites the graffiti writers Fab Five Freddy (Frederick Brathwaite) and Futura 2000 (Lenny McGurr) to be guest curators. Their exhibition, *Beyond Words*, proves to be a major cultural event.

On April 9, Clemente attends *Beyond Words* opening. Meets Jean-Michel Basquiat (exhibiting under the name Samo), Futura 2000, Haring, and Kenny Scharf. Basquiat exhibits *Flats Fix* (collection of Francesco Clemente).

In April, again in the little apartment on Greene Street, paints a series of twenty frescoes, approximately 79 x 59 inches each, a selection of young artists, musicians, philosophers, *maîtresses*, and Taylor Mead. Each is an individual allegorical portrait of a New York personality. DeAk, Jimmy De Sana, Fab Five Freddy, Schnabel, Terrence Sellers, Duncan Smith, etc.: each is pictured with an enigmatic attribute. Rene Ricard is represented nude, life size, balanced on a large egg, holding a smaller one in each hand. The cast of characters is curated by Diego Cortez, to whom Clemente had been introduced by Boetti in the early 1970s, when Cortez was still a Conceptual artist.

New York is in the surge of hip-hop culture, with a constant series of events in a city seemingly without a racial divide. The sudden accessibility of black culture was simpatico to the young artist, who quickly made friends outside the art world, in the nightly spectacle of the clubs. "Africa is closer to the Mediterranean than New York."[3]

On May 2, opening of second solo show at Sperone Westwater Fischer. It includes frescoes and the twenty-four miniatures, *Francesco Clemente Pinxit*, which are shown in a custom-built wooden cabinet. The miniatures, remaining intact as a group, are purchased by Sydney and Frances Lewis for the Virginia Museum of Fine Arts, Richmond. The opening was another event in the scene, a stop somewhere between the Roxy and the Mudd Club, with the same crowd. The wanderer was beginning to find a home.

In Harlem, attends an all-city jam of rap stars with deAk. They run into Fab Five Freddy. A riot breaks out.

Throughout the year, Clemente is tutored in Sanskrit at Columbia University.

In June, Angela Westwater finds him and Alba, who are reluctant to leave New York, a large loft in Tribeca, where they stay a month. Taking advantage of the space, stretches a canvas roughly 13 feet wide. Paints a "self-portrait in New York" of a blind man with a cane on a tightrope stretched between two tall buildings. In the background is a view of the gravestones in the cemetery that is one of the first things a visitor sees coming from the airport. Using a wax medium, explores the possibilities of small paintings on Frederix ready-stretched canvases, one of which, *Titire*, he gives to Ricard, who carries it around town everywhere he goes for two weeks. Most of these paintings are discarded. The big one is cut into scraps.

Walking down Broadway, sees a vacant corner loft. He walks in off the street. A girl there gives him the realtor's home number.

On July 15, Nina Clemente is born in Piacenza, Italy, using the Le Boyer method of nonviolent birth. He cuts his daughter's umbilical cord.

In August, visits Bischofberger in Appenzell. Bischofberger convinces Clemente to call the realtor in New York from a car phone. He buys the Broadway loft with money advanced by Bischofberger for the paintings that will be in his next show.

On September 19, opening of first show with Bischofberger in Zurich. The enamel painting *Arme Clemente* (cat. no. 38) is included.

On September 21, moves into studio on Broadway. During his first night in the raw loft, dreams he is naked on the New York streets in a downpour of human excrement. Unused to working from oneiric influences, will later paint *Perseverance* (1982, cat. no. 20) directly from this dream. In it, he holds a model of the Pantheon in a rain of shit.

Before buying a stove or a bathtub, buys a Mynah bird. Names the bird Rama. With the children, Alba arrives in New York to an empty loft.

In December, meets Warhol.

1982

In January, Warhol paints a three-panel portrait of Clemente wearing a suit and tie. Clemente exchanges three geometrically shaped canvases with stitched-in padding for the portrait. These have never been exhibited.

In February, Warhol's *Interview* publishes an interview with Clemente. DeAk is the interlocutor. The photograph accompanying the article is by Robert Mapplethorpe. Clemente's appearance is striking. He patronizes the Astor Place barbershop, where for $5 they machine-clip his hair and beard, leaving a short stubble. This "three-day growth" will be extensively copied by fashionable men.

During April–June, the Solomon R. Guggenheim Museum presents a survey show of young Italian painters, curated by Diane Waldman. To his consternation, Clemente is not included.

Meets Henry Geldzahler, the Commissioner of Cultural Affairs for the City of New York under Mayor Ed Koch. Former Curator of Twentieth-Century Art at the Metropolitan Museum of Art, Geldzahler is a close friend of David Hockney and Warhol.

Through Geldzahler, meets Raymond Foye, who will become his cicerone in the world of living poets.

Completes *The Fourteen Stations* (1981–82, cat. nos. 154–65), a cycle of twelve large paintings. "To me these paintings look as if they were made in a dark church in Naples; but to a friend in Italy they may look as if they were made in the winter light of New York."[4]

1989: From bottom left: one of the twins (Andrea or Pietro Clemente), Nina Clemente, Melia Marden (with glasses); directly above Marden: Aurora Pellizzi; right foreground, in profile: Keith Haring; and in right background, looking out: Teresa Scharf. Photo by Allen Ginsberg.

1990: The face, Francesco Clemente, the hands, Nina Clemente. Photo by Paul Blanca.

During July–September, paints twelve "replicas" of *The Fourteen Stations*, entitled *Midnight Sun*, on the terrace of a rented house on the Bay of Naples, in Capri.

In September, at the Broadway loft, is introduced to the composer Morton Feldman by Pellizzi.

With the portrait of Nell Garret, a sister of the painters Jedd and Dana Garret, begins what will become a massive series of watercolor portraits.

On October 2, opening of Schnabel exhibition at the Mary Boone Gallery, New York. It includes *The Raft*, a monumental plate painting. Clemente posed for the face of the lonely figure on the raft.

On October 15, on site at the Martin-Gropius-Bau, Berlin, finishes *My House* (cat. no. 1) for the *Zeitgeist* exhibition. This is his largest painting to date.

1983

On January 7, *Francesco Clemente: The Fourteen Stations* opens at Whitechapel Art Gallery, London.

On January 8, *Francesco Clemente: The Midnight Sun* opens at Anthony d'Offay Gallery, London. D'Offay sells the twelve canvases of *The Fourteen Stations* to Charles Saatchi under the condition that they remain together as a group.

In March, Foye and Geldzahler introduce Clemente to Ginsberg in New York. The following day, he and Ginsberg begin a collaboration of poems and watercolors called *White Shroud* (cat. no. 173). Many more collaborations will follow.

In white chalk on black paper, executes the drawing for the cover of *Primitive Cool*, Mick Jagger's second solo album.

Foye brings William Burroughs by while Clemente is working on lithographs for an edition of Alberto Savinio's *The Departure of the Argonaut* at Petersburg Press on Lafayette Street. Clemente immediately takes out his block of paper and executes a portrait of Burroughs.

Goes out to a Brooklyn garbage dump with artist Jim Long. They find broken bits of rusted machinery, which he will bring back to the studio and paint on in fresco. These pieces appeal to other artists. One is acquired by Helen Marden and another by Schnabel.

On April 24, the cover of the Sunday *New York Times Magazine* is a photograph of Clemente in his studio. The accompanying article by John Russell is entitled "The New European Painters."

During the summer, waiting for a green card and unable to leave the country, accepts a position teaching fresco painting at Skowhegan School of Painting and Sculpture in Maine, where he replaces George Schneeman. Is visited there by Alex and Ada Katz. (Katz arranges to do a large portrait of Clemente and Alba when they are back in the city, the first of many portraits.) Rammellzee also visits from New York. He lectures on "Gothic Futurism and Iconoclast Panzerism." The effect on Clemente's students is predictable.

A friend from Milan, Mabi Tosi, sends a mass of scenic backdrops from old Covent Garden productions of Sergey

Diaghilev ballets, some by Alexandre Benois. In Skowhegan, begins to paint on them: *Purgatory, Unborn, Son* (cat. nos. 39, 40, 42), among others.

In September, paints a large fresco, *Mice, Rice, and Dice,* in Julian and Jacqueline Schnabel's newly built loft on 20th Street in New York.

In October, the Clementes rent a small house with a garden on Chamiers Road in Madras.

Collaborating with the craftsmen who make large figures for temple processions, executes two suites of papier mâché sculptures: a set of sixty figures each four feet tall with nine holes perforating each one in correspondence with the nine orifices of the body, and a set of twenty-one figures the same height, each one standing on a papier mâché egg, meant to lean precariously against a wall.

In the garden of Prema Srinivasan's house is an indigo pit for traditional block printing on cotton. Here, Clemente makes *The Indigo Room* (1983–84, cat. no. 167).

Srinivasan and Lindy Dufferin, the Marchioness of Dufferin and Ava, take him to lunch with J. Krishnamurti, whose lectures he has attended through the years.

1984

Jean-Christophe Ammann and Pellizzi visit. They and the Clementes, traveling by train, go to the great Siva temples of southern India. It is harvest time, a time of festival and religious celebration: Pongal. They see the Ramana Maharishi ashram, the Great Temple of Chidambaram, and the early Chola bronzes in Tanjore.

On March 16, a show of pastels opens at the Nationalgalerie, Berlin. He remains in India.

During May–June, at the Kunsthalle Basel, Ammann mounts a show of all the work produced that winter in India. Clemente attends the opening.

During the summer, in New York, at Bischofberger's instigation, Clemente, Basquiat, and Warhol collaborate on seventeen paintings; Basquiat and Clemente paint two.

Basquiat and Clemente, neighbors, become close friends during this period, which will be looked back on nostalgically by Clemente.

In August, Basquiat accompanies the Clementes to Rome. Here, the two painters will title the collaborations they did with Warhol, for example, *Alba's Breakfast* (cat. no. 188). In Mandrione, at di Giambattista's, Clemente paints *Sky* (cat. no. 135) using pigments ground from shale.

In September, the family returns to New York. Feldman and Bunita Marcus move a 1905 Steinway half-grand piano into the loft. Over the next few years, Feldman will present a number of concerts here, with premieres of compositions by John Cage, John Lurie, and Marcus, among others, and, of course, Feldman himself, performed by such musicians as Ake Takahashi and the Kronos Quartet.

1991: The two laughing people on the left are Rene Ricard and Francesco Clemente. The three serious poets, from left to right, are Michael McClure, Allen Ginsberg, and Andrei Voznesensky. The location is the Clemente backyard. This historical photo is by Camilla McGrath.

1993: Andrea (left) and Pietro Clemente. On the beautiful Amalfi coast. Photo by Sante D'Orazio.

Marcus gives piano lessons to the reluctant Chiara.

In November, shows *The Indigo Room*, *Celtic Bestiary* (pastels), and frescoes at the Arts Council Gallery in wartorn Belfast. Dufferin drives him to Clandeboy, her home outside Belfast, where he paints a portrait of her favorite dog.

1985

In February, with Warhol and *Interview*'s advertising director, Paige Powell, goes frequently to amateur night at the Apollo on 125th Street and wastes time in Harlem after-hours clubs.

In March, exhibits simultaneously in three galleries: Sperone Westwater, Leo Castelli, and Mary Boone. Russell in the *New York Times* and Robert Hughes in *Time* both single out the same paintings for comment: Russell claiming they are masterpieces, and Hughes slamming them as bogus. For the first time, shows eighteen small oils on wood, portraits of friends, including *Luigi Ontani* (cat. no. 185), *Fab Five Freddy* (cat. no. 186), *Allen Ginsberg* (cat. no. 187), *Wendy Whitelaw*, and *Suzanne Malouk* (Basquiat's ex-girlfriend); they enter Thomas Ammann's collection as a group. Ammann and his sister Doris become his friends and the foremost collectors of his work.

In May, the Palladium opens. Steve Rubell and Ian Schrager, former owners of Studio 54, hire the Japanese architect Arata Isozaki to design an enormous club in the old Academy of Music on 14th Street. They commission Geldzahler to select a group of young painters to decorate the interior. Basquiat, Haring, and Scharf participate. Clemente paints a fresco on a landing of the stairs leading to the main dance floor. Rubell goes on record saying, "The rock stars of the '80s are the painters."

During the summer, Alba and the children are in Italy. He remains in New York.

In September, back on Chamiers Road in Madras with family. Foye arrives. On first seeing India, he wants to take the next plane out, but the New York flight is canceled. He stays on and takes the responsibility of tutoring Chiara, who is now eight and whose schooling has been interrupted by constant travels.

D'Offay and his son Tim visit. Clemente takes them to meet Pandimalai Swami, a *siddha*: a miracle man who materializes objects and urinates rose water.

Always fascinated by the idiosyncratic presentation of Indian book design, particularly the 3-x-4-inch devotional books sold at temple gates, Clemente and Foye conceive of a series by contemporary poets to be published in this format. The result is the Hanuman imprimatur, printed in India by Nachiappan. This series will eventually comprise fifty titles, beginning with the Boston poet John Wieners. Hanuman is the Hindu monkey-god, friend of Rama: "He is associated with bravery, healing, and dedicated friendship."

In November, the monsoon floods them out of Chamiers Road. Foye rescues 109 watercolors from destruction. Although Clemente painted 109 works, the set is called *CVIII* (cat. no. 119). These will be acquired by Dieter Koepplin for the Öffentliche Kunstsammlung Basel, Kupferstichkabinett.

On December 24, Christmas Eve, in southern Italy, as the family is playing a card game, Beuys appears at the door. During this visit, Beuys proposes an exchange of work, enquiring if Clemente's studio floor "can support a lot of weight." Beuys dies February 17, 1986, and the exchange never occurs.

1986

In March, returns to New York. Chiara and Nina are enrolled in the United Nations School.

AIDS is causing a massive social upheaval. Siege mentality begins to overtake New York. Among many directly affected friends is Mapplethorpe.

Alba and the children summer in Italy.

In May, attends opening of show at the Dallas Museum of Art. The curator, Michael Auping, calls the survey exhibition "an introduction" rather than a retrospective. Originating at the John and Mable Ringling Museum of Art, Sarasota, it provides the first overview of his work.

A young, deaf, Italian painter, Paolo Malfi, instigator and muse to Clemente, suggests that he rent a car and drive to New Mexico. He does this.

During July–August, with Maurice Payne, he executes 108 monoprints. This is the number of beads in the Hindu rosary. The word D.E.A.T.H. reappears in these prints. The entire series is a reworking of one plate.

A sedentary year. Remains in New York throughout summer. Richard Avedon takes his portrait. Clemente's face is half covered with his hand. He feels this photograph makes him look harsh and urban: "a New Yorker."

In December; with Alba and Bruno and Yoyo Bischofberger, visits the mortuary chambers in the Valley of the Kings in Egypt: "Strongest visual impact since Velázquez at age eight."

1987

On February 22, Warhol dies. Warhol had been working on a series of nude portraits of women. The one of Alba is never completed.

The Broadway neighborhood has completely changed. From being quiet and deserted at night, it changes to a scene of stores and restaurants, making daily traffic almost as impenetrable as the sidewalk on weekends.

In March, rents a small north-lit studio on the tenth floor of the Chelsea Hotel.

Alba pregnant.

In April, lectures Thomas Krens's class at the Williams College Museum of Art in Williamstown, Massachussets. Krens has, in the basement of his house, a disassembled printing press and suggests bringing Nachiappan from Madras, reassembling the press, and printing an artist's book there. This suggestion is not taken up.

During April–May, exhibition of six large frescoes at the Fundación Caja de Pensiones in Madrid, curated by Maria de Corral, includes *Maternal* and *Honey, Silver, Blood* (cat. nos. 151, 152).

Accompanied by Alba, Pellizzi, and Maria de Corral, visits Toledo, Córdoba, Granada, and Seville. It is the week before Easter and the oranges are in flower. Looks at the ceilings of the Alhambra.

1993: Francesco Clemente and Jaye Davidson, star of Neil Jordan's *The Crying Game,* as a modern-day Jon Hall and Maria Montez in Clemente's Broadway loft. Photo by Sante D'Orazio.

1997: Francesco Clemente's double-portrait fresco of Ettore Sottsass (left) and himself in Yoyo and Bruno Bischofberger's bathroom in Zurich,

The room was designed by Sottsass, who took this photograph.

Chuck Close paints *Francesco I*, and, in 1988, *Francesco II*.

In May, with Alba and Bill Katz, finds the isolated studio of a cowboy sculptor, near El Rito, New Mexico. In the 1990s, will return and, with Katz as architect, build a home and studio here.

On May 2, opening of a drawing show, curated by Koepplin, at the Museum für Gegenwartskunst, Basel. This exhibition of over three hundred drawings is culled entirely from the museum's collection.

In August, in a lighthouse owned by Pellizzi in Argentario, in Tuscany, directly across from the island of Elba, Clemente paints *The Argentario Paintings*, nine very wide canvases, in an extremely thin, rarefied oil medium.

In September, Alba settles into an apartment above the Broadway studio, on the sixth floor.

During October–December, at the instigation of Westwater, a show of *The Argentario Paintings* is held at the Art Institute of Chicago.

On November 23, at Beth Israel Hospital in New York, Pietro and Andrea Clemente, twins, are born. Mapplethorpe and Ettore Sottsass are named godfathers, with Powell and Barbara Radice as godmothers.

In late December, at the Chelsea Hotel, paints a score of large, horizontal tempera works on unprimed linen. Entitled *Funerary Paintings* (see cat. no. 52), these evoke memories of the Valley of the Kings. "In every tradition, between the 25th of December and the 5th of January the armies of the dead arrive."

1988

Continues through the year to work on the *Funerary Paintings* exclusively.

The family summers in Southampton, Long Island, in a big house found for them by Geldzahler, a five-minute walk away from his own house. Alba will stay in Southampton with the children throughout the winter.

In June, with Prince Michael of Greece and his daughter Alessandra, visits Damascus, Palmyra, and Aleppo. Cenotaphs of figures holding overflowing cups that he sees in Palmyra will appear later in his work.

In June, shows seven paintings in the Italian pavilion of the Venice *Biennale*. These mystical works associated with the *Funerary Paintings* are derived from occult sources: magic squares and numerology. For example, *Earth, Paradigm, Honey and Gold*, and *Signature* (cat. nos. 93, 96–98). These paintings contain figures surrounded by the outlines of vases, reminiscent of ancient burial urns.

On August 12, Haring and Kenny and Teresa Scharf are present at Chiara's birthday party in Southampton. A phone call informs them that their friend Basquiat has just been found dead in his studio on Great Jones Street.

During June–December, in Southampton, completes sixty-four pastels, many of urns with flowers growing in them. These pastels also begin to focus on female genitalia. For example, *Flower, Clouds, I Hear, Unus omnes*, and *Silence* (cat. nos. 44–48). A book of the pastels will be published by Bruno Bischofberger with an accompaniment of poems by Robert Creeley. This inaugurates the publication of Clemente's books in collaboration with American poets.

Clemente will spend the next ten years working almost exclusively on images derived from female anatomy.

In October, the Dia Art Foundation shows the *Funerary Paintings* at its 22nd Street location.

In November, Helen Marden, a close friend, finds a house suitable for the Clemente family in Greenwich Village. It was once the home of Bob Dylan. Work on the place is completed in the fall (the architect is Richard Gluckman), and they move in in time for Thanksgiving dinner with Foye, Ginsberg, and Haring.

During the summer, at the Broadway studio, paints *The Gold Paintings*. Inspired by Indian roadside altars, these include *The Dark in Me*, *Speak Not of Byzantium*, and *Februarian Sky* (cat. nos. 49–51).

Bischofberger publishes *The Gold Paintings* as a collaboration with poems by Gregory Corso.

1989

During January–February, tours Orissa, in India, alone. Visits Bhubaneshwar, Puri, and Konarak. At each place, makes a book. These tall narrow books, twice as tall as they are wide, introduce the double square into his work. The Orissa books—*The Red Book*, *The White Book*, and *The Black Book* (cat. nos. 129–31)—are concerned with the female form and sexuality. *The Black Book* shows couples (and triples).

Attached to the Jagannath temple in Puri are villages of miniature painters. Utilizing the possibilities of these craftsmen, Clemente executes *Story of My Country*, ninety-nine miniatures in the folkloric Orissa style (see *Story of My Country I*, cat. no. 127).

On March 9, Mapplethorpe dies in Boston.

On July 8, a show of five small oil paintings, *The Vowels*, organized by Geldzahler, opens at the Dia Art Foundation's location in Bridgehampton, Long Island.

During the summer, Alba and the family return to her hometown in southern Italy. She and Clemente are visited here by Haring. Together they go to Naples, where Philip Taaffe has a house.

In conjunction with a show of pastels at the Anthony d'Offay Gallery, London, d'Offay publishes a book with eleven accompanying poems by Ricard.

1990

On February 16, Haring dies of AIDS, at thirty-one, in New York. Haring had been very close to the two older Clemente children, Chiara and Nina. For Nina's seventh birthday, he made an elaborate book called *Nina's Book of Little Things*. In his will, he leaves the two girls works by himself and Basquiat.

During the spring, Clemente and Alba are taken to see vogueing performances in the New York clubs. Vogueing is an extreme form of competitive dance performed by gay crews called "houses"; the moves are based on the exaggerated poses of fashion models. They meet Karl of the House of Extravaganza, who becomes a friend. Under this influence, completes seven monumental black paintings with interlocking female profiles. Where the mouths connect is a pink triangular semaphore. Although innocuous in description, these paintings contain a potent sexual charge, for example, *Black Muse*

1997: Faithful friend Bill Katz and Francesco Clemente scale the heights in Truchas, New Mexico. Photo by Hudson Wright.

1993: Portrait of Francesco and Alba Clemente by Bruce Weber.

Twice (cat. no. 109). From the central pink shape will evolve the rest of the year's work, as well as some paintings of the following year. These mostly centrifugal compositions, done in matte water-based paint on unprimed linen, include *Contemplation, Oblation, Seed, Foot, Necessity, Friendship,* another *Foot, Meditation,* and *Broken Hearts* (cat. nos. 100–7).

In June, accompanies the family back to Alba's hometown in southern Italy.

During July–August, alone in Madras. Again with the sign painters, produces two sets of three works each in the large, billboard format. These gouaches recall paintings like *The Two Painters.* Wanting to do work based on the five senses, he achieves three (cat. nos. 121–23). Also paints *Contemplation; Sound, Point;* and *Birth* (cat. nos. 124–26).

Bruno and Yoyo Bischofberger visit, and they all have their fortunes told by the palm-readers of Tanjore.

On October 20, *Francesco Clemente: Three Worlds,* a large show of works on paper, curated by Ann Percy, opens at the Philadelphia Museum of Art. "The three worlds are: inside, outside, and beyond; Italy, India, and New York." The Indian art scholar Stella Kramrisch contributes to the catalogue. This is a personal coup for Clemente, who has always admired her writing.

1991

On January 1, 1 A.M., in the house in Greenwich Village, a crowd of friends ring in the New Year: Johnny Dynell, Deborah Harry, Lauren Hutton, Alex and Ada Katz, Michael and Marina of Greece, Maripol, Earl and Camilla McGrath, Gita and Sonny Mehta, John Reinholt, Ricard, Marina Schiano, Chi Chi Valenti, Daniel Wolf, etc.

The Greenwich Village house will provide Alba with a wonderful place to receive people. She begins having friends come on Sundays. This will continue throughout the decade.

In March, paints *Symmetry* (cat. no. 68) at Port Antonio, Jamaica, a forgotten resort of the 1940s. *The Book of the Sea* is a group of extraordinarily big watercolors on paper (see cat. nos. 67–70). With the tropical air and its 100-percent humidity, he is able to work wet on wet on the prohibitively extensive surfaces without fear of drying.

During September–November, exhibits a series of canvases entitled *Testa Coda* at Gagosian Gallery, New York. Koepplin writes an introduction for the accompanying catalogue and Michael McClure contributes an essay and interview with Clemente.

During September–October, Norman Rosenthal presents the Philadelphia show *Francesco Clemente: Three Worlds* at the Royal Academy of Arts, London. Bill Katz assists in hanging the works. This inaugurates Katz's participation in the design of Clemente's installations.

In November, in Moscow, Aidan Salakova opens the first private gallery in the newly liberated Soviet Union with an exhibition of Clemente works, including *Necessity.* The artist visits Boris Pasternak's house with Andrei Voznesensky, who contributes a text for the exhibition catalogue. Accompanying him on this trip are Powell and Gus Van Sant from Portland, Oregon.

1992

In February, makes more paintings for *The Book of the Sea,* including *The King and the Corpse* (cat. no. 70), in Benares.

In a small room on the Ghats of the Ganges, paints *The Evening Raga* in watercolor.

While in Delhi is introduced by the writer Naveen Patnaik to Jyotindra Jain, scholarly curator of the Folk Art Museum in Delhi and advocate for the living artists of rural India. Clemente is delighted and surprised to find that Jain is familiar with his work.

In March, meets Alba and children in Negril, Jamaica. They drive to Port Antonio. He paints more pages for *The Book of the Sea.*

During the summer, in Long Island City, casts *Sun, Moon, Mercury* (cat. no. 117), and *Saturn* (cat. no. 118) from papier mâché into brass, copper, tin, and lead, respectively. Also casts *Mothers of Letters* (cat. no. 128) in solid iron.

1993

During the spring, after returning from Mexico City and still influenced by a visit to Diego Rivera's studio, begins what will become a comprehensive series of large female heads in pastel on paper. Among the *New York Muses* are *Fabiola, Akure*, and *Lysa*, (cat. nos. 30–32). When completed and framed, this set, leaned against the wall, will surround the studio.

In March, shows sculpture at the Anthony d'Offay Gallery. From there, goes to Port Antonio, where he paints *Tree* (cat. no. 69) for *The Book of the Sea.*

In April, in New York, begins extensive work on what will be the *Black Paintings*. These will incorporate new techniques such as silk-screening and the use of metallic paint.

Spends the year preparing for an exhibition at the Sezon Museum of Art, Tokyo.

On June 9, Thomas Ammann dies, at forty-three, in Zurich. "Sometimes, to sit in front of a painting can be like sitting in front of a fire. You don't need to speak about it, you just sit there and keep yourself warm and we have been doing that together."[5]

On August 5, arriving with the monsoon at Pushkar Lake, Rajasthan, the site of the only Brahma temple in India, Clemente watches the empty lake fill with water. More work on the large watercolors comprising *The Book of the Sea*, including *Fountain* (cat. no. 67). Passes the time with a sadhu who lives on the banks of the lake.

During September–December, in New York, executes three separate groups of paintings simultaneously:

Mother of Hope is thirteen square paintings in black-and-white tempera on ocher-prepared canvases. After many years of celebrating the fecundity and sexuality of women, he treats women as threatening, even as hags, in such paintings as *In Silence, Mandala*, and *Mother of Hope* (cat. nos. 139–41). Though the series is entitled *Mother of Hope*, these are paintings of warfare. The eponymous painting even depicts tanks and helicopters across its surface, imagery taken from Afghani carpets, woven during the Soviet occupation of the 1980s, that Clemente collects.

Purgatorio is five large-scale temperas on old theatrical backdrops (see cat. no. 63). These paintings are finely drawn and vaporous.

1997: From left to right: Francesco, Pietro, Nina, and Andrea Clemente sitting shivah for Allen Ginsberg at Naropa headquarters in Manhattan. The rectangular shape behind Francesco is the coffin covered with a ceremonial drape. Directly behind the coffin, over the altar, is a painting by the late Trungpa Rimpoche, Ginsberg's guru. Photo by Shawn Mortensen.

1995: Francesco Clemente in a moment of attainment at Kali Temple, Mount Abu, Rajastan.

Meditation is twelve large horizontal works painted in enamel and silk-screened on gessoed canvases (see cat. nos. 136–38). These depict scenes from Clemente's theater of the mind, complete with proscenium curtains and audience. This voyeuristic set-up is a formula he has occasionally returned to throughout his career.

1994

During January, in Rome, visits Boetti, who has been diagnosed with cancer.

In February, at the ancient bronze foundries of Tanjore, India, casts the five separate pieces of *The King and the Corpse* (cat. no. 120) in five different metals. As is Clemente's custom, the title, taken from a book by Heinrich Zimmerbut, bears only a glancing reference to the actual inspiration for the work, which in this case is about making love to a corpse, with its folkloric Hindu connotations of Shakti.

On April 24, Boetti dies in Rome.

After a week in Tanjore, returns to little studio behind Nachiappan's print shop in Madras. The slight malaise that had inconvenienced him in New York now assails him with force. He feels constantly dizzy and "seasick." Panicking, he checks into the Madras Holiday Inn—TV, air-conditioning. Watches the Winter Olympics and draws 108 works in ink on paper. These will eventually become the studies for the pastels *Ex Libris Chenonceau* (see cat. nos. 72–75).

In March, abruptly curtails trip to India to seek medical attention in New York. After a full work-up of tests, the doctors can find nothing wrong with him and prescribe a powerful drug, Xanax, that knocks him out but does not help. Discards pills.

During the spring, Geldzahler is terminally ill in New York. Clemente draws several pastel portraits of him.

During July 2–9, having driven to Colorado from New Mexico, attends a tribute to Ginsberg at Naropa Institute, Boulder. Meets Gelek Rimpoche, Tibetan incarnate Lama, teacher of Tibetan Buddhism. At Gelek Rimpoche's request, Clemente joins Ginsberg and Philip Glass on the board of Jewel Heart, a foundation devoted to the continuation of Tibetan Buddhism.

On August 12, a retrospective, suggested by Kenichi Kinokuni, opens at Sezon Museum of Art, Tokyo, with a catalogue text by Tatsumi Shinoda, as well as text and interview by Geldzahler. With Anthony d'Offay, Clemente goes to Kyoto to visit Tim d'Offay, who lives there.

On August 16, Geldzahler dies in New York.

On August 22, under the advice of a friend, seeks treatment with a reflexologist and healer named Michelangelo in Milan. Spends three days undergoing physical therapy and dietary instruction. Health improves over the following year.

During September–October, shows *Purgatorio* paintings and other works at Gagosian's uptown gallery in New York. Exhibition is accompanied by a book of six poems by Creeley.

On October 26, opening of an exhibition of works on paper, curated by Béatrice Salmon, at the Musée National d'Art Moderne, Centre Georges Pompidou, Paris. With the help of Bill Katz, Clemente installed the exhibition. Catalogue has a text by Harry Mathews, with whom he had previously collaborated on the book *Singular Pleasures* in 1988.

In November, works on *Ex Libris Chenonceau* pastels in New York.

1995

In January, begins *Mother of Paintings* (cat. no. 142), a mural-size tempera on backdrop. He will paint on it intermittently throughout the following year. (Clemente frequently reuses titles. *Mother of Paintings* and *Meditation*, for instance, are titles used more than once.)

In March, finishes the last of *Ex Libris Chenonceau* pastels in his new studio in New Mexico.

On March 27, mother dies in Rome. Flies to Naples for the funeral.

In May, with Krens, visits construction site of the new Guggenheim Museum Bilbao.

During June–September, at the Venice *Biennale*, in a little room, shows seven small paintings in tempera, including *Seed*, *Friendship*, and *Meditation*.

Is in Venice before the opening of the *Biennale*. With Alba, takes their sons, Andrea and Pietro, on a tour. They visit Giulio Romano's Palazzo del Tè in Mantua, where Francesco sees the Sala dei Gigante for the first time. In Siena, revisits the Palazzo Pubblico and Simone Martini's fresco of the Guidoriccio di Fogliano, a favorite. In Ferrara, the Palazzo Schifanoia is frescoed by Francesco del Cossa and Ercole di Roberti in a three-tiered allegory of time and the seasons, of special interest to Clemente as the model for *The Cantos* by Ezra Pound.

Ginsberg visits the Clementes in southern Italy. The poet makes little ink sketches of the landscape and titles them *Deva Loka* ("land of the Gods" in Sanskrit). Ginsberg stays ten days and then accompanies the family by train (the Palatino) to Paris and from there to Chenonceau, France.

On June 25, an exhibition of pastels opens at the Château de Chenonceau. On the spot, Allen writes his "Pastel Sentences" (see pp. 152, 154, 156, 158), a caption for each of the 108 pastels.

On June 26, in the town of Saché, near Chenonceau, Mary Rower, Alexander Calder's daughter, opens Calder's studio and home to the Clementes and Ginsberg.

Arrives in Bombay. The monsoon gets there the following day. Travels north to Mount Abu, sacred to the Jain religion. The monsoon follows him there and breaks at his arrival. Always traveling north, drives to Jodhpur, where the monsoon, three days later, floods the hotel. With nowhere dry to sleep, flies out of India. The trip, however, results in *Fifty-one Days on Mount Abu* (see cat. nos. 76–81).

On August 20, a large exhibition of Clemente's work, organized by the painter Silja Rantanen, opens at the Helsingin Taidehalli as part of the Helsinki Festival.

1996

During January–February, in New York, executes six very large pastels, nude self-portraits. With these works in shades of gray, begins a prolonged investigation of grisaille techniques (see cat. nos. 33–36).

In March, with Alba and the children, Clemente is on spring break in Port Antonio. Paints *The Book of the Arrow*, a suite of thirty-nine watercolors.

On March 29, visits his show at the Gagosian Gallery in Beverly Hills.

During April, in New York, begins a series of large heads of poets in charcoal and gray pastel: Ginsberg, McClure, Bernard Picasso, Ricard.

During April–July, painting again on old ballet and opera backdrops using tempera, executes the seventeen paintings that will hang in the gallery devoted to his work when the Guggenheim Museum Bilbao opens in October 1997. Some of these paintings are enormous, but energized by the scale, Clemente executes them without assistance in three months. The group, entitled *La Stanza della Madre*, reinvestigates imagery begun in January 1995 with *Mother of Paintings*.

In May, Alfonso Cuarón, director of the film *A Little Princess*, visits the studio and asks Clemente if he will provide the actual paintings to be used in Cuarón's film based on Dickens's *Great Expectations*, rewritten as the story of a young painter. He enthusiastically accepts.

During July, in New Mexico, executes *The Paintings of the Gate* and works on drawings for *Great Expectations*.

During August, in New York, draws portraits of the cast members of *Great Expectations*: Anne Bancroft, Robert De Niro, Gwyneth Paltrow. Paints the portrait of Paltrow that will become the poster for the movie.

During September–October, *The Book of the Arrow* watercolors are shown at the Städtische Galerie Altes Theater, Ravensburg, Germany. While in Germany is taken by Bruno Bischofberger on a tour of Baroque churches. Is amused to discover the extensive use of grisaille frescoes in their decoration.

Invited to Bali by Ugo Jereissati, a Brazilian expatriate who has lived there for years. Stays in his house for a month with Alba, the twins, and their tutor. Jereissati's house is the former residence of Walter Spies, the Russian painter who was the first to notate gamelan music in the 1930s. Paints more pages of *The Book of the Sea* in grisaille. Bali has a traditional school of painting in black-and-white.

During October–December, in Kerala, India, still with the family and tutor, travels with Raman Schlemmer to the camel fair in Pushkar. While there, completes the three books of *The Early Morning Ragas* in watercolor.

On Christmas Eve, as usual, the family has a small party at home in New York.

1997

Atop Rome's Spanish Steps, behind Trinita dei Monti, is a sixteenth-century corridor frescoed in anamorphic perspective. When looked at from one precise point, the wall contains the image of a tree. But a monk appears on the same wall when seen from the opposite side. In January, in New York, painting on a coarse canvas that takes the oil paint in a way that suggests pastel, Clemente makes six large-scale anamorphic paintings, including *The Swan* and *The Skull* (cat. nos. 143, 144).

In March, while preparing for an exhibition of portraits at the Andy Warhol Museum, Pittsburgh, realizes that not a single portrait of Alba has been included in the show. On a large, double-square canvas, paints a monumental portrait of Alba reclining in evening clothes, his largest portrait to date (cat. no. 37). This begins a series of women's portraits in the same grand format.

On April 4, Glass calls at 10 A.M. to say that Ginsberg has had a stroke. At Ginsberg's 13th Street apartment, sits with Alba, George and Anna Condo, Foye, Robert Frank, Lichtenstein, Larry Rivers, Oliver Reis, and Patti Smith. At 5 P.M., Gelek Rimpoche and two monks arrive to perform rites. Clemente and Alba leave at midnight. At 1:30 A.M., Ginsberg is dead.

On April 12, an exhibition of eighty portraits, curated by Mark Francis, opens at the Andy Warhol Museum. Creeley and Wieners read their poetry.

In May, with Powell, flies to Toronto, where he spends one day acting the role of a hypnotist in Van Sant's film *Good Will Hunting*.

During July, in New Mexico, begins work on four mural-sized canvases of very coarse texture. One of these derives its imagery from Sassetta's painting of Saint Anthony and Saint Jerome hugging before a cave, which Ginsberg had hanging as a postcard on his refrigerator. As of 1999, these paintings are still being worked on.

Spends the summer in New Mexico.

During September, in New York, paints eleven small squarish grisaille self-portraits in oil (see cat. no. 33).

On November 20, *Francesco Clemente: Indian Watercolors*, an exhibition of one of the books of *The Morning Ragas*, organized by Holly Day, Curator of Contemporary Art at the Indianapolis Museum of Art, opens at the Metropolitan Museum of Art. Another exhibition of Indian art, *King of the World: A Mughal Manuscript from the Royal Library, Windsor Castle*, is also on view at the Metropolitan Museum of Art.

1998

In February, Nachiappan, Clemente's friend and printer of his books for twenty years, has decided to become a Hindu monk. They travel together to Nachiappan's ancestral home in Chettinadu country, where he has been asked to become the abbot of a monastery. Since he has dissolved all earthly ties, Hanuman Books are now effectively terminated.

During April, in New York, using the large double-square format on coarse linen, through this year and into the next, paints monumental reclining portraits of Ellen Gallagher, Fran Lebowitz, Helen Marden, Gita Mehta, Toni Morrison, Diane von Furstenberg, and Gloria von Thurn und Taxis. Also receives four commissions for portraits in this format.

During the summer, stays in New York and paints twelve anamorphic self-portraits (see cat. nos. 34, 35). The distortions accentuate the appearance of age. He has been concerned with aging for a while now, and these works are an attempt at reconciling himself, reluctantly, to the inevitable.

On September 19, having driven from New York with Simeral Achenbach—artist, Sufi, and occasional assistant—attends the opening of *Francesco Clemente: Indian Watercolors* at the Indianapolis Museum of Art. On the afternoon of the night Clemente is scheduled to lecture at the museum, he and Simeral are pulled over by traffic police, who find a joint of marijuana. Simeral is thrown in jail. After a short delay, they resume their drive to New Mexico.

In October, Susan Cianciolo publishes *The Run Seven* book at Alleged Press. For this, Clemente draws in charcoal on three pages torn from R. D. Laing's *The Politics of Experience*, a book that was important to him in his youth.

In October, hosts a fund-raiser for Jewel Heart at his New York studio. Glass performs on the piano Feldman had installed in the loft. "I prefer religions one is born into rather than religions one converts to. One is born a Hindu or a Jew; one converts to Buddhism, to Christianity or Islam."

During November, in New York, Chandraleika, radical Madrasi choreographer, tells Clemente that the colors of India are "black, white, and red." He is bemused by this, since Diana Vreeland has already told us that "pink is the navy blue of India." Paints three works entitled *Black, White, and Red*. A table designed by a famous architect is depicted in each. One of these, *Black, White, and Red* (cat. no. 145), pictures a cardboard table by Frank Gehry.

1999

During January, in New York, works on three square paintings in red and green including *Skull* and *Scissors and Butterflies* (cat. nos. 147, 148). Has returned to a "more explicitly tantric palette."

During March, in Port Antonio, paints eight more pages of *The Book of the Sea*.

During May–September, exhibition of watercolors and pastels, curated by Danilo Eccher, is shown at the Galleria d'Arte Moderna, Bologna. Many old friends attend the opening, including Paola Betti, Diego Esposito, Luigi Ontani, and Remo Salvadori. Clemente and Bill Katz installed the exhibition.

Drives through northern Latium and lower Tuscany alone. Visits Etruscan tombs in Tarquinia.

In June, visits show of paintings, pastels, and tapestries at the Anthony d'Offay Gallery, London. The tapestries were woven in Guadalajara under the direction of Robert Evren. Some of the anamorphoses are shown.

David Hockney draws his portrait in graphite heightened with white.

In Paris, at the hotel La Louisiane, paints twenty-one small square watercolors reprising the imagery in the red and green square paintings.

In Milan, presents contractor with drawing for a mosaic commission. The festive imagery contains a boat carrying an orange tree, clouds becoming hands holding pomegranates, and snakes holding diamond rings. Oversees printing of *Life Is Paradise* by Powerhouse Books. A selection of portraits, the book has a text by Vincent Katz.

In New York, works on a book for Aperture with photos of Clemente in his studio by Luca Babini and text by Rene Ricard.

In the midst of preparations for his Guggenheim retrospective, to the consternation of the museum's staff, flies to Egypt with the twins and Nina. Visits Luxor by train.

During July, while in southern Italy with his sons and daughter, revisits the tomb of the diver in Paestum. Its mural, one of the masterpieces of Greco-Etruscan painting, has had singular importance to him from early on and has been a tutelary painting for his own work.

Unattributed quotations are from Francesco Clemente's conversations with the author in 1999.

1. Francesco Clemente, "Apricots and Pomegranates," in Lynne Cooke and André Magnir, *Worlds Envisioned: Alighiero e Boetti and Frédéric Bruly Bouabré*, exh. cat. (New York: Dia Center for the Arts, 1995), p. 60.
2. Rainer Crone and Georgia Marsh, *Clemente: An Interview with Francesco Clemente* (New York: Vintage Books, 1987), p. 26.
3. Clemente, untitled essay, in *Jean-Michel Basquiat Portraits*, exh. cat. (Zurich: Edition Galerie Bruno Bischofberger, 1996), unpaginated.
4. Clemente, qutoed in Edit deAk, "Francesco Clemente," *Interview* (New York) 12, no. 4 (April 1982), p. 70.
5. Clemente, eulogy for Thomas Ammann, Solomon R. Guggenheim Museum, New York, November 18, 1993.

Selected Exhibition History

Compiled by Melanie Mariño

Exhibition entries contain information about related catalogues and artist's books, and are followed by related articles and reviews. For further information about artist's books cited in this section, see "Artist's Books" in the bibliography.

Solo Exhibitions

1971
Galleria Valle Giulia, Rome, solo exhibition, Dec.

1974
Galleria Area, Florence, solo exhibition, dates unknown.

1975
Massimo Minnini, Brescia, Italy, solo exhibition, dates unknown.

Franco Toselli, Milan, solo exhibition, Feb.

Gian Enzo Sperone, Turin, solo exhibition, opened Feb. 28.

Gian Enzo Sperone, Rome, solo exhibition, opened June 26.

1976
Lucrezia de Domizio, Pescara, Italy, solo exhibition, opened April 21.

Gian Enzo Sperone, Rome, solo exhibition, opened Dec. 17.

1977
Paola Betti, Milan, solo exhibition, dates unknown.

1978
Centre d'Art Contemporain, Geneva, *Gratis*, opened Feb. Artist's book.

Galerie Paul Maenz, Cologne, *Francesco Clemente P.M.F.C.*, May 3–16.

Art & Project, Amsterdam, *Undae Clemente Flamina Pulsae*, July 3–28. Artist's book.

1979
Galleria d'Arte Contemporanea Emilio Mazzoli, Modena, Italy, *Vetta*, dates unknown. Artist's book with text by Achille Bonito Oliva.

Giuliana de Crescenzo, Rome, solo exhibition, May.
—Lamberelli, Roberto. "Francesco Clemente, de Crescenzo/ Roma." *Flash Art* (Milan), nos. 90–91 (June–July 1979), p. 60 (in Italian).

Art & Project, Amsterdam, *Emblemi e colpi della pittura di fortuna*, May 2–27. Catalogue.

Lucio Amelio, Naples, solo exhibition, opened Oct. 27.

Lisson Gallery, London, solo exhibition, Nov. 20–Dec. 21.

Gian Enzo Sperone, Turin, *Non Scopa*, Dec. Artist's book.
—Linker, Kate. "Obsessed—and Repelled—by the Past." *Artnews* (New York) 80, no. 5 (May 1981), p. 76.

1980
Padiglione d'Arte Contemporanea, Milan, *Francesco Clemente*, dates unknown. Catalogue with text by Germano Celant.

Sperone Westwater Fischer, New York, solo exhibition, April 2–19.
—Rickey, Carrie. "Taste Test." *The Village Voice* (New York), May 15, 1980, p. 83.

Galerie Paul Maenz, Cologne, *Francesco Clemente*, Oct. 16–Nov. 8. Catalogue.

Gian Enzo Sperone, Rome, and Mario Diacono, Rome, solo exhibition, opened Nov. 22.

Art & Project, Amsterdam, *New Works*, Dec. 11, 1980–Jan. 10, 1981. Catalogue.

1981
Sperone Westwater Fischer, New York, solo exhibition, May 2–June 6.
—Blau, Douglas. "Francesco Clemente, Sperone Westwater Fischer." *Flash Art* (Milan), international edition, no. 104 (Oct.–Nov. 1981), p. 54.
—Kramer, Hilton. "Expressionism from Italy Arrives." *The New York Times*, June 5, 1981, p. C19.
—Lolis, Merope. "Francesco Clemente." *Arts Magazine* (New York) 56, no. 1 (Sept. 1981), p. 23.

Art & Project, Amsterdam, *Frescoes*, Aug.

University Art Museum, University of California, Berkeley, *Francesco Clemente/Matrix 46*, Aug.–Oct. Traveled to The Art Museum and Galleries, California State University, Long Beach, *Centric I: Francesco Clemente*, Oct.–Dec.; Wadsworth Atheneum, Hartford, Connecticut, *Francesco Clemente/Matrix 70*, Feb. 20–April 18, 1982. Brochure with text by Mark Rosenthal.
—Lewallen, Constance. "Matrix: Clemente, Eno, Hagemeyer." *University Art Museum Berkeley*, July–Aug. 1981, p. 2.
—Wilson, William. "Clemente: The Uses of Naiveté." *Los Angeles Times*, Nov. 2, 1981, part 6, pp. 1–5.

Anthony d'Offay Gallery, London, *Francesco Clemente Pinxit*, Sept. 2–Oct. 10. Artist's book.
—Feaver, William. "Peacocks at a Private View." *The Observer* (London), Sept. 13, 1981.
—"London Calendar." *Burlington Magazine* (London) 123, no. 944 (Nov. 1981), p. 708.
—Von Gehren, Georg. "Bericht aus London." *Das Kunstwerk* (Stuttgart) 34 (Oct. 1981), pp. 53–54.

Galerie Bruno Bischofberger, Zurich, *Francesco Clemente: New Works*, Sept. 19–Oct. 10. Catalogue with text by Rainer Crone.
—Gassert, Siegmar. "Unverfrorener Bildervagabund." *Basler Zeitung* (Basel), no. 231 (Oct. 1981), p. 45.

1982
Galerie Daniel Templon, Paris, solo exhibition, June 5–July 16.
—Liebmann, Lisa. "Francesco Clemente, Daniel Templon." *Artforum* (New York) 21, no. 3 (Nov. 1982), p. 83.
—Moore, John M. "The Return of the Emotive." *Connaissance des Arts* (Paris), no. 26 (March 1982), pp. 54–61.

Galerie Paul Maenz, Cologne, *Francesco Clemente: Il viaggiatore napoletano*, Nov. 26–Dec. 23. Artist's book with texts by Rainer Crone and Paul Maenz.

Galerie Bruno Bischofberger, Zurich, *Francesco Clemente: Watercolours*, Dec. 4, 1982–Jan. 22, 1983. Artist's book with text by Rainer Crone.

1983
Akira Ikeda Gallery, Tokyo, *Paintings*, Sept. 5–30. Catalogue, *Francesco Clemente: Paintings*.

Whitechapel Art Gallery, London, *Francesco Clemente: The Fourteen Stations*, Jan. 7–Feb. 20. Traveled to Groninger Museum, Groningen, The Netherlands, April 1–May 8; Badischer Kunstverein, Karlsruhe, Germany, May 24–July 3; Galerie d'Art Contemporain des Musées de Nice, July 14–Aug. 31; Moderna Museet, Stockholm, Sept. 17–Oct. 30. Catalogue with foreword by Nicholas Serota and texts by Mark Francis and Henry Geldzahler.
—Farber, Jules B. "Holland Focus: 2 High C's from Italy." *International Herald Tribune*, May 7–8, 1983, p. 7.
—Feaver, William. "Quick and Slow." *The Observer* (London), Jan. 30, 1983, Review/Arts.
—Fisher, Jean. "Francesco Clemente, Whitechapel Art Gallery, London." *Flash Art* (Milan), international edition, no. 113 (summer 1983), pp. 66–67.
—Gooding, Mel. "Francesco Clemente, Whitechapel and Anthony d'Offay." *Arts Review* (London), Jan. 21, 1983, pp. 10–11.
—Halder, Johannes. "Francesco Clemente, Erich Reiling, Badischer Kunstverein, Karlsruhe." *Das Kunstwerk* (Stuttgart) 36 (Jan. 1984), pp. 168–69.
—Shone, Richard. "London: Francesco Clemente." *Burlington Magazine* (London) 125, no. 959 (March 1983), p. 182.
—Taylor, John Russell. "Tearing Passion to Tatters." *The Times* (London), Jan. 11, 1983.

Anthony d'Offay Gallery, London, *Francesco Clemente: The Midnight Sun*, Jan. 8–Feb. 22.
—Feaver, William. "Quick and Slow." *The Observer* (London), Jan. 30, 1983, Review/Arts.
—Gooding, Mel. "Francesco Clemente, Whitechapel and Anthony d'Offay." *Arts Review* (London), Jan. 21, 1983, pp. 10–11.
—Shone, Richard. "London: Francesco Clemente." *Burlington Magazine* (London) 125, no. 959 (March 1983), p. 182.
—Taylor, John Russell. "Tearing Passion to Tatters." *The Times* (London), Jan. 11, 1983.

A Space, Toronto, *Francesco Clemente: Drawings*, Feb. 14–26.

Sperone Westwater, New York, April 2–May 10, and Mary Boone Gallery, New York, April 2–30, *Francesco Clemente*.
—Cannell, Michael. "Francesco Clemente." *Arts Magazine* (New York) 57, no. 10 (June 1983), p. 4.
—Cohen, Ronny. "Francesco Clemente, Mary Boone, Sperone Westwater." *Artnews* (New York) 82, no. 6 (summer 1983), pp. 189–91.
—Kuspit, Donald B. "Francesco Clemente at Mary Boone and Sperone Westwater." *Art in America* (New York) 71, no. 10 (Nov. 1983), p. 227.
—Larson, Kay. "Freezing Expressionism." *New York Magazine*, April 25, 1983, pp. 95–96.
—Lawson, Thomas. "Francesco Clemente." *Artforum* (New York) 21, no. 10 (June 1983), pp. 75–76.

Kunsthalle Basel, *White Shroud*, May 13–June 24. Catalogue.
—Väth-Hinz, Henriette. "Mystik in schwarz und weiß." *Wolkenkratzer Art Journal* (Frankfurt), no. 3 (June–Aug.), pp. 70–74.

1984

The Institute of Contemporary Art, Boston, *Currents: Francesco Clemente*, January. Brochure with text by Elisabeth Sussman.
—Temin, Christine. "The ICA's Barely Installations." *The Boston Globe*, Jan. 26, 1984, pp. 47–48.

Nationalgalerie, Berlin, *Francesco Clemente, Pastelle 1973–1983*, March 16–May 13. Traveled to Museum Folkwang, Essen, Germany, June 15–Aug. 19; Stedelijk Museum, Amsterdam, Sept. 27–Nov. 18; Fruitmarket Gallery, Edinburgh, Nov. 28–Dec. 30; Kunsthalle Tübingen, Tübingen, Germany, Jan. 12–Feb. 24, 1985. Catalogue edited by Rainer Crone with texts by Crone, Zdenek Felix, Lucius Grisebach, and Joseph Leo Koerner.
—Ohff, Heinz. "Francesco Clemente." *Das Kunstwerk* (Stuttgart) 37 (Aug. 1984), pp. 64, 77.
—Thomson, Richard. "Clemente in Edinburgh, Tübingen and Belfast." *Burlington Magazine* (London) 127, no. 983 (Feb. 1985), pp. 112–15.

Kunsthalle Basel, *Francesco Clemente*, May 13–June 24.
—Idone, Carol. "Francesco Clemente, Barbara Kruger, Jenny Holzer." *Flash Art* (Milan), international edition, no. 119 (Nov. 1984), p. 46.

Akira Ikeda Gallery, Tokyo, *New Paintings*, July 23–Aug. 25. Catalogue, *Francesco Clemente: New Paintings*.

Arts Council Gallery, Belfast, *Francesco Clemente in Belfast*, Nov. 1–24. Catalogue with interview by Giancarlo Politi.
—Beaumont, Mary Rose. "Francesco Clemente, Arts Council Gallery, Belfast." *Arts Review* (London), Nov. 9, 1984, p. 560.
—Shone, Richard. "Clemente in Edinburgh, Tübingen and Belfast." *Burlington Magazine* (London) 127, no. 983 (Feb. 1985), p. 115.

Kestner-Gesellschaft, Hannover, *Francesco Clemente: Bilder und Skulpturen*, Dec. 7, 1984–Jan. 20, 1985. Catalogue with text by Carl Haenlein.

1985

Sperone Westwater, New York, March 30–April 23, Leo Castelli Gallery, New York, March 30–April 23, and Mary Boone Gallery, New York, March 30–April 20, solo exhibition.
—Cone, Michèle. "Francesco Clemente, Castelli, Sperone Westwater, Boone." *Flash Art* (Milan), international edition, no. 123 (summer 1985), p. 55.
—Garcia-Herraiz, Enrique. "Francesco Clemente en dos galerías de SoHo." *Goya* (Madrid), no. 186 (May–June 1985), p. 385.
—Gardner, Paul. "Gargoyles, Goddesses, and Faces in the Crowd." *Artnews* (New York) 85, no. 3 (March 1985), pp. 52–59.
—Heartney, Eleanor. "Francesco Clemente, Sperone Westwater, Castelli Greene Street, Mary Boone." *Artnews* (New York) 84, no. 7 (Sept. 1985), p. 132.
—Hughes, Robert. "Symbolist with Roller Skates." *Time* (New York), April 22, 1985, p. 68.
—McEvilley, Thomas. "Francesco Clemente, Mary Boone Gallery, Leo Castelli Gallery, Sperone Westwater Gallery." *Artforum* (New York) 24, no. 2 (Oct. 1985), p. 123.

The Metropolitan Museum of Art, New York, *Francesco Clemente Prints 1981–1985*, May 14–June 9. Catalogue with introduction by Henry Geldzahler and interview by Danny Berger.

Galerie Bruno Bischofberger, Zurich, *Francesco Clemente: New Paintings*, June 8–July 7.
—"Bischofberger, Zürich: Francesco Clemente." *Basler Zeitung* (Basel), June 27, 1985, p. 35.

Museum für Gegenwartskunst, Basel, *Il viaggiatore napoletano. 73 Zeichnungen von 1971–1978*, July 13–Sept. 15.
—"Gegenwartskunst in der Gegenwartskunst." *Neue Zürcher Zeitung* (Zurich), Aug. 7, 1985, p. 31.

John and Mable Ringling Museum of Art, Sarasota, Florida, *Francesco Clemente*, Oct. 9–Dec. 8. Traveled to Walker Art Center, Minneapolis, Jan. 11–March 2, 1986; Dallas Museum of Art, March 30–May 18, 1986; University Art Museum, University of California, Berkeley, June 9–Sept. 21, 1986; Albright-Knox Art Gallery, Buffalo, New York, Nov. 14, 1986–Jan. 4, 1987; The Museum of Contemporary Art, Los Angeles, Feb. 8–March 29, 1987. Catalogue with texts by Michael Auping and Francesco Pellizzi in collaboration with Jean-Christophe Ammann.
—Freudenheim, Susan. "Berkeley, California: Francesco Clemente." *Burlington Magazine* (London) 128, no. 999 (June 1986), p. 458.
—Marcus, Stanley E. "The War and the Peace of Francesco Clemente." *Artweek* (San Jose, California), April 26, 1986, p. 1.
—Riddle, Mason. "Francesco Clemente, Walker Art Center." *New Art Examiner* (Chicago), no. 13 (June 1986), p. 57.

1986

Akira Ikeda Gallery, Tokyo, *Watercolors*, July 7–31. Catalogue, *Women and Men*.

Anthony d'Offay Gallery, London, *Recent Paintings*, Sept. 4–30.
—Januszczak, Waldemar. "Jumping the Mystic Wall." *The Guardian* (London), Sept. 10, 1986.
—Kent, Sarah. "Spirit World." *Time Out* (London), Sept. 10, 1986.
—Taylor, John Russell. "Francesco Clemente, Anthony d'Offay." *The Times* (London), Sept. 16, 1986.
—Watson, Gray. "Francesco Clemente, Anthony d'Offay." *Flash Art* (Milan), international edition, no. 131 (Dec. 1986–Jan. 1987), p. 93.

The Museum of Modern Art, New York, *The Departure of the Argonaut*, Nov. 6, 1986–Feb. 10, 1987.
—Bleecher, Stephanie. "The Departure of the Argonaut." *Arts Magazine* (New York) 60, no. 10 (summer 1986), p. 114.
—Henry, Gerrit. "The Departure of the Argonaut—A Departure for Clemente." *The Print Collector's Newsletter* (New York) 17, no. 3 (July–Aug. 1986), pp. 87–89.
—Spector, Buzz. "The Departure of the Argonaut." *Artforum* (New York) 25, no. 6 (Feb. 1987), p. 114.

Sperone Westwater, New York, *Francesco Clemente*, Nov. 22, 1986–Jan. 6, 1987. Artist's book, *Two Garlands*.
—Jones, Alan. "Francesco Clemente." *Flash Art* (Milan), international edition, no. 133 (April 1987), p. 81.
—Kuspit, Donald. "Francesco Clemente, Sperone Westwater." *Artforum* (New York) 25, no. 8 (April 1987), p. 125.

1987

Fundación Caja de Pensiones, Madrid, *Francesco Clemente Affreschi: Pinturas al fresco*, April 7–May 17. Catalogue with texts

by Diego Cortez, Rainer Crone, and Henry Geldzahler.
—Albertazzi, Liliana. "Francesco Clemente." *Artefactum* (Antwerp) 4, no. 21 (Nov. 1987–Jan. 1988), pp. 6–9, 60–61, 65 (in French with summary in English).

Museum für Gegenwartskunst, Basel, *Francesco Clemente: Zeichnungen und Aquarelle, 1971–1986*, May 2–July 5. Traveled to Groninger Museum, Groningen, The Netherlands, Sept. 9–Oct. 10; Ulmer Museum, Ulm, Germany, Nov. 8–Dec. 6; Musée de la Ville de Nice, Jan.–Feb. 1988; Museum Ludwig, Cologne, March 15–April 24, 1988; Frankfurter Kunstverein, Frankfurt, June 22–July 24, 1988; Musée Cantonal des Beaux-Arts, Lausanne, Switzerland, Sept. 1–Oct. 16, 1988; Galerie im Taxispalais, Innsbruck, Austria, Dec. 1988–Jan. 1989. Artist's book, *Francesco Clemente CVIII: Watercolours Adayar 1985*, with introduction by Dieter Koepplin.
—Dienst, Rolf-Günter. "Francesco Clemente, Museum für Gegenwartskunst, Basel." *Das Kunstwerk* (Stuttgart) 40 (Sept. 1987), pp. 134–35.
—Koepplin, Dieter. "Francesco Clemente: Aquarelle aus Indien." *Du* (Zurich), no. 5 (May 1987), pp. 76–79.
—Kuspit, Donald. "Francesco Clemente." *Artforum* (New York) 26, no. 3 (Nov. 1987), pp. 149–50.
—Schenker, Christoph. "Francesco Clemente, Museum für Gegenwartskunst, Basel." *Flash Art* (Milan), international edition, no. 136 (Oct. 1987), pp. 117–18.

Galerie Bruno Bischofberger, Zurich, *Zeichnungen: Verschiedene Werke aus den Jahren 1977–1979/Works on Paper 1977–1979*, June 13–Sept. 5.

Galerie Bruno Bischofberger, Zurich, *Neue Werke: Funerary Paintings*, Sept. 12–Oct. 10.

The Art Institute of Chicago, *The Argentario Paintings*, Oct. 6–Dec. 6.

1988
Milwaukee Art Museum, *Francesco Clemente: The Graphic Work*, Jan. 21–March 27. Traveled to The Saint Louis Art Museum, April 15–June 5; Museo Italoamericano, San Francisco, July 14–Sept. 11.

Cabinet des Estampes, Geneva, *Le Départ des Argonautes et autres estampes*, Feb. 18–April 3. Catalogue.

Mario Diacono Gallery, Boston, solo exhibition, April 15–May 14.
—Bonetti, David. "Francesco Clemente at the Mario Diacono Gallery." *The Boston Phoenix*, May 6, 1988, p. 14.

Museum of Contemporary Art, Chicago, *Francesco Clemente: Fourteen Stations of the Cross*, April 23–June 19.

Fundació Joan Miró, Barcelona, *La Partenza del Argonauta*, June 16–Aug. 28.

Dia Art Foundation, New York, *Funerary Paintings*, Oct. 7, 1988–June 18, 1989. Artist's book.
—Chua, Lawrence. "Francesco Clemente." *Flash Art* (Milan), international edition, no. 144 (Jan.–Feb. 1989), pp. 110–11.
—Decter, Joshua. "Francesco Clemente, Funerary Paintings." *Arts Magazine* (New York) 63, no. 5 (Jan. 1989), pp. 105–06.
—Pellizzi, Francesco. "Charon's Boat." *Artforum* (New York) 27, no. 3 (Nov. 1988), pp. 112–17.

Galerie Paul Maenz, Cologne, *Francesco Clemente: Major New Work*, Nov. 11–Dec. 23.
—Magnani, Gregorio. "Francesco Clemente, Paul Maenz, Cologne." *Flash Art* (Milan), international edition, no. 145 (March–April 1989), p. 119.

1989
Galerie Bruno Bischofberger, Zurich, *Francesco Clemente: The Gold Paintings*, Jan. 4–31. Artist's book with poem by Gregory Corso.

Galerie Yvon Lambert, Paris, *Francesco Clemente: Pastels*, May 20–June 30.

Anthony d'Offay Gallery, London, *Francesco Clemente, Story of My Country: Paintings, Sculptures, Frescoes, Tapestries, Pastels, Miniatures*, May 23–June 21. Artist's book, *Sixteen Pastels*, with poems by Rene Ricard.
—Buck, Louisa. "A Nomad's Postcards Home." *The Weekend Guardian* (London), June 10–11, 1989.
—Burn, Guy. "Prints." *Arts Review* (London), June 16, 1989, pp. 462–63.
—Carpenter, Merlin. "Francesco Clemente, Anthony d'Offay." *Artscribe* (London), no. 77 (Sept.–Oct. 1989), pp. 73–74.
—Feaver, William. "A Quiver of Quick Arrows." *The Observer* (London), June 4, 1989.

Dia Art Foundation, Bridgehampton, New York, *The Vowels (a e i o u): Paintings by Francesco Clemente*, July 8–Oct. 9. Catalogue with text by Henry Geldzahler.
—Smith, Roberta. "On Long Island: Vienna, Video, and Visions of Nature." *The New York Times*, Aug. 4, 1989, p. C22.

Fundación Cultural Televisa, Centro Cultural Arte Contemporáneo, Guadalajara, Mexico, *Francesco Clemente: Cinco Tapices Realizados en el Taller Mexicano de Gobelinos (Guadalajara, Jalisco, Mexico)*, Oct. 1989–Feb. 1990. Catalogue with texts by Raymond Foye, Henry Geldzahler, and Sylvia Navarette.

1990
Anthony d'Offay Gallery, London, *Francesco Clemente: Pastels*, May 19–June 15.

Vrej Baghoomian Gallery, New York, *Francesco Clemente: Ten Bad Mothers*, May 26–June 23.

Sperone Westwater, New York, *Francesco Clemente*, Oct. 20–Nov. 10.
—Denson, G. Roger. "Francesco Clemente: The Color of Desire." *Flash Art* (Milan), international edition, no. 156 (Jan.–Feb. 1991), p. 124.
—Heartney, Eleanor. "Francesco Clemente, Sperone Westwater." *Artnews* (New York) 90, no. 1 (Jan. 1991), pp. 143–44.
—Kalina, Richard. "Francesco Clemente at Sperone Westwater." *Art in America* (New York) 79, no. 3 (March 1991), pp. 136–37.

Philadelphia Museum of Art, *Francesco Clemente: Three Worlds*, Oct. 20–Dec. 23. Traveled to Wadsworth Atheneum, Hartford, Connecticut, Jan. 27–March 17, 1991; San Francisco Museum of Modern Art, April 11–June 2, 1991; Royal Academy of Arts, London, Sept. 20–Oct. 27, 1991. Catalogue with texts by Raymond Foye, Stella Kramrisch, Ann Percy, and Ettore Sottsass.

—Burn, Guy. "Prints." *Arts Review* (London), Oct. 18, 1991, p. 513.
—Francis, Mark. "Philadelphia, Museum of Art, and Hartford, Wadsworth Atheneum, Francesco Clemente: Three Worlds." *Burlington Magazine* (London) 133, no. 1055 (Feb. 1991), p. 148.
—Jenkins, Steven. "An Immortal Approaches Forty: Francesco Clemente at the San Francisco Museum of Modern Art." *Artweek* (San Jose, California), May 16, 1991, p. 20.
—Larson, Kay. "On the Line." *New York Magazine*, Nov. 19, 1990, pp. 117–18.
—Mahoney, Robert. "Francesco Clemente: Three Worlds." *Flash Art* (Milan), international edition, no. 155 (Nov.–Dec. 1990), p. 170.
—Neff, Eileen. "Francesco Clemente, Philadelphia Museum of Art." *Artforum* (New York) 29, no. 6 (Feb. 1991), pp. 130–31.
—Norrie, Jane. "Francesco Clemente, Royal Academy." *Arts Review* (London), Oct. 4, 1991, pp. 499–500.
—Spears, Dorothy. "Francesco Clemente." *Arts Magazine* (New York) 65, no. 6 (Feb. 1991), p. 88.
—Zimmer, William. "One Man's Vision Combines Three Worlds." *The New York Times*, Feb. 10, 1991, section 12, p. 16.

1991
Kunsthalle Basel, *Francesco Clemente: The Black Book*, Jan. 27–March 17. Artist's book.
—Arici, Laura. "Gottliche Umarmung: Francesco Clemente-Ausstellung in der Kunsthalle Basel." *Neue Zürcher Zeitung* (Zurich), Feb. 5, 1991.
—Schiess, Robert. "Robert Filliou—Francesco Clemente." *Basellandschaftliche Zeitung* (Basel), Jan. 28, 1991.
—Wagner, Thomas. "Transavantgardia: Francesco Clemente in Basel." *Frankfurter Allgemeine Zeitung* (Frankfurt), March 9, 1991, p. 29.

Perry Rubenstein, New York, *Francesco Clemente: Early Self-Portraits*, March 26–April 19.

Galerie Beyeler, Basel, *Francesco Clemente*, June 7–Sept. 27. Catalogue with text by Urs Albrecht.

Museum für Moderne Kunst, Frankfurt, *Francesco Clemente: Bestiarium*, July 6, 1991–Jan. 30, 1992. Catalogue with text by Jean-Christophe Ammann.

Gagosian Gallery, New York, *Francesco Clemente: Testa Coda*, Sept. 28–Nov. 16. Traveled to Museum für Gegenwartskunst, Basel, Dec. 8, 1991–March 2, 1992; Kunstverein, Ulm, Germany, March 15–April 20, 1992. Artist's book with introduction by Dieter Koepplin and text and interview by Michael McClure.
—Decter, Joshua. "Francesco Clemente's *Testa Coda*." *Arts Magazine* (New York) 66, no. 4 (Dec. 1991), pp. 80–81.
—Heartney, Eleanor. "Francesco Clemente, Gagosian." *Artnews* (New York) 90, no. 9 (Nov. 1991), p. 133.
—Koepplin, Dieter. "Clemente Back to Front." *Flash Art* (Milan), international edition, no. 162 (Jan.–Feb. 1992), p. 147.
—Kuspit, Donald. "Francesco Clemente, Gagosian Gallery." *Artforum* (New York) 30, no. 5 (Jan. 1992), p. 98.
—Mahoney, Robert. "Francesco Clemente, Gagosian." *Flash Art* (Milan), international edition, no. 162 (Jan.–Feb. 1992), p. 129.

Galerie Daniel Templon, Paris, *Francesco Clemente: Oeuvres Récentes*, Oct. 30–Nov. 30.

First Gallery, Moscow, *Francesco Clemente*, Nov. 2–Dec. 2. Two artist's books, *Mental'nyi limon/The Water's Skeleton*, *Francesco Clemente: Sixteen Watercolours* and *Francesco Clemente: Nine Drawings/Andrei Voznesensky: Five Poems*, with foreword and poems by Andrei Voznesensky.

1992
Perry Rubenstein, New York, *Francesco Clemente*, Jan.
—Heartney, Eleanor. "Francesco Clemente at Perry Rubenstein." *Art in America* (New York) 80, no. 1 (Jan. 1992), p. 120.

Leccese Spruth Gallery, Cologne, *Francesco Clemente: Works on Paper 1979–1983*, Feb.–April 4.

Galerie Bruno Bischofberger, Zurich, *War Usury Pestilence Death*, June 11–Sept. 5.

Gagosian Gallery, New York, *Francesco Clemente: Watercolors*, Sept. 19–Nov. 17. Artist's book, *Francesco Clemente: Evening Raga and Paradiso*, edited by Raymond Foye with discussion by Clemente, Allen Ginsberg, and Peter Orlovsky.
—Cotter, Holland. "Francesco Clemente." *The New York Times*, Oct. 23, 1992, p. C28.

Galerie Michael Haas, Berlin, *Francesco Clemente: Gemälde. Aquarelle. Pastelle*, Dec. 5, 1992–Jan. 30, 1993. Catalogue.
—Lan, Werner. "Kurswechsel ohne Knicke." *Tagesspiegel* (Berlin), Jan. 5, 1993.
— "Mit und ohne Drachen: Neues von Clemente." *Die Welt* (Bonn), Jan. 23, 1993, p. G7.

1993
Anthony d'Offay Gallery, London, *Francesco Clemente: Paintings, Sculptures and Works on Paper from India*, March 11–April 30. Catalogue with text by Dieter Koepplin.
—Graham-Dixon, Andrew. "Flirting with Hippie Chic." *The Independent* (London), April 20, 1993.
—Kent, Sarah. "Sarah Kent on Francesco Clemente." *Time Out* (London), March 17, 1993.
—Renton, Andrew. "Francesco Clemente: Unrelaxed Cosmology of Floating Symbols." *Flash Art* (Milan), international edition, no. 171 (summer 1993), p. 110.

Gagosian Gallery, New York, *Francesco Clemente: The Black Paintings*, Nov. 16, 1993–Jan. 8, 1994. Artist's book, *Life & Death*, with poems by Robert Creeley.
—Bonami, Francesco. "Francesco Clemente." *Flash Art* (Milan), international edition, no. 175 (March–April 1994), p. 101.
—Bourdon, David. "Francesco Clemente at Gagosian." *Art in America* (New York) 82, no. 6 (June 1994) p. 99.
—Kino, Carol. "Francesco Clemente, Gagosian." *Artnews* (New York) 93, no. 4 (April 1994), pp. 159–60.

1994
Galerie Bruno Bischofberger, Zurich, *Tree of Life*, Feb. 19–April 30.
—Trepp, Judith. "Francesco Clemente, Bruno Bischofberger." *Artnews* (New York) 93, no. 5 (May 1994), p. 168.

Sezon Museum of Art, Tokyo, *Francesco Clemente: Two Horizons*, Aug. 12–Oct. 16. Catalogue with interview by Henry Geldzahler and text by Tatsumi Shinoda.

Gagosian Gallery, New York, *Francesco Clemente: Purgatorio*, Sept. 10–Oct. 15. Artist's book, *There*, edited by Raymond Foye with poems by Robert Creeley.

Musée National d'Art Moderne, Centre Georges Pompidou, Paris, *Early Morning Exercises: Oeuvres sur papier 1971–1994*, Oct. 26, 1994–Jan. 16, 1995. Catalogue with preface by Béatrice Salmon and texts by Harry Mathews and Ettore Sottsass.
—"Drawings on Exhibit." *Drawing* (New York) 16, no. 3 (Sept.–Oct. 1994), p. 63.

1995
Museum für Moderne Kunst, Frankfurt, *Mothers of Hope*, Jan. 27–May 15. Artist's book with introduction by Jean-Christophe Ammann.
—Auffermann, Verena. "Ein Votum fur die Malerei." *Frankfurter Rundschau* (Frankfurt), Feb. 4, 1995.
—Gropp, Rose-Maria. "Erzahler im Raum." *Frankfurter Allgemeine Zeitung* (Frankfurt), Feb. 21, 1995.

Anthony d'Offay Gallery, London, *Francesco Clemente: Frescoes and Pastels, 1970–1995*, Feb. 22–March 31.
—Searle, Adrian. "Francesco Clemente, Anthony d'Offay." *Time Out* (London), March 8, 1995.

Galerie Rigassi, Bern, *Francesco Clemente*, May 3–June 10. Catalogue.

Jablonka Galerie, Cologne, *Francesco Clemente*, May 19–July 15. Artist's book, *Francesco Clemente/Peter Handke*, with poems by Peter Handke.
—Goodrow, Gerard A. "Francesco Clemente." *Artnews* (New York) 94, no. 7 (Sept. 1995), p. 154.

Château de Chenonceau, France (organized by Galerie Bruno Bischofberger, Zurich), *Ex Libris Chenonceau*, June 25–Nov. 5. Artist's book.
—Dordeit, Olivier. "Francesco Clemente au Château de Chenonceau: Astète ou estète?" *Parcours* (Paris) 1, no. 3 (summer 1995), pp. 48–49.
—Pythoud, Laurence. "Francesco Clemente Pastels." *L'Oeil* (Paris), no. 474 (Sept. 1995), p. 98.
—Suchère, Eric. "Clemente joue la Séduction." *Beaux Arts Magazine* (Paris), no. 137 (Sept. 1995), p. 112.

Helsingin Taidehalli, *Francesco Clemente* (part of Helsinki Festival), Aug. 20–Oct. 1. Catalogue with foreword by Silja Rantanen, text by Tatsumi Shinoda, and interview by Barbaralee Diamonstein.
—Hannula, Mika. "Hienovaraisen liikkeen ensisijaisuus." *Taide* (Helsinki) 35, no. 3 (1995), pp. 32–33.
—Hannula, Mika. "Desire: ja haviavan herkka kosketus." *Taide* (Helsinki) 35, no. 6 (1995), pp. 12–14.

Peter Blum, New York, *Francesco Clemente: Works from 1980 to 1990*, Nov. 10, 1995–Jan. 20, 1996.
—Hainley, Bruce. "Francesco Clemente." *Artforum* (New York) 34, no. 8 (April 1996), p. 101.
—Mac Adam, Alfred. "Francesco Clemente." *Artnews* (New York) 95, no. 3 (March 1996), p. 112.
—Russell, John. "Francesco Clemente's Provocations." *International Herald Tribune*, Dec. 30, 1995, p. 6.

1996
Galerie Daniel Templon, Paris, *Francesco Clemente*, Feb. 17–March 20.

Gagosian Gallery, Beverly Hills, California, *Francesco Clemente: New Works*, March 23–April 27.

Städtische Galerie Altes Theater, Ravensburg, Germany, *Francesco Clemente: The Book of the Arrow, Aquarelle*, Sept. 8–Oct. 27. Catalogue edited by Tilman Osterworld and Thomas Knubben with texts by Dieter Koepplin and Osterworld.

Galerie Bruno Bischofberger, Zurich, *Francesco Clemente: Paintings of the Gate*, Sept. 9–Oct. 19.

1997
Galerie Jérôme de Noirmont, Paris, *Francesco Clemente: The Paintings of the Gate*, April 2–May 31. Catalogue with text by Démosthènes Davvetas.
—Attias, Laurie. "Francesco Clemente, Jérôme de Noirmont, Paris." *Artnews* (New York) 96, no. 6 (June 1997), p. 136.
— "Clemente, dualité." *Connaissance des Arts* (Paris), no. 539 (May 1997), p. 30.

The Andy Warhol Museum, Pittsburgh, *Francesco Clemente: Portraits*, April 12–Aug. 31.
—Shearing, Graham. "Warhol Show Makes Portraits 'New.'" *Tribune-Review* (Greensburg, Pennsylvania), April 20, 1987, p. E6.

Anthony d'Offay Gallery, London, *Fifty One Days on Mount Abu*, April 24–May 31. Artist's book with text by Clemente.
—Lucie-Smith, Edward. "Critic's Diary." *Art Review* (London) 49 (June 1997), pp. 26–29.

Gagosian Gallery, New York, *Francesco Clemente: Anamorphosis*, May 1–June 14. Artist's book edited by Raymond Foye with poems by Robert Creeley.
—Carrier, David. "New York: Spring Exhibitions." *Burlington Magazine* (London) 139, no. 1133 (Aug. 1997), pp. 570–71.
—Wei, Lilly. "Francesco Clemente at Gagosian." *Art in America* (New York) 85, no. 11 (Nov. 1997), p. 126.

The Metropolitan Museum of Art, New York, *Francesco Clemente: Indian Watercolors*, Nov. 20, 1997–Feb. 8, 1998. Traveled to Modern Art Museum of Fort Worth, Texas, May 31–Aug. 2, 1998; Indianapolis Museum of Art, Sept. 19, 1998–Jan. 3, 1999. Brochure.
—Cotter, Holland. "Many Shows and Many Indias." *The New York Times*, Dec. 26, 1997, pp. E43, E45.
—Seeman Robinson, Joan. "Francesco Clemente, Indianapolis Museum of Art." *Artforum* (New York) 37, no. 4 (Dec. 1998), p. 134.

1999
Anthony d'Offay Gallery, London, *Francesco Clemente: Painter's Wardrobe*, April 29–June 16.

Galleria d'Arte Moderna, Bologna, *Francesco Clemente: Opere su carta*, May 29–Sept. 12. Catalogue with discussion by Clemente, Danilo Eccher, and Francesco Pellizzi.

Jablonka Galerie, Cologne, *Francesco Clemente: Broken Women, Neue Pastelle*, June 4–July 31.

Group Exhibitions

1973
Museum of the Philadelphia Civic Center, Philadelphia, *Italy Two—Art Around '70*, Nov. 2–Dec. 16. Catalogue with texts by Furio Colombo and Alberto Boatto and Filiberto Menna.

1974
Studenteski Center, Belgrade, group exhibition, dates unknown.

1975
Galleria Diagramma, Milan, *Campo Dieci*, dates unknown.

Galleria l'Attico, Rome, *24 ore su 24*, Jan.
—Bonita Oliva, Achille. "Spazio a Tempo Pieno." *Casabella* (Milan) 41, no. 407 (Nov. 1975), pp. 32–35.
—Bonita Oliva, Achille. "24 ore su 24." *Studio International* (London), no. 190 (Sept.–Oct. 1975), pp. 154–55.
—Corà, Bruno. "24 ore su 24." *Data* (Milan), no. 15 (spring 1975), pp. 2–5.

Parco Ibirapuera, São Paulo, *XIII Bieñal de São Paulo*, Oct. 17–Dec. 15. Catalogue.

1976
Gallerie Communale d'Arte Moderna and Sala del Ridotto del Teatro Regio, Parma, Italy, *Foto & Idea*, April–May. Catalogue.

Gian Enzo Sperone, Rome, *Francesco Clemente, Mario Merz, Vettor Pisani*, opened April 14.

1977
Studio Cannaviello, Rome, *Drawings/Transparency*, dates unknown. Catalogue with text by Achille Bonito Oliva.

Gian Enzo Sperone, Rome, *Wednesday 16 Feb. 1977*, Feb. 16.

Palais de Tokyo and Musée d'Art Moderne de la Ville de Paris, *Xe Biennale de Paris*, Sept. 17–Nov. 1. Catalogue.
—L. L. P. "La Biennale di Parigi—Problema." *Domus* (Milan), no. 576 (Nov. 1977), pp. 50–53 (in Italian and French).

1978
Galleria la Salita, Rome, *Pas de deux*, opened May 16.

1979
Galerie Paul Maenz, Cologne, *Arte Cifra*, June 21–July 21. Catalogue with text by Wolfgang Max Faust.

Kunstaustellungen Gutenbergstrasse, Stuttgart, *Europa '79*, Sept. 30–Oct. 26. Catalogue.
—Pohlen, Annelie. "Europa 79: 2. Kunstvorstellung in Stuttgart." *Flash Art/Heute Kunst* (Milan), nos. 94–95 (Jan.–Feb. 1980), pp. 70–71.

Galerie Yvon Lambert, Paris, *Parigi: O Cara*, Oct. 20–Nov. 24.

Palazzo di Città, Acireale, Italy, *Opere Fatte ad Arte*, Nov. Catalogue with text by Achille Bonito Oliva.

Castello Colonna, Genazzano, Italy, *Le Stanze*, Nov. 30, 1979–Feb. 29, 1980. Catalogue with texts by Achille Bonito Oliva and Mario Merz.
—Ferrari, Corinna. "Le Stanze del Castello." *Domus* (Milan), no. 604 (March 1980), p. 55 (in Italian and English).

1980
Bonner Kunstverein, Bonn, *Die enthauptete Hand—100 Zeichnungen aus Italien: Chia, Clemente, Cucchi, Paladino*, Jan. 20–Feb. 28. Traveled to Städtische Galerie Schloss Wolfsburg, Wolfsburg, Germany, March 9–April 6; Groninger Museum, Groningen, The Netherlands, June 6–July 6. Catalogue with texts by Achille Bonito Oliva, Wolfgang Max Faust, and Margarethe Jochimsen.

Francesco Masnata, Genoa, Italy, *Sandro Chia, Francesco Clemente, Enzo Cucchi, Nicola De Maria, Mimmo Paladino*, March.

Mannheimer Kunstverein, Mannheim, *Egonavigatio: Sandro Chia, Francesco Clemente, Nicola De Maria, Mimmo Paladino*, March 30–April 27. Catalogue with texts by Jean-Christophe Ammann, Achille Bonito Oliva, Germano Celant, Wolfgang Max Faust, and Margarethe Jochimsen.

Kunsthalle Basel, *Sandro Chia, Francesco Clemente, Enzo Cucchi, Nicola De Maria, Luigi Ontani, Mimmo Paladino, Ernesto Tatafiore*, May 11–June 22. Traveled to Museum Folkwang, Essen, Germany, Oct. 17–Nov. 30; Stedelijk Museum, Amsterdam, Dec. 12, 1980–Jan. 13, 1981. Catalogue with texts by Jean-Christophe Ammann, Achille Bonito Oliva, and Germano Celant.
—Ammann, Jean-Christophe. "Espansivo-Eccessivo." *Domus* (Milan), no. 593 (April 1979), p. 45.
—Franzke, Andreas. "7 Junge Künstler aus Italien." *Pantheon* (Munich) 39, no. 1 (Jan.–March 1981), pp. 7–8.
—Payant, René. "From Landuage to Landuage: En suivant quelques oeuvres peintes italiennes." *Parachute* (Montreal), no. 23 (summer 1981), pp. 27–33 (summary in English).

Venice, *XXXIX Biennale di Venezia: L'arte negli anni settanta/Aperto '80*, June 1–Sept. 28. Catalogue with texts by Achille Bonito Oliva, Michael Compton, Martin Kunz, and Harald Szeeman.
—Celant, Germano. "Biennale '80: Sonni e Risvegli/Venice: Sleep and Sparks." *Domus* (Milan), no. 608 (July–Aug. 1980), pp. 48–55 (in Italian and English).
—Gendel, Milton. "Ebb and Flood Tide in Venice." *Artnews* (New York) 79, no. 7 (Sept. 1980), pp. 118–20.
—Pincus-Witten, Robert. "Entries: If Even in Fractions." *Arts Magazine* (New York) 55, no. 1 (Sept. 1980), pp. 116–19.

Sperone Westwater Fischer, New York, *Sandro Chia, Francesco Clemente and Enzo Cucchi*, Sept. 20–Oct. 4.
—Larson, Kay. "Bad Boys at Large! The Three C's Take on New York." *The Village Voice* (New York), Sept. 17, 1980, pp. 35, 37.
—Lawson, Thomas. "Chia, Clemente and Cucchi, Sperone Westwater Fischer." *Flash Art* (Milan), international edition, no. 100 (Nov. 1980), p. 43.
—Nadelmann, Cynthia. "Sandro Chia, Francesco Clemente, Enzo Cucchi." *Artnews* (New York) 79, no. 10 (Dec. 1980), p. 193.
—Rickey, Carrie. "Francesco Clemente, Sperone Westwater Fischer Gallery." *Artforum* (New York) 19, no. 4 (Dec. 1980), pp. 70–71.

Galerie Rudolph Zwirner, Cologne, *Neuerwerbungen*, Oct.

Galerie Daniel Templon, Paris, *La transavantgarde Italienne: Sandro Chia, Francesco Clemente, Enzo Cucchi, Nicola De Maria, Mimmo Paladino*, Dec. 6, 1980–Jan. 8, 1981.

Galleria la Salita, Rome, *"il ritratto,"* opened Dec. 17.

Annina Nosei Gallery, New York, *Drawings and Works on Paper*, Dec. 20, 1980–June 17, 1981.
—Casademont, Joan. "Drawings and Paintings on Paper, Annina Nosei Gallery." *Artforum* (New York) 19, no. 8 (April 1981), pp. 65–66.

1981

Rheinhallen der Kölner Messe, Cologne, *Westkunst*, May 30–Aug. 16. Catalogue with texts by Marcel Baumgärtner, Laszlo Glozer, and Kasper König.
—Ammann, Jean-Christophe. "Westkunst in Cologne." *Flash Art* (Milan), international edition, no. 104 (Oct.–Nov. 1981), p. 51.
—Armstrong, Richard. "Heute, Westkunst." *Artforum* (New York) 20, no. 1 (Sept. 1981), pp. 83–86.
—Feaver, William. "Talismans and Trophies: Vintage Modernist at 'Westkunst.'" *Artnews* (New York) 80, no. 7 (Sept. 1981), pp. 132–35.
—Marmer, Nancy. "Isms on the Rhine." *Art in America* (New York) 69, no. 9 (Nov. 1981), pp. 112–23.

Musée National d'Art Moderne, Centre Georges Pompidou, Paris, *L'Identité Italienne: Art en Italie depuis 1959*, June 25–Sept. 7. Catalogue with introduction by Germano Celant.
—Ammann, Jean-Christophe. "Identité Italienne: Una scleta per Parigi." *Domus* (Milan), no. 621 (Oct. 1981), p. 57.
—Bonito Oliva, Achille. "Cosi Celant tutti." *Domus* (Milan), no. 621 (Oct. 1981), pp. 58, 62.
—Gruterich, Marlis. "Italienische Identität oder reiche arme Kunst." *Kunstbulletin* (Bern), no. 2 (Feb. 1982), pp. 2–9.

Sperone Westwater Fischer, New York, *Sandro Chia, Francesco Clemente, Enzo Cucchi, Carlo Mariani, Malcolm Morley, David Salle, Julian Schnabel*, Sept. 19–Oct. 17.

Crown Point Gallery, Oakland, California, *Italians and American Italians: Etchings*, Sept. 20–Oct. 30. Brochure with text by Kathan Brown.

Galerie Paul Maenz, Cologne, *Die Erotik der neuen Kunst*, Oct. 17–Nov. 11. Catalogue with texts by Jean-Christophe Ammann, Germano Celant, Wolfgang Max Faust, and A. Wildermuth.

Galleria d'Arte Contemporanea Emilio Mazzoli, Modena, Italy, *Tesoro*, Nov. Catalogue with text by Achille Bonito Oliva.

Albright-Knox Art Gallery, CEPA Gallery, and Hallwalls, Buffalo, New York, *Figures: Forms and Expressions*, Nov. 20, 1981–Jan. 3, 1982. Catalogue with texts by Robert Collignon, William Currie, Roger Denson, Biff Henrich, Charlotta Kotik, and Susan Krane.

The Squibb Gallery, Princeton, New Jersey, *Aspects of Post-Modernism*, Dec. 7, 1981–Jan. 10, 1982. Catalogue with text by Sam Hunter.

1982

Galleria Civica del Commune di Modena, Modena, Italy, *Transavanguardia: Italia/America*, March 21–May 2. Catalogue with text by Achille Bonito Oliva.

Aurelian Wall, Rome, *Avanguardia Transavanguardia 68, 77*, April–July. Catalogue with text by Achille Bonito Oliva.
—Clarke, John R. "Up Against the Wall, Transavanguardia!" *Arts Magazine* (New York) 57, no. 4 (Dec. 1982), pp. 76–81.
—Cocuccioni, Enrico. "Avantgarde–Transavantgarde (Mura Aureliane/Roma)." *Flash Art* (Milan), international edition, no. 109 (Nov. 1982), pp. 70–71.

Marlborough Gallery, New York, *The Pressure to Paint*, June 4–July 9. Catalogue with texts by Diego Cortez and David P. Robinson.
—Russell, John. "Marlborough Offers Sampler of 17 Paintings." *The New York Times*, June 11, 1982, p. C26.
—Silverthorne, Jeanne. "The Pressure to Paint, Marlborough Gallery." *Artforum* (New York) 11, no. 2 (Oct. 1982), pp. 67–68.

Museum Fridericianum, Kassel, Germany, *Documenta 7*, June 19–Sept. 28. Catalogue (2 vols.) with texts by Saskia Bos, Germano Celant, Rudi Fuchs, Johannes Gachnang, Walter Nikkels, Gerhard Storck, and Coosje van Bruggen.
—Ammann, Jean-Christophe. "Documenta: Reality and Desire." *Flash Art* (Milan), international edition, no. 109 (Nov. 1982), pp. 37–39.
—Frackman, Noel, and Ruth Kauffman. "Documenta 7: The Dialogue and a Few Asides." *Arts Magazine* (New York) 57, no. 2 (Oct. 1982), pp. 91–97.
—Owens, Craig. "Bayreuth '82." *Art in America* (New York) 70, no. 8 (Sept. 1982), pp. 131–38, 191.
—Politi, Giancarlo. "Documenta 7." *Flash Art* (Milan), international edition, no. 109 (Nov. 1982), pp. 34–36.
—Russell, John. "A Palace of Pleasure for Art." *The New York Times*, July 11, 1982, section 2, pp. 1–11.

Anthony d'Offay Gallery, London, *Five Painters: Chia, Clemente, Kiefer, Salle, Schnabel*, June 23–July 25.
—Einzig, H. "Chia, Clemente, Kiefer, Salle, Schnabel." *Arts Review* (London), July 16, 1982, p. 373.

The Museum of Modern Art, New York, *New Work on Paper 2: Jonathan Borofsky, Francesco Clemente, Mario Merz, A. R. Penck, Giuseppe Penone*, July 28–Sept. 21. Catalogue with text by Bernice Rose.
—Linker, Kate. "New Work on Paper 2." *Artforum* (New York) 21, no. 3 (Nov. 1982), pp. 76–77.
—Russell, John. "Drawings, Reticent and Bold, at the Modern." *The New York Times*, July 30, 1982, p. C24.
—Smith, Roberta. "Drawing Fire." *The Village Voice* (New York), Aug. 17, 1982, p. 74.

Groninger Museum, Groningen, The Netherlands, and Kunsthalle Wilhelmshaven, Wilhelmshaven, Germany, *kunst nu/kunst unserer zeit*, Sept. 4–Oct. 10. Catalogue with introduction by Antje von Graevenitz.

Martin-Gropius-Bau, Berlin, *Zeitgeist*, Oct. 15, 1982–Jan. 16, 1983. Catalogue with foreword by Christos Joachimides and texts by Karl-Heinz Bohrer, Paul Feyerabend, Hilton Kramer, et al.
—Faust, Wolfgang Max. "The Appearance of the Zeitgeist." *Artforum* (New York) 21, no. 5 (Jan. 1983), pp. 86–93.
—Rose, Barbara. "In Berlin, 'The Spirit of the Times': Zeitgeist." *Vogue* (New York) 173, no. 2 (Feb. 1983), pp. 296–301, 349.
—Russell, John. "A Big Berlin Show that Misses the Mark." *The New York Times*, Dec. 5, 1982, p. 33.
—Simon, Joan. "Report from Berlin: 'Zeitgeist,' The Times and the Place." *Art in America* (New York) 71, no. 3 (March 1983), pp. 33, 35, 37.

The Parrish Art Museum, Southampton, New York, *How to Draw/What to Draw: Works on Paper by Five Contemporary Artists*, Nov. 14, 1982–Jan. 3, 1983.
—Harrison, Helen A. "Showing How and What to Draw." *The New York Times*, Dec. 5, 1982, Long Island Weekly Section, p. 36.

1983
Anthony d'Offay Gallery, London, *New Paintings and Watercolours*, Jan. 8–Feb. 22.

Fundación Caja de Pensiones, Madrid, *Italia: La Transavanguardia*, Feb. 1–March 5. Catalogue with texts by Achille Bonito Oliva and V. Cambalia.

The Museum of Modern Art, New York, *Prints from Blocks: Gauguin to Now*, March 6–May 15. Catalogue with text by Riva Castleman.
—"Museum and Dealer Catalogues, Museum of Modern Art." *The Print Collector's Newsletter* (New York) 14, no. 2 (May–June 1983), pp. 68–69.

Bonner Kunstverein, Bonn, *Concetto–Imago: Generationswechsel in Italien*, March 18–May 1. Catalogue with texts by Zdenek Felix and Margarethe Jochimsen.

Kunsthalle Bielefeld, Bielefeld, Germany, *Sandro Chia, Francesco Clemente, Enzo Cucchi: Bilder*, April 29–July 3. Catalogue with texts by Wolfgang Max Faust and Ulrich Weisner and interviews with the artists by Heiner Bastian.
—Friedrichs, Yvonne. "Angerührt vom Geheimnis: Chia, Clemente, Cucchi in Bielefeld." *Du* (Zurich), no. 4 (April 1983), pp. 80–81.
—Winter, Peter. "Chia, Clemente, Cucchi, Kunsthalle Bielefeld." *Das Kunstwerk* (Stuttgart) 36 (summer 1983), pp. 156–57.

Solomon R. Guggenheim Museum, New York, *Recent European Painting*, May 20–Sept. 4.

Galerie Beyeler, Basel, *New Work on Paper: Drawings, Watercolors, Collages*, June–Oct.

The Parrish Art Museum, Southampton, New York, *The Painterly Figure*, July 24–Sept. 4. Catalogue with text by Klaus Kertess.

Tate Gallery, London, *New Art*, Sept. 14–Oct. 23. Catalogue with text by Michael Compton.
—Beaumont, Mary Rose. "New Art, Tate Gallery." *Arts Review* (London), Sept. 30, 1983, pp. 534–35.

The Boibrino Gallery, Stockholm, *Det Italienska Avantgardet*, Sept. 17–Oct. 16. Catalogue with text by Cecelia Stam.

Galerie Beyeler, Basel Art Fair, Basel, *Expressionist Painting Beyond Picasso*, Oct.–Dec. Catalogue with text by Siegfried Gohr.

Ateneumin Taidemuseo, Helsinki, *Ars '83 Helsinki*, Oct. 14–Dec. 11. Catalogue with texts by Yrjana Levanto, Barbara J. London, Mats B. J. O. Mallander, Pauli Paaermaa, Leena Peltola, and Matti Ranki.
—Madoff, Steven Henry. "Ars 83 Helsinki." *Artnews* (New York) 83, no. 1 (Jan. 1984), pp. 120–26.

The Museum of Contemporary Art, Los Angeles, *The First Show: Painting and Sculpture from Eight Collections, 1940–1980*, Nov. 20, 1983–Feb. 19, 1984. Catalogue with texts by Julia Brown, Pontus Hulten, Bridget Johnson, and Susan C. Larsen.

Mary Boone Gallery, New York, *Paintings*, Dec. 3–31.

1984
National Gallery of Art, Washington, D.C., *The Folding Image*, March 4–Sept. 3. Catalogue with foreword by Michael Komanecky and texts by Janet W. Adams, Virginia Fabbri, and Komanecky.

Akira Ikeda Gallery, Nagoya, *Painting Now: Basquiat, Chia, Clemente, Cucchi, Salome, Schnabel*, March 5–31. Catalogue with foreword by Kazuaki Mitsuiki and text by Nobuyuki Hiromoto.

Sidney Janis Gallery, New York, *Modern Expressionists: German, Italian, and American Painters*, March 10–April 7. Catalogue.

Musée d'Art Contemporain, Montreal, *Via New York*, May 8–June 24. Catalogue with texts by Phillip Evans-Clark, France Gascon, André Menard, and Robert Pincus-Witten.

The Museum of Modern Art, New York, *An International Survey of Recent Painting and Sculpture*, May 17–Aug. 19. Catalogue with text by Kynaston McShine.

Mary Boone Gallery, New York, *Drawings*, June 2–30.

BlumHelman Gallery, New York, *Francesco Clemente, Bryan Hunt, David Salle*, June 6–July 27.
—Robinson, John. "Francesco Clemente/Bryan Hunt/David Salle." *Arts Magazine* 59, no. 1 (Sept. 1984), p. 34.

San Francisco Museum of Modern Art, *The Human Condition: San Francisco Museum of Modern Art Biennial III*, June 28–Aug. 26. Catalogue.
—Levy, Mark. "Confronting the Human Condition." *Artweek* (San Jose, California), Aug. 11, 1984, p. 1.

The Chicago Public Library Cultural Center (organized by Chicago Council on Fine Arts and The Renaissance Society at the University of Chicago), *Contemporary Italian Masters*, June 30–Sept. 8. Catalogue with texts by Henry Geldzahler and Judith Russi Kirshner.

Anthony d'Offay Gallery, London, *Beuys, Clemente, Gilbert & George, Kiefer, Long*, July 31–Aug. 24.

The Guinness Hop Store, Dublin, *ROSC '84: The Poetry of Vision*, Aug. 24–Nov. 17. Catalogue with texts by Rosemarie Mulcahy, Patrick J. Murphy, William Packer, Michael Scott, Ronald Tallon, and Dorothy Walker.

Galerie Bruno Bischofberger, Zurich, *Collaborations: Basquiat, Clemente, Warhol*, Sept. 15–Oct. 13.
—Wechsler, Max. "Collaborations, Galerie Bruno Bischofberger." *Artforum* (New York) 23, no. 5 (Feb. 1985), p. 99

Walker Art Center, Minneapolis, *Images and Impressions: Painters Who Print*, Sept. 23–Nov. 25. Traveled to Institute of Contemporary Art, University of Pennsylvania, Philadelphia, March 15–April 28, 1985. Catalogue with text on Clemente by Rainer Crone.
—Larson, Philip. "New Expressionism." *The Print Collector's Newsletter* (New York) 15, no. 6 (Jan.–Feb. 1985), pp. 199–200.

Hirshhorn Museum and Sculpture Garden, Smithsonian Institution, Washington, D.C., *Content: A Contemporary Focus, 1974–1984*, Oct. 4, 1984–Jan. 6, 1985. Catalogue with foreword by Abram Lerner and texts by Howard Fox and Miranda McClintic.

1985

Kunsthalle Tübingen, Tübingen, Germany, *7000 Eichen*, March 2–April 14. Traveled to Kunsthalle Bielefeld, Bielefeld, Germany, June 2–Aug. 11. Catalogue with texts by G. Adriani, Heiner Bastian, and U. Weisner.

Grande Halle du Parc de la Villette, Paris, *La Nouvelle Biennale de Paris*, March 21–May 21. Catalogue with texts by Achille Bonito Oliva, Georges Boudaille, Alanna Heiss, et al.

Castello Colonna, Genazzano, Italy, *Nuove Trame dell'Arte*, June 21–Oct. 31. Catalogue.
—Clarke, John R. "Circuses and Bread: Achille Bonito Oliva's *Nuove Trame dell'Arte* at Genazzano." *Arts Magazine* (New York) 60, no. 2 (Oct. 1985), pp. 34–39.

Kunsthalle Basel, *Von Twombly bis Clemente: Ausgewahlte Werke einer Privatsammlung/Selected Works from a Private Collection*, July 14–Sept. 15. Catalogue with texts by Jean-Christophe Ammann and Roman Hollenstein.

Anthony d'Offay Gallery, London, *Unique Books*, Sept. 5–Oct. 2.

The Museum of Modern Art, New York, *India and the Contemporary Artist*, Oct. 16, 1985–Jan. 21, 1986.

Museum of Art, Carnegie Institute, Pittsburgh, *The Carnegie International*, Nov. 9, 1985–Jan. 5, 1986. Catalogue with texts by Benjamin H. D. Buchloh, Hal Foster, Rudi Fuchs, et al.
—van der Marck, Jan. "The Triennial Revisited." *Art in America* (New York) 74, no. 5 (May 1986), pp. 49–55.

Joslyn Art Museum, Omaha, Nebraska, *New Art of Italy*, Nov. 22, 1985–Jan. 21, 1986. Traveled to Dade County Center for the Fine Arts, Miami, Feb. 1–March 23, 1986; The Contemporary Arts Center, Cincinnati, April 4–May 23, 1986. Catalogue with text by Holliday T. Day.
—Benson, Timothy. "Cincinnati: The New Art of Italy." *Burlington Magazine* (London) 128, no. 996 (March 1986), p. 242.

Castello di Rivoli, Turin, *Ouverture*, opened Dec. 13. Catalogue with text by Rudi Fuchs.

1986

Whitechapel Art Gallery, London, *In Tandem*, March 27–May 25. Catalogue with text by Lynne Cooke.

Städtische Galerie im Lenbachhaus, Munich, *Beuys zu Ehren*, July 16–Nov. 2. Catalogue with texts by Johannes Cladders, Bernd Kluser, Armin Zweite, et al.

Museum Ludwig, Cologne, *Europa/Amerika*, Sept. 6–Nov. 30. Catalogue with texts by Rainer Crone, Johannes Gachnang, Siegfried Gohr, et al.

Galerie Bruno Bischofberger, Zurich, *Clemente, Salle, Schnabel: Three Large Paintings*, Sept. 23–Nov. 15.

Philadelphia Museum of Art, *Philadelphia Collects Art Since 1940*, Sept. 28–Nov. 30. Catalogue with introduction by Mark Rosenthal.

1987

Palais des Beaux-Arts, Charleroi, Belgium, *L'Exotisme au Quotidien*, Feb. 7–April 5.

Los Angeles County Museum of Art, Los Angeles, *Avant-Garde in the Eighties*, April 23–July 12. Catalogue with text by Howard Fox.

Minnesota Museum of American Art, Saint Paul, *The International Exhibition to End World Hunger*, Sept. 13–Nov. 8. Traveled to Sonia Henie-Neils Onstad Foundation, Høvikodden, Norway, Dec. 8, 1987–Jan. 20, 1988; Göteborgs Konstmuseum, Göteborg, Sweden, Feb. 27–April 4, 1988; Kölnischer Kunstverein, Cologne, April 21–May 29, 1988; Musée des Arts Africains et Océaniens, Paris, June 10–July 20, 1988; Barbican Art Gallery, London, Aug. 4–Oct. 2, 1988.

Miriam and Ira D. Wallach Art Gallery, Columbia University, New York, Dec. 4, 1987–Jan. 30, 1988, Leo Castelli Gallery, New York, Dec. 5–22, and Ileana Sonnabend Gallery, New York, Dec. 2–22, *Similia/Dissimilia: Modes of Abstraction in Painting, Sculpture and Photography Today*. Catalogue with introduction by Rainer Crone and text on Clemente by Linda Norden.

1988

Galeria Eude, Barcelona, *Paladino — Cucchi — Clemente*, Jan.

Winnipeg Art Gallery, Winnipeg, Canada, *The Impossible Self*, April 10–July 10. Catalogue with artists' statements.

Museo d'Arte Contemporanea, Prato, Italy, *Europa Oggi—Europe Now: Arte contemporanea nell'Europa occidentale*, June 25–Oct. 20. Catalogue with texts by Carlo Bertelli, Achille Bonito Oliva, Bruno Corà, Gillo Dorfles, and Helmut Draxler.

Venice, *XLIII Biennale di Venezia: Il Luogo degli Artisti/Aperto '88*, June 26–Sept. 25. Catalogue with introduction by Giovanni Carandente and texts by Guido Ballo, Achille Bonito Oliva, Pier Luigi Tazzi, et al.

Carnegie Museum of Art, Pittsburgh, *The Carnegie International*, Nov. 5, 1988–Jan. 22, 1989. Catalogue with foreword by Phillip M. Johnson and texts by John Caldwell, Vicky A. Clark, Lynne Cooke, Milena Kalinovska, and Thomas McEvilley.

The Museum of Modern Art, New York, *For 25 Years: Crown Point Press*, Nov. 20, 1988–March 8, 1989. Catalogue with text by Riva Castleman.

1989

Royal Academy of Arts, London, *Italian Art in the Twentieth Century*, Jan. 14–April 9. Catalogue with texts by Paolo Baldacci, Carlo Bertelli, Germano Celant, et al.

Rheinhallen der Kölner Messe, Cologne, *Bilderstreit*, April 8–July 2. Catalogue with texts by Hans Belting, Michael Compton, René Denizot, et al.
—Beyer, Lucie. "Bilderstreit, Rheinhallen Fair Center, Cologne." *Flash Art* (Milan), international edition, no. 147 (summer 1989), p. 154.

Musée National d'Art Moderne, Centre Georges Pompidou, Paris, *Magiciens de la Terre*, May 18–Aug. 14. Catalogue with texts by Homi Bhabha, Mark Francis, Pierre Gaudibert, et al.
—Heartney, Eleanor. "The Whole Earth Show, Part II." *Art in America* (New York) 77, no. 7 (July 1989), pp. 91–96.
—McEvilley, Thomas. "Marginalia: Thomas McEvilley on The Global Issue." *Artforum* (New York) 28, no. 7 (March 1990), pp. 19–21.

Museum des 20. Jahrhunderts, Vienna, *Wiener Diwan — Sigmund Freud — heute*, May 29–July 16. Catalogue edited by Thomas Zaunschirm with texts by Matthias Boeckl.

Fundación Cultural Televisa, Centro Cultural Arte Contemporáneo, Guadalajara, Mexico, *Paul Klee, Francesco Clemente, Papunya Tula*, July 5–Oct.

1990

Franklin Furnace Archives, New York, *Contemporary Illustrated Books: Word and Image, 1967–1988*, Jan. 12–Feb. 28. Traveled to The Nelson-Atkins Museum of Art, Kansas City, Missouri, April 5–June 3; University of Iowa Museum of Art, Iowa City, Feb. 8–April 7, 1991.

Massimo Audiello Gallery, New York, *Disturb Me*, March 17–April 7.

Galerie Bellier, Paris, *Renaissance du polyptique chez les artistes contemporains*, June 14–July 20. Catalogue.

Nippon Convention Center, Makuhari Messe Exhibition Hall International, Tokyo, *Pharmakon '90*, July 28–Aug. 20. Catalogue with foreword by Kikuko Amagasaki and texts by Jan Avgikos, Achille Bonito Oliva, and Motoaki Shinohara.

1991

Brooke Alexander Editions, New York, *Poets/Painters: Collaborations*, March 13–30.

Matthew Marks Gallery, New York, *Artists' Sketchbooks*, March 20–April 5. Catalogue with text by Guy Davenport.

Studio d'Arte Cannaviello, Milan, *Clemente, Paladino, Gli Anni '70*, May 1–June 5. Catalogue.

Louver Gallery, New York, *Clemente, Dorner, Iglesias, Mol, Sarmento*, June 1–July 5.

Kunstmuseum Basel, Sept. 1–Dec. 8, and Berowergut, Riehen, Switzerland, Sept. 1–Oct. 20, *Zeichnungen des 20. Jahrhunderts: Karl August Burckhardt-Koechlin-Fonds*. Catalogue with foreword by Dieter Koepplin.

Museum für Gegenwartskunst, Basel, *Emmanuel Hoffmann-Stiftung 1980–1990*, Sept. 13–Nov. 25. Catalogue with foreword by Vera Oeri-Hoffman and texts by Jean-Christophe Ammann, Coosje van Bruggen, Dieter Koepplin, et al.

Institute of Contemporary Art, University of Pennsylvania, Philadelphia, *Devil on the Stairs: Looking Back to the Eighties*, Oct. 4, 1991–Jan. 5, 1992. Traveled to Newport Harbor Art Museum, Newport Beach, California, April 16–June 21, 1992. Catalogue with texts by Peter Schjeldahl and Robert Storr.

Stedelijk Museum, Amsterdam, *Wanderlieder*, Dec. 7, 1991–Feb. 9, 1992. Catalogue with texts by Wim Beeren, Sir Isaiah Berlin, H. J. A. Hofland, Heiner Müller, and Cees Nooteboom.

1992

The Museum of Modern Art, New York, *Allegories of Modernism: Contemporary Drawing*, Feb. 16–May 5. Catalogue with texts by Emily Kies Folpe and Bernice Rose.

Musée d'Art Moderne et d'Art Contemporain de la Ville de Nice, *Le portrait dans l'art contemporain*, July 3–Sept. 27.

Kunsthal Rotterdam, *Warhol — Kiefer — Clemente: Werken op papier*, Nov. 1, 1992–Jan. 3, 1993. Catalogue with texts by Ruud Schenk.

Claudia Gian Ferrari Arte Contemporanea, Milan, *Transavanguardia: Sandro Chia, Francesco Clemente, Enzo Cucchi, Nicola De Maria, Mimmo Paladino*, Nov. 26, 1992–Jan. 23, 1993. Catalogue.

1993

Sperone Westwater, New York, *The Spirit of Drawing*, May 1–June 12.

Tony Shafrazi Gallery, New York, *1982–83, Ten Years After*, May 8–Aug. 6.

Museumsquartier Messepalast and Kunsthalle Wien, Vienna, *Der Zerbrochene Spiegel*, May 26–July 25. Traveled to Deichtorhallen, Hamburg, Oct. 14, 1993–Jan. 2, 1994. Catalogue with introduction by Kasper König and Hans-Ulrich Obrist.

Peggy Guggenheim Collection, Venice, *Drawing the Line Against AIDS*, June 8–13. Catalogue with texts by John Cheim, Diego Cortez, Carmen Giménez, and Klaus Kertess.

Salzburger Festspiele and Galerie Thaddaeus Ropac, Salzburg, *Utopia: Arte Italiana 1950–1993*, July 24–Aug. 31.

National Portrait Gallery, London, *The Portrait Now*, Nov. 19, 1993–Feb. 6, 1994.

1994

Marlborough Gallery, New York, *Metamorphosis: Surrealism to Organic Abstraction 1925–1993*, Jan. 12–March 5.

Luhring Augustine Gallery, New York, *The Ossuary*, Feb. 19–March 19.

Anthony d'Offay Gallery, London, *Painting, Drawing and Sculpture*, March 2–April 8.

Museum Moderner Kunst Stiftung Ludwig, Vienna, *Malfiguren: Francesco Clemente, Jörg Immendorf, Per Kirkeby, Malcolm Morley, Hermann Nitsch, Cy Twombly*, July 7–Sept. 18. Catalogue with texts by Achille Bonito Oliva, Otto Breicha, Rainer Fuchs, Lorand Hegyi, and Edwin Lachnit.

Castel Trento, Trento, Italy, *L'incanto e la transcendenza*, July 10–Aug. 28. Catalogue with texts by Achille Bonito Oliva, Danilo Eccher, Ermanno Olmi, and Crispino Valenziano.

1995
Museum für Moderne Kunst, Frankfurt, *Szenenwechsel*, Jan. 27–May 14.

Venice, *XLVI Biennale di Venezia: Identità e alterità*, June 11–Sept. 4. Catalogue with texts by Maurizio Bettini, Marc Fumaroli, Cathrin Pichler, et al.
—Couturier, Elizabeth. "Biennale: Les jeux sont faits." *Beaux Arts Magazine* (Paris), no. 135 (June 1995), pp. 68–73.

Galerie Thaddaeus Ropac, Paris, *Muses: Transformation de l'image féminine dans l'art contemporain*, Sept. 26–Nov. 18. Catalogue with texts by Alan Jones, Sydney Picasso, Peter Schjeldahl, Caroline Smulders, Elizabeth Stuart, and Barbara Wally.

1996
Sperone Westwater, New York, *Francesco Clemente, Julian Schnabel, Cy Twombly: Three Large Scale Works*, Jan. 13–Feb. 17.

Claudia Gian Ferrari Arte Contemporanea, Milan, *Nudo e Crudo corpo sensibile/corpo visibile*, Jan. 25–March 16. Catalogue with texts by Manlio Brusatin and Claudia Gian Ferrari.

Museum Fridericianum, Kassel, *Collaborations: Warhol, Basquiat, Clemente*, Feb. 4–May 5. Traveled to Museum Villa Stück, Munich, July 25–Sept. 29; Castello di Rivoli, Turin, Oct. 17, 1996–Jan. 19, 1997. Catalogue with foreword by Tilman Osterwold and texts by Trevor Fairbrother, Mark Francis, Keith Haring, et al.

Art Gallery of New South Wales, Artspace, and Ivan Dougherty Gallery, Sydney, *Tenth Biennial of Sydney: Jurassic Technologies, Revenant*, July 27–Sept. 22. Catalogue with introduction by Lynne Cooke and texts by Leslie Camhi, Jonathan Crary, Sarat Maharaj, and Elisabeth Sussman.

1997
Peter Blum, New York, *Drawing the Line and Crossing It*, Jan.–March.

Claudia Gian Ferrari Arte Contemporanea, Milan, *Metamorphosis: Il tempo della mutazione*, Jan. 16–March 1.

Galleria d'Arte Moderna, Bologna, *Materiali Anomali*, Feb. 28–May 4.

The Museum of Modern Art, New York, *On the Edge: Contemporary Art from the Werner and Elaine Dannheiser Collection*, Sept. 20, 1997–Jan. 20, 1998. Catalogue with introduction by Kirk Varnedoe and text by Robert Storr.

Guggenheim Museum Bilbao, *The Guggenheim Museums and the Art of This Century*, Oct. 19, 1997–June 1, 1998.

Galleria d'Arte Moderna, Bologna, *Arte Italiana: Ultimi quarant'anni, Pittura Iconica*, Nov. 28, 1997–March 8, 1998.

1998
Museum Würth, Künzelsau, Germany, *Transavanguardia*, Feb. 26–June 1. Catalogue.

Culturgest, Lisbon, *Anos 80/The Eighties*, May 12–Aug. 31. Catalogue with texts by Dan Cameron, Maria Corral, Jose Gil, and Alexandre Melo.

Bibliography

"Artist's Books" and "Interviews and Statements" are arranged chronologically. "Articles and Essays" is arranged alphabetically. For information about exhibition catalogues and exhibition reviews, see the exhibition history.

Artist's Books

Castelli di sabbia. Naples: L'Arte Tipografica, 1964.

Pierre Menard. Rome: Edizioni GAP, 1973.

6 Fotografie. Brescia, Italy: Banco, 1974.

Gratis. Geneva: Centre d'Art Contemporain, 1978.

Undae clemente flamina pulsae. Amsterdam: Art & Project, 1978. Edition of 800.

Vetta. Modena, Italy: Emilio Mazzoli, 1979. Edition of 1,000.

Non Scopa. Turin: Gian Enzo Sperone, 1979.

Chi pinge figura, si non può esser lei non la può porre. Basel: Kunsthalle Basel, 1980.

Francesco Clemente Pinxit. London: Anthony d'Offay; Rome: Gian Enzo Sperone, 1981. Edition of 500.

Il viaggiatore napoletano, ed. Paul Maenz. Cologne: Gerd de Vries, 1982.

Francesco Clemente: Watercolours. Zurich: Edition Bruno Bischofberger, 1982. Edition of 1,000.

White Shroud. 1983. With poem by Allen Ginsberg. Unique book.

Images from Mind and Space. 1983. With poem by Allen Ginsberg. Unique book.

Black Shroud. 1985. With poem by Allen Ginsberg. Unique book.

Early Morning Exercises. 1985. With poems by John Wieners. Unique book.

The Departure of the Argonaut. New York: Petersburg Press, 1986. With text by Alberto Savinio (trans. George Scrivani). Edition of 200.

Francesco Clemente: The Pondicherry Pastels. London: Anthony d'Offay, 1986. Edition of 1,000.

Francesco Clemente: Two Garlands. New York: Sperone Westwater, 1986.

India. Pasadena, California: Twelvetrees Press, 1986. Edition of 3,050.

Francesco Clemente CVIII: Watercolours Adayar 1985. Basel: Museum für Gegenwartskunst, 1987.

Singular Pleasures. New York: Grenfell Press, 1988. With text by Harry Mathews. Edition of 350.

Funerary Paintings. New York: Dia Art Foundation, 1988.

It. Zurich: Edition Bruno Bischofberger, 1989. With poems by Robert Creeley. Edition of 2,500.

Sixteen Pastels. London: Anthony d'Offay Gallery, 1989. With poems by Rene Ricard. Edition of 1,000.

The Gold Paintings. Zurich: Edition Bruno Bischofberger, 1990. With poem by Gregory Corso. Edition of 1,000.

Testa Coda. New York: Gagosian Gallery, 1991.

Mental'nyi limon/The Water's Skeleton, Francesco Clemente: Sixteen Watercolours and *Francesco Clemente: Nine Drawings/Andrei Voznesensky: Five Poems*. Zurich: Edition Bruno Bischofberger, 1991. With poems by Andrei Voznesensky. Edition of 1,110.

Francesco Clemente: The Black Book. Basel: Kunsthalle Basel, 1991.

Francesco Clemente: Evening Raga and Paradiso. New York: Gagosian Gallery and Rizzoli, 1992.

Cathay. New York: Limited Editions Club, 1992. With poems by Ezra Pound after Li Po. Edition of 350.

Life & Death. New York: Grenfell Press, 1993. With poems by Robert Creeley. Edition of 70.
There. New York: Gagosian Gallery, 1994. With poems by Robert Creeley. Edition of 1,000.
Ex Libris Madras. Madras: Kalakshetra Press, 1994. Edition of 2,000.
Francesco Clemente/Peter Handke. Cologne: Jablonka Galerie, 1995. With poems by Peter Handke. Edition of 1,000.
Ex Libris Chenonceau. Madras: Kalakshetra Press, 1995. Edition of 2,000.
Mothers of Hope: Francesco Clemente. Madras: Kalakshetra Press, 1995. Edition of 1,100.
Anamorphosis. New York: Gagosian Gallery, 1997. With poems by Robert Creeley.
Fifty One Days on Mount Abu. London: Anthony d'Offay Gallery, 1997.

Interviews and Statements

"Prezentazione: Francesco Clemente." *Domus* (Milan), no. 577 (Dec. 1977), pp. 52–54 (in Italian, French, and English).
Ammann, J. C., Paul Groot, Pieter Heynen, and Jan Zumbrink. "Un altre arte." *Museumjournaal* (Amsterdam) 25, no. 7 (Dec. 1980), pp. 288–301.
Zaya. "Conversación con Francesco Clemente: Sustancia de lo imaginario." *Guadalimar* (Madrid), no. 56 (1981), pp. 14–15.
White, Robin. "Francesco Clemente." *View* (Oakland) 3, no. 6 (Nov. 1981), pp. 2–27.
Berger, Danny. "Francesco Clemente at the Metropolitan: An Interview." *The Print Collector's Newsletter* (New York) 13, no. 1 (March–April 1982), pp. 11–13.
deAk, Edit. "Francesco Clemente." *Interview* (New York) 12, no. 4 (April 1982), pp. 16–21.
Bastian, Heiner. "Samtale med Francesco Clemente." *Louisiana Revy* (Humlebaek) 23, no. 3 (June 1983) pp. 40–44.
Clemente, Francesco. Statement in Achille Bonito Oliva. *Dialoghi d'artista: Incontri con l'arte contemporanea 1970–84*. Milan: Electa, 1984 (in Italian and English).
Politi, Giancarlo. "Francesco Clemente." *Flash Art* (Milan), international edition, no. 117 (April–May 1984), pp. 12–21.
Courtney, Cathy. Interview with Clemente. *Art Monthly* (London), no. 100 (Oct. 1986), pp. 39–40.
Clemente, Francesco. Statement in Kynaston McShine, et al. *Andy Warhol: A Retrospective* (exh. cat.). New York: The Museum of Modern Art, 1987.
Crone, Rainer, and Georgia Marsh. *An Interview with Francesco Clemente*. New York: Vintage Books, 1987.
Marsh, Georgia. "Francesco Clemente: Faire quelque chose à partir de rien." *Art Press* (Paris), no. 113 (April 1987), pp. 4–10.
Philipps, Lisa. "Clemente: Les chemins de la sagesse." *Beaux Arts Magazine* (Paris), no. 69 (June 1989), pp. 90–95.
Kent, Sarah. "Turtles All the Way: Francesco Clemente Interviewed by Sarah Kent." *Artscribe* (London), no. 77 (Sept.–Oct. 1989), pp. 54–59.
"Manners Entice: A Discussion between Alex Katz and Francesco Clemente." *Parkett* (Zurich), no. 21 (Sept. 1989), pp. 48–56.
Kuspit, Donald. "Clemente Explores Clemente." *Contemporanea* (New York) 2, no. 7 (October 1989), pp. 36–43.
Geldzahler, Henry. "Francesco Clemente." *Interview* (New York) 21, no. 11 (Nov. 1991), pp. 54–56.
Burroughs, William S. "The Creative Observer: Conversation with Francesco Clemente." *Flash Art* (Milan), international edition, no. 127 (Oct. 1993), pp. 36–38.
Clemente, Francesco. Untitled essay. In *Jean-Michel Basquiat Portraits* (exh. cat.). Zurich: Edition Bruno Bischofberger, 1996.
———. "The City and the Painter." In *Alex Katz* (exh. cat.). Cologne: Jablonka Galerie, 1997.
Sischy, Ingrid. "fc." *Interview* (New York) 27, no. 7 (July 1997), pp. 74–81.

Articles and Essays

Ammann, Jean-Christophe. "Espansivo-eccessivo: Osservazioni sulla giovane arte italiana." *Domus* (Milan), no. 593 (April 1979), pp. 45, VI, VII (in Italian, Dutch, and English).
———. "Was die siebziger Jahre von den sechzigern unterscheidet: Der Weg in die achtziger Jahre." *Kunstforum International* (Cologne), no. 39 (March 1980), pp. 172–84.
———. "Francesco Clemente et l'Inde." *Artstudio* (Paris), no. 7 (winter 1987–88), pp. 64–69.
Anderson, Alexandra. "Art Boom in New York: The Sudden Arrival of Francesco Clemente." *Harpers and Queen* (London), Feb. 1983, pp. 134–35.
Argan, Giulio Carlo, and Achille Bonito Oliva. "Avanguardia e transavanguardia." *Iterarte* (Bologna) 24, no. 8 (June 1982), pp. 3–32.
Ashbery, John. "Under the Volcano." *Interview* (New York) 18, no. 3 (March 1988), pp. 62–70.
Attias, Laurie. "C'mon Let's Twist Again." *Artnews* (New York) 95, no. 10 (Nov. 1996), pp. 124–26.
Baker, Kenneth. "Clemente Aims for the Heart." *San Francisco Chronicle*, Nov. 15, 1990, p. E3:1.
———. "Clemente Keeps Polishing His Image." *San Francisco Chronicle*, April 13, 1991, p. C3:2.
Bienek, Horst. "Wenn er traumt, verandert er die Welt." *Art, das Kunstmagazin* (Hamburg), no. 10 (Oct. 1988), pp. 30–46.
Bonito Oliva, Achille. "Process, Concept, and Behaviour in Italian Art." *Studio International* (London), no. 979, vol. 191 (Jan.–Feb. 1976), pp. 3–10.
———. "The Italian Trans-Avantgarde." *Flash Art* (Milan), international edition, nos. 92–93 (Oct.–Nov. 1979), pp. 17–20.
———. "The Bewildered Image." *Flash Art* (Milan), international edition, nos. 96–97 (March–April 1980), pp. 32–35, 38–39, 41.
———. "Francesco Clemente." *Domus* (Milan), no. 613 (Jan. 1981), pp. 52–53 (in Italian and English).
———. "La pazienza del vincitore." *Segno* (Pescara) 6, no. 29 (Nov. 1982–Feb. 1983), pp. 8–11.
———. "Les raisons poétiques de la trans-avantgarde." *Artstudio* (Paris), no. 7 (winter 1987–88), pp. 64–69.
Bourdon, David. "Battling the Masters." *Geo* (New York) 4, no. 8 (August 1982), pp. 30–45.
Bozzi, Elisabeth. "Francesco Clemente: En parcourant les mondes, il s'est trouvé lui-même." *New Art International* (Paris), nos. 3–4 (May 1987), pp. 17–20.
Capetillo, Marta. "A Life with Art." *Casa Vogue* (Milan), no. 261 (April 1994), pp. 130–37, 230.
Castle, Ted. "A Bouquet of Mistakes." *Flash Art* (Milan), international edition, no. 108 (summer 1982), pp. 54–55.

Celant, Germano. "The Italian Experience—Touched Upon." In *Paul Maenz Jahresbericht, 1978*. Cologne: Paul Maenz, 1979.

Cortez, Diego. "Francesco Clemente: L'affresco della Piscina." *Domus* (Milan), no. 684 (June 1987), pp. 8–9 (in Italian and English).

Cotter, Holland. "Francesco Clemente." *Parkett* (Zurich), nos. 40–41 (June 1994), pp. 6–23.

Cronau, Sabine. "Drei Stars tauschen ihre Leinwande." *Art, das Kunstmagazin* (Hamburg), no. 2 (Feb. 1996), pp. 92–93.

Crone, Rainer. "Clemente and His Pictorial Symbolism." *Parkett* (Zurich), no. 9 (April 1986), pp. 70–81.

Curtis, Cathy. "Straddling Grace and Decadence: Francesco Clemente." *Artweek* (San Jose, California), Sept. 12, 1981, p. 16.

Davvetas, Démosthènes. "Le paradoxe de Clemente." *Artstudio* (Paris), no. 7 (winter 1987–88), pp. 56–63.

deAk, Edit. "A Chameleon in a State of Grace." *Artforum* (New York) 19, no. 6 (Feb. 1981), pp. 36–41.

———. "The Critic Sees through the Cabbage Patch." *Artforum* (New York) 22, no. 8 (April 1984), pp. 53–60.

——— and Diego Cortez. "Baby Talk." *Flash Art* (Milan), international edition, no. 107 (May 1982), pp. 34–38.

——— and Ingrid Sischy. "A Light Opportunity." *Artforum* (New York) 23, no. 5 (Jan. 1985), pp. 48, 60–63.

de Bure, Giles. "L'art aux bains." *Beaux Arts Magazine* (Paris), no. 136 (July–Aug. 1995), pp. 108–13, 118.

Di Felice, Attanasio. "Painting with a Past: New Art from Italy." *Portfolio* (New York) 4, no. 2 (March–April 1982), pp. 94–99.

———. "The Italian Moderns." *Attenzione* (New York) 4, no. 3 (March 1982), pp. 62–63.

Dubrow, Norman. "Clemente's *Farsi degli Amici*." *Drawing* (New York) 7, no. 5 (Jan.–Feb. 1986), p. 105.

Eckhoff, Sally S. "Lit Bits." *The Village Voice* (New York), Oct. 31, 1989, p. 67.

Faust, Wolfgang Max. "Arte Cifra? Neue Subjektivität? Trans-Avantgarde?" *Kunstforum International* (Cologne), no. 39 (March 1980), pp. 161–71.

Feaver, William. "Dispirit of the Times." *Artnews* (New York) 82, no. 2 (Feb. 1983), pp. 80–83.

García, Aurora. "Vanguardia, retaguardia, transvanguardia." *Lapiz* (Madrid), no. 3 (Feb. 1983), pp. 54–57.

Geldzahler, Henry. "On Tape: Henry Geldzahler, Commissioner of New York City's Department of Cultural Affairs." *Express* (New York), no. 2 (spring 1982), pp. 4–5.

Groot, Paul. "Alchemy and the Rediscovery of the Human Figure." *Flash Art* (Milan), international edition, no. 126 (Feb.–March 1986), pp. 42–43.

———. "Die achtziger Jahre: Von pathologischer Anatomie, digitalen Arbeiten und Neo-Duchampiana." *Jahresring: Jahrbuch für Moderne Kunst* (Munich), no. 39 (1992), pp. 192–205.

Hawthorne, Don. "Prints from the Alchemist's Library." *Artnews* (New York) 85, no. 2 (Feb. 1986), pp. 89–95.

Hill, Andrea. "Meandering: Francesco Clemente's Pastels." *Artscribe* (London), no. 50 (Jan.–Feb. 1985), pp. 44–47.

Hjort, Oystein. "Firhaendigt med historien: Kort forbemaerkning til tre ung italienske malere." *Louisiana-Revy* (Humlebaek) 23, no. 3 (June 1983), pp. 32–35.

Hughes, Robert. "Raw Talk, but Cooked Painting." *Time* (New York), April 3, 1989, pp. 77–78.

Hutton, Lauren. "La Dolce Vita." *Harper's Bazaar* (New York) 125, no. 3,370 (Oct. 1992), pp. 80–86.

Jodidio, Philip. "Rigeur et déclin." *Connaissance des Arts* (Paris), no. 406 (Dec. 1985), pp. 112–19.

Jones, Alan. "Hanuman and His Books." *Arts Magazine* (New York) 63, no. 3 (Nov. 1988), pp. 13–16.

Keziere, Russell. "Tiresius Unbound." *Vanguard* (Vancouver) 13, no. 7 (Sept. 1984), pp. 8–12.

Kontova, Helena. "From Performance to Painting." *Flash Art* (Milan), international edition, no. 106 (Feb.–March 1982), pp. 16–21.

Kramer, Hilton. "Expressionism Returns to Painting." *The New York Times*, July 12, 1981, section 2, pp. D1, D3.

Kuspit, Donald. "The Only Immortal." *Artforum* (New York) 28, no. 6 (Feb. 1990), pp. 111–18.

Larson, Kay. "Between a Rock and a Soft Place." *New York Magazine*, June 1, 1981, pp. 56–58.

———. "Their Brilliant Careers." *New York Magazine*, Oct 24, 1988, pp. 150–52.

Lawson, Thomas. "Last Exit: Painting." *Artforum* (New York) 20, no. 2 (Oct. 1981), pp. 40–47.

Levin, Kim. "The Miniature Marauder." *The Village Voice* (New York), May 20, 1981, p. 81.

Marcadé, Bernard. "Francesco Clemente Symboliste." *Cardinaux* (Paris) 2 (spring 1987), pp. 29–37.

Martin, Henry. "The Italian Art Scene: Dynamic, Argumentative and Highly Charged." *Artnews* (New York) 80, no. 3 (March 1981), pp. 70–77.

Morera, Daniela. "Artisti nel loro studio: Francesco Clemente." *Vogue* (Rome), Feb. 1988, pp. 232–37, 256–59.

Ottmann, Klaus. "Painting in an Age of Anxiety." *Flash Art* (Milan), international edition, no. 118 (summer 1984), pp. 32–35.

Pellizzi, Francesco. "Images of the Material and the Manner of Taste: Reflexions (from F. C.)." *Parkett* (Zurich), no. 9 (April 1986), pp. 44–69.

Pernoud, Emmanuel. "Mythologies contemporaines." *Nouvelles de l'estampe* (Paris), no. 122 (April–June 1992), pp. 63–69.

Perrone, Jeff. "Boy, Do I Love Art or What." *Arts Magazine* (New York) 56, no. 1 (Sept. 1981), pp. 72–78.

———. "Entrées: Diaretics: Entreaties: Bowing (Wowing) Out." *Arts Magazine* (New York) 59, no. 8 (April 1985), pp. 78–83.

Phillips, Deborah C. "No Island Is an Island: New York Discovers the Europeans." *Artnews* (New York) 81, no. 8 (Oct. 1982), pp. 66–71.

Pincus-Witten, Robert. "Becoming American." *Arts Magazine* (New York) 60, no. 2 (Oct. 1985), pp. 101–03.

Pohlen, Annelie. "Eine Minderheit auf dem Weg zum morgen im gestern und heute: Zum italienischen Beitrag für 'Europa 79.'" *Kunstforum International* (Cologne), no. 36 (June 1979), pp. 88–156.

———. "Cosmic Visions from North and South." *Artforum* (New York) 23, no. 7 (March 1985), pp. 76–81.

Ratcliff, Carter. "On Iconography and Some Italians." *Art in America* (New York) 70, no. 8 (Sept. 1982), pp. 152–59.

———. "Dramatis Personae, Part II: The Scheherazade Tactic." *Art in America* (New York) 73, no. 10 (Oct. 1985), pp. 9–13.

Ricard, Rene. "Not About Julian Schnabel." *Artforum* (New York) 19, no. 10 (June 1981), pp. 74–80.

Robbins, D. A. "The Meaning of 'New'—The '70s/'80s Axis: An Interview with Diego Cortez." *Arts Magazine* (New York) 57, no. 5 (Jan. 1983), pp. 116–21.

Rubinstein, Meyer Raphael. "Singular Volumes: Artists' Collaborations with Harry Mathews." *Arts Magazine* (New York) 64, no. 7 (March 1990), pp. 29–34.

Russell, John. "The New European Painters." *The New York Times Magazine*, April 24, 1983, pp. 28–33, 36, 40–41, 71–73.

Schjeldahl, Peter. "Treachery on the High Cs." *The Village Voice* (New York), April 27, 1982, p. 96.

———. "Up Against the Wall." *Vanity Fair* (New York) 46, no. 2 (April 1983), pp. 92–97.

Schwarze, Dirk. "Collaborations: Warhol, Basquiat, Clemente." *Kunstforum International* (Cologne), no. 134 (May–Sept. 1996), pp. 416–18.

Shapiro, David. "Maxima Moralia: On the Art of Francesco Clemente." *Parkett* (Zurich), no. 9 (April 1986), pp. 16–43.

Smith, Roberta. "Healthy Egos." *The Village Voice* (New York), March 3, 1983, p. 100.

———. "Clemente: Slouching Towards Anonymity." *The New York Times*, Dec. 2, 1990, pp. 2, 41.

Stevens, Mark. "Revival of Realism: Art's Wild Young Turks." *Newsweek* (New York), June 7, 1982, pp. 64–70.

Storr, Robert. "Realm of the Senses." *Art in America* (New York) 75, no. 11 (Nov. 1987), pp. 132–45, 194.

Strasser, Catherine. "Francesco Clemente: Le son du corps." *Art Press* (Paris), no. 59 (May 1982), pp. 24–25.

Taylor, Paul. "How Europe Sold the Idea of Postmodern Art." *The Village Voice* (New York), Sept. 22, 1987, pp. 99–102.

Tomkins, Calvin. "The Art World: Seminar." *The New Yorker*, June 7, 1982, pp. 120–25.

Tucker, Marcia. "An Iconography of Recent Figurative Painting: Sex, Death, Violence, and the Apocalypse." *Artforum* (New York) 20, no. 10 (June 1982), pp. 70–75.

Venturi, Luca. "Nuovi Artisti." *Data: Practice and Theory of Art* (Milan) 4, no. 14 (winter 1974), pp. 68–79.

Vetrocq, Marcia E. "Utopias, Nomads, Critics." *Arts Magazine* (New York) 63, no. 8 (April 1989), pp. 49–54.

Index of Reproductions

Catalogue numbers appear in bold.

Photo Credits

Many color transparencies were provided by Thomas Ammann Fine Art, Zurich; Galerie Bruno Bischofberger, Zurich; Anthony d'Offay Gallery, London; Gagosian Gallery, New York; and Sperone Westwater, New York. Unless otherwise noted, black-and-white photographs are courtesy Francesco Clemente. In addition, the following credits are specified: Frontispiece, p. 452: © Estate of Robert Mapplethorpe. Used with permission; cat. no. 1: RB/Art; cat. nos. 2–8, 168: Martin Buehler; cat. nos. 9, 24, 27 , 44-48, 54, 58-59, 95, 104, 136-38, 140, 150, 188: Roland Reiter, Zurich; cat. no. 14: Paul Maenz, Cologne; cat. nos. 16, 53, 76–81, 167: Prudence Cuming Associates Ltd. ; cat. nos. 19, 23, 26, 41, 50, 55, 64, 66: courtesy Alesco AG, Zurich; cat. nos. 21, 39, 93: Zindman/ Fremont; cat. nos. 22, 111, 128: David Heald; cat. nos. 29, 57, 74, 120, 129–31, 147, 148, 173, 184: Ellen Labenski; cat. nos. 30, 33–35, 72, 73, 75, 82-84, 146: Beth Phillips; cat. nos. 31, 32, 37: Nic Tenwiggenhorn; cat. no. 42: © Albright-Knox Art Gallery, Buffalo, New York; cat. nos. 49, 51: Phillips/Schwab; cat. no. 52, 85–91, 94, 96-99, 101, 103, 105–7, 109, 121–23, 126, 174–83: Dorothy Zeidman; cat. no. 112: Steven Sloman; cat. no. 115: Naomi Fisher; cat. no. 135: courtesy Sperone Westwater; cat. nos. 144, 145: Tom Powel; cat. no. 149: J. Littkemann; cat. no. 152: Martçi Gasull, Barcelona; cat. no. 170: R. + B. Reiter, Zurich; p. 460: courtesy Bill Katz.

Francesco Clemente, May 1993. Photo by Sante D'Orazio.